Why did he have to kiss her as though he needed her—as a woman, as a lover?

He'd been angry with her, of course. That was no reason to hold her so perfectly, to kick her needs into overdrive. And that raw, primitive kiss wasn't what she'd expected, that unshielded hunger, the heat pouring from him. She hadn't expected the heat or the passion from Hogan—or herself. She hadn't expected the hard sensual jolt in her lower body, the need to bear him to the ground and have him.

She'd left him there, pushing away that fragile tenderness and struggling to her horse; left him standing with boots wide spread upon the earth, his face dark and brooding and terrifying—or was she terrified of what sprang from her? That need to take him, to claim him, had come from deep inside her, not her usual calculating, logical choice. She didn't want that need, ever.

Dealing with a brooding, intense man who seemed to look straight into her soul wasn't part of her life plan.

*Other Avon Contemporary Romances by*
**Cait London**

THREE KISSES

# Cait London

# Sleepless in Montana

AVON BOOKS ◆ NEW YORK

AVON BOOKS, INC.
1350 Avenue of the Americas
New York, New York 10019

Copyright © 1999 by Lois Kleinsasser
Inside cover author photo by Sothern Studio
Published by arrangement with the author
Library of Congress Catalog Card Number: 99-94451
ISBN: 0-380-80038-1
**www.avonbooks.com/romance**

First Avon Books Printing: November 1999

AVON TRADEMARK REG. U.S. PAT. OFF. AND IN OTHER COUNTRIES, MARCA REGISTRADA, HECHO EN U.S.A.

Printed in the U.S.A.

WCD 10 9 8 7 6 5 4 3 2 1

# In Appreciation

My appreciation to editor Lucia Macro and Avon Books, for letting me enjoy writing about the Kodiaks, a family torn apart and struggling to mend; to Montana's Big Sky country, especially the people of Sweet Grass County, who let me fudge a bit in my fictional location and legends. (I did love writing this contemporary love story of Jemma and Hogan, and incorporating Montana's great history into it.); and to my readers, who have encouraged and supported my stories for years. I adore you!

*Cait London*

# prologue

*Life's circle is broken*

"The old man will blame me if you drink that." Hogan noted the six-pack of beer that his teenage brother, Aaron, had just hauled in from the cold, snow-fed Montana stream. After a hot August day of hauling hay, Aaron and an adopted brother, Mitch, were sprawled on the stream's grassy bank. Under a rising, full moon, they were primed to split a fast-food bucket of fried chicken. The teens were ripe from a raging battle with Ben Kodiak, their father. They'd be talking big, about women—always women and sex—fast cars, and leaving the big Bar K Ranch.

At twenty-one, Hogan was leaving Sweet Grass County as soon as he tossed his battered suitcase into his old pickup. He'd leave a part of his heart in Montana, and it would always beckon to him—Sweet Grass County. The Kodiak ranch—all twelve thousand acres, in alfalfa fields and natural grass—would always be in his heart. He already stayed overlong for his brothers' sake, taking the edge off Ben's rough handling.

Today, he scanned the rolling, moonlit hills and noted a summer lightning storm brewing in a high mound of clouds. After the fall frost, the buffaloberries along the stream would be sweet, and quaking aspens would turn fiery yellow. In the spring, serviceberry bushes would begin to bloom, bitterroot—once dug by the Indians— would bloom in pink and white. In the distance, the snowcapped Crazy Mountains with their lava upthrusts, rugged beauty, and haunting winds would always call to him.

Hogan turned away from land he loved and focused his attention on the six-pack of cola he was carrying. He tossed Mitch and Aaron each a can and grinned as they scowled at him. Hogan understood the arrogance of teenagers resenting older brothers. "You're under drinking age."

He ripped off his leather gloves and thanked the wild horse he'd been breaking for trimming his anger. The teens weren't going anywhere soon, and if they drank the beer they'd gotten illegally, Ben would make them pay the next day.

Hogan inhaled the musky scent of hay mixed with the heavy damp summer night. His dark coloring and black, straight hair proved he had Indian blood that hadn't come from the fair-haired, blue-eyed Kodiaks.

Who was his mother? Even bastards had mothers— who was she? His father had hoarded the secret of Hogan's birth, but he was his father's son, after all, and cold clear through. He reached for a cold beer and settled down on the lush grass of the creek bank, dissecting the churning bitterness within him.

While Mitch and Aaron ate chicken, sipped the lowly cola, and wondered how they could manage "the old man," Hogan scanned the tops of the trees dancing in the slight breeze and sank into his dark thoughts.

Ben had married once, and it wasn't to Hogan's mother. It was to Dinah, who had saved his life in a tractor mishap. He'd hated her for that trespass—because big, tough Ben Kodiak had lost one leg. And that accident, rather Ben's pride, had torn the Kodiak family apart.

The canyon owl hooted in the distance, the eerie sound matching Hogan's dark mood. Who was his mother? Hadn't she wanted him? Why wouldn't Ben talk about her? Ben's silence said that he was ashamed of his half-blood son.

"There's no goddamn marriage certificate," Ben had raged when Hogan was just twelve and had once more worked up courage to question his father. "But you're my son, and I took you. You've got my name—Kodiak. Remember it, that's who you are—my son—and that's all you have to know."

Ben had given Aaron, his younger white son, his own father's name—not Hogan.

*Hogan Kodiak, the bastard*, Hogan thought bitterly, though Ben had never used the word and had taken apart men who had. Hogan tipped up the beer bottle and welcomed the bitter brew sliding down his throat. He was only four when Ben took his white wife, and Hogan felt like even more of an outcast when his blond brother and sister were born. His teen years had been spent in an uneasy relationship with Ben, and now it was time to leave.

"You look like the old man laid you out again," Mitch said. "Snake" was Mitch Kazimierz Kodiak's Chicago street name, before Ben Kodiak had hauled him out of a Chicago juvenile court and into Montana. Adopted at thirteen, Mitch still reflected his harsh, neglected childhood, and more than once Hogan and Aaron had had to drag him out of a brawl. A former hoodlum, and now seventeen, Mitch likely had gotten the beer, but it wasn't Ben who haunted him—it was his past.

"I'm leaving," Hogan stated, lifting his beer bottle in a toast to the Montana night and the worldly freedom that awaited him. "I'll let you know where I'm at, and I'll come back if you need me. I ordered your school clothes from the catalog and they'll be in next week. Keep up those dentist checkups and your grades. You're both going to college."

Mitch glared at him. "Yes, Mother. At least you won't be pushing us around anymore. And you didn't go to college anyway. Why do we have to?"

"Because you're smart, that's why. And because I say so." Hogan lifted his beer bottle in a toast. "To my ticket out of here—that art scholarship in France."

Would his brothers and half sister, Carley, be all right without him? Or would Ben turn his bitterness toward them? "Make sure you call me. If you have trouble, I'll get here somehow."

"He'll work us to death without you standing up to him." At sixteen, Aaron was a blond replica of Ben Kodiak. He reached for the six-pack of beer and glared at Hogan, who had just firmly placed his boot on it.

Hogan rested his arm across his knee. Later tonight, Penny Morales would ease his mind and bruised body, and in the morning, Hogan would be gone, driving his old pickup as far away as he could. He smiled tightly; he'd probably starve—that's what artists were supposed to do, but he wasn't taking anything that wasn't his from the ranch. He glanced at Aaron, marked by Ben's blue eyes and blond waving hair and build. Hogan wasn't jealous of Aaron, and he'd defended him against Ben's demands. Ben expected his sons to be as hard as he was.

Big Ben Kodiak wasn't happy with Hogan's artistic talent. "A man doesn't paint pictures and draw all day. He makes a living."

Hogan inhaled the damp, richly scented night air. He

might fail, but he didn't think so—he intended to put his stubborn Kodiak blood to good use.

Mitch worked to get a good wad of spit, then sailed a high arc into the tumbling, cold-water creek. Always competitive, Aaron sailed his spit into the night. "I'm going to make enough money to buy Dad out of this place. Carley may have stayed in Seattle with Mom, but I came back here to stay when I was twelve. This is Kodiak land, and the old man isn't running me off."

Mitch belched, grinning with pride as Aaron tried to work up a louder-sounding one. "He may be sleeping with Maxi Dove, but he's still in love with your mother. Carley looks just like her," Mitch said.

Aaron forgot about award-winning belching and eyed Mitch. "You come near my sister, and I'll—"

"Back off. She's my sister, too. Anyway, I think of her that way." Mitch's tone was disgusted.

"That skinny Seattle friend of hers, Jemma, is nothing but trouble on skinny legs. She's bossy, and I wish she wouldn't come here in the summer. Man, she's bad news."

"She can outride you any day," Hogan offered, wanting to equalize the brothers' battle. Hogan was proud of his half sister, all bright and shining and new, filled with life and joy. She touched his dark side and brightened his life, but she'd created more of a rift between Ben and him. Ben was too hard on Carley, wanting more from her than a girl her age could do, working from morning until night. With his brothers, Hogan had defended her.

That only made matters worse, because Ben Kodiak could not tolerate a family member who could not defend him- or herself. Yet every summer and holidays, Carley came to visit the Bar K. From Seattle, her mother would call, anxious about Carley's safety. Hogan had decided to stay the summer to protect Carley from Ben's bitter tongue; it wasn't Carley's fault that she looked like Dinah.

"Sometimes I wonder what the old man was like before he lost that leg," Aaron said, flopping on his back to look up into the starlit Montana night. "My mother had to see something in him. She should have stayed with him, stuck when the going got rough."

"And you should have stayed with her in Seattle and not had to work your butt off for the old man, living up to his expectations," Mitch said. "You could have it soft."

Hogan knew that Aaron was enough like Ben not to take the easy road on anything, and Aaron loved the land, just as Ben did.

Bitterness churned inside Hogan. It wasn't Aaron's fault that Ben openly preferred his all-white son.

"How old were you when he lost that leg, Hogan? Can you remember what happened?"

"I was eight, or so. Carley was just one and you were three. Dinah tried to make it work for a year after the accident, and then she had to go. It wasn't pretty then, with Ben slashing at her." Hogan had lots of memories and none of them sweet, except for Dinah trying to hold him. He couldn't allow that, a strange sweet-smelling woman wanting to cuddle him. As Ben's son, and a motherless child, he didn't understand gentleness, and he'd lashed out at her. For a time, she'd softened Ben, especially when Aaron and Carley came along.

Hogan pushed back his hair, worn in a long braid to irritate his old-fashioned father. "The day Ben went under that tractor, his leg was crushed, and they took it at the knee, everything changed. He couldn't stand to have Dinah around. He started yelling at her, and she tried to stay. It wasn't her fault that Ben started drinking again.

Then she packed up one day, tears streaming down her face, and left with you and Carley."

Out of habit, Hogan fingered the scar on his cheek. He'd been just three, just after old Aaron had died. Seeking security in an uncertain world, he'd gone to Ben, who promptly shoved him away. He'd fallen, cutting his cheek badly, and Ben had told him not to cry, but to stand still. Ben cleansed, sewed the wound closed, and pressed yarrow—a natural herb to stop the bleeding—against Hogan's cheek. After a moment of watching Hogan and making certain that he didn't cry, Ben nodded and went back to work, breaking horses.

So much for tenderness. The adult Hogan knew that he wouldn't qualify as a husband or father—he had that same cold streak inside him.

"He's not so bad." Mitch fished the other six-pack out of the creek and scowled at Hogan, who took it away and tossed another cola at him. "You're like him, Hogan, in more ways than one. Arrogant, keeping to yourself, and hard clear through. I know I'm a hell of a lot better off here than in jail. Old Ben went to bat for me, pulled legal strings, and I hated his guts. But I'm alive, and the reason is probably Ben Kodiak. There's worse men in the world—sick creeps . . . I like Montana. I might come back to visit after I've made my first million."

The other males knew that Mitch's Chicago life had been bad and didn't challenge him.

"Yeah," Aaron said wistfully, lifting his face to inhale the summer breeze, scented of hay and the approaching summer storm. "I had to come back. It wasn't the same in Seattle."

"There's that old owl up in the pines," Hogan noted as he drew Montana's familiar sounds and scents into him. "It's time for me to leave."

Aaron and Mitch met his eyes. "The infamous art world, huh?"

Hogan lifted his beer in a toast. "Paris and babes. Envy me, children."

"You'll be showing in high-priced art galleries, and we'll be slaving here," Aaron grumbled.

"Maybe." Hogan didn't know if he was talented, if his work would sell. But the spirit moved in him, shadowy forms, his fingers needing to touch and examine and shift his emotions into art. His high school art teacher had loved his sketches and watercolors. But uncertain of his talent, he could fail, and knew he'd need a fair share of luck to survive. He listened to the owl, and a cold trickle sped up his spine. "Old Joe Blue Sky says that when you hear an owl hoot like that, something bad is going to happen—"

Then a girl's terrified scream pierced the sweet Montana night air.

# one

*Eighteen years later*

Hogan watched the headlights coming toward his home, zigzagging and slicing through the Montana night. He held his breath—Jemma Delaney still drove like a kamikaze fighter, soaring over the creek's narrow wooden bridge.

In the silence of his living room, he ran his hand down a large bronze eagle statue; it leaned toward the hunt, wings slightly spread, talons tight on a branch. His creation reflected his emotions at twenty-one—surging into the world and Paris, hungry and ready, inhaling life as if it were sweet cream. Beneath his fingertips, the metal was smooth, cool, and predictable—unlike his thoughts about Jemma Delaney.

Tonight, Hogan had no time for Jemma's offbeat ideas to promote whatever venture she currently favored. A gypsy whirlwind who had been his sister's best friend since they were eight, Jemma had always been a ragged, vivid tear in Hogan's streamlined life. He regretted answering her telephone call and agreeing to her demand that he "stay put until I arrive."

He'd come back to Sweet Grass County. In late

March, the sprawling alfalfa, timothy and "needle and thread" grass fields were coming to life. Soon, fed by the snow water from the mountains, the irrigation ditches would fill, be dammed, and overflow onto the fields, a ritual necessary to rich grasslands.

In the night, the jutting, snow-covered Crazy Mountains and their haunting winds called to him. He listened to the ceiling fan, the crackle of box elder fire, and hunted for harmony. It wouldn't come; his elements were not in alignment. Had they ever been? Too restless to create, or to rest, he swirled the fine wine in his glass and studied the amber liquid. His emotions were like the eagle's, hunting prey.

At thirty-nine, Hogan knew that he couldn't go on until he resolved the unanswered questions in his life and had returned to Montana the previous November. He'd taken time from his growing business before to refresh his creative needs. But this time he wondered, was he burned out, the images and color gone? Or had he sold what was in him and there was nothing left? He'd made a dive into the commercial designs that were certain to sell; he'd packaged himself along the way, developing a persona that drew attention. Now he was bone tired, stretched to the limits, and unhappy with his work. Hogan shrugged; he'd made a fortune. Did that cold hole eating at him really matter?

He was on edge, unable to sleep, prowling through the nights and the brittle memories of his home place. He'd bought land that had been Ben Kodiak's. Was it out of revenge? Or the need to hold what was his birthright?

Did a bastard have birthrights?

Hogan opened his free hand on the ceiling-to-floor window overlooking Kodiak land. Nearly ten thousand acres and six hundred head of Hereford cows and their calves—white-face Angus, or "baldies"—from an Angus bull, spread in front of him. He could almost hear the winds whispering to him. Some said an Indian or a white—whichever they preferred—went mad on the prairie and found a haven in the mountains; that madness was protection from Indians, who left him alone. Then those who believed in the Celestial Virgins said they ached for their homeland.

Across the rolling natural grass and alfalfa fields stood the house in which he'd grown up—stark, two-story, weathered, windows like the steel-patched holes in his heart—another monument.

He studied his reflection in the floor-to-ceiling windows, taking in the brutal stamp of the Kodiak family—his coloring was different from the fair, blue-eyed family, a reminder that he was not really one of them. He considered his dark, deep-set, haunted eyes, soaring black eyebrows, the blunt Kodiak nose, and harsh cheekbones. His cheeks were in shadow, laying bare the grim line of his mouth, the angular Kodiak jaw. The dark warlord in the glass was a man incapable of softness and joy . . . or was he?

He studied his hands—large, long, artistic hands, but with broad flat palms that said he'd dug his share of postholes and shoveled his share of manure. He'd found a refuge in his talent, but who was he?

"You're frozen in time, Hogan," he murmured to himself. "You're as unfeeling as your father." His hand opened near the reflection, the glass as cool and smooth as his emotions.

His cool exterior—sophisticated, classy, charming when necessary, lacked—lacked what? He'd done what he'd set out to do, and yet he wasn't at peace.

An image of a boy, dressed in worn jeans, running freely through the mountain meadows, lying lazily upon the grassy stream banks, fishing for trout, flashed across the glass—or was that a memory of the freedom he wanted in his soul? Undefined need drew him back to Montana, to the clean air and rugged mountains, to the streams and forests he'd known and loved. Hogan frowned; the need was stronger than he'd suspected— deeper, more troubling. His need concerned him as a man, the essence of man, and it was elusive. Unable to sleep, prowling through his memories and his creative senses blocked, he'd given himself to remodeling the house and to familiar ranch work, hoping to cleanse away whatever drove him—

He found his hand in a fist against the glass, a reflection of his turmoil. Or was it because he was his father's son—hardened early, too cold, and too complete. But he wasn't, was he? Complete? What was that aching dark hole within him? When would it fill?

Hogan ran a fingertip down the length of the eagle's head, turned slightly at an angle, his eyes watchful. He hadn't expected or received an invitation to Ben's Christmas dinner table, nor had Carley returned for the holidays. Hogan knew by her guarded telephone conversation at Christmas that his sister was troubled.

She'd never been the same since that night and the attempted rape; once vibrant, she'd become frumpy, quiet, and guarded. Hogan frowned as he thought of his sister, rage swirling deep inside him.

That night Mitch had been the first to find her. She'd been hiding in the bushes with Jemma. She and Jemma were set to play a prank on Carley's brothers and had separated. And someone had gotten to Carley, held her down, and had described vividly what he would do to her and called her his "Celestial Virgin." Those moments of horror had changed carefree Carley into an overweight, quiet shadow.

Carley's plea echoed in the firelit room as Hogan's eyes flicked around the massive, stark room filled with his large paintings and sculptures. *"Don't tell Mom and Dad! Please don't! Mom won't let me come back to Montana. I've been coming here since they were divorced and she'll blame Dad and they'll fight—oh, please don't—"*

He preferred working with metal and stones, because inevitably when he painted, he'd find an image of Carley's sheet-white face, her eyes huge and filled with horror. Her attacker was never identified, and she'd been trapped in an unending nightmare without closure.

*Closure.* Hogan needed that now, more than he needed sleep—to finish whatever drove him back to Montana and Kodiak land. Miles from the Kodiak Bar K was a town named for the first Kodiak—Hogan inhaled and wondered again why the land of his ancestors called to him.

His ranch was small and neat; the newly remodeled house contained an airy studio and a business center. He might purchase a few horses and beef cattle, because the sight of them grazing on the lush pastures seemed eternal, and pleased him visually. Although he had hated working for Ben, Hogan wanted to tend his own land and livestock—to replenish himself, rather than to profit.

After all, Hogan's land had once been Ben's, sold to protect the major portion of the Bar K. The outsiders with California tans and soft hands had left—rather ran from Montana's harsh weather—and now the land was Hogan's. The bastard's land, cast off to preserve the rest.

Hogan braced his hand against the gray, smooth river stone of the fireplace and studied the flickering fire within the huge open grate. A fireplace insert would have been more practical, but Hogan wanted the color and flow of fire, the arc of sparks. He frowned and followed his darker thoughts: He'd come home, and he ached for something that had always eluded him. He would find it—here, where he belonged.

Headlights speared his windows, forcing his thoughts back to Jemma Delaney. He sighed wearily, used to years of Jemma's pushy demands. He tolerated her because of her unwavering love and absolute devotion to Carley. What did Jemma want of him now?

He knew Jemma too well. Through the years, she'd never missed a chance to make money. She intended to marry money and get more money. She'd been everything from a bartender to a nurse's aid, and she knew how to hustle, to promote. Carley had said that Jemma's family was poor, but that was all that Hogan knew of Jemma's young life. He didn't care to know more. He didn't want to understand her.

He dreaded her visit, the brisk familiarity, the verbal jabs. Jemma was illogical, self-centered, and maddening—except when it came to Carley. His sister's friend had come to stay at the ranch during the summers and holidays. At five-foot-eight, Jemma wasn't intimidated by the tall Kodiaks, but sailed right into the midst of them for Carley's sake. Vivid and fierce, she'd rip into anyone who pushed Carley about laying the past aside and creating a new life as a woman. Jemma had a call-it-as-I-see-it personality and a sharp, protective tongue when Carley was challenged. Jemma wasn't afraid to pit herself against Ben, and he liked her, often laughing at her sassy mouth. Hogan frowned; that sassy, fast mouth had taken strips off him, digging at him, when they were younger.

Now, headlights lasered into the shadows of his home and died as quickly as they appeared. A car door slammed outside his house and with a slow, painful sigh Hogan opened his front door. "Nice," he said, noting the black four-wheeler.

"Rented," Jemma returned in the years of shorthand conversation that suited their relationship. Leggy and lithe, and bundled in a bulky hot pink jacket, Jemma sailed by him to stand before the blazing fireplace—her muddied, knee-high yellow boots stood on the long, soft, Egyptian cotton rug. Hogan preferred to lie naked upon that rug to watch the fire's designs. It was typical of Jemma to tear into his home and destroy his simple, ordered peace.

She lifted her hand to her ponytail and tugged the yellow ruffled band from it. A river of dark red waves spilled into the firelight. Cut in layers, the tips of her hair seemed to ignite, a fiery halo gleaming around her head as she stood in front of the fire. She shook her head and pushed her hands through the thick mass. The feminine gesture caught Hogan, forced the air from his lungs. On another woman, he might have thought the action was erotic and sensual. But he knew Jemma too well—she had a mind like a full-steam-ahead locomotive, deterred by nothing when she wanted something. *And she always wanted something.*

"So this is the cave where you hide from the world— I heard that pained sigh. It sounds like Aaron's and Mitch's, like you'd like to avoid me and can't. It's a doomed sigh. I've had years of dealing with all you male Kodiaks, and none of you are going to escape me. Shut the door, the heat is getting out," she said, just as Hogan was closing the door.

He paused, then pushed the door closed, making it click on his terms, not hers. He turned slowly to her and her gray eyes ripped down his body, clad in a black silk shirt and loose flowing slacks, his feet bare on the smooth cool wood. "Ben would hate that outfit. You probably wear it just because you know it gets to him when you dress like an artist. Or an Indian."

Hogan closed his eyes, inhaled slowly, and withdrew into his control. Jemma was right, of course, but he didn't like people seeing past his walls. He liked quiet people and a smooth, uncomplicated life. He liked harmony, quiet, soothing colors, and Jemma tore into both. His sister's friend knew how to irritate and dig, yet she was devoted to Carley. If Carley needed attention, Jemma was the first to notice and she didn't hesitate to call anyone to tell them what they could do for Carley. She'd never left Carley after the attempted rape, sleeping with her when the nightmares tore his sister apart. They'd become women, and still that bond held true. For that, he tolerated Jemma. "What's this about?" he asked.

He studied her face, the bone structure that would serve her well as she aged. He could almost feel that pale, fine skin, a contrast to the living flame of her hair. The bones beneath her skin were delicate, fascinating, and he wondered what her face would feel like beneath his hands—He tossed that idea into the fire.

"You look awful. From the shadows under your eyes, you're not sleeping. Missing Mama?" She referred to Simone D'Arcy, Hogan's Paris lover of years ago and now his friend. Jemma ripped off her hot pink coat, sailed it to a cream-colored angular couch with matching throw pillows, and glanced around the room. She tugged up the sleeves of her bulky pink sweater, the soft cowl neckline framing her pale face. Her tight, flower-decked jeans slid down long legs into high yellow boots. As always, Jemma's color choices raked Hogan's need for visual harmony; so did her reference to Simone D'Arcy.

Ignoring her taunt, he settled into the shadows. He studied Jemma, who was a chameleon, adjusting to the role that suited her at the time. In Seattle he'd seen her elegantly dressed for the theater and in a tailored, gray suit for business. She could be flirtatious to a potential male backer, and in the next instant suck profit from him and stroll away without a backward glance.

But now she was free, the real Jemma, who hid nothing from the Kodiaks, including her love of vivid, irrational clothes. For years, she'd twisted through their lives like the myriad facets of sunlit citrine in a dark, shadowy room. In business, she shielded her expressions, but with the Kodiaks, that oval, honed face changed expressions within a heartbeat—a lift of an eyebrow, the tilt of her head, all easily read. In her power-woman role, alive with color, she had a reason for coming to Hogan, and he probably wasn't going to like it. She wasn't a creature of whimsy, but had dedicated herself to earning millions—and pasting the Kodiaks together for Carley's sake. And she knew how to get what she wanted—

Hogan frowned. He braced himself for Jemma's pleas to make peace with Ben, to make life easier for Carley. Hogan resented the woman striding into his shadows, slashing at the Kodiaks with the freedom no one else dared. Not even his family.

The firelight caught on her wild dark red mane, and she impatiently pushed it back from that angular fascinating face, the expression that ran through her like a tumbling stream. Her hair had always reminded Hogan of a rich carnelian stone with varying shades. The tendrils and waves fell below her shoulders, a living mass of color that clashed with her vivid clothing.

She scanned his uncluttered, peaceful living room and tore into its harmony. "It's big and too dark. Needs plants and a few color cushions. Think about pink and rust. Where's the kitchen?"

When she hurried off, exploring without waiting for

an answer, Hogan shook his head—his tranquil home threatened by a tornado of clashing colors and nonstop woman. He followed her into the kitchen, resenting the need to be herded or to follow Jemma Delaney anywhere. "Carley's Whirlwind" hadn't changed—she ate voraciously, she bossed and prodded, and she loved Carley without qualification.

He frowned at the artist awakening in him—the need to touch, to smooth that lithe taut female body between his palms, absorbing the curves into him, to store for use in his work. He'd always had the need to touch, to draw into him, and he resented the need to feel Jemma's body beneath his palms, to smooth those narrow hips and stroke those firm, long thighs, to wrap his hand around her ankle, an image of male capturing a female. Her uptilted breasts had taunted him since she'd matured years ago.

He pushed away the artist and slid into the man who knew Jemma too well—she always wanted something, and she wasn't sweet.

In the kitchen, Jemma bent, studying the contents of Hogan's double-wide refrigerator. "I'm starved."

"What else is new?" In contrast to his rounder, shorter half sister, Jemma's lithe, restless body never reflected her bottomless-pit eating habits.

The artist within him awakened at her smooth, graceful movements, her slender, eloquent hands that could— Hogan inhaled sharply when he realized that his skin had tightened almost sensually.

Jemma was not a sensual woman, never stopping to enjoy a texture or image. In constant motion, she disturbed Hogan's naturally methodical senses, creating a tidal wave in his smooth, calm, pensive waters. She flew her own plane. A top entrepreneur, she'd been an arctic bush pilot. She had as much sensitivity as a block of marble and, except for her deep affection for Carley, Jemma was strictly geared to stuffing her checkbook.

She scanned his spacious, gleaming kitchen. "Nice place. Expensive and classy. Cold, though. But it suits you, I suppose, all this gleaming stainless steel. Yes, it does suit you."

"Now I'm 'stainless steel.' The last time I was Mr. Granite Heart."

"You've always worn armor, as long as I've known you. You never let anyone get too close—all the doors swing shut—even with your family. That's awfully hard on people who love you—but then, you don't care about that, do you? You know—family, loved ones."

Hogan leaned against the wall and crossed his arms. Jemma's whirlwind manners had always irritated him. The comparison to stainless steel grated. He resented the quick glance in the kitchen window to see his reflection, to see if he was that easily read. Nettled that Jemma could distract him so easily, he turned to her. The sooner he got answers, the sooner she'd leave. "What about Carley?"

"She's in trouble. You're going to help." Jemma opened the refrigerator door and bent down, scanning it.

Hogan tried not to notice the tight fit of her jeans across her hips. He frowned, certain that the sudden jarring he'd just felt was the awful sunflower pattern clashing with his artistic sensibilities. He had the awful image of gathering those soft, sunflower-decked hips into his open hands—His body jolted to alert, the primitive need to take, startling him. Hogan lowered his lids and wished the slight tic at his temple would stop—he had no interest in Jemma's body. He needed sleep; his raw edges were showing. Jemma Delaney did not appeal to him.

Jemma retrieved half of a blackberry pie from the refrigerator and placed it on the counter. She withdrew a roast turkey breast and mashed potatoes. Hogan's eyes narrowed as she hacked at the neatly cut meat, slapping it onto a plate, and plopped a generous helping of mashed potatoes beside it. She bent to study his microwave, punching the buttons. "You must have a cook."

He noted the slivers of meat and dollops of potatoes Jemma had left on the counter and wiped them away. He neatly replaced the wrapping on the roast turkey breast, replacing the food in the refrigerator.

Hogan saw no reason to explain that Maxi Dove, Ben's housekeeper, and her daughter, Savanna, came and went in his home as well. He appreciated the meals, laundry, and housekeeping. When neither would take money, Hogan had funneled regular payments in their names to Aaron's brokerage company in New York. Neither woman knew that they owned shares in Kodiak Designs.

He'd wondered at times if Savanna was his sister, her sleek, dark, Native-American coloring matching his own. Maxi was Assiniboine and Blackfoot—what was he, in a land of Blackfoot, Crow and Cheyenne, and Kootenai? He treated Maxi with respect, and she had acted as his mother. Clearly Ben honored her, protected her when she had Savanna outside of marriage—Who was Hogan's mother?

"About Carley?" he asked, pushing away that cold, haunting, and familiar ache.

Jemma pushed a fork filled with turkey into her mouth, chewed and closed her eyes. "Mmm. Good." She reached for a wooden pepper grinder, used it, and carried the pie and plate of food into the living room. She sat cross-legged near the fire and flicked an impatient glance at Hogan. He was nettled by having to follow her through his house to discover why she had come. Jemma had always managed to place him in positions he didn't like. "Stop hovering. I'm not going to hurt you," she said.

In typical Jemma fashion, she ate the pie first, all of it, stuffing it into her mouth with a spoon. She licked the last bit of blackberry from her lip and dived into the roast turkey. "Ben still doesn't know about that summer when Carley and I were hiding in the bushes. I circled around, because I thought if you guys went skinny-dipping, I wanted to see it all. Anyway, I've always felt guilty that I left her and that creep, whoever he was almost raped her."

Hot rage slapped at Hogan, the fierce need to protect his sister. He didn't like feeling helpless, and Carley's haunted expression made him want to—

"You're blaming yourself again for not catching him that night. The rest of us are humans, Hogan. We accept that we make mistakes—but you're an unforgiving, cold heart, even with yourself. You're almost terrifying when you look like that, Hogan. I wonder sometimes what would have happened to him, if you had caught him. I don't think he would have lived—you're very protective of your family, and that's your only value to me." Her fork paused over the mashed potatoes. "Steamed brown rice would be healthier—You don't have gravy, do you? No, you wouldn't."

"I've had a plate or two of fettuccini Alfredo in my time." Hogan resented the way Jemma could put him on the offensive so quickly. In the way that had served for years, he quietly returned the barb—just a little warning tap to remind Jemma that he could defend himself. "You were married, weren't you? About four years ago?"

The color of brewing thunderclouds, her eyes flicked at him as she disregarded his question. "Sit down. You're making me nervous. You haven't changed.

You're just as moody-looking, intent like a cougar waiting to spring. I see you've still got the long hair Ben hates, though that's probably a high-priced designer cut, tied at the back with a leather thong. The short ponytail at your nape works. It's better than that long braid. You know how to market yourself. I like that.''

"Get to the point," Hogan said, and instantly regretted the sharp edge to his usual quiet tone. "You came here for a reason. What is it?"

Jemma's expression tightened into fury and words burst from her like bullets. "That bastard who nearly raped Carley has followed her. He's been sending her little messages. Eighteen years, and he's still after her. *Hogan, she hasn't slept in all these years—not unless you or Aaron or Mitch or Ben were in the vicinity.* No one is sleeping, it seems, haunted by that night and watching Carley come apart. Now, it's like she's afraid something is going to happen to Dinah, too. One night I found Carley sitting in the kitchen with a knife in each hand, just sitting there, staring at the door. You know she's never told anyone—even Dinah—and now he's started the threats. Dinah is terrified, and Carley won't leave work. She's a sitting duck right now. I promised I wouldn't say anything before this—before he started up again—he might have died meanwhile, anything could have happened, and I was hoping Carley would forget. But she can't now. *Because he's back, and we have to do something.*''

Hogan's blood ran cold; this time he couldn't push his rage back into the shadows, and his fist hit the wall. He knew then that he was capable of murder, if not of love. Jemma shoved back her hair and crossed her arms as she stared out into the night. In a typical, restless, abrupt motion, she turned, walked to the wine decanter, and filled their glasses. "There's one thing about you,

Sasquatch, I can always count on you for Carley's sake. We may not like each other, but you'll be there for her and for Dinah.''

''We shouldn't have run over those tire prints that night, trying to get him,'' Hogan said, lashing at himself. *Because he's back, and Carley can't take a second attack.*

Jemma slashed out a hand. ''That's old stuff—the area was rocky anyway. He could have stolen any car; no one around here used to bother to take their keys out of the ignition. Let it go. We've got a real problem. Dinah is scared, and she's called Mitch and Aaron. They're tying up business and they'll both be here for as long as it takes. She knows good and well that Ben and Carley's brothers are the best men to protect Carley.''

Jemma took a deep breath, her gray eyes steady upon his. ''Dinah and Ben never knew anything about that summer, or the messages the bastard has sent Carley through the years. Dinah only knows that Carley is being threatened now—Dinah opened a package addressed to Carley. It was a pair of panties. 'Wear this when we meet,' he'd written. Sick weirdo. Dinah thinks it's because some creep got mad at Dinah's Temporary Employment Service, because they wouldn't hire him. I don't think so. It's the same guy. He also sent her own panties from that night—Hogan, he's had them all these years, saving them. He's so sick and he wants to get her.''

Despite his rage and fear for Carley, Hogan noticed that Jemma was shivering and pale. ''Sit down.''

She swung a fist into the couch, then her nails dug deep into the woven material. ''I can't. I'm so mad.''

''You didn't know that would happen, Jemma,'' he began reasonably. How many times had each of them

crucified themselves for not protecting sweet young Carley that night?

"Didn't I? I should have—a girl, unprotected and
somewhere she shouldn't be," she said too tightly, and
again Hogan suspected that Jemma's life had not been
easy. She walked to Hogan and shoved a finger into his
silk-clad chest. "Dinah and Carley are coming here. And
we're all going to stay at Ben's house. You're going
along with this, Hogan, and you're going to make
friends with Ben. We're all going to be one big happy
family until this is over. You are not—repeat not—going to upset Carley or Dinah even more by tangling with
Ben."

While Hogan was dealing with the idea of Carley,
endangered and terrified, and Jemma's ordering him into
a relationship with Ben, she sailed in for another hit on
him. "For Carley's sake, to get her out of Seattle, Ben
has agreed to fake a terminal illness. He's agreed to this,
Hogan, and you're not ruining it. If Ben can give, so
can you. Dinah knew that this was no time for pride and
the past, not when Carley's life was involved, and she
asked him to help. He called Carley and requested that
all his family be together."

Hogan withheld his need to lash out at her, his temper
simmering. He pushed her finger aside; it returned to jab
at him again. "I'm in the middle of this one, bub. You're
not shoving me away like you do Dinah and the rest.
They love you, though I don't know why. You're in on
this whether you like it or not. One wrong move from
you, and I'll crucify you."

His temper did surge, fired by her stormy mood. He
wrapped her hand in his, holding it away. "You think
I'd endanger Carley? Or hurt her?"

"She's hurt every time you and Ben go at it. Not the
hot kind of mad, where everything is out in the open,

but the cold, slashing, bitter kind that is worse. You tear her apart, the both of you. I've watched it happen for years."

Hogan flung away her hand. "You're not one of the family. You don't know what goes on."

"Tell that to Carley or to Ben. *He* appreciates me."

"He's got Maxi Dove, his housekeeper, to keep him happy. She moved in—ready to give birth to Savanna— just after Dinah moved out. Maxi has never named Savanna's father, but then, moving in with Ben said a lot, didn't it?"

"Will you stop growling? Ben saw Maxi as someone in need, the way Mitch was in Chicago. He needed a housekeeper and a sitter for you, and she needed a refuge for her baby. It's worked out, and Dinah has never said one thing about their relationship, so why should you? Dinah will do what has to be done to protect Carley, just as the rest of us will. The police can't find traces of this guy and at least here, she'll have good protection. If there is one thing I know about Kodiak men, it's that they won't let anyone harm their loved ones."

Her eyes flashed, the color of steel, slicing at him. "You won't let your family down, not even Ben, if it came down to it. I know it. You know it. So don't try that dark stormy look at me. You may terrify other people, but you don't me. I know you too well."

Hogan fought for calm. "Fine," he managed tightly. "What's being done to find him?"

"You're the hunter, so are your brothers. If it started here, he'll probably trace her back here. Then you Sasquatches will take him out. That's the plan. You're hunters, and you know what you're doing. You'll get that rat."

Hogan eased onto the couch, staring at the fire. Jemma was right. Carley's best protection lay in her father and brothers. Kodiaks did know how to protect their own, and in a small rural community, an outsider would be noticed immediately. "What's your part in this family get-together? How are you going to keep Carley from suspecting anything is wrong? Ben is hard and healthy as ever."

Jemma flopped down at the other end of the couch and lay back, stretching, her arms behind her head. She placed her booted feet across his lap. "That's the beauty, Hogan, old buddy. I've worked a neat little plan. Savanna is a nurse, she'll help."

"You always have a plan, if not ten." Hogan noted the mud bits that had crumbled onto his silk slacks. He eased Jemma's feet to the floor.

"Hey! I'm tired and I've got a hard night ahead of me, driving back to Big Timber and flying back to Seattle. We've just got time for this little chat, and then I'm on my way. My feet are tired."

"Your mouth isn't." With a sigh, Hogan allowed her boots to return to rest across his thighs.

"You could save money by wearing imitation silk, not the real thing. These days polyester is really amazing," Jemma noted, but Hogan was frowning at the fire, thinking back to that night—

# two

"Not bad at all," Jemma was saying as she studied the firelight dancing on the boards of his varnished, gleaming cathedral ceiling. The ceiling fan's shadows circled rhythmically, breaking the firelight patterns. Her hair ripped dark red streaks across his cream-colored upholstery, matching Hogan's seething anger at the attacker. Once more, Hogan saw Carley's white face, the terror in her silvery eyes, and realized he was crushing the cushioned arm of his couch.

"You've got that look, all drawn in and dangerous." Jemma sat up in a startling typically Jemma-move and tapped her fingers on Hogan's *Crying Woman* statue and picked it up to study it. "Not bad. I could run a gallery for you here while I'm shooting the television pilot. You know, we could market a line of these babies, maybe pour plaster over them or something and mass produce them for tourist shops."

With a sigh, Hogan took the statue away from her. An early piece, *Crying Woman* held his young whimsy and dreams; he'd kept it to remind him of when he'd wanted a home and family of his own. Now, he felt old

27

and worn and restless, and he didn't like the hard, quick way Jemma appraised his work, calculating dollars and profit. "What television pilot?"

She grinned at him. "That's the beauty of it. Carley thinks I need her support when I make my pilot effort. With Ben's illness going for us, one backup plan or the other will keep Carley here, and she's looking forward to her favorite Sasquatches turning up. Until this is over, we're all going to be one happy family, like it or not."

"You keep forgetting that you're not one of the family." Familiar with Jemma's money-making schemes, Hogan studied her. He'd seen her work, driving hard; he'd seen her play men to give nothing and get everything. Jemma could be seductive and feminine, and sometimes she played that game with his brothers, who obviously enjoyed her teasing. Hogan didn't. "Don't tell me. You've found some hot-pants-for-brains backer for another can't-lose project. You're going to make money while we're protecting Carley. Waste not, want not, right?"

Jemma's agile mind almost frightened him.

"I just love it when you look like that, as if waiting for a ton of bricks to fall on you and not knowing which way to run." She threw out her arms, and her husky laughter echoed in the shadowy room. "You got it. I'm going to be 'Fly Fisher Woman.' If this works out, I'll be peddling a weekly television segment on Montana fly fishing. You know, teach women how to do it. Who knows? Maybe I can set up vacation fly-fishing schools?"

Her eyes gleamed at him as she shot out her hands. "I could develop a whole resort idea off this. Health retreats, meditation, couple getaways . . ."

Hogan stared at her. Jemma always could stop his thoughts. When they started to move again, he tried for a calm tone and realized it came out strangled. "Unless you've changed, you've never liked the outdoors. When did you learn how to fly fish?"

"Phooey, smooey. I never have. I've never known how to do most of the things I've done, including working on a trawler off the coast, or shucking oysters. But all of you know how to fish just great. I've got until July to learn. Les doesn't want to get caught in a freak snowstorm, and I've promised him beautiful weather. I remember watching all of you while I was lying on the bank reading fashion magazines. You were the best, or at least a close second to Ben. I don't want him mad at me—he's got that thin Kodiak patience—so you're the logical choice. Mitch and Aaron are likely to lose it too quick. You've always been the coolest of the lot, though you've lost it once or twice with me. You get to teach me, bud."

Hogan almost choked again; he had just sipped to steady his nerves. The idea of Jemma slinging a fly rod, line, and hooks around his head gave him the chills. "Not a chance."

"I want to be here for Carley, Hogan," Jemma said softly. "I can't afford to take time away from work—"

He eyed her; she'd never failed to slash through the easy, planned rhythms of his life. "You should have that first million by now, the way you're going. What are you doing anyway? The last time I heard you were a radio sports announcer."

"Gave that one up. They wanted to tie me down with five-year exclusive contracts, that sort of thing. I'm not going exclusive for anyone but myself. Sold limousines for a time, but I made a bundle. I'm into stocks and trading—Aaron helped me get started. By the way, I see you have a computer. I'd like to check my latest investments and see how they're doing."

"Fine. Do what you want. You will anyway," Hogan said, leaning his head back to study the fan and firelight shadows upon the ceiling. Jemma's mind could roll in twenty directions at once; his was still prowling through the past and Carley's attack—who was her attacker? Whoever he was had to know about the local Celestial Virgin story, or knew someone who lived in the area. He had to know where Carley was that night—

Jemma bounced to her feet and headed toward his office. After staring into the fire, hating Carley's attacker, and wondering how he could manage a relationship with Ben, even a short-term one, Hogan sighed and went to find Jemma. She was busily punching keys on his computer. "I knew that investment in Slinky Lace would pay off. Working women don't like to wear plain cotton bras anymore. They've got a few more dollars to spend, and they're spending it on great underwear. Yeah! I've tripled my investment since this morning."

She stood and stretched, arms over her head, revealing a smooth expanse of creamy stomach. Again, Hogan's throat dried. He looked away, stunned by his impulse to flatten his dark hand upon that pale skin, to feel the curved form move and arc beneath his touch. The line was perfect, feminine, and soft, a visual reminder that a woman's body could hold life and nurture—He inhaled her feminine scent and frowned. He didn't want to enjoy any part of Jemma and her computer-for-profit brain.

Jemma looked at him. "Mitch and Aaron can be trusted to make things run smoothly. I came here early to get your promise that you won't cause trouble with Ben. They still love each other, you know."

"Dinah married another man. That doesn't sound like love."

"It wasn't love. It was companionship. Joseph helped set her up in the temporary work business. She kept the

Kodiak name, not Joseph Merrick's last name. Joseph gave her warmth and protection when she needed it. She gave him the family he'd always wanted and made certain that Carley and Aaron knew who their father was and keeping Kodiak as their names as well. It was a fair exchange that suited them both for a time." Jemma pushed her hand through her hair, studied Hogan, then touched his cheek. "You look so much like Ben."

"Aaron looks like Ben. Old Jedidiah, Ben's grandfather, and Aaron, Ben's father, all have that same blunt, hard look—wide forehead, deep-set eyes, broad high cheekbones, an ordinary blunt nose, a hard line for a mouth, and a jaw that could cut granite."

"What a description. Those are your ancestors, too, Hogan. Jedidiah was your great-grandfather and old Aaron was your grandfather. Aaron has wavy blond hair and is blue-eyed. But you are a reflection of Ben in every way, and he knows it. Maybe that's why you can't get along, because he resents himself as a younger man. That senseless old dog, new dog stuff. Do you ever wonder how beautiful life would have been if he hadn't lost that leg?"

"Skip the psychology. Ben never wanted me, the bastard son." The words were bitter on his tongue. Life hadn't been beautiful for Hogan; his earliest memories were those of trying to please a man who treated him coldly.

"Still feeling sorry for yourself, aren't you? Aaron and Carley saw you as their protector, the big brother they could depend on. When they came back to visit, it was you who protected them, made certain they stayed. You were there, supporting them, when they would have run back to Dinah and Seattle the first time Ben lit into them for saddling a horse wrong. You were almost as much parent as he, telling them stories about Montana,

making them love the ranch and country life. You were
the one who gave him the idea to get Mitch involved
with dogs and calves. I know who spent time with Carley, explaining that sex wasn't dirty—Ben jumps and
looks hounded when the subject is brought up. You had
an easy way of explaining everything. You kept that
family together, and probably Ben, too, after they broke
up, and it took a big chunk out of you.''

"Are you done yet?'' Hogan disliked the harsh tone
of his voice and disliked her ripping into his life.

"No way. I've been in this war for years, Hogan. I
saw how you deflected Ben when he wanted too much
from Aaron and Carley—I saw how you put softer ideas
into him, like buying Carley a locket that time. And he
listened. He respected your input. You could have taken
off long before you did, but you kept all the Kodiaks
together. I know you got up in the night with Carley
more than I did. That you talked that soft, easy way to
her until dawn, and then you went out to work on the
ranch. I know you jerked Aaron out of trouble that could
have sent him back to Seattle, and I know what you've
done for Mitch. You stood up for Dinah when Aaron
said everything was her fault—that the family came
apart because of her leaving Ben. Their stories about you
say that you've paid a big price.''

"That's over.'' He wanted her to stop dragging out
the painful memories—

"No, it's not. It's buried inside you, festering. You
were an adult before your time, almost a parent to the
others. Maybe that's why you don't know how to laugh
or play.'' Jemma took a deep breath and fired again. ''I
know what you've done, coming back here, remodeling
this place and putting yourself right in front of Ben—
you're out to take Ben to task for everything you've held
against him. You are absolutely, truly, one hundred per-

cent certified perverse. You think it's time and—''

"Take it easy," Hogan warned, uncertain if his leashes would hold when Jemma pushed too close to his raw, exposed edges. None of them knew how deeply he'd needed to know about his mother, needed to know who he was; he hadn't let them inside to see that gaping pain and uncertainty.

"Don't think I didn't understand how you felt, a dark-skinned, black-eyed member of the family—Hogan, you positively wallowed in that status, looking down at the rest from your lofty perch. I know how that feels, not being a part of a family. I wanted something in my life, too, and it just wasn't there. Did I step into a big dark hole and pull it around me? No. But you did. You'll tear them apart and yourself. Right now, you're like some big, dark thunderstorm that can erupt at any minute. But I may lay off you. I just may, if it will help Carley. I know that you will do everything in your power to protect her. I want your promise that you will not upset Dinah or her by arguing with Ben.''

"I haven't seen him in years. I can't promise any-thing—" Hogan looked down to Jemma's fist crushing the silk covering his chest. She'd ripped into him, sparing nothing. "I can laugh," he said, his pride jarred by her statement a moment ago.

"Really? I've never heard you, in all these years. I've never seen you really smile—You may not have seen Ben, but you've been tracking him. I've seen your expression when Carley or the rest say something about him. You're storing every word, adding and subtracting. I know that look—I invented it and know what it means. You know his property value and how many cows he has—''

"Cattle," Hogan corrected automatically and a bit

sharply, with the impatience of a man bred to the West, dealing with city mentality.

"Fine, schmine. Cattle, then. You know what he's got in the bank. I'm into computer tracking myself, and I found your marks all over anything concerning Ben Kodiak. We both know you could buy him out easily." She pushed her face close to his. "Now get this, Kodiak. I intend for this gig—everyone here, in Montana, at the same time—to work. I do not want anything to go wrong, to allow any arguments to leave Carley unprotected."

She paused for breath, glaring up at him. Then she leaned forward, eyes smoking, fists tight, and started hacking at him again. "Do you know how much work it is to get a mule-headed, slow-minded, dipped in bad memories and dysfunctional family like the Kodiaks all together in the same place? I've done it, and you're not going to dig the scars deeper, Hogan Kodiak. I've worked too hard."

For a moment, Hogan stared at Jemma, her eyes flashing like lightning ripping across steel swords. She wasn't afraid to step into the past, or the future, and she wasn't backing off.

"Take your hand off me, Jemma," Hogan said too quietly, and knew that in another minute—he looked down to where her pale hand rested against his bare chest. The contrast of male and female, light and dark, startled and excited him. Textures, colors, and forms, trapped in movement, had always been his downfall, his fascination, and Jemma was a mixture of all of them.

Stunned that his thoughts could run to Jemma-the-woman, he brushed away her hand and smoothed his wrinkled shirt, just as he would have liked to smooth away her interference in his life. Jemma planted her body in front of him, her expression fierce. "Do you promise that you will try to get along with Ben?'' she asked too carefully.

After warring with his need to end his passage, his quest for peace, Hogan nodded. "For Carley," he said carefully.

"Yes, for Carley." Her expression was worried now, looking up at him. "Do you think it's a good plan, Hogan? Do you? She wouldn't have left her work for any other reason than her family's welfare. Do you think you and your brothers can protect her?"

At her first uncertainty, her concern for his sister, Hogan weakened. The dark circles beneath Jemma's eyes said she'd missed sleep. He couldn't resent Jemma when she loved Carley and would protect her with her life. "You shouldn't feel guilty about this, Jemma."

She ran her trembling hands over her face. "I love her as much as you do."

"She'll be protected here," Hogan said, meaning it.

"I know. It's as if the Kodiak men were bred to protect her, as if destiny made you all so hard and tough for just this moment. You'll catch him, won't you, Hogan?"

For the first time, Jemma looked weak and tired, her usual vibrancy darkened by worry. She looked helpless and delicate and wounded, and even as he reached for her, Hogan knew she would make his life unbearable. "Yes, like that," she whispered against his shoulder as his arms enclosed her. "I'm so scared, Hogan. You always know the right things to say. When things are coming apart, you've always been rock-solid. Say them now."

"Carley will be safe. We'll get him." Against her vibrant hair, he murmured what she needed to hear, though fear ran through him like an icy stake. She nestled against him, slender and feminine within his arms.

He resented the need to hold her closer, to protect her. He'd known her since she was eight, scrambling up the roof with Carley to toss balloons filled with water at the Kodiaks. He shouldn't have thought of her as a woman, but as his sister's friend. He frowned because, experienced in life, Hogan knew that Jemma had just aroused his sensual, prowling side. He didn't like the idea, or the woman who huddled in his arms. He held his body taut, away from hers. "You should have told me sooner, Jemma."

"I know. You always know how to make things right, but I thought the detectives could catch him—they couldn't. I thought I could manage and not let it come to this, and Carley still doesn't want Dinah or Ben to know about that night. She's too afraid of hurting them—she's just too afraid of anything."

Hogan held her a distance away. "You said there were detectives. I'll want their report files. Do you want to stay here tonight?"

She shook her head, and a ripple of dark red hair caught the firelight. "Their visit is a secret between you and me. I don't want the others to know that I want you to try with Ben. Do it for Carley's sake, Hogan. You will, won't you? For Carley? And for Dinah?"

He raked her hair back from her face, fisting it, and she didn't flinch as her face lifted to his. "I'd die for Carley and you know it."

Her smile was all slow, knowing, feminine pleasure. "I know. But I had to be certain that you wouldn't ruin it by fighting with Ben."

Hogan searched her pleading gray eyes and tried to isolate what fascinated him, that Jemma could reach into him and squeeze his emotions. "You're asking a lot."

"You'll give a lot . . . for Carley and Dinah, won't you?" she asked again.

"I would. Let me get this straight. Ben is sick, but not really. This is the reason we're all going to make like a family, right? There's a flaw in your masterpiece. A healthy-looking Ben when he's supposed to be sick?"

"I'll work on it. Now hold me just a bit more before I have to leave. I never break down, but—" When she began to shake and tears filled her eyes, Hogan tugged her into his arms and held her tight. "I knew I could count on you," she murmured against his chest. "I always could."

After a time, she stopped shaking, and Hogan eased her away, disliking the unsteady emotions she could arouse in him. He'd wanted to hold her closer, to stroke that long curved back and fill his hands with her bottom—"You'd better be going."

She smiled brightly, pushing her hand through the fabulous red mane he longed to hold like living fire in his hands. "Sure. Thanks. Don't forget Mitch and Aaron will be here next week. Dinah, Carley, and me the week after. See you in two weeks. Bye."

At the doorway, she turned to him. "Help me make this work, Hogan. Do not start with Ben. Let's get through this. Find that bastard and make him pay."

As her headlights ripped through the night, Hogan settled down into his thoughts, prowling through them. He couldn't ignore his body's need for Jemma, even as his mind told him that she was dangerous to him, to what he wanted. After a moment, he turned and hurled his wineglass into the fireplace. "I'll do what I have to do. I will find that bastard. Nothing is going to happen to Carley "

He looked up to the firelight dancing between the rotating shadows of the fan's blades. Hogan breathed deeply, inhaling the fragrance Jemma had left behind—and the excitement. He didn't like how his senses responded to her body, not at all. With a groan, he picked up the ringing telephone. Jemma's voice came across her car phone—''Don't feel too bad about burning out, Hogan. You've got enough work out there, and we can mass produce the designs, use cheaper grades of stones and market discount—''

He hung up and stripped off his silks, jerking on worn jeans. He needed a good mean horse and a long midnight ride to get the woman out of his mind. Her taunts jabbed at him, and Hogan stalked out of the house, nettled that Jemma had once more gotten to him. One minute she was pure Jemma—hard, slashing, and fast-moving and the next she'd moved into his arms with the natural ease of a lover. Hogan eyed his bronze eagle. ''I do know how to laugh.''

''*I will have Carley Kodiak as my bride*,'' the man at the top of the stairs murmured, heady with power after killing the old man. A dentist and an amateur mystery sleuth, the old man presented a potential problem and had to be eliminated. Now the fragile old man lay broken like a rag doll at the bottom of the stairs.

The Kodiak family together had always been powerful, though the killer was much smarter and in the end, he would have Carley for his Celestial Virgin, his sexual slave. As teenagers, the Kodiak brothers had dreamed of finding the legendary cave where the Chinese women were taken when they were of no more use to the frontier prospectors. The Kodiaks imagined they could ease the restless maidens' spirits, returning their bones to China. The Kodiaks thought they were smart, but they weren't. They hadn't found the cave, didn't believe it existed—but it did, and it waited for Carley . . . They'd had everything, the Kodiak golden gods—each was talented, successful, charming. As high school sports stars, they were untouchable, and Hogan's dark sensuality drew women—The Kodiak brothers had swaggered through town, showing off at rodeos. He wasn't jealous, of course, because he was superior to them. They'd had girls, but he would have what none of them had ever attained, a virgin. He would also have Carley—and in the cave, no one would hear her screams of pleasure. . . .

He clutched the file folder he'd made the old man give him. He lit the old kerosene lamp, and tossed it into the cluttered office where it would catch on cloth drapes, quickly setting the house on fire. It would look like the old man was running for help and tripped, falling down the stairs. . . .

The murderer laughed wildly and spotting an antique carved jade Buddha, swept it into his coat pocket—after all, old Doc Medford wouldn't need it anymore.

"I can handle this; everything is going just as planned. There's plenty of time to get everything right." Morning sunlight skimmed the clouds below her as Jemma circled the light plane over the Seattle runway approach. She automatically checked the instruments as she waited for permission to land. She was too tired, badly needing rest, but all the pieces were in place. She could trust the Kodiaks to act as a family to protect Carley. She would accept that Ben wanted his family together as he wound toward death. Mitch would come back from his social services work in Chicago, and Aaron would fly in from his brokerage firm in New York. They'd put their lives on hold to protect Carley, and Ben would try to be less—just Ben, demanding, bitter, hurting.

"There isn't any place safer for Carley than with her father and brothers," Jemma said firmly, believing it with all her heart and soul. "Hogan isn't ruining it. He knows it's for Carley."

Hogan was the same as he'd been when she'd seen him five years ago at Dinah's home in Seattle. Only harder, more stoic, as if he'd held in his storms too long, and they had eaten too much of him. He still resented his father, and, in his house, the bitter waves had slammed around her almost instantly.

Jemma slashed away tears. She blamed her unsteady emotions on the tension of flying over the mountains in bad weather. She'd had to sweet-talk an aging playboy fight controller, land on an icy runway to refuel, and battle mountain currents with a small plane. She was in no mood for Hogan to be tearing at her senses. "Blast him. Hogan still gets to me. He just always looks so lonely and brooding. I'm a sucker for that look, though I know he hasn't a bit of softness in him."

He'd had to be tough, surviving and caring for all of them through the years. He was always there, always calling—at graduations, sending presents, and he'd gotten a little colder each time, appeared more lonely, despite his success. A whole big piece was missing from Hogan, and she'd die for a real smile from him—just one really warm smile that reached those lovely, veiled black eyes.

She wiped away the tears streaking her cheeks and checked her instruments again. At six feet three inches, Hogan towered over her, and when he'd held her, there wasn't a bit of softness in that hard rangy body. Always a man who liked to touch, drawing textures and images into him, Hogan's body moved gracefully within his silk clothing as if it could be shed at any moment, as if he was accustomed to roaming his lair without it. He had smelled like—like man, a clean, arousing scent that she associated only with Hogan. His face seemed chiseled, planes gleaming, shadows defining his harsh features, that almost sensuous mouth. Except for his anger and obvious distaste for her, she couldn't define what thoughts lurked in those black, black eyes guarded by the long sweep of his lashes. "No man ought to have lashes like that. Not when I spend a fortune on high-priced mascara," she muttered.

Holding her close against him, Hogan's body was hard and safe and his loose silk pants were worn without underwear; she'd felt his sex nudge against her stomach, but she hadn't been thinking then of anything, anyone but Carley and the danger to her. The black silk had flowed around him, the shirt open and loose. She'd been aware of how beautiful he was, gracefully padding after her, that nettled, hounded look almost shielded from her. Dedicated to her finances, Jemma had few entertainments, but one of them was upending Hogan's famed control.

He'd known how to hit back and had gone right to the barb—"You were married, weren't you? About four years ago?"

"You knew I was. You just like playing games," she batted back into the empty cockpit.

"What was that, pilot Jemma?" the flight controller asked sharply, cutting into her dark thoughts about Hogan—the brother who pretended to be an outsider, when he loved the family deeply. Hogan loved Ben, though he didn't know it—the layers of fighting and coldness were too deep. For his part, Ben had dug in, refusing to relent, and the Kodiaks were at an impasse, each locked in his own cave. Jemma intended to change the rules where Ben and Hogan were concerned. They were going to relate if it killed her. "Dysfunctional, stubborn, mule-headed bulldogs tearing at each other—"

"What was that, pilot Delaney?" the controller asked again.

"Just checking my instruments. They're fine." Jemma wasn't about to explain to Hogan the sordid, embarrassing details of her marriage. She hadn't wanted love, but respect and security would have filled the gap. Donald Gillis ultimately gave her neither. The son of a banking family, he quickly pointed out her lack of society training and respectable background. "I'm the daughter of migrant workers who had ten children. How much time between tending babies and moving from shack to shack did Donald think there was for classes on how to entertain?" she muttered.

But Donald was what she'd wanted—classy, connected in society, wealthy, and pushable. She liked having things her own way, and Donald had been easy enough to direct without too many problems—until it came to her acting as a proper hostess. Once married, he'd laid down too many laws—including no flying and no business wheeling-dealing and no independent woman as his wife.

She could do without a husband and marriage tethers; she had always done just fine on her own. Jemma glanced around the neat interior of her small Cessna jet. She'd traded a neat little stationery business she'd started for the jet; later, she'd trade it for a customized travel camper van. She couldn't afford to have a Kodiak battle explode while she was promoting her fly-fishing idea to the producer. She knew how to bargain, and she wasn't letting anyone make her feel incapable and dumb again. "I thought it might be worth the try. Win some, lose some," she muttered, aware of the bitterness in her tone.

She fastened her mind on Les Parkins, the producer of a men's outdoors television program. Attracted to her, he wanted an affair. He wasn't having her, of course,

but she wasn't blocking any doors to financial oppor-
tunity. By July, she'd have him hooked on the idea. A
mild flirtation with Les wouldn't hurt, not when Jemma
stood to gain a television series. "He's coming along
nicely."

Hogan's image seared back to Jemma's mind. Trust
Hogan to look as he had, dressed in a black-silk shirt,
open to reveal his tanned chest and the ridges of his
stomach. Swaggering, arrogant, disdainful, his body had
moved gracefully within the flowing silk. The firelight
had gleamed upon his smooth chest, reminding her of a
polished metal statue. She'd wanted to place her hand
on those hard layered ridges, to smooth her palm down
to . . . Jemma glanced at a DC9 passenger plane gliding
through the blue sky, preparing to land. The white trail
in the blue sky was like Hogan, tearing across her life.

The firelight had touched his cheekbones, on that
blunt masculine line of his nose, those black fierce eyebrows, scowling at her as they always did. She smiled
tightly. She knew how to get to him, dig at him, torment
him. She always had. On her, Hogan had the effect of
a fire that needed fueling. She delighted in pushing him,
the layers cracking just a bit before all those wary angles
locked into place.

Her leather gloves gleamed as she gripped the controls
tightly, her thoughts veering back to Hogan. Always Hogan. Aloof, distant, dark, swirling in emotions about his
home place and his past. The protector of the Kodiak
family when Ben came undone, when Dinah left, Hogan
could rally the others around him, even Ben. His father
respected Hogan as a man who could match him any
day. He saw himself in Hogan, and understood him.
Wary opponents, they'd coldly slashed at each other
through the years, and forgiveness was eons away.

Aaron hid his bitterness for Dinah, for leaving Ben,

but it was there. Carley's defenses were a mile high, despite the warmth running beneath those drab, loose fitting clothes and her too serious expression. More than anything, Jemma wanted Carley to have the best, to have a life that filled her. Jemma dreamed of Carley smiling— free and happy—before that night.

Jemma considered the stormy dynamics of the Kodiak family. To her, they were dysfunctional pieces in a puzzle, never quite fitting exactly right. Hogan clung to his outsider status and fought Ben, who was powerless to escape the grip his own father's harsh ways had upon him. Then there was Dinah, loving them both, and her children. Touched by a rawhide past and Ben's accident, they were a family of high pride and warring emotions, a hard family to understand, but Jemma loved them. They were hers. Her family. Even Mitch, the street orphan, who loved them all, was hers; and Dinah had protected her, fought for her. Growing up, Jemma practically lived with Dinah; the Delaneys hadn't noticed, continuing to have other babies.

*Dinah.* A strong woman, Dinah still loved Ben, and she looked forward to having all of her family—and her family included Hogan—together. "This is going to work. They are going to be a family again, whether Hogan likes it or not."

Jemma slashed away another tear. She hated crying; it was only because she was too tired. She regretted grabbing Hogan like a lifeline. She'd never let him see her fears, shielding the heart of her, because Hogan could hurt her.

*Hogan.* Jemma wondered if he could ever be anyone's. "He's a lone wolf, that's what he is, and he's licking his wounds. He's going after Ben, positioning himself for the kill, and I won't have it."

Still, she could trust him and his unwavering love for

Carley, Dinah, Mitch and Aaron. Jemma didn't like him—that cold, stony silence, or the way he walked away from her, all lithe and rangy in that hunter's stride, but she wanted him. She wanted to scoop all those dark corners into her and make him better, to please him. "I am truly sick and demented. What woman would possibly want to cuddle Hogan Kodiak?" she muttered.

He'd held her wrists once when she was fifteen and trying herself against a twenty-three-year-old man of the world. He'd flown to Dinah's from his studies in France, looking tough in faded jeans and a tattered black T-shirt. She'd grabbed him, tumbled into his lap as she would with Mitch and Aaron to scuffle and laugh. But Hogan hadn't laughed. Fire and passion had leaped in his eyes, searing her, before he pushed her away with a look of disgust.

She didn't want fire and passion, she wanted men she could control, just as she controlled her life, and Hogan wasn't one of them. "I can trust him. He won't do anything to endanger Carley."

She'd wanted to hear Hogan tell her that her plan would work. She was terrified it would fail, and Carley would pay. Jemma hit the leather flight bag in the empty seat beside her. He'd held himself away from her, disdaining to touch her. "Too bad, buddy. We're in it for the duration."

"Nice view, Hogan. You can see the ranch perfectly, and this ranch was originally on the Kodiak homestead before Ben sold it. But that was the plan, wasn't it? To prove to the old man that you'd made it? That you're not going away?"

At dusk on the first week of April, the white rumps of antelope bounced away into the shadows of the Crazy Mountains. Newborn calves suckled cows in the Kodiak pastures and the foothills beyond the grassy expanse would have a blanket of light frost in the morning.

Mitch tossed aside his black-leather jacket, leaned back, and sipped his brew. He shared a look with Aaron, a replica of his blue-eyed, blond father. "So Jemma has a plan."

"Dad is supposed to fake a terminal illness, or so goes her plan. Trust her to come up with drama." Aaron kicked off his expensive Italian leather shoes, and propped his stockinged feet on Hogan's massive coffee table. He leaned back against the couch, his beer braced on his stomach. He flipped open the buttons of his shirt. "Jemma probably has a dozen backup plans. I've still got scars from the last ones. We'd better pull this off quick—"

"Or that creep will go underground for another eighteen years," Mitch finished roughly.

Crouched by the fire, Hogan studied his two brothers: Quick to smile and laugh, with black waving hair and the black sweatshirt, Mitch's black jeans, and biker's boots heightened his bad-boy looks. Aaron was smoother, harder, his jeans meticulous, pressed to a sharp crease, and his shirt custom-made. "We'll have to stay at the ranch—all of us. I don't like the idea of Dad's faked illness, but it is a good cover, especially if Carley won't leave Seattle. We can protect her better here."

Mitch snorted. "What about you, Hogan? You've got a house here. You can't logically stay at the old place."

"I'll be there often enough," Hogan said. He nodded toward the thick file Jemma had mailed overnight to him. He almost appreciated her quick mind for details. The report was thorough, mostly due to her relentless prodding; the detectives would have closed their case long before, except for Jemma's insistence that they continue. She'd paid the bill, not wanting to alarm Dinah or Carley. From the letters and faxes, Jemma had insisted on a list of every offender in the area eighteen years ago. She'd paid to have each located and their lives examined.

Hogan noted Jackson Reeves's name. When they were in high school, Jackson hadn't liked Hogan taking away his switchblade and breaking the blade. That and Hogan's blocking of his bullying might be the motive to hurt Carley. Jackson would know of the Celestial Virgins rumor and Jackson liked to hurt the unprotected—Hogan decided to chat with Jackson.

"A suspected serial killer and no one knows," Mitch stated grimly as he flipped through the file. He whistled at the fee Jemma had paid to separate agencies. "She's good. She's hacked, bullied, and flirted her way getting info from the police who don't want to alarm anyone by releasing the facts. Missing women. Known virgins. Three of them in ten years."

"He spread it out," Hogan noted.

Aaron studied the file Mitch had handed him. "Jemma paid a chunk for all this. Those women are all the same body type and coloring as Carley."

Mitch knew about women being stalked; working for social services, he'd seen too much. "Now he wants to finish the job."

"He's not getting Carley," Hogan said, meaning it.

After the brooding silence, Aaron chuckled. "You have to hand it to Jemma. Carley is in danger and wouldn't leave work or let Mom sell the business. Ben's request that his family be together was a great plan."

Hogan sat back to enjoy his brothers' expressions as he dropped a Jemma-fact into their laps. "She's got others. Jemma's trying to get a producer interested in starring her in a women's fly-fishing television series."

Mitch scratched his head and shook it. Aaron closed

his eyes as if reliving a nightmare. "I see hooks flying everywhere. I remember when we were kids and she tried that beauty-operator thing—"

"You looked great with orange hair." Mitch almost spewed his beer as Aaron elbowed him. Mitch rubbed his side, bruised by a terrified little boy who had been living in the streets; the boy had thought he wanted more than to comfort. The couple who took the boy knew how to handle him; he'd be safe. "Watch it."

"I thought old Ben would faint when he saw Carley's spiked orange hair. But he didn't. He just said, 'Fix it,' and walked out the door."

Aaron hefted his brew, toasting Jemma's escapades. "Remember that time she wanted to be a chef? And if she starts on that 'relate and express your feelings' psychology—"

Mitch lifted his glass. "To Jemma. Aren't we glad she's adopted our family? Aren't we all just looking forward to her schemes to bring us closer together? To make us better men? *To make us hug?*"

"Sorry, but if I'm going to be hugging, it's going to be a woman. I'll be damned if I'll take up knitting as therapy, and I'm not into visualizing flowers in fields and harmony. They should bar booksellers from selling any self-help books to her—everyone suffers," Aaron muttered. They all groaned and unspoken memories filled the silence. They'd called each other through the years, but building lives and careers had taken time. Now they had Carley to protect.

Mitch studied Aaron and Hogan. "I've been working with street kids. Hugs can do miracles—if they're not too terrified that you're out to hurt them."

"Sissy," Aaron sneered.

Hogan's thoughts ranged outside his brother's conversation. In his arms, Jemma had felt like a fragile little shaking bird. He resented how he had tilted his head just so to feel that untamed river of fiery silk on his skin, catching Jemma's scent—elusive, exotic and far more beckoning than expensive fragrances.

"Have you seen the old man, Hogan? I came back about three years ago and he wasn't pleasant. I caught something about being a city-sissy when I didn't want to shovel manure." Aaron didn't want to show how anxious he was about returning to the old house.

Hogan shook his head. He wasn't looking forward to seeing Ben so soon, either. He'd wanted to wait and think. He'd been too busy remodeling the house to include a studio and office, transferring his business equipment to the ranch—to script the dialogue. Or harden the shields of his heart.

"I've been back, last spring. I needed to see the fields and the new calves in it, replenishing life, spring in Montana where the air wasn't gray with exhaust. I meant to send a note to you both, but forgot," Mitch said. "Dropped in on him because I missed his sweet temperament. He gave me a life, and I respect him, because I know what could have happened to me if he hadn't. He's rawhide rough as always. Old Aaron's portrait still hangs over the fireplace with old Jubal's sprawling horns and that old bear-stopper buffalo gun. Dad says that Jubal was the first Kodiak Texas longhorn bull that made the Bar K. But the place is run-down. He and old Joe Blue Sky can't manage. We'll be working our butts off."

Aaron shot a sharp look at him. "Run-down? Kodiak ranch? Twelve thousand acres and six hundred baldies? How's that possible?"

Mitch nodded grimly. "Twelve thousand minus the two hundred acres that Hogan just bought. The old man probably knew that the family wouldn't stay in boring old rural Montana. Carley and Jemma didn't want to ask us for help, because Ben wouldn't have it. But we're here now, and he's low on cash. He'll lose the place if he doesn't get help.''

"He won't ask for it.'' Hogan hated that tenderness for Ben, for a man who kept his pride and would lose it if he lost his family homestead.

"We'll get him out of this jam,'' Mitch said quietly.

"He's not losing Kodiak land,'' Aaron stated firmly.

They looked at each other, hounded men who would protect Ben, even as they disliked how he had treated them as youths. Hogan didn't like the idea of helping Ben, because he knew the battles it would bring—but he wasn't letting the land go. All those years ago, when Dinah moved out, Hogan had managed accounts Ben forgot to pay. At fourteen, Hogan already knew how to bargain for credit, and how to make payments. Ben had cursed and fought the credit idea, nursing his pride. But he knew cattle and the land, and with Hogan working beside him, the ranch had stood firm. Hogan wondered if Ben would ever forgive him; the son taking matters into his hands, saving the ranch from the auction block. At fifteen, Hogan was winning track medals, making straight "A's" and working past midnight on Kodiak accounts. Sometime in those hours, he had worked on the ranch beside Ben.

Ben had resented Hogan's strength, the same as he'd admired it, and he never once said, "I'm proud of you." It wasn't Ben Kodiak's way and Hogan hadn't expected hugs.

"Cow piles,'' Mitch said flatly. "I've always hated 'em. Give me a city street any day.''

"Tractors at dawn.'' Aaron groaned the words. "Physical ranch work, not a nice sweet office and an accommodating staff. How I love to walk into the office and have some pretty young thing hand me a cup of

coffee and a smile. I like to smell their hair in the morning, just after they've washed it. Starts my day off right.
Barn manure doesn't have the same appeal.''

"I'm betting on that ladies' man charm, bro," Mitch
said. "Old Snake did a good job training you."

Hogan couldn't resist riffling Aaron and Mitch's
smooth waters. "She'll want to learn how to shoot, if
she doesn't know already."

Mitch sat up, instantly wary. "Carley and Dinah can
knock the eye out of a fly."

"Damn. He means Jemma," Aaron muttered in a
doomed tone and sank lower into the cushions. "We'll
all be dead."

"Shot in the butt, or hooked in the butt. Gentlemen,
which do you prefer?" Mitch offered dramatically.

Hogan stared off into the night and prayed they'd get
the stalker. "He'll come, and we'll be waiting." He
looked at his brothers. "I guess there's just one thing to
do—"

Aaron chafed his hands together, grinning at Hogan.
"Play poker. By the way, old man, Jemma says you
never laugh and that you're not fun."

Hogan raised his eyebrows and leered. "She's got it
wrong. Women like me, boys. I'm a charmer."

"Oh, man, she's already gotten to you," Mitch said,
laughing so hard he rolled off the couch. "She says
you're the worst caveman of the lot ... worse than
Ben."

"I'd think she could adopt another family, or stand
still long enough to make her own. She's had guys after
her, but she either scares them off, or she's running too
fast for them to catch up. If she starts that hugging stuff,
I'm riding out," Aaron promised darkly. "Yeah, Hogan,
you're all worked up, looking like a thundercloud. She
cut right to the chase, didn't she? Laid you open and

bleeding, and she probably walked away without a scratch.''

"Back off.'' Hogan promised himself that Jemma wasn't getting to him again.

With a feeling of grim determination, the brothers settled down to enjoy their last night before returning to the Bar K, Ben, and the shattered shadows of their lives.

# three

Ben Kodiak sat in his kitchen, his morning chores already done. Maxi was busy preparing his six-thirty breakfast. A branch from the old maple tree outside scratched on the kitchen window as he drank coffee and slid into his unsettled emotions. He knew his sons would come—for Carley. He was ashamed of the house and land, the way he'd let it go, but when Dinah called, he'd offered it and his life gladly. Her voice had quivered, coming across the telephone lines, telling how much she feared for Carley.

The girl was a Kodiak all right. His daughter wasn't letting a stalker run her away from her work. At first he'd hated the idea of faking a terminal illness, of seeing the pain in his daughter's eyes, but then the thought of his family all together under one roof had tempered the blow to his pride. Jemma was shrewd and unafraid; he liked and respected her.

He ran his hand over his chest, the faded flannel shirt covering the gold wedding ring he always wore on a chain. *Dinah, his wife—the mother of his children—was coming back to him.* He'd always loved her, from the

53

first time he saw her on that Seattle street corner—a classy, well-dressed blond, not a hair out of place, as she hurried to pick up her groceries, dropped on the sidewalk. He'd stopped to help her, and his heart had stayed for a lifetime. He'd wanted her to marry again, but it had hurt. Someone else could give her tenderness, financial stability, and a whole body.

Ben gripped his thigh, the part of his leg that belonged to him, and damned the rest, the prosthesis. She'd been the bright flower of his life—in his heart, she'd always be. She'd added to his joy and pride in Hogan by giving him two more fine children, Carley and Aaron. She'd brought happiness into the old house that his father had built and ruled.

He had too much of his father, old Aaron, in him. He didn't know how to tell Hogan how he felt. He hadn't told Dinah, either, except with his body. Then, after the accident, he couldn't bear for her to see him—less than he was. Lovemaking was impossible; not a whole man any longer, he'd feared how she would look when she saw him that first time. A strong man, he couldn't bear her distaste, and so he had forced her away.

He'd forced away a soft, tender part of his heart, and now she was coming back.

Ben looked at the shabby kitchen that Maxi kept clean, the old appliances barely working, the rugs worn and the furniture battered. The old house was too quiet after the boys left, one by one. Hogan had been the first, soaring off in that beat-up old pickup. Ben slapped his open hand on the table, jarring his coffee mug. Something had happened that summer, eighteen years ago, and his children weren't talking—they'd locked some dark secret inside them, and they didn't trust him enough to share it. Carley was at the focus of that night, and she'd become a shadow of the woman she should have been—what was it his children kept from him?

Maxi wiped up the spill, her Native-American eyes soft upon him. "It won't be so bad."

"Dinah should have better."

"She's coming to you to protect your child. The mother in her knows what is best. The woman in her still wants you, Ben Kodiak."

"That was over the day that tractor tipped over the bank and crushed my leg," Ben said firmly.

"It's over the day she says it is, and she hasn't said that yet."

"Maxi, you've been sipping that tequila again. That was thirty-two years ago, and then Dinah married another man."

"Cow poop," Maxi remarked eloquently, labeling what she thought of Ben's defense.

Dressed in her nurse's uniform, Savanna, Maxi's daughter, hurried into the kitchen, poured her morning coffee into a mug, and kissed her mother. She'd stayed the night to visit with her mother, but her town apartment served her needs for privacy. "Hi, Mom. 'Morning, Ben. Are you taking those calves to sale today?"

Ben hated to let the calves go. They were prime, pretty little Hereford and Angus cross "baldies," with white faces and black bodies. By fall they'd be fat on grazing. "I may."

"Got to go. The clinic will be busy on a Monday. I think they save the disasters over the weekend, just so they can make it rough. Susan McRoy had her baby Saturday night. A boy."

Savanna patted his shoulder, a brief show of affection that Ben hoarded in his heart. She was almost like his daughter, and like Jemma. Like Maxi, Savanna still visited Hogan, and Ben was too proud to ask about his eldest son. He clung to the bits they fed him about his son—how he looked, if he ate well, the progress on his remodeling of the house.

According to Maxi, Hogan wasn't sleeping nights and had a hawkish, shadowy look. He worked too hard, sometimes all night, ripping into the house, remodeling it. The boy always had his demons, and he'd paid for Ben's inexperience at being a father. Ben damned himself for his errors; his own father hadn't been a loving one. He knew about sleepless nights, his memories tangling through the shadows of the old house.

Ben regretted his inability to give Hogan what he needed. He was only eighteen when Hogan was born. They'd started out badly, and old Aaron had hated his dark-complected grandson. He'd tolerated Hogan because if he hadn't, Ben would have taken his son and left the big Bar K forever. The first years of Hogan's life were spent in bitterness, as Ben battled old Aaron, and somehow the pattern continued after Aaron died.

Ben swallowed roughly, remembering his little baby boy—his first son. He'd held Hogan close against him, a young teenage father faced with too much and a ranch to run. But there was no going back. With the Bar K needing him, Ben had pushed Hogan aside as soon as he could. Memories of Willow had curled around him, like the scent of sweet grass, and Hogan reminded Ben of her—his first sweetheart.

Then Hogan had taken care of him, the roles reversed after Dinah left. Hogan had saved the Bar K in those dark days, paying dearly with the loss of his teenage years, and Ben understood—because he'd done the same for old Aaron. His pride kept him from talking with Hogan, the bitterness between them too deep. *"You drove her away, Ben"* . . . *"Call me Dad"* . . . *"I will when you act like it."*

The echoes of their arguments slashed at him, and he'd been so wrong—

Aaron and Carley were a part of Dinah, his love and his wife, but Hogan was a reflection of himself and another time, a sweet good time. Hogan sensed the land more deeply, the shadows and the scents, the seasons, just as Ben did, drawing them into himself for solace. But his son was better than he, Ben thought. In his quiet, certain way, Hogan had the ability to draw the rest of the Kodiaks to him.

"The boys are coming in. They called this morning." His boys. His daughter. His wife. A family. His children were grown now and still torn by storms. Carley had sunk into a shadow of her early self and Mitch couldn't find peace. Aaron had started drawing women to him early, but he was restless, unwilling to commit. Ben wanted to see the reaction on Aaron's face when he saw Savanna again. She'd been a thin little thing, all elbows and knees and big, black eyes when Aaron had come home those times. She'd been off to nurse's training the last time he'd been home, and now she filled out her uniform. A sensible girl, Savanna wasn't likely to fall for Aaron's lady-killer ways. She knew men, liked them, but she wasn't getting caught as her mother had, unmarried and pregnant.

In the kitchen's morning light, Savanna smiled brightly, her blue-black hair neatly pinned into a twist. She took the money Ben handed her from his battered wallet. "Mom and I made the beds. I've got the grocery list."

She studied Ben's expression for a moment, saw more than he wanted her to, and quickly bent to kiss his cheek. "Everything is going to be just fine, Ben. Carley won't know that you're healthy as a horse. Those nursing classes you funded will pay off, and I'll help keep you alive for a time. You'll just have to go die some other time. She'll have all the protection she needs here, with you and your sons."

He studied the worn linoleum kitchen floor. "Maybe we should get some things for Dinah's room, a nice rug and a little table like she used to have—to put her perfume and such on." He loved watching her comb her silky blond hair at that silly little table, cluttered with tiny colorful bottles and jars. His hands had been too rough to touch her, but she had given him everything—looked at him with those clear blue eyes as if the sun set on him, and, for a time, he believed they would make a life despite the harshness he'd gotten from old Aaron. Together the city girl and the rough-hewn cowboy had made a home and children and had loved.

His hand smoothed his worn jeans to where his leg ended and the prosthesis began. Habits, he thought. Old Aaron had taught him that rawhide-rough way of looking at life. The unfit didn't survive. Dinah had said his missing leg didn't matter, that they could go on as before, but his own pride damned him. Ben breathed shakily; he couldn't bear for her to see him—half a man.

Maxi looked at his fingers, sunken into his thigh, and smiled at him. "It's going to be a home again, Ben Kodiak, with your family in it. You stop worrying."

"My boys stayed the night at Hogan's. He won't come home even for a meal. Does that sound like they're missing home?"

"Sounds to me as if they needed one last powwow—the beer-buddy kind. You know where men lament the old days, and see who can belch the loudest? Maybe they needed to talk about their Celestial Virgins."

When he was young, Ben hadn't had time to explore what other boys did, but he knew that his three sons had probably done just that. The subject of women was always close to the surface when his boys were together. He rubbed the ache in his heart and remembered how they were—strong, young, arrogant—with Hogan leading the pack in a quiet, but certain way that said he knew who he was and where he was going.

Ben inhaled roughly. He'd never been anywhere, except Chicago. His sons would find him even more behind times than when they left all those years ago. "Well, hell, I'm nervous, Maxi. You two women stop staring and wringing your hands over this old bear. I'll mind my manners and won't run them off before they eat a bite."

Then he hid a grin as Savanna rumpled his hair, teasing him, as she left for the clinic.

Later, when Aaron's silver Land Cruiser, a high-class sport utility vehicle, slid into the driveway, Ben's heart leaped. My son, he thought with pride as Aaron stepped out of the four-wheeler, shading his eyes against the midday sun. From the corral where he'd been saddling his gelding, Ben stopped to admire what he and Dinah had created. Clean-cut and dressed in a brown-leather jacket and jeans, Aaron directed his blue eyes at Ben. The impact knocked Ben back a step. *Beautiful*, he thought. *Perfect. A fine son.*

Mitch's big black Harley purred into the ranch yard. Riding without his helmet, Mitch sported rumpled black hair, his leather jacket and biker's boots showing his city roots. He'd only been a quick-minded scamp when Ben caught him hot-wiring his car in Chicago. Now, Mitch was a man, a Kodiak who battled the Chicago streets that had sired him.

Ben's heart kicked up and locked when Hogan's shiny new black pickup, layered with good Montana mud, pulled up beside Mitch's expensive rig. Ben's eldest son had been home for months and hadn't contacted him.

He'd heard stories about Hogan's rebuilding the old
Holmes ranch. The jutting contemporary-styled addition
with huge silver windows glinting in the dying sun, sat
exactly opposite the Kodiak house.

*Perfect*, he thought as his sons stood together, all
tough and arrogant, broad in the shoulder and with long,
healthy legs. They'd come home for Dinah and Carley,
to protect them. They walked toward the corral, and frozen—terrified that old Aaron would surface in him—
Ben stood still. For Dinah, he could change. He *would*
change. "Good morning, boys," he said, perhaps a little
too roughly, because his emotions were running away
from him.

"Dad," Aaron said smoothly.

"Dad," Mitch said, acknowledging the man who had
dragged him away from a life he had returned to—this
time to help others.

"Ben." Hogan's greeting was cool, his thumbs
hitched in his jeans, weight on one leg, the other apart,
hip-slung just as Ben used to do before—*What did he
expect?* Ben thought desperately. This was the son he'd
kept despite old Aaron's objections. Ben should have
known that the boy needed more. Dinah's tender ways
had shown Ben how it should have been—

Hogan's hair was tied back at his nape, just long
enough to almost make Ben smile. Hogan was like that,
testing him, and Ben was proud of his son, making his
own life against all odds. He admired him. He should
have left old Aaron and the Bar K like Hogan did eighteen years ago. Instead Ben had stayed and spread that
unloving darkness into his children. For a time, Dinah
had made a difference—until Ben had ruined it. He'd
carry that sorrow all his life, how he couldn't bear to
have her help him, look at him, feel sorry for him.

"Supper is at six," Ben said, unable to bridge the

distance between his sons and himself, especially Hogan. Anger tore at Ben. He should have given Hogan what he needed, held him more, loved him more, and now from the hard set of Hogan's expression, the taut line of his body, it was too late. There would be no redemption for Ben with Hogan, but Hogan would not fail Carley. Running away from his emotions and the inability to deal with them, Ben swung up into the saddle. "I've got work to do."

"Still the same," Aaron stated flatly as the brothers watched Ben ride to the natural grass fields where the small longhorn herd—descendants of old Jubal, a Texas bull—were grazing.

"The place isn't," Hogan said. He'd seen that the house badly needed painting, one window was broken and patched with linoleum. Close inspection revealed a worse picture: The front porch needed boards, the door wasn't hanging straight on the hinges, and the roof's shingles needed replacement. "I've got the power tools. We'll bring them over."

His earliest memories included Ben working to make the house presentable to the woman he would marry— Dinah. Hogan had been eager to help, eager for his father's approval, which never came. Now, he scanned the twenty horses in the field; once there had been two hundred and a nice income after they were broken. But back then, he'd done his share of breaking and showing the horses—Hogan missed that, handling horses, talking to them softly, and gaining their trust. He enjoyed the full mound of a mare's belly, the unborn foal's tiny leg protesting the touch. The wonder of birth always stunned and pleased him—and shapes stirred around him, colors and images, never defined.

Hogan slid back into his thoughts, prying at the images, trying to understand, because he knew as surely as he was in Montana, that the sensations came to him for a reason. *What was it?*

"Home sweet home," Mitch said, taking in the two-story building. "It really was. When Ben brought me here, I had enough to eat for the first time. And I was thinking every minute what I could take when I ran. What I could turn into cash. But I stayed. As long as I played by the rules, life was okay. When I didn't, Ben let me know hell. Kids sometimes need that, to know the rules, what is right from wrong, because they haven't been taught."

"That fat psychology degree probably taught you that, not Ben," Aaron stated.

"Ben told me that I wasn't a street kid anymore, that I was a Kodiak with a new name and a new start and that now there were rules. I respected and hated him at the same time."

Hogan stepped inside his emotions, not listening to his brothers. He watched Joe Blue Sky try to chop wood. The feeble old man had been a child when he first came to the Bar K, working for old Aaron Kodiak. Then Joe had seen Hogan through those first years. When Joe turned to him, shadows moved across the old man's face and Hogan wondered what tangled inside him.

Maxi Dove, the woman who had taken care of him as a baby and for those first years, hurried out the back door with the slop bucket for the pigs. Hogan didn't want to think about the work that needed to be done inside and braced himself against the memories that could swallow him. Hogan glanced at his brothers. "It's going to cost."

"Plenty," Aaron agreed. "And that's not counting the barn—it needs shoring up, part of the metal roof is torn off. Look at that fence—"

"May as well see what's inside," Hogan said, and

walked toward the house. He'd spent his young life there, fearing and hating Ben, and never free of his shadows. This time, he intended to settle his life. "It looked just like this before Dinah came. He put it back together for her. I guess we can do the same."

"He's too cool," Aaron said quietly, studying Hogan's set expression, the knee-locked, wide spread of his legs, as if nothing could tear him away from Kodiak land.

"Too much is going on inside him. He's holding."

Aaron winked. "Jemma never did like that—when Hogan pulled back into himself."

"True," Mitch agreed with a grin. "She'll get under his skin in no time."

"Twenty dollars says it'll take one week."

"I've got fifty on the first day. She'll track him down like a dog the first day, and destroy that famous cool."

Hogan lifted a wary eyebrow; his brothers knew too well how Jemma could hound him into a corner and test his control. He turned to the knoll overlooking the Bar K. Ben sat in his saddle, looking down at the ranchyard, a pose as eternal as the West.

"So much for homecoming," Aaron muttered darkly.

"He doesn't know how to handle it," Mitch said quietly and glanced at Hogan, who stood apart, staring up at Ben. Hogan's expression lacked emotion.

Aaron inhaled, already preparing for the old battles. "He won't like you footing the bill for repairs, Hogan. We're all chipping in."

"Uh-huh." Hogan remembered Ben, clenching every dollar, resenting the needs of a growing boy who had worked like a man.

Aaron and Mitch looked at each other; they knew that quiet, thoughtful tone. Hogan wasn't backing off this time. With the experience of a peacemaker, Mitch hooked his arms around Hogan's and Aaron's necks and said, "Well, sons of Ben Kodiak, we only have a week to get this place in shape before Dinah and Carley arrive. Jemma will have our hides if we don't pitch in."

"She can be nasty. I remember that time she tied me up in the bedsheets, sat on me, and told me just how nice I was going to be at the supper table. And if I said anything to make Carley think about the poor dead bunnies we were eating—that were her pets—Jemma had a backup plan to murder me—slowly." Aaron groaned, but Hogan moved aside, his stare locked on Ben.

"My mud flaps are going to be dirty." Jemma grimaced when her custom camper-van hit a solid Montana rock on the way to the Kodiak Bar K. She glanced in the opposite direction to Hogan's stark home, the bleak windows catching the evening sun. In mid-April, white-faced black calves were frolicking in the field, the snow-covered Crazy Mountains rose behind Ben's home. The rambling red barn and various sheds softened the no-frills house.

A yearling colt ran beside the fence, racing with Jemma's van and then off into the field. Foals nursed at the mares, and she remembered how young Hogan had looked, walking among the horses, talking, and touching them. She adjusted her sunglasses to buffer the brilliant sundown ricocheting off the gold van. "Hogan had better be at the ranch."

"Ben said that he would be and neither one ever breaks a promise." Dinah turned to her, a cool, classy woman, dressed in a gray merino sweater and neatly tailored slacks. She'd tried to hide her excitement and fought the flush on her cheeks—she was, after all, too old to be feeling so heady about seeing her first love again. Would she look old to him?

She quickly glanced down at her body, still trim, but not the same. She almost placed the simple gold band he'd given her back on her finger, and then had scoffed at herself for dreaming. Ben had been so terrifyingly masculine, so rugged and yet incredibly gentle and somewhat afraid of the lady he had captured. His shyness of her, yet his need, was more potent than heady wine and fancy words. "If Ben isn't there, we'll make ourselves at home. It's not like we haven't all lived at the ranch, one time or another. But he'll be there."

In the rear seat, Carley drew the sight of Kodiak land into her, holding it close to her heart. Unwillingly, her eyes slid to the distant rise—beyond that lay the stream that watered Ben's cattle. There, along the willow and brush, she'd been shoved down and—she pushed away the terror that always found her; her father needed her desperately. "I can't believe Dad is so ill. He was just fine last fall when I flew back to see him."

"Things happen fast," Jemma said, and hoped the Kodiaks would catch Carley's stalker soon. She was terrified that her plan wouldn't work, that Carley's stalker would succeed. Worse. She was afraid she'd do more damage than good in the stormy Kodiak family, hurting them all.

"*Ben*," Dinah said simply, tasting the name. She'd loved him on sight, that gentle, quiet-spoken cowboy who stooped to help her with her parcels. Her hand trembled as it rose to smooth her hair, a neat boy-cut in silky gray. He'd always loved smoothing her hair, a little embarrassed as he brushed it, a rawhide-rough Montana cowboy tending his wife's hair. And then the accident—

From that one day, when Ben's leg was mangled and taken from him, the Kodiaks' perfect life had been torn apart. She'd seen old Aaron in him then, killing the love his family felt for him, denying what they could all have.

He'd wanted to die, and she didn't let him. For that, he'd never forgiven her.

"I wonder how much time Dad has," Carley worried for the thousandth time.

Dinah turned to her daughter; she'd lie to protect her daughter, yet it did not sit well upon her. "He doesn't want anyone to know, Carley. Please don't mention it to anyone outside the family. You know your father—he'll be embarrassed to show any signs of frailty."

He'd been so white, fainting from pain and loss of blood, his tall body crumpled beneath that tractor. *"No, dammit, woman. Let me die a whole man, not some . . . thing."*

But she hadn't listened, dragging him from under the tractor and tying off the mangled leg with his shirtsleeve and later, his belt—and he'd hated her.

Jemma gripped the steering wheel tighter. She wasn't going to let this family drift farther apart. God help her, she had looked at the danger to Carley as a way to bring the Kodiaks together—they'd never let anyone down, and Carley was the most precious of the lot. If this didn't work to protect Carley—Jemma tossed away that thought. If there was a family who knew how to fight and survive, it was the Kodiaks—and Hogan, perhaps the most unpredictable, dark warrior of the lot, tried to keep himself outside emotion, but he felt it—it was there, stark love for every one of them, even Ben.

"Dad's pride is everything, of course," Carley murmured. "Yes, I can respect that. I won't say anything."

*Pride.* Jemma damned Hogan's and Ben's pride. She hadn't time to worry about her own, and theirs had cost too much pain and wasted too much time. Time was something she did not have, and the Kodiaks were going to be shoved back into a family, and they were going to like it, even if it killed her—and Hogan.

"Shut up and watch for big bumps and fresh cow piles—any cow pile. We're all going to be with Ben, and that's what he wants," Jemma said softly, with the ease of a friend who could nudge and love. She reached to tug Carley's hand from her mouth. "I'm the only one allowed to bite nails, and I'm not doing it. I'm driving and nervous, and I've got a producer coming in July. I don't remember these roads being so narrow," she said, as one tire slid off the dirt road.

"Stop muttering to yourself. This luxury boat isn't narrow," Carley said. "And you're not a good driver."

"Hey, babe, I've driven taxis, limos, and fishing trawlers. I'll get the hang of it," Jemma noted, concentrating on her plan. Carley inhaled sharply, and Jemma forced back a smile. Carley had edges that could be pricked; she wasn't always sweet, and beneath her angelic appearance, she had that high-wide Kodiak pride. Jemma glanced at Carley—tense, sitting too straight, her fine blond hair hacked into an unflattering Dutch-boy cut, and her body layered with clothing. Overweight, reclusive, and too quiet, Carley preferred dull colors and ate to fill an unending ache inside her.

There was rage inside her, too, and Jemma knew that hot slap of her own as she remembered how Carley had been held down and—

"I hope *he* doesn't come here," Carley worried again. "I don't want anything to happen to my family, not because of me."

*Dear God, please don't let him hurt my family. They've been through so much, and now Dad is dying,* Carley prayed. She fought the tremor that ran through her—her eyes locked in the direction of the meandering stream where *it* had happened eighteen years ago. She'd

been terrified to come back after that, terrified that her
mother would discover the attack and forbid her to return. But she'd loved Montana, despite the horror of that
night. Her heart belonged here, on Kodiak land. She felt
the tug of home with each hour she was away.

Carley balled her fists on her sweatpants. She knew
how to fight now; she'd had hours of self-defense
classes—urged into them by Jemma, who never stopped
protecting her. Carley glanced at Jemma—quick mind,
strong, eager for a new experience, completely and desperately driving herself to fill her bank account. But
Carley saw something in Jemma that was rare and true—
selfless love. Jemma had given Carley back a measure
of her pride; Jemma had prodded and insisted, but Carley's deep fear of men remained. She welcomed the time
with her father and brothers; she could relax a bit.

"Ben wants his family together. Just being here is the
best thing for him," Dinah was saying. In an awed
tender tone, she straightened, leaning forward to better
see the old ranch house. Love nestled in her tone, not
bitterness. "There's the ranch house."

Her hand covered her mouth, her blue eyes alight and
eager. "Oh! There's Ben and the boys."

Jemma wanted to cry at the aching tenderness in Dinah's voice, cry for the Kodiak family and all they'd
missed. A perfect family torn apart by an everyday farm-
ing accident, they were hers now, and she was determined to mend the rifts. She'd lined up the players, and
it would be a war, but Jemma wanted Dinah and Carley
to have a homecoming to remember.

# four

Home. Jemma felt the same thrill as she had when she came with Carley that first summer. The house was weathered, a stark two-story white house with a big sprawling porch. Wooden rocking chairs swayed as though just vacated. There was a picnic table in the backyard and—Jemma's throat tightened, despite her determination to remain in control—there were sheets flapping in the clean Montana wind, just as there had been on that first day she came. There was so much heavenly space.

There were two Sasquatches—Hogan and Aaron—when she'd first visited as an eight-year-old. Hogan was just sixteen and too silent, a dark foil to the other Kodiaks. A loner, he'd been tall, dark, and impervious to her best smile; she'd hated him on sight. Aaron was the playful brother she'd never had. Later, when ''Snake'' arrived, she'd had another brother to torment.

Hogan had been broody, dark-skinned with beautiful glossy black hair, standing apart from the blond, blue-eyed Kodiak family. He had that tall, rangy look, wrists too long for his sleeves, a red bandanna tied around his

forehead. Already swaggering, that loose, free stride of
a long-legged hunter, to her he looked like a god—arrogant, disdainful of girls, untamed, and perfect for tormenting. At eight, she'd told him that he was beautiful,
and that had sent him running. When she'd seen him
breaking horses, riding them until they were too weary
to fight, she'd been totally fascinated.

Jemma tossed her hair back from her face—she still
knew how to put Hogan on edge. She had always delighted in scoring hits on his cool, dark, remote shields.
He was so easy to read—once she had him in her grasp,
she intended to make him squirm. That image slid
away—Hogan was too tough, too worldly now, but if
there was truly a sport in her life, it was getting to Hogan.

Jemma pushed away the lingering bitterness about her
parents. Her parents had been no more than careless children themselves, not tending their brood of ten children,
and now they were all gone. She'd survived, and sometimes hated herself for doing so. But she'd gone on,
living and working to build a comfortable portfolio. She
had one weakness—the Kodiaks. They loved deeply,
and she'd loved them all—even Hogan and his shadows—at first sight. They'd had everything, but it had
been torn apart by the accident.

"I remember the first time I came here with Carley,"
Jemma said, floating into her memories. "Ben scooped
her up and held her tight. He looked like a tough cowboy, but with his face against Carley's throat, I saw just
one tear. It glittered on his lashes, then dropped onto my
hand. It felt like love, and I knew I'd love him forever
then. And then he swung me up onto his other hip, a
tall gangling eight-year old, as if I were his daughter,
too."

Amid the early mid-April alfalfa fields, the house had

stood for more than a hundred years. It had been remodeled here and there, and in Jemma's transient young
life, it had been heaven to know that a house and a
family would always remain in one place, that they
could come home.

Under the pretense of smoothing her hair, she wiped
away a tear. From what she knew of the Kodiaks, they
had been perfect until Ben's accident. A beautiful loving
family with a future ahead of them. Given time, Dinah
would have won Hogan into her keeping. Jemma caught
the love she felt for this family and held it tight—they
were hers, the only family she'd known.

The Kodiak men, lined up and waiting, presented a
homecoming to remember. Dressed in jeans, their white
dress shirts blazing in the late-afternoon sun, standing
with their legs spread wide and their rangy bodies outlined, they took her breath away.

*Hogan.* Jemma fought for breath, then scowled. She
wasn't wasting any time with a man who hated her, who
avoided her.

When Jemma stopped the van, she sat in the shadows,
watching the family she loved. Pale, fine hair tossed by
a cold Montana breeze in the dying sunlight, Dinah and
Carley hurried toward their loved ones. Aaron scooped
Carley into his arms and Mitch hugged Dinah. Always
a step back and holding to himself, Hogan stood,
crossing his arms. Aaron was stiff with Dinah, bending
to kiss her cheek and rigid when she wrapped her arms
around him.

Clearly uncertain what to do, Ben's gaze skimmed
across to the horses. Jemma knew that he wanted to ride
out, but he locked his boots and stayed, a big powerful
man obviously riding emotions too much for him, his
fists clenched at his side.

Jemma pushed open the door and circled the van. She

noted Hogan's earring—an expensive-looking, dangling black bead and silver affair—certain to snag Ben's temper. "Hi, babe," she said to Hogan, just to start him simmering.

"Flashy," he said coolly, indicating the golden metallic camper with a nod.

"Gold has always been my color. Goes with green, the color of money," she flipped back at him and stopped in midstep when she saw Dinah stand in front of Ben. They just stood there, a man and a woman in the April Montana sun, their eyes saying more than spoken words. Then Dinah lifted her hand to touch the gray at Ben's temples and as if no one else existed, he took her hand to his mouth, placing his kiss within her palm.

They'd been apart for over thirty years and yet they looked young—the gesture was so humbling that Jemma looked away, the intimacy between Ben and Dinah also striking Aaron and Mitch. Carley brushed away tears, her bottom lip trembling. Jemma chanced a look up at Hogan's tanned, usually impassive face and caught a sharp fleeting emotion, gone before it could be defined. "They're perfect, aren't they? Standing together like that?" he asked quietly.

"What do you mean?" Jemma looked up at him and found that fleeting glimpse of Hogan's scars, his loneliness and shadows.

He shook his head and retreated from her, and she hated him with a fury. "You just went into your cave, Hogan Kodiak. You know how I detest that."

His smile was cold and tight. Hogan rarely cared what people thought. "You're not ruining this moment," she stated firmly. "Try and I'll kill you."

She turned to the Kodiak family—the family she loved and wanted to be happy. Ben's expression held her like magic. His expression was soft, whimsical, as if he'd had everything he wanted right then and there. His look at Jemma was grateful as he swung Carley into a tight, fierce hug. Jemma waited just a heartbeat, just time enough to give him a moment with his daughter, then she launched herself upon him. "Hey!" Ben exclaimed in delight. She stood back and grinned at him a moment before she turned to Mitch and Aaron, kissing them soundly.

Both reacted the same—that slight catch, that momentary friction of an experienced man holding a woman in his arms. And both had shot her a satisfying leer that was all play. Filled with success and high on love, Jemma turned to Hogan and, with a Devil-made-me-do-it attitude, flung her arms around him, lowered one hand out of sight of the others, and patted his hard butt. "Gotcha," she said, and stepped back before he could push her away.

Then Hogan's hand shot out, gripped her upper arm and he tugged her close for a light kiss that lingered for just a heartbeat, shocking her. She stepped back again, stunned. The kiss wasn't friendly, but firm—a challenge of a male to a woman who taunted him.

He was trying to get to her, of course, trying to put her in her place and warn her not to test him. Jemma glared at him, tossed her hair back carelessly, to show him that she could easily shed any surprises he threw at her.

Dinah hugged Mitch and held Aaron tight, because she'd seen them through the years, and Hogan, too. She turned to Hogan and took his hand. "My son," she whispered in a reverent motherly tone that couldn't be challenged.

Hogan's body tensed; he wasn't unaffected. He glanced at Ben, who placed a hand on Dinah's shoulder. "I'm glad you're home. We all are. This is where you should be. You'd better come rest now," he said quietly.

"Rest? But I just got here—uh!" Dinah jerked as Jemma nudged her with her elbow.

Then Ben bent and lifted Dinah in his arms, walking toward the house. There was just that bit of hesitation as his right boot settled onto Kodiak land, a slight hint that his body wasn't complete. Clearly stunned, Dinah looked back, then settled into Ben's arms. Jemma, who couldn't help giggling as she hooked an arm around Carley. "Well, well, well. You Kodiaks ought to see yourselves, all of you, standing with your mouths open. You're all so easy, and so emotional."

"Dad doesn't look sick at all," Carley said quietly.

"Ben doesn't want it to show. You know him," Jemma returned quickly, and hated the lie. Still. She'd do anything for Carley—

While Mitch, Aaron, and Carley were stunned, Hogan scowled darkly at the man carrying Dinah into the house. Jemma nudged him with her shoulder. "That frown has to hurt."

Mitch, Aaron, and Carley hurried to unpack the van and follow Ben, but Hogan remained standing, immovable, arms crossed in front of him. She was tired, riding on nerves, and Hogan wasn't making anything easy. "You're going to be difficult, aren't you?" Jemma asked wearily.

"Miss Fix-It," Hogan said tightly, anger rimming the hard planes of his face, the tight, rhythmic cord in his jaw.

"Look, you. I don't want any fights straight off, but if you're asking, I can deliver. Just try to be sweet for today, okay? If it isn't too much of a strain?" she shot back. She turned to look at the house, the new white paint and repaired boards. In an attempt to remain cool and civil, she said, "I see you've all been working."

At her side, Hogan murmured, "Mitch bribed the lo-

cal high school teacher's shop department. We had more
trouble than the teenage labor was worth. They expected
beer and didn't get it. There's a fair amount of spit and
body fluids in that paint.''

"Don't tell me you don't have Ben in your blood,
always mulling in the dark side,'' she muttered.

But when she turned around, Hogan was striding toward his pickup. "Who needs you anyway, babe?'' she
asked softly, and knew from the hard set of his broad
shoulders that Hogan's emotions were tearing at him.

She couldn't bear for him to be alone and an outsider
to the Kodiaks and yet torn by love for them. Hogan
had never accepted himself. She hurried after him, hook-
ing a hand in the back of his tooled Western belt. A
powerful man set on a fast getaway, Hogan caused her
to skid along behind him until he stopped and swung
around to her.

"How about a ride in my new van?'' she asked, hoping to trim the edge off his stormy mood. She slid him
her best thousand-watt smile. It hit Hogan and crumpled
into the dirt at his boots.

He swung a disdainful look at her golden baby, all
shining silver mud flaps and studded with antennas,
gleaming in the twilight. "I want to live.''

She was trying, damn him. "What's eating at you?
Come on, don't be shy.''

Hogan's dark eyes flicked at the house. "He'll hurt
her. She's too soft for him. He'll start jabbing and hurting—''

"He will not. Any man who looks at a woman like
that is a man who feels blessed. He's romantic, carrying
her into the house like that.''

"What would you know about it? How a man feels?
It's common knowledge that he's sleeping with Maxi
Dove. Now he wants Dinah in his bed.''

"That is pure manure, and you know it. Ben took Maxi in when she was pregnant with Savanna and her family had turned her away. He's raised Savanna as his own daughter. He paid for her nurse's training."

"Maybe she is his daughter. Maybe he's been paid for that favor." Bitterness curled around his harsh tone, his eyes glinting dangerously at her.

Jemma pushed her face up to his; Hogan wasn't intimidating her with tough looks. "Savanna hasn't got that nasty Kodiak streak, like you do. You're just looking for trouble, and if you want a whole lot of it, just try me."

Hogan braced his hands on his hips. Tired, nerves stretched too thin and aching to take him on, Jemma did the same, lifting her face to his dark rugged one. "You are not going to ruin this, Hogan. You are coming inside and we're all going to be civilized and then, after a time, you'll excuse yourself and leave quietly."

Hogan reached past her to jerk open his pickup door and Jemma flattened herself against it. "Don't even think about it. I'll make your life so miserable, you won't be able to breathe."

He lifted a black, sleek brow. "This isn't *your* family. Or have you forgotten?"

"I'm in it now, and I'm sticking," she said, and blinked at the slight softening of his mouth, the warmth of his eyes. "So can you manage to be human, or not? I'll lay off, if you will."

"Tell Dinah and Carley that I'll be back in the morning," he said, and gently nudged her away with his shoulder.

Hogan wasn't setting his terms, when and where he could be reached. Jemma narrowed her eyes. "You're going to start this shindig off right at the breakfast table tomorrow morning. If you're not here for breakfast and in a sweeter mood, I'll bring everyone over in the morning. I've got room in the van. Ben will want a ride in it.''

She reveled in that quick black slap of temper, Hogan's stoic mask pulled aside. "The hell you will. You stay out of this."

"Brunch at eleven with sweet rolls, coffee, and orange juice is okay. Stop at the grocery store and get some of those bake-it-yourself ones. I like the thought of you cooking for me," Jemma said lightly, and, with a toss of her head, turned and stalked back to the house. In another minute, she'd have her hands around his big thick arrogant neck—

"Jemma." The quiet solid thud of her name hit her like a brick.

She stood still as Hogan walked to her and tugged the ruffled band from her ponytail. She fought the quiver of her senses as his scent and his body heat reached her. He leaned down to place his angular jaw against her own and to whisper in her ear. "Don't play games with me, Jemma. I'm not being molded and packaged for the family plan because you want it. It's a little late for that."

"See you tomorrow, bud, either really early here, at the breakfast table—or later at your place. They'll come for a ride with me, and we'll just happen to all land at your house. But while you're sulking over there in that fort, don't forget, this is for Carley . . . to protect her. If Dinah—or Ben—gets a few perks along the way, their family together again, then that suits me, too." She shot a solid elbow back into his stomach, noted the satisfactory grunt, and continued walking.

From the window, Ben spared a glance away from Dinah, who was hugging Maxi Dove. He noted Hogan's scowl, the quick dark heat of his eyes on Jemma's swaying hips, and the fury written on the young woman's.

Hogan was snarling again, and Jemma wanted her way. The girl had good moves, tearing away Hogan's reserve, and she wasn't giving up. A pain old and familiar shot through Ben's chest as he turned to look at the woman he'd always loved; he shouldn't have given up either.

Jemma shoved her body up the steps of the ranch house and forced her fist to uncurl before she took a deep, steadying breath and opened the new door. She pasted a smile on her face—as a survivor and making her way too soon in the world, she'd had plenty of practice in covering her emotions. Hogan could be a beast, when he wanted, but he wasn't getting to her—he wasn't.

She pushed aside her anger at Hogan and slowly studied the house she'd come to think of as her real home. The Kodiak house would always stand like this, solid, battered by weather and years and yet it remained, big, clean, and neat, clearly masculine. Ben's old leather chair was near the huge stone fireplace, the flickering flames adding to the sheen of the varnished floors.

The dangling crystals of an imitation Tiffany lamp speared a myriad of light into the room. Ben would have brought it down from the attic upstairs, where it had been stored since Dinah left. A huge battered pigeonhole desk was layered with paper, Aaron's sleek little portable computer closed by the telephone. Old Aaron's portrait and Jubal's sprawling horns over the fireplace were gone, the ancient buffalo gun remaining. The bedrooms upstairs were meant to accommodate a family and had before Ben's accident. He'd slept downstairs since then, and when Carley and Jemma had come home, he'd ordered the "Sasquatches" to the bunkhouse.

"The boys will be staying here in the house," he was saying quietly to Dinah. "It's better that way."

Her blue eyes met his. "Yes, it is. Thank you, Ben."

"I want you here," he said, and looped an arm around Carley and Jemma, drawing them close.

"How are you, Dad?" Carley asked, snuggling close, her flyaway straight blond hair almost silver, contrasting with Ben's crisp, dark blond-and-gray waves.

"Better," he said, with a meaningful look at Jemma. "Much better."

When Dinah exclaimed about the new linoleum floor in the large family kitchen, Ben scowled. The way he settled back into the shadows, reminded Jemma of Hogan. "Cost a fortune," Ben grumbled. "I'll have to sell off the place to pay back Hogan. He likes that, me indebted to him. Why the hell didn't he stay? Maxi fixed a special dinner, and this is Dinah and Carley's first night home."

"Not beef?" Jemma asked hopefully. "I really hate the thought of those poor little calves—"

"Beef," Ben stated, a Montana rancher protecting his life and income against marauding bean-curd vegetarians.

Jemma nudged him with her shoulder. "You'll have to manage by yourself, handsome. Hogan isn't here to protect you. I'd really like you to teach me something about guns."

His blue eyes lit with humor. "Don't sweet-talk me. I'm not teaching you how to shoot. Putting a gun in your hands would be asking for another missing leg."

Jemma resented the way Ben could head off her plans. "I'm not that bad, and what if Carley needs me—"

"Carley can handle a gun, if she needs. You're too hot-tempered. But don't let her go anywhere by herself. The boys and I are sticking close—one of us will be with her. Thank you, Jemma, for helping us."

"I'm good at wicked plans. The Kodiaks are too honest. I love you, Ben," Jemma said, meaning it and

watched the shy, embarrassed flush creep up his face.
She kissed his weathered cheek. "Get used to it."

Dinah hurried past them, her eyes shimmering with
emotions. She peered out of the window. "I have to—
Where's Hogan?" Dinah asked.

"Gone," Ben stated flatly, bitterness curling around
his tone.

"He'll be back in the morning." *Or I'll drag him
back*, Jemma thought. "Let's eat. I'm starved."

Mitch grinned and eyed her lean body. "You're always starved. Where do you put it?"

"Calories can't move fast enough to catch her. Mine
come to stay," Carley said cheerfully.

"Girls upstairs—Aaron, too. He's taking the corner
room. Jemma, you and Carley have to share a room this
trip. Mitch and I will bunk downstairs," Ben stated.
"Go wash up."

"Great, now I'm with the girls," Aaron muttered.
Everyone but Carley knew his presence was more for
protection than for accommodations. The "corner
room" had been built as a lookout by the first Kodiak,
with a small tower that overlooked the entire Bar K.

"Better be careful, Aaron, or I'll dye your hair again.
You looked snazzy in orange," Jemma teased.

"I love when you threaten. You get all hot and
wicked looking—uh!" Aaron hopped and rubbed his
backside. "No pinching."

At one o'clock that morning, Carley gathered her
worn flannel robe around her and sat curled in Ben's
chair. The fire had died, banked for the night with ashes,
and the old house had settled in creaks and sighs. The
past swam before her, two parents, each scarred and hurt
by the other, yet loving her. Her brothers, "the Sasquatches," were men hardened by life, lines and love

on their faces as they looked at her, trying to see below
the surface, blaming themselves. She slapped a palm
down on the smooth curled wood of the chair. *"You're
never going to forget me,"* he'd rasped that night, his
hands hurting her budding breasts. He'd jammed himself
against her, hurting her and yet not penetrating, though
he'd tried. Her body had resisted his and it only angered
him more.

He'd torn her mouth, though, bitten and hurt, and his
rage had slammed into her. When she was thirteen, those
fifteen minutes had been an eternity. Now, eighteen
years later, she was still haunted—Her hand stopped the
soft wounded cry, and she turned to the man moving
from the shadows. "Mitch."

He crouched in front of her chair, and, still filled with
her terror, she pulled her hands from his. "Baby," he
said so softly that the sound of her beating heart almost
buried it. "Baby, I'm here."

The firelight gleamed off his bare angular shoulders,
the old scars he never explained. His black waves were
rumpled as if he'd been running his hands through them.
He stood suddenly, a fit angular, beautiful man, dressed
only in jeans and brooding by the fire. He turned too
suddenly, surprising her. "Damn it, Carley. He's won if
you keep up like this. He meant to hurt you, and you're
letting him."

She pushed away that wave of anger, then let it roll
over her. "How would you know?" she shot at him.
"How would you know what it feels like?"

"I'd know, honey," he said, reminding her of the
scarred youth Ben had adopted.

"You don't know *this*. You don't know how I feel."

His answer cut like a knife. "It's written all over you.
You've pulled your life into a hole. I saw it in Seattle.
I saw how you shrank back when a man came near you,

someone you didn't know. You're afraid to be a woman.''

''Oh, well. Now that's something you'd know about—women. You've had your share.'' Mitch's attraction for women was legendary, and he was so smooth, so easy as he drew them to him.

She'd never know that flirtation, didn't want to. Didn't want to be under a man's body again or hurt and told how dirty she was—

''I like women. It's natural, Carley. Your fear of men isn't. If you need someone to talk to—''

''That's right. Pull out those big psychology degrees. I do not want to be your study, Mitch. Leave me alone.''

''That's just the problem, Carley. Everyone has left you alone. I don't intend to. I just wanted you to see me coming.''

She shot to her feet, smaller than he, but raised with the same hard steel. ''Ben won't have it.''

His smile was cold and tight, and there was nothing left of the boy who had been her brother all those years. ''That's right. Hide behind Ben.''

''I'm not hiding behind anyone.'' She knew she sounded like a Kodiak, and only Mitch could taunt that steel out of her.

''You're hiding from yourself,'' he said sadly, and reached to tug her hair. ''Darling, you're still a virgin, hoarding yourself. I'll bet you haven't had a kiss yet.''

''Why, Snake,'' she cooed, fury licking at her. ''Not everyone kisses and tells.''

He chuckled at that, then in a lightning change of expression, frowned down at her. ''Talk to me when you want. It's killing them to see you like this, like a scared little mouse, fear in your eyes when a man comes too close.''

To prove him wrong, she tried not to flinch as Mitch

curled his hand around her nape, his fingers stroking her skin. She'd known him for most of her life, saw him change from street-smart "Snake" to a man. But she couldn't stop the tremble that moved up her body, the quick edging away from him. "Don't play the do-gooder with me, Mitch. I have a life and I like it. Ben is—"

"He wants you here, and you came. That's family, Carley. Let me help."

Because she couldn't bear more, those soft concerned eyes, the way his body gleamed in the firelight, Carley tipped her head. "I'm going upstairs. Good night."

"You're running, Carley, and we both know it. You have to do this for yourself. I can help. I'm trained to help."

Her eyes were clear, glinting in the firelight, that fine Kodiak tempered steel that would see her through life—if she'd let it. "You know where you can stuff your help, don't you, Mitch? I'm not buying."

After she had gone, the house settling again, Mitch placed a hand on the rough-hewn wooden mantel and stared at the banked fire. He'd given her too much time to grow up, to shed the damage done to her at a tender age. And there would be hell to pay when Ben discovered Mitch had always wanted Carley. "Some way to pay Ben back, by craving his daughter," Mitch muttered darkly, and damned the stalker for hurting her all those years ago.

Then he remembered the steel in Carley's tone, that quick slap of her temper, and knew she remained a Kodiak beneath the layers. "She just hasn't been pushed, and I intend to push plenty. She's wallowed in that night enough."

He wanted the woman within—that sweet tender bud that had been nipped too soon and too harshly would have been more woman than—Was he pushing for her sake? Or for his own?

Hogan was home before he realized he wore Jemma's black ruffled band around his wrist. He ripped it from him and tossed it to the living-room floor on his way to the bedroom. The room was stark, the flat pillowless bed covered with a lush woven blanket, Native American in style. The large baskets held much of his work, a clutter of sketchbooks by his bed for the hours he couldn't sleep. Hogan clicked on the sound system and tried to let the notes of a solitary flute curl around and soothe him. He tried to concentrate on paperwork, to return his e-mail messages and failed.

Whatever stirred inside him now had nothing to do with his commercial drive. It had to do with finding his soul—

He toyed with the carnelian beads he would use in his designs. *Jemma.* All bold, fast-talking, pushing woman, an outsider who wouldn't allow herself to be, easily blending in with the rest of the Kodiak family. Sunlight had caught in her hair, the strands layered in deep waves. There was that proud, defiant lift of her chin, steely anger in her gray eyes. All passion-ripe, heat pouring from her, Jemma would fill his needs, but the consequences would be dear. She wasn't an easy woman, filled with pride and needs that almost devoured every breath. Her love for Carley redeemed her, and the bond to Dinah was clearly strong.

Jemma would keep her promise to invade his privacy—his "lair." She grated on his nerves; she excited him on a sensual level.

He damned his need to touch and stroke Jemma's body. Brittle with emotions, Hogan crouched to build a fire and spotted the ruffled band lying on the gleaming

wood floor. He picked it up, and, in the firelight, a long
fiery strand of hair erotically slid along his dark skin.
He wrapped it around his fingertip, smoothing the silky
texture with his thumb. After all the years he'd known
her, he knew little about her. What drove her to mend
the deep tears in his family? Why was she so desperate,
jabbing away at calculator buttons and figuring profit
and losses the moment she latched on to an idea?

She'd haunted him for years and he'd filled his body's
hunger with other women, but the need was still there,
ripe and hot and waiting.

Hogan padded to his sleek uncluttered office, apart
from his studio to keep from business distractions. If
Jemma wanted to dig at his family roots, it was time to
learn about hers. At his uncluttered glass-and-chrome
desk, Hogan picked up the copies of the stalker's notes
to Carley, included in Jemma's file. Cut and pasted letters would be hard to trace.

Hogan remembered Carley's scream that night and
Jemma's startling, too-adult rage. There was more to this
than a protective friend, much more. He rubbed the old
scar Ben had given him and prayed that Carley would
not be hurt.

*All the Kodiaks were gathering around sweet Carley,
and now she was so close to being his—He'd always
hated the Kodiaks and the mongrel Ben had adopted,
and now he would tear the heart from them.* Dear, sweet,
virginal Carley would be his. He had to have her, the
virgin she remained after all these years, waiting for him.
She would be pure, he knew, but the others weren't.
They'd shared their bodies, pretended to be virgins to
the world, but they weren't. Only Carley would be
unique, perfect, clean, and pure.

He'd changed her. Since that night other men hadn't

been interested in her with her frumpy clothes and shy temperament. The added weight was appealing, because he knew that was a protection to keep her for him. She had few male friendships, sidling away—he'd watched her grow into an adult, a professional, dedicated to her work, running the temporary employment service. She was very good, very thorough, his Carley, but then he deserved her—an intelligent, pure woman.

He frowned, hating the Kodiak men, tall tough men bred to the West. Mitch, Ben's adopted son, was just as physical. Women loved them, of course—stupid women. But they couldn't have Carley—because she was his. Because his darling, perfect virgin had waited to give her body to him.

# five

"Jemma got Hogan to come to the breakfast table. She's smart and tough, just like my son. They're a good match," Ben said to Sagebrush, a sturdy, ordinary-looking brown quarter horse. Sagebrush responded to Ben's uninjured leg better than any other horse; when tested, Sagebrush had a fighting spirit, just like his sons.

Ben settled back in the saddle, letting the horse pick his way up the fir-and-spruce-studded knoll to the old line shack. His sons didn't think he knew that it was their place to come when the storms were raging in the family. As a teenager, Hogan had stayed at the shack more than he stayed at the house or bunkhouse. As a teenager rebelling against old Aaron, Ben had stayed there, too.

He smiled briefly and checked the gasoline can tied to his saddle horn. From the sounds behind him, he knew another horse followed. "That would be Hogan, coming to set the rules of this fandango."

Like Ben, Hogan liked boundaries, used them to protect himself. Ben smiled again and raised his face to the clear Montana sky, letting the scents drift into him. This son was a tracker, bred to it, and could follow a cold-dead trail through a midnight rain. Hogan would know that the shack would provide a perfect overlook to the ranch. To keep Carley safe, it had to be destroyed.

"He's a hard son of a gun," Ben said, admiring his son. "Went his own way. Made his life and fortune. An artist—what do you think of that, Sagebrush? Would you think that a Kodiak could have that in him? He reached for the stars, and got them, too." Ben acknowledged the pride in his voice. "Ah, he's a lonely man, Sagebrush. And if he doesn't watch it, he'll throw away his chance for happiness, just like I did mine. We're alike, you know, and the trail is set too deep. Dinah has hope in her eyes that things will change between us, but I ruined it once, and I may do it again."

He slowed Sagebrush just that small bit, to let his son's Appaloosa gelding come alongside him. His son had picked a fine strong horse with good lines; Moon Shadow was probably out of Mike Blue Feather's herd. Hogan always knew horses, how to pick them. He knew how to talk gently, touching and gaining trust for a rider. There was nothing like seeing Hogan ride in the rodeo, except seeing him with the horses, how they came to him. Animals knew a good heart, and Hogan's was true. Ben's heart skipped a beat and went sailing into the sunlight; it felt good to ride beside his son, clean cold Montana air upon his face and the horse riding over Kodiak land. His family was together again, and a man couldn't ask for more—

*Dinah.* Ben lifted his face to the breeze scented of pines and the earth that lay waiting for his tractor. Dinah still filled his heart every time he thought of her, coming home to him, just as she had as a bride. There was that quick glance to the shambles that had been her pride, her garden. The slow drift of her hand over the old furniture that had belonged to his mother. As a bride, she'd stripped away the black varnish, and the wood gleamed new now, the old claw-foot buffet, and the sprawling spool-leg table. In the bedroom, she'd babied a free-standing closet into life—an ''armoire,'' she called it.

There would be plants and flowers in the house this summer, silly little things that showed a woman's touch. Ben swallowed the emotion tightening his throat. Before his accident, she'd just started a little business, pouring jam into pretty little jars, sealing them, and placing gingham cloth over the lids. She'd loved herbs, wanting to share her little pots of chives and oregano. He'd wanted to provide for her, to give her everything, and couldn't. Sunlight died in him the moment she walked out of his house.

He pushed away a smile, the good and the bad memories twisting inside him like a horsehair lariat—she'd seduced him into agreeing to let his wife be a business-woman, to make a little profit, his lovely Dinah. At first, he'd been uncomfortable with a woman's touch, the changes in his life—putting his dirty clothes in a hamper and not dropping them on the floor, going to church on Sunday morning, and going to dances and potluck dinners. His mother had abided by old Aaron's strict rules; she'd died young, used and empty, leaving Ben with a harsh father. Ben gripped his saddle horn with one leather-covered fist. He should have known what a boy like Hogan needed.

Moon Shadow came alongside Sagebrush and from the corner of his eye, Ben admired the fine loose Western way his son sat in the saddle, commanding the horse. It was a fine feeling riding beside a grown son; Ben's heart filled with pride. They rode together in silence, neither acknowledging the other. Both knew that the old

shack had to be destroyed. Hogan dismounted, already
striding inside the cabin before Ben could ease his prosthesis to the ground. He admired his son's movements,
prayed that nothing would happen to that young, strong
body—Hogan had had enough pain.

"He's been here. City shoes . . . new," Hogan said
grimly.

Ben nodded, walking around young serviceberry
bushes crushed by a four-wheeler. "Likes toys."

They worked quickly, efficiently, and Ben paused to
look at his family gathered in the ranch yard. The blaze
scrolled up into the midday sky, destroying the shack
that old Aaron treasured. It had been built by Jedidiah
Kodiak, a drover who didn't want to go back to Texas.

Then Hogan ripped off his gloves, tucked them in his
back pocket and turned to Ben. "Let's get this straight."

The hard punch of the words raised Ben's anger, a
familiar battle between father and son. He'd pushed his
own father just like this, and inside him pride swelled—
his son was a man. "You're talking to me, boy. I set
the rules."

Hogan's anger flashed back. "If I want to make Dinah
welcome here, I will. A few boards and paint charged
to my account shouldn't hurt you. We're not labeling
who pays for what this go-around. I don't like feeling
like I'm taking food from your breakfast table."

"I pay my own bills, and she's your mother. Call her
that." Ben heard the snarl in his voice and regretted it.

Ben refused to back down or apologize. The boy
should know he wasn't stabbing at him; he just wanted
his family fed and well, putting good solid food into
their bodies. He didn't have the sweet way of saying it,
but that was what was in his heart.

He couldn't help fighting back; Aaron had bred that
hard edge into him. "The pup wants to fight with the

old dog, does he? Why didn't you stay last night, if you're so concerned? Why didn't you stay to supper?''

Hogan's quick flash of pain should have told him to back off, but Ben had had his heart set on seeing his family together at the supper table. The empty chair that first night had mocked and hurt him.

Hogan's cold words slashed at Ben. ''Your table? Ben Kodiak food? Why do you think I didn't stay?''

*Because you're too much like me, unable to show your emotions, and so you hide.* Ben ached for his son and regretted the damage he'd done.

''I want to know about my mother, Ben. My *real* mother, not Dinah,'' Hogan stated, slapping his Western hat along his thigh.

Ben hadn't wanted to hurt the boy, and he didn't want to hurt the man. ''That's best left alone. She's buried now anyway. And you've got trouble coming right now. Probably more than you can handle.''

Hogan's black eyes flashed, a man who took challenges and hurled them back. ''What do you mean? Is that a threat?''

''Hell, I knew when I saw that damned earring in your ear and that black getup this morning that you were out for blood. What kind of a righteous man wears black jeans? It isn't me that you have to worry about now. Look.'' Ben nodded toward the trail winding upward to the knoll. ''She sure can't ride.''

Her hair fiery in the sunlight, Jemma bounced along on Sandy, a gentle quarter horse, the saddle slipping a little to the side. The girl loved color, Ben thought, the hot pink jacket contrasting with a purple sweater and tight jeans. The yellow boots were meant for city streets, not Montana dirt and mud and cow piles. Ben smiled as Hogan slapped his Western hat against his thigh, this time hard. He slapped it again as Jemma bounced into the shack's clearing. She almost spilled out of the saddle and came up with a too-bright smile, clearly an intruder out to make peace with warring men. "Hi. Did anyone bring the marshmallows?"

"You still can't ride worth a damn, city girl." Ben tossed a board onto the fire. While he loved her, the battle with Hogan and the past left a rough, angry edge to his voice.

"Of course I can't ride well. I was meant to ride in a padded seat on a smoothly moving, very expensive car. I haven't really wanted to bruise my backside that much. But I can outshop you any day, and that's important. As a matter of fact, who is going to loan me a pickup? I'm not getting my pretty rig dirty, and Dinah wants loads of potting soil."

"More money," Ben grumbled, and hated himself for being stingy.

"It's potting soil, not gold. Leave her alone." Hogan straightened, his body language challenging Ben's. "No one asked you for anything."

"It's my house." Ben's words shot into the sunlight like cold steel, and the sound of old Aaron's voice tore at him. Maybe he was too old to change, his father's son.

"Of course it is your house, but—" Jemma began, her wide gray eyes glancing at one, then the other tall Kodiak.

"Dinah doesn't like it?" Ben asked curtly, more wounded than if his heart had been sliced from him, but shielding that pain with anger.

"I like plants, but mine die. Dinah and Carley want houseplants, and they want the garden plowed. If you can't bother, then I will. Driving a tractor and plowing a garden can't be that hard. Hogan will lend his pickup for the potting soil, won't you, Hogan?"

Hogan stared at the brilliant blue sky and wondered how Jemma always managed to use him as her backup plan. "Let it go."

Ben didn't back off, digging in to argue. He wasn't letting anything go, furious with himself. He remembered raging at Dinah about potting soil, asking her why Montana cow manure and dirt wasn't good enough. He'd been so wrong. "The girl doesn't know how to saddle a horse. She's lucky she didn't fall off with that loose cinch."

"Boys," Jemma purred, moving smoothly between them, placing a hand on each of their chests. Her fingers moved slightly across Ben's buttoned shirt, and she frowned before looking up at Hogan, who had pushed her hand away. "Why are we having a bonfire? And where's the marshmallows?" she asked lightly.

"Look." Both men said at the same time, pointing down to the Kodiak ranch yard, clearly visible from the knoll.

Jemma expression darkened immediately. "He can see everything from up here."

"We're just not making him comfortable," Ben said.

"Well, then you'd just better hug and make up, because Carley is going to need each of us, not a war between you two. This morning, something set you both off. What was it? Ben? What got to you?"

"That damned earring," he muttered, looking away to the foothills of the Crazy Mountains.

"Hogan looks good in anything. It's an in-thing to do. See his black jeans? I'll get you a pair when we get to town. You'll be dynamite, and we've got to do something about these old flannel shirts, too. Maybe a sweater or two."

Jemma rubbed Ben's cheek lightly. "You need a new razor. Hogan wears his own designs. They suit him. He can be pretty when he wants, not all dark and broody-looking.''

Ben scowled at the onyx earring and because he needed to push the man who hoarded too many secrets, Hogan removed his earring and handed it to Ben. ''It's yours.''

It wasn't a peace offering; it was a challenge. This time Ben looked hounded. He looked at the fragile earring in his callused, scarred palm. ''It's a strange thing for a son to give his dad. I won't wear it, of course.''

Hogan inhaled—his work wasn't a trinket, but Ben would see it as silliness.

''You'd look cool with it on. Very exciting and studly.'' Jemma slung her arm around Ben and rested her head on his shoulder. She touched the earring in his palm, prodding and turning it. ''Isn't it pretty? It's a beautiful gesture, Ben. Take it. Doesn't he do marvelous work?''

Ben frowned, his expression something that Hogan couldn't define, and he blamed it on disgust. ''I design jewelry, Ben. You'll have to swallow that.''

''Kodiak Designs sell all over the world, in the best shops,'' Jemma said. She prodded it, revealing a tiny printed Kodiak with an arrow beneath it. ''See? Kodiak. *Your* name. There are expensive stores just waiting to get on his client list.''

''Do you have some of it?'' Ben asked softly, still studying the earring.

''I can't afford it, but Carley gave me earrings and Dinah gave me a ring to match, from his Fire Bird collection. They're in my safe-deposit box in Seattle. I think they'll become collectors' items, and I can make a mint off them.''

Ben stared at the earring in his rough palm, rolling it gently to catch the sunlight. Then he tucked it in his flannel shirt pocket, carefully buttoning the flap over it. Hogan braced himself for the taunts, but instead Ben's glance skimmed the old cabin, in full blaze. He nodded to Jemma, walked to his horse, and swung up, shooting a dark look at his son. "That's old Aaron's cabin. It's gone now."

Hogan returned the hard look; the cabin was a monument to rawhide-rough men and old Aaron. Then Jemma nudged him aside, and, unwillingly, Hogan's gaze dropped to the neat curve of her backside in tight jeans. "Wait!" she said. "Ben, I thought you might like to show me how to fly fish. I've got that producer coming, and I have to learn a little bit to make the series sell. If you could just point me to a stream with some hungry fish in it. I bought all this great stuff, and I have a license—"

"Oh, no. Not me. I want my skin all in one piece, and I don't fancy wearing fishhook jewelry on my backside. And I'm not showing anyone my fishing hole," Ben returned with a rich chuckle Hogan hadn't expected. "You tell my sons to get that old chest down from the attic. Not the camelback, but the old blue footlocker. Dinah will be wanting to have pictures of you children around her."

"I suppose I can make do with Hogan teaching me how to fish, and I've got until July anyway," Jemma muttered. She placed her hand on Ben's shoulder and kissed him again. "We'll be changing the house a bit, Ben. You'll help, won't you? Not hide out? Men and women manage households together now. You and Dinah could go grocery shopping—"

Hogan looked at Montana's blue sky. The rule-setting he had planned with Ben had turned into a "father-and-son-relate" session. From there, Jemma had driven the conversation into grocery shopping.

Ben cast a wary, cornered look at Hogan. "Maybe. Maybe, I'll help her."

"Aaron and Mitch and Hogan are all helping redo the house, and you did say for us to make ourselves comfortable, Ben. You're helping, too, aren't you?"

Because Ben was clearly uncomfortable with a man entering what he considered a woman's domain, Hogan smiled. "Okay, Ben. I'll wash, you dry."

When Ben shook his head and left the clearing to ride down the hill, Jemma turned to jab a finger in Hogan's chest. "Don't you start with him. Didn't you hear how he says, 'my son,' as if his heart is bursting with pride? You came to breakfast with a big chip on your shoulder, aching for a fight. From those shadows under your eyes, you were probably up all night planning on how to make life rough for Ben."

"I was there, wasn't I?" Hogan didn't feel like explaining his dark moods. Part of his lack of sleep was due to the woman who battled him now, that fire warming his cold shadows.

Her slap on his back was companionable, a coach to a student; instead, it nettled. "I knew I could count on you. He's wearing his wedding ring beneath his shirt. I just felt it. He still loves Dinah, and she loves him. You're not tearing them apart a second time."

Hogan turned toward her, his defenses rising. He remembered Ben lashing at Dinah, her crying behind closed doors. "You're blaming their split on me?"

"No. They both wanted something different. You're inventive, Hogan. You've got the ability to step back, analyze, and proceed logically. But maybe you could have engineered a reconciliation if you weren't so busy running away. Maybe." She followed Hogan to her horse, where he flipped up the stirrup and tightened the cinch. She hit his shoulder. "See what I mean? You're always running. I'm exhausted, standing between you two snarling yard dogs, and my butt hurts.'' She rubbed her bottom and tossed him a winner's smile. ''Horses are really wide, you know.''

''Someday you'll get tired of bossing me around, little girl,'' Hogan said, his senses pumping up, because he knew Jemma would rise to the bait.

Jemma crossed her arms. ''I know that we're decorating that house with a few of your canvases, to make Carley and Dinah happy. We could use a statue or two, nothing too big, and dramatic, like that awful eagle with the claws. Nothing too savage or scary.''

''Eagles have *talons*, and I don't paint anymore,'' Hogan corrected, noting the fine edge of her jaw, the way the sun painted a sheen on her smooth skin. He saw her with a headband, a curving brass affair, playing up to her Celtic heritage and bone structure. Still raw from his encounter with Ben, he fed his need to set off that fine fiery temper, to see that heat in her eyes and feel her passion surround him, burn him. ''How's your love life lately?''

''It's mine—private—and that's the point.'' Few people interfered with her, or pushed her, and Hogan was clearly gearing up to do just that.

''I know you're used to pushing men around to get what you want, and then you move on. It's a wonder you got married.''

''I had a different picture of married life than he did. He wanted children and a sweet little helpless wifey. I didn't like the picture. End of story—'' She looked down to the wild grass field and the small herd of longhorns. ''Oh, look. Ben isn't out on his tractor or fixing fence, he's down there just sitting on his horse and staring at that cow herd. He's thinking about all of you being home—how nice it is, and he's wanting things to change.''

"Don't change the subject and don't push me, Jemma," Hogan murmured, meaning it.

She placed her palms on his chest and shoved. Hogan didn't move back; instead, he backed her closer to the horse, framing her with his hands on the saddle. Jemma glared up at him. "I'm making this happen, Hogan. You're not stopping it."

"Ah, the real Jemma-agenda. Protecting Carley is essential. We agree on that, but you've got another plan, don't you? Could that be reuniting Dinah and Ben? Making the Kodiaks all one, big happy family? All of us hugging?" He enjoyed the feminine toss of her head, fiery hair swirling around her like a sunburst. Jemma, beneath all that hurry-hurry, human dynamo, was a very feminine woman.

He reached out to smooth the gleaming strands that had come free from her ponytail and watched the curtains come down. She edged away from him, gray eyes dark and wary.

Without an escape route, backed against the horse, Jemma looked down on to the sprawling fields, cut with irrigation ditches. Baldies dotted the pastures, calves frisking around cows, an Angus bull lying on the ground, overlooking his Hereford harem. She edged her jaw away from Hogan's prowling finger, a contrast of dark skin and fair. "You're playing with me. You and Ben are enough to exhaust a saint—too stubborn, cut out of the same cloth—and I don't have the time or energy."

"I do," he said, lowering his lips to taste hers, just a brush of his mouth, following that silky shape of hers, her scent curling around him. Hogan reached around her, capturing her arms against her body. He flattened his hand low on her spine and with his other, fisted that dark red thick mane, holding her face up to his. Her pink coat prevented him from locking her curved, lean body to his, but that was exactly what he wanted—Jemma close and tight against him.

"I'll get you," she said breathlessly, after a struggle that Hogan enjoyed, the softness of her body exciting his. Now there was just that stubborn set of her jaw, the steely flash of her eyes. Heat poured from her—live, twisting around him, igniting angry little edges and making them hunger.

"Mm. I'm looking forward to that." Then he slanted his mouth to hers and took. She tasted like freedom, sunlight, and life—she tasted like woman, erotic, darkly sensual, heat, and storms. She tasted like dreams that had died in him long ago—she tasted like life . . .

Jemma worked her hands free and slid them into his hair, fisting it as he held her, meeting him, an even match. Usually controlled with women, Hogan took the kiss deeper, tasting her mouth with his tongue, and Jemma's quickening breath set off a sensual need to have her—there beneath the clear Montana sky.

Then she shivered, her head jerking back, her body taut, and he caught her fear of him, of what he wanted, and Hogan gentled the kiss, seeking out the tender edges of the woman who called forth the darkness and the heat in him.

When the first of May lay green upon the land, the recent rains feeding the creeks and fields, Hogan leaned back against his extended-cab truck. At one o'clock in the afternoon, Kodiak was like any other quiet Western town, and he'd missed the friendly warmth of families he'd known. He'd grown to enjoy the shopping trips with Dinah, Carley, and Jemma and it was time for more potting and planting.

He was just discovering how much he liked the feminine spring ritual. When Jenna bent over the pots, digging with her spade, her hair all propped up into a cute little topknot, her hips were nice and round and just about two handfuls—if he'd dared.

Hogan sighed. All in all, he was enjoying the himself—if only Carley were not in danger. He'd missed rural Montana, the timeless spring planting and the town he'd known all his life.

Kodiak was a single main street lined with two-story adobe stores that had been redone with contemporary signs. Jedidiah Kodiak, the drover who never returned to Texas after the cattle drive, had married a mountain-man's daughter. His statue stood in the center of the small city park. Small dark taverns that had operated since the town's rip-roaring gold days now had neon beer signs, and the two small friendly cafés were always busy.

A small bakery, a real-estate office, the sheriff's department, a combination drugstore and dry goods store completed the picturesque street. Just off Main Street, new and used tractors were sold and repaired near a gas station that still catered to teen boys and their vehicles. The lumberyard stood on the other side of the street.

Cars and trucks lined Kodiak's streets, talk of cattle prices, horse breeding, and crops drifted pleasantly on the air. The two-story house with the big painted sign in the front yard was the local museum, tended by Kodiak's Historical Society.

Hogan turned his face up to the sun and thought of Jemma. He'd enjoyed that quick flash of awareness when she came too close. Wrapped in the novelty of letting a woman know that he was coming after her, that he wanted her for his own was a game he'd learned to enjoy.

Wary of him now, Jemma did not come near him,

clearly on the run. Teasing her with a brush of his finger across her cheek had become addictive. Sitting beside her, nudging her with his knee, putting his arm across the back of her chair at meals—he made a point not to miss meals at his father's now—was sheer pleasure. Jemma was as aware of him as a mare of a stallion—and he intended to claim her.

*Claim her.* Hogan smiled at his thoughts as a familiar boy tossed a softball to him. Hogan tossed it back and settled into his thoughts about Jemma. Hogan had never actively pursued a woman, or wanted to make her his own, exploring his fascination. He'd known experienced women who wanted no more from a relationship than he; Jemma delighted him, filled him in some way he hadn't known, and tangled his shadows with sunlight. As eager as a boy, just looking at her walk set him off, drooling. It was a fine time in life for an experienced man to discover that a special woman excited him, made him feel alive and eager. But then he'd never been a boy flirting with girls; he'd taken and given, but not that dark, deep essence of himself.

He did not like the thought of Les Parkins, her would-be producer, and Jemma in her van. He disliked her blatant flirting, the softening of her voice when she talked to him on the telephone.

Hogan glanced at Jackson Reeves, who glowered at him from across the street. Jackson was a potential candidate as Carley's attacker. The gas-station mechanic hadn't been cooperative when questioned about his activities and whereabouts. He hadn't liked Hogan since grade school. With a long criminal record of abuse toward women, Jackson had begun a brawl with Hogan. That was a mistake. Hogan's contempt for a man who hurt women, children, and animals who could not fight back was put into a few neat jabs. He left Jackson sprawled on the station's greasy cement floor with a promise to keep checking on him. "I'll get you," Jackson had snarled.

"I'll be waiting," Hogan had returned, meaning it.

He glanced down the street and locked on to Jemma. With her hair aflame in the sunlight and her jeans hugging her hips and long legs, he turned to pleasanter thoughts.

"He's still got it. Doesn't have to do a thing, just stand there and women hover like flies." Jemma watched Hogan, a worldly man at ease in the small Western town named after the Kodiaks. He seemed to be enjoying the day. In a black sweatshirt and black jeans, his hair tied at his nape with a leather thong, he'd captured the attention of several women, who had stopped to talk with him.

Carley shifted the catalog of upholstery swatches to her hip. "I can't believe he's in such a good mood. He's so easygoing. He actually volunteered to take us shopping—not a drop of fear. Aaron and Mitch ran like the hunted. Ben actually paled, and they all headed for a tractor that needed repair."

Jemma shivered just looking at Hogan's long, dark, sensual stare at her. She hadn't suspected that Hogan would want her, and as a prospective lover, he terrified her.

A carload of teenage boys whistled at Carley and Jemma as they walked toward Hogan's extended cab pickup. A three-year-old girl ran to him, lifting her arms to be held. With a quick grin, he picked her up, tossed her lightly in the air and braced her on his hip. An attractive woman, dressed in a green sweater and jeans, hurried out of the grocery store, obviously in search of her child who was now sitting on Hogan's shoulders, busily braiding his hair. The mother talked with Hogan, obviously enjoying his company, then lifted the girl down onto her hip. The girl stretched out her arms and Hogan bent for a kiss.

"Apparently, a woman's age doesn't matter." Jemma tightened her arms around the cardboard box of paint, linoleum, and carpeting samples. She refused to look at the man she still tasted on her lips. She hadn't anticipated the easy, seductive brush of his mouth, lifting, testing, and yet never connecting.

She knew how to kiss, how to pull back, how to tempt and yet not give. She wasn't a tease; she merely refused to give more of herself than she wanted. But Hogan had made her come for him, demand from him. She hadn't expected that slow seductive touch of his hands, those long fingers tracing her spine, stopping just above her hips.

His hands had moved over her, lightly, not caressing, just brushing, sensitizing her body and every nerve until she ached. She could taste the hunger, his desire, yet he controlled his body while hers was flung off into the white heat, aching for each touch.

She turned to glare at him now, and Hogan's black stare revealed nothing. Then he began a slow devastating smile, and Jemma wished she could pick up the fifty-pound bag of potting soil and—she inhaled sharply.

She set the rules in her relationships, not that Hogan was a potential relationship. She knew him too well. She chose the men she liked and never allowed them too close. A few dates, dinner and dancing, and she'd have enough. That raw edge to Hogan was not acceptable at all. Nor was the beguiling tenderness she hadn't expected.

She had to remember his skill with animals. He could be seductive, and suddenly he was riding them—Jemma shivered again, the image of Hogan's tall dark rangy body locked with her pale one. She swallowed and missed a step. Hogan was definitely in pursuit and undaunted by her sharp barbs, or evasion of him. He just kept coming.

He'd framed her with his hands, blocking her exit of the barn. "Afraid?" he'd asked in a husky tone that raised the hair on the back of her neck. She could have killed him for his knowing grin.

She hadn't expected that hot slap of desire, nor the tenderness and a feeling of coming home when she'd settled into his arms after that kiss on the mountain—his hands stroking her gently, his cheek nuzzling hers. Even more terrifying to her than his stormy hunger was the sense that he needed her, too.

She hadn't expected the leaping of her heart when she saw him, when he turned and met her eyes as if he knew they were going to be lovers.

A small boy came to slowly lean back against the pickup, mimicking Hogan. He studiously adjusted his small body in the same long-legged stance as Hogan's, and crossed his arms over his thin chest. Hogan looked down at the boy and rolled one shoulder; the boy rolled his. Hogan studied the clear sky, and the boy lifted his head.

Jemma tried to breathe as the idea of Hogan, as a father, invaded her. She'd seen his patience with animals, who responded to him, but she hadn't seen him win a small child's heart. Clearly the boy adored him. She wondered, briefly, if Hogan had adored Ben in just the same way, watching and copying the typical male stance.

Then Hogan reached into his pocket, carefully unwrapped a small lollipop, and stuck it in his mouth. After a moment, he gave one to the boy, and Hogan crossed his arms again, clearly relaxed and enjoying the sunlight.

The boy stuck the sucker in his mouth, checked Hogan's stance, mimicked it, and crossed his small arms. Both males were clearly enjoying each other, the lollipop shifting as Hogan smiled. The boy's sucker moved, and they grinned at each other. The boy reached into his pocket and showed Hogan a large white marble. Hogan crouched, took the marble, and shot it expertly against the adobe storefront, watching it roll back to him. He nodded approvingly and handed it to the boy, who seemed delighted, running down the street to catch his mother.

"Jemma?" Carley asked. "You look a little woozy. Are you okay?"

"I'm just fine." Why did Hogan have to jolt her with unexpected softness? Why couldn't he just be the same old dark, brooding male she loved to torment?

Dinah came out of the feed store and Richard Coleman, the small town's only doctor, walked beside her, his arms full of her purchases. Hogan took them from Richard, placing them in the truck, and Richard smiled at Carley and Jemma. "Savanna said you'd come home. Welcome back."

"Hi, Richard," Carley said, hoisting the thick catalog of swatches into the back of the truck.

"Hi, yourself. I don't suppose you still have that ring I gave you years ago?"

She nodded. "You were always so sweet."

"So are you. If that hay fever starts to bother you when the alfalfa blooms, come in, and I'll check you for a prescription."

"Hi, Richard. Are you still collecting butterflies?" Jemma asked, and instantly felt sorry for the man who had taken over his father's medical practice. Richard was too shy, but nice, really sweet—unlike Hogan. Richard's glasses glinted in the sun, his hair meticulous.

His narrow face brightened at the mention of his collections. "I'm into antiquity now. You should come to the house and see my collections. Just got in a Mayan bowl. You, too, Hogan. I understand you're quite the artist. Your work might be a good investment for me. I'd like to see it."

Hogan nodded and flicked Jemma a lazy look that said he remembered their kiss that morning. She sniffed, turned up her nose, and looked away, just to show him she had no idea what his look meant. But inside, her senses jumped into high gear, tasting the kiss once more.

"Mom is planning a party as soon as we can. You'll come, won't you, Richard?" Carley asked.

"Just let me know. I'll be there. Come to the house sometime. Mother would like to see you, I know." He got into a sedate black Cadillac and spoke through the open window. "Got to get back to the work. Had to run home to check on Mother. She's developed a few problems, but I'm just a call away. If you talk to her, you'll note she's a bit forgetful and says odd things. Age, you know, and the shock of Father's dying. I'd better go. Savanna is holding down the clinic."

"Poor guy," Carley said after Richard's car rounded the street corner. "His parents always wanted so much out of him. Savanna likes working with him. She says he's very good and patient. He's never married. He's so shy, but nice. I remember how Jemma terrified him. He was never certain of what she would try or do."

"I felt sorry for him. I know his father thought I was an evil influence. That old man had a nasty look I didn't like. I once saw him pick up Richard by the back of his neck and drag him away from us because Richard hadn't completed his college-level math project—it was summer and he was only a sophomore in high school. Savanna was younger than he, but says if Richard got less than an 'A' he was terrified. Mrs. Coleman was always so nice, but she acted like all the life had been pumped out of her.''

"You, Jemma Delaney, are an evil influence on anyone," Carley agreed with a grin. "And you're used to acting as you want. We lesser mortals sometimes have to do what our families want.''

# six

Hogan walked out to the porch, shouldering a door and placing it across the battered wooden sawhorses. He enjoyed sanding and finishing the heavy solid wood, feeling and seeing the grain awake in his hands. Working on the porch, he was free of the battles inside the house.

The May air was fresh and cold; steam was shooting from the horses' nostrils as they pranced in the field. The sprawling porch was cluttered with plant starts, potting-soil bags, and clay pots. He glanced at the cup of herbal tea that Jemma had left to chill near the rocking chair. One wary look at him, and she'd gracefully surged to her feet and hurried inside. For a moment, Hogan luxuriated in the heady sense that for once, he had her on the run.

He ran his hands across the scarred door, taking the grain into him, feeling its flow beneath his fingers. Jemma didn't know how to take that kiss, but the taste of her haunted him, and he planned another—not quite so hungry. He intended to take the next kiss very slow, dissecting Jemma's effect upon him. His fierce desire to lock her to him, to take everything, had shocked him. When he'd expected resistance, she'd dived into the heat too quickly, the part of her lips surprising him. Jemma liked to hurry, racing through life; he didn't. He intended to taste her again, to explore what hunger rode him now. He wanted to know why his body tightened when he saw her. She'd blushed just that once when he'd cornered her in the barn and he'd upped the ante by leaning close.

Hogan settled into a comfortable mood. He definitely had Jemma on the run after all these years and intended having the upper hand.

The lingering scent of morning coffee and Dinah's bacon-and-egg breakfast curled comfortably around Hogan. Maxi Dove had taken the week off, deciding to stay in Savanna's town apartment.

Everything beyond the house was peaceful, quiet, as it should be, Hereford cows and baldies grazing in the field. Hogan pulled the peace around him, sank into it, and pushed Jemma's constant redo-this and move-that demands away from him. She clearly was at her height, organizing, ordering—but she wasn't bothering him as she had. For a man who had been sought by women, stalking one who tasted like fire and matched his hunger was heady and addictive. An unlikely woman to attract him, Jemma had done just that. He picked up the electric sander—

"Hogan! Aaron! Mitch! Help!" Jemma yelled from on top of the roof, where she had been cleaning windows.

Hogan shook his head, Jemma's call for help familiar through the years. He noted the order of the names and decided that this time, he didn't mind being first on the list. He stepped from the porch, shaded his eyes against the morning sun. He found Jemma flattened and clinging to the edge of the roof. She was safe enough and impatient as always—he intended to slow her a bit and enjoy the full-blown feminine froth. Then Jemma scowled at him. "Don't just stand there. I'm stuck, and you know it. Move the ladder from the back side of the house, so I can get down. It's easier there."

Hogan liked having her at his terms. "Drop. I'll catch you."

"Get the ladder."

"I told you to wear shoes with better traction." He locked his work boots to the ground and crossed his arms, waiting.

"Oh, that's just great. I'm about to break my neck, and you're pulling that 'I told you so' business ... Ben!" Jemma yelled, searching for an alternative Kodiak male.

A second-story window jerked open, and Ben called roughly, "I'm busy up here. Get one of the boys to help you."

"Mitch and Aaron won't leave their bathroom plumbing job. I'm stuck with you, and I know that stubborn look." Jemma glared at Hogan, then sprang off the roof.

Reeling back from the impact, Hogan staggered and went down on the ground, Jemma on top of him. He gasped air into his lungs and tossed away his confident male in pursuit of female, good-morning mood. He realized his hands had immediately gripped her bottom. He'd thought about doing just that—filling both hands with Jemma's softness and holding her tight against him. He blew away the silky hair teasing his lips. "I said 'drop,' not 'jump.' "

"And I said to get the ladder. Hogan, your hands are on my butt." She wriggled upon him, reaching behind her to push his hands away.

He resettled them higher on her back and Jemma

braced her hands on the dirt beside his head, pushing
away from him. The movement sent her breasts against
him, and Hogan inhaled, deepening the contact. Jemma's
eyes were steely, her tone cold. "You can let me go
now. I've got to go take the cake out of the oven."

"Do you?" he asked, suddenly fascinated by the sunlight firing her hair, the sweep of her smooth cheeks,
and the lush curve of her mouth. Hogan wanted to keep
her just a bit longer there in the bright morning sunlight
scented of new grass and spring beginnings.

Heat and sensual tension quivered in the inches between their faces. Then Jemma wriggled upon him again
and Hogan fought a groan. He realized his hand was
sliding upward to cup her breast, and his body had just
taken a sensual jolt. "What's wrong with you?" she
asked curiously, peering down at him. "You're holding
me too tightly. I can't move. I can't breathe. Let go."

Just there, on the side of her pale throat, a telling pulse
beat too quickly. He wanted to taste that creamy skin,
to open his mouth over the flavor of her. "Is that so?"

"Hogan, let me go. You're just being perverse as always. This is just like that time you tied me up to keep
me from following you Sasquatches." She pushed her
hands on the dirt by his head, levering away, her eyes
wary before she scrambled to her feet. She hurried toward the house, her loose sweat suit flowing around her
long legs. The wary glance over her shoulder both questioned and denied that heated, hungry quiver that had
passed between them.

Left with his frustration, an annoying sense that he
had to kiss Jemma, Hogan surged to his feet. His hands
flexed with the memory of Jemma's taut body, his appreciation of her waist and curved hips and the rise of
her bottom. Her position over him had excited, her rich

red mane cascading down, brushing his face.

He regretting that momentary tightening of his hands on her hips, the instinctive sensual rise of his body to hers. With Jemma around, anything could happen. As if on cue, her window-cleaning spray bottle tumbled down from the roof. With the ease of anyone in Jemma's vicinity, he automatically reached to catch it in one hand.

"You're strangling that bottle, and you look as if you'd like to tangle with a bear," Aaron said inside the living room. "To think I left my nice quiet penthouse for this," he muttered while drying his hands. "There is no system whatever in this hell-bent, steamrolling drive to redo the house. It's been a month of fetch this, do that. Mitch is enjoying the whole mess, so is Jemma. Dammit, I'm in charge of the biggest account in my company, and I've left it in a beginner's hands. That creep better turn up fast, or I'm going after him."

Hogan suspected Aaron wasn't frustrated with his work alone—his mood stemmed more from the growing relationship between Dinah and Ben. Aaron also wasn't expecting Savanna's light treatment of him, dismissing his flirtation with her own and then walking away.

Aaron's uneasy mood was matched by the other Kodaks, each for a different reason. The family coming together amounted to several small battles with the war still to go. At any minute the whole family could be torn apart by the very lies that had brought them together. "Whoever attacked her will wait until he feels safe. He'll come, and he'll know that we couldn't use alarms or sensors because of the wildlife and cattle. He's not going to act soon. He's getting the rhythm of our schedules. When he's comfortable with that, he'll make his move."

"I'm going to make him pay for this hell, and if he

manages to hurt Carley, I'm killing him,'' Aaron stated harshly.

"He won't wait long. He's too hungry, and he's waited too long. Right now, he's just waiting for us to settle down into a predictable schedule.''

Upstairs, Ben and Dinah were arguing loudly. In the living room, Carley was arguing with Mitch about moving the bookcase again. With a surprising display of temper, Carley had hooked her foot behind Mitch's and tossed him to the hardwood floor. Hands on hips, she looked down at him. "You do not have all the answers to my life, Mitch. I am not a neat freak. I just think that we should take everything out of the living room before we try to redo the hardwood floor. It only makes sense, Dumbo.''

He stood up slowly, rubbed his butt, and planted his hands on his hips, towering over her. Carley, dressed like Jemma in sweatpants and a T-shirt, raised a furious face to him. "Don't try that older brother bully stuff on me. Lay off,'' she ordered.

"You're working me to death and expect me to take it?'' he raged. "Where did you learn that self-defense move?''

"Jemma and I have trained for years. Expect a lot of sitting on your butt if you try to muscle me around,'' she said, bending to roll a large braided rug.

"Ooo. I'm so scared.'' Mitch said, studying her as she tromped away. He glanced at Aaron and Hogan and wiggled his eyebrows in a leer. "She's so sexy when she gets mad.''

Upstairs, Ben raged, "What do you mean I've 'been living in a cave'? I get out. I go to the tavern—''

"You are not hiding out at the Lucky Dollar, Ben Kodiak. If I have to, I'll come after you this time. Don't you dare walk out on me,'' Dinah yelled furiously.

"You're going to fill all those nail holes and sand them. You're the one who made all the bullet holes. Light seafoam green is just the perfect color for this bedroom. Once the brass is polished on the bed, it will pick up the light from the window. Here—use this window cleaner and rag—"

Silence preceded Ben's explosion. "I've got better things to do than act like a mop boy. Hell, no. I'm not cleaning windows. I've got a ranch to run."

Aaron's expression was grim. "Home sweet home. Just like old times. She'll take off."

"Don't count on it," Hogan returned, remembering how Ben had greeted his ex-wife, like the love of his life. "Dinah is tough. She started and built a good business."

Aaron's tone was bitter. "She had help from the man she married after Dad. She left a man who needed her and moved on with her life. She tore apart our family."

"She had little choice. Ben wasn't sweet back then, to any of us. I remember him saying that Kodiak men didn't have good luck with wives."

"The old man was right. None of us are married. My ex-fiancée had a lot to say about my not fitting the bill as a husband. Then let us not forget that I was actually married—you were the best man."

"I'm sorry that didn't work out. I thought maybe with Christina you would find what you needed. She was a sweet girl."

"That's the problem. She was too sweet and giving. I kept tearing her up all the time, and I reminded myself of Dad. I didn't like the image. She's better off without me and I heard that she married a nice guy and they're expecting their third baby. I didn't want kids . . . I wasn't ready to settle down."

"Here." Jemma leaned out of the kitchen and handed

a bowl filled with frosting mix to Hogan. She slapped a large wooden spoon in his free hand. "You're an artist. Mix. Think of it as paint or clay or something."

Teasing as she had always done when he frowned at her, Jemma grinned up at him and dipped a finger into the chocolate mix and stuck it into his mouth. Hogan caught her finger between his teeth, just for an instant, just to let her know she'd better stop teasing him. "Beast," she muttered, scowling at him.

When she soared upstairs, Aaron began to laugh. "Hogan, my man, you should see your face. If it weren't you, I'd say the expression was pure lust."

"I've lusted a few times in my day," Hogan said, uncomfortable that his brother had so easily read his desire for Jemma.

"Not me. I'm pure as the driven snow," Aaron returned with a cheeky grin that said he wasn't.

Just then Dinah came down the stairs, her expression glowing. Ben followed, whistling a cowboy tune. He patted Hogan on the shoulder. "You boys need to lighten up," he said cheerfully. "Women need to be understood."

"They're killing us, Dad," Aaron muttered.

"I imagine we'll all live. They're just making their nests. Women do that before they can settle down. You've got chocolate on your mouth, boy." He studied Hogan, who was holding the frosting bowl and glaring at him; Ben quickly turned away, shielding a grin.

"What's that?" Mitch asked, strolling over to Hogan. He dipped a finger into the frosting, tasting it. "Mmm. How much does she need for the top of a little cake anyway?"

"Let's adjourn to the barn. Grab the poker deck," Hogan said quietly, and walked out the door, carrying the frosting bowl. Feeling cornered, assigned tasks by

Jemma and unsettled by Ben's cheery turnaround, Hogan had had enough of the Kodiak household for the moment.

Forty minutes later, Aaron spread his royal flush upon the hay bale, raked up the dollar bills, and studied the near empty bowl. "We're dead men."

"One of us is," Mitch agreed, as Jemma stormed out into the ranch yard, her hands on her hips. One swipe of Mitch's finger took that last of the frosting before he called, "Hey, Jemma! Hogan ate all the frosting."

A week later, the mid-May night was fragrant outside Hogan's home, and he tried to concentrate on the promotion of his new Kodiak "Autumn" line. Naked and comfortable after working on his barn roof, he padded into the living room. Across the small valley, the lights of Kodiak house were ablaze.

His need for Jemma sprang alive at every turn, and she was too aware of him, blushing when she looked at him and hurrying in the other direction. The tension dancing between them was new to Hogan, making him feel alive. He was giving her so much time and then—

On his drawing board, his new sketch for Kodiak's Fire Feathers collection waited. His new line of jewelry was intended to be light and flexible, but what had stirred beneath his drawing pencil was vibrant, almost alive, and almost pagan. He preferred the subtle light designs, not the bold layered, almost flamelike, feathers. The day of the Kodiaks' emotions firing at every turn, tempers battling, flashing over the dinner table had taken their toll upon his creative mood.

Tranquillity was not a Kodiak family trait. During the day, tempers soared. Adults, no longer children and coming back to their home place, demanded equal respect. Ben was clearly on edge, but for once he hadn't run for the safety of ranch work.

A huge truck had brought a huge moonlike disk for receiving television programs, and a big-screen television; Aaron said he needed his "sports fix." After a battle with Carley and Jemma about soap operas—which Ben had strangely begun to watch in the afternoons with Dinah—Aaron moved the big screen setup to the bunkhouse. Old Joe Blue Sky spent most of his time catching up on Western movies. He made notes about the mistakes on the portrayal of Native Americans. Joe's damning of the Italian actors, who played the warriors' parts, could blaze at any moment.

The memory of Jemma's slender, agile and curved body upon his own stirred Hogan's shadows. His body had responded too quickly, escaping his cool control for just that instant. That kiss on the mountain pursued him in his dreams, and when he awoke with a painfully hardened body, he immediately hurried into a cold shower.

With a frustrated groan, Hogan drew on his jeans, shoved his feet into his moccasins, and lashed them. He threw on a light denim shirt and left the house. The night called to him, the slight wind drifting through his hair, moonlight on the rolling pastures—shapes curled around him again, and he allowed them to flow into him.

"So much for peace." Moments later, riding Moon Shadow, Hogan sat in the moonlight and watched Jemma's gleaming van glide toward his house. His hunger for her immediately leaped to life, reminding him of how long it had been since he'd been sensually satisfied—or had he ever, choosing women who played the same game? All he needed to do to start real trouble was to jump into a flammable, sensual relationship before the rules were laid down—and tonight he wasn't that certain about himself, or his need to kiss those sweet, sassy lips.

He wanted to keep to his dark shadows tonight—alone.

"After that kiss, she should know better than to come after me. Another woman would—oh, no, not her," he muttered and groaned as the van missed the curve and lumbered down a slight incline. "Oh, hell."

Jemma revved the motor, but the van's tires were sunk too deep into the mud. The incline was not steep, or dangerous, but slanted enough to prevent escape. She only hoped the mud did not contain cow manure. But manure or the world on fire couldn't stop her from hunting down Hogan in his lair and talking sense into him. She jerked open the door, gauged the moonlit distance to the ground, and leaped into the night.

Hogan's solid body and grunt stunned her as he struggled for balance, held her, and toppled to the ground. In the moonlight, his fierce scowl almost frightened her. He released his grip on her and opened his arms wide on the ground, away from her body. "That's twice today. The first time I saw you coming."

After hours of planning how she could run him down and trap him for a private conversation, Jemma struggled not to rapid-fire her concerns at him. Hogan did not react well when pushed too far—in his way, he was like a hot summer thunderstorm rolling across the mountains. "What are you doing here?"

"What does it look like? I'm not having a conversation with you on top of me. Get off me," he said between his teeth in a tone that reminded her of a yard dog's warning growl.

"Oh." She scrambled to her feet and held out a hand to help him. She knew that he wanted her, but she'd put her mission ahead of her safety. Hogan hadn't made any move to get closer to Ben, and it was time he did so.

Her other reason for coming to Hogan was that she

wanted to set up rules about the way he looked at her, those stunning little brushes of his fingertips across her cheeks. He had her so rattled, she couldn't keep track of ongoing business and had made too many mistakes her bankbook couldn't afford. She needed her senses, and right now she was on Hogan-alert, and unbalanced whenever he came near her.

Hogan shook his head and came agilely to his feet without touching her. "If you want to mash me, do it on something softer."

"I was coming to see you." She walked around him and brushed off his back side. "Mud. You'll have to use spot cleaner before you wash those jeans. I think it will come out though, but if you're going to throw them away, I'd like them. I've got an idea to make jean quilts—"

"Uh-huh." He shifted away from her hand that had just brushed the crushed leaves from his bottom. He faced her, his arms crossed, his expression forbidding, dark jutting planes and black hair catching the slight night breeze.

Hogan's quiet, solemn nature never failed to set her off. "Well, what are you doing out here anyway? I would have thought you would have been working, or relaxing, or sleeping."

"Don't try to boss me around now, Jemma. We're not on Kodiak land, we're on mine."

"You *are* a Kodiak, Hogan." When he shook his head and started to walk toward his horse, Jemma hurried to follow. "You're not going to leave me here . . . alone . . . at night, are you?"

She listened to an eerie sound that lifted goose bumps on her body. "Is that a coyote howling?"

"Yes." Hogan gripped the saddle horn and surged up into the saddle. "I'd prefer to leave you here."

She couldn't have him get away, not when she had to talk with him. "I was coming to see you," she repeated. "The least you can do is help me. What if Carley's stalker gets me?"

"He won't want you, once you start sassing him. You've got two choices—ride my horse back to Ben's— or wait out the night here. Either way, I'm going back to my place, not Ben's."

"And leave my beautiful van? Or stay by myself out here?" she repeated and wished she hadn't almost screamed. She found her hand on his hard denim-covered thigh.

The muscle beneath the cloth tensed, then Hogan removed her hand. "Your van is probably equipped with a telephone—call them."

Jemma shook her head. "You know what will happen. Ben will find out that you could have helped and you didn't—I might not be able to keep myself from telling him. You and he will argue. Carley and Dinah will cry. Mitch and Aaron will hunker off somewhere looking like orphans. Then I'll have to just try harder to get everyone happy again."

"Uh-huh. And we'd all suffer." Hogan stuck out a boot and his hand. "If you want to ride back to my place, my tractor can pull you out."

She hadn't expected the ease with which he lifted her into the saddle behind him. Because he made her feel safe and protected, Jemma wrapped her arms around his waist and placed her head on his shoulder. Hogan stiffened within her arms, but said nothing. "I'm really tired, Hogan, and I just want everything to go well. I think it is going well, don't you? We're all learning how to make adjustments."

He didn't answer. Jemma couldn't resist the sudden emotions flying free of her control. She'd been pushing too hard, wanting to protect Carley, and fearing for her. She hated lying to Carley and if she discovered that Ben's illness was staged—She hit his back lightly with her fist. "I love this family. You know that, Hogan Kodiak."

His grunt confirmed nothing, but that he'd prefer her to be quiet. Hogan liked silence and shadows and thoughtful answers while she raced on in life, frustrated by him. She wiped her face against his shirt, drying the sudden tears that leaped upon her when she was too tired. The shadows of her life were there, too, but she could push them back now, riding in the clear moonlit night with her arms around Hogan Kodiak, his horse moving smoothly beneath them.

Hogan wanted quiet, and she gave him that much until they reached his barn. He dismounted and held the horse, standing back to wait for her. Holding the saddle horn, Jemma was too impatient and got her running shoe caught in the stirrup and hopped with the other foot as the horse pranced nervously. "Hogan!"

His arm looped around her waist and he lifted her free. There was just that tightening of his body, his arm bringing her close and hard, and Jemma stopped breathing, caught by his fierce expression. "What is it?"

Shaking his head, Hogan set her aside gently, walked to the tractor, and started it. Then he slowly drove it out into the moonlit field, leaving her behind. Hurrying behind him, Jemma was out of breath when he slowed, held down a hand, and levered her up onto his lap. Once his arms closed around her, Jemma shuddered. "You're a pure beast, Hogan Kodiak. You know I'm terrified of the dark."

"Just don't touch anything," he said, and for a moment there was that low dark curl of amusement in his voice. Jemma sat very still, too aware of the hard male body beneath hers.

"Stand back," he said later, adjusting a chain to pull the van up onto the road. "Stay back," he repeated before climbing onto the tractor.

"As if I would want to be crushed by a tractor or my van," she muttered as the van was pulled up onto the dirt road. "Well, that was easy," she said, as Hogan bent to unloop the chain from her van.

When he didn't answer, she swatted him on the back. He straightened slowly, then turned to her. "Don't. Just don't hit me with your elbow, swat me, punch me, or pat me. I've had enough for one day."

She loved teasing Hogan, watching those dark solemn eyes light with temper and just that little bit of male nostril-flaring was delightful. But he knew her too well, and he wouldn't play by her rules. Their kiss and his dark, searing looks, his teasing had shaken her safety. She wanted him to be as he had always been for her— safe and predictable. "I'm doing my best. When you want to get someone's full attention, it's best to touch them."

"That's the problem. Don't. Your best is pure trouble."

His hands-off surprised her; she'd been familiar with him for most of her life. Hogan wanted to withdraw into his lone-wolf, solitary male image; he wasn't avoiding her, not when she had to talk with him. "I brought you some carrot juice. You left before we could make it. I'd like you to see my new van, Hogan. It's beautiful inside. I bought it with the idea of filming some cute little camping recipes in my new show. Oh, Hogan, you've got to see it. It's so cute."

Jemma knew how to maneuver men into business deals, to sweet-talk and "ooo, you're so smart," if she had to, but Hogan was another matter. He was a part of her life, a part of the Kodaks, and his opinion mattered. "I spent a fortune on my van, Hogan. Traded in my Cessna. I want you to tell me that I didn't make a mistake."

He smoothed back a strand of hair from her face, studying her, his features rugged, impassive, unable to be read in the moonlight. She caught his wrist. "It's important to me, Hogan."

"You should have a fat bank account by now, Jemma. You've been wheeling and dealing for years. You're a good businesswoman with a talent for making money. You shouldn't worry about failing. You've already succeeded. Why can't you take this time to relax?"

She couldn't hide her fear from him. She wouldn't burden Carley and Dinah. With Aaron and Mitch, Jemma made light of her bartering, but not with Hogan, whose shadows were as great as her own. "Hogan, I know what it's like to have nothing, and I'm never going back there."

His finger stroked her face, traced her cheekbone, and followed her jawline down to her throat. She should have moved away—she couldn't, trapped by the excitement racing through her. The night breeze carried a strand of his hair across his jaw and throat, making him appear more intense, more rugged and yet almost mysterious. "Are you still collecting those buttons?"

"I brought them. They're still in the van, little bits from clothing of people I've known and loved. Don't you dare make fun of me." But Hogan had never laughed at her love of remembering people who had touched her life.

"Show me," he said quietly.

\*     \*     \*

In the clutter of Dinah's new and still-disorganized upstairs office, the best place for viewing the distance between the Kodiaks and Hogan, Mitch put aside the binoculars he'd been using to trace Jemma's night trek. He cut a slice of Jemma's unfrosted chocolate cake and took a bite. "I knew she was up to something. She was too quiet after he left, steaming about something. Jemma is usually all out there, every emotion defined. He's pulled her van onto the road with his tractor. Now they're in it."

Unsettled by his telephone call to Jimmy, a ten-year-old boy who needed him, Mitch needed Montana and the Kodiak family. Burned out and raw, he had to re-fresh—or a part of him would tear away, and he'd never be able to help kids again. He'd wired Jimmy money for food and prayed that Jimmy's mother wouldn't get it. Mitch looked down at his hands, locked into fists, and knew that once Carley was safe, he'd be going back into the nightmare.

Aaron yawned and shut off the laptop, he used to catch up on business. If he wasn't there to make deals, at least he could input and watch the fun. Like Mitch, he cut a slice of cake and ate it from his hand. "See? I told you Hogan would help her. If we would have charged out there and pulled that seduction van onto the road, Hogan would have gotten a whole night to himself, to relax, like I need to. He's a good sacrifice. A whole day of our family together is worse than ten major ac-counts wanting action at the same time."

Dinah, dressed in a long black-satin robe, tied at the waist, came into the office. "What's up?"

Mitch lifted the cake, a signal his mouth was too filled to talk. Carley, dressed in loose men's flannel pajamas, padded into the room. "There's what's left of the cake. Give me that." She scooped up the plastic container and tucked it under her arm. "Why are we here?"

"Well, little girl, Jemma has just gotten Hogan into her van. She's up to something," Mitch said, taking in Carley's rumpled look and loving her, as always.

"Don't say anything about how I look, or I'll flatten you," she hurled at him.

Mitch's shadows evaporated at Carley's fierce expression. She gave him an eagerness for the bright side of life and its goodness. Caught in her own nightmare, she wasn't ready to accept him as a man, but one day. "You can try. Now I know about the self-defense stuff."

Ben paused at the doorway, scanned the room filled with his family, and slowly took in Dinah's robe. He swallowed, flushed, and said shakily, "I've got to check that injured calf in the barn. Need to put salve on those barbed-wire cuts."

"I'll help you," Dinah offered, moving toward him.

"No," Ben snapped, hurrying down the hall.

"He's so stubborn," Dinah muttered. "I'm going out to that barn if it kills me. Don't tell him that Jemma has Hogan in her van. He still thinks you're all children. He'll rush out there and probably ruin the first peace anyone has had around here today. If you're still hungry, go down and make sandwiches. There's a beef roast perfect for slicing, but don't tell Jemma. I hid it behind that stack of tofu."

"I love that woman," Mitch exclaimed after Dinah left the room. "With Jemma around, beef is scarce and guilt-ridden. Mixed grains do not a hamburger make."

Carley picked up the binoculars and found Jemma's van. "What do you suppose she's up to?"

"Who wants to bet on which one comes out of that alive?" Aaron asked with a chuckle. He was hoping to get Savanna in a small, tight place, and very soon.

He could feel the heat simmering off her body, and her looks at him said she felt the same.

"Jemma has always gotten the best of Hogan, you know that."

"Maybe not this time," Aaron purred in the tone of a man who recognized another man in pursuit of a woman.

Carley turned to glare at Mitch's closed expression as he studied her, too slowly and too carefully. She didn't like anyone trying to see inside her, where she had been hurt and felt dirty. "What's wrong with you?"

"Why, angel, I think you're cute, all rumpled and cuddly-looking," he answered slowly, sincerely and smoothed her chopped pale hair back from her cheek.

"Just let me out of here before the explosion," Aaron said, moving out of the room.

"Define 'cute,' " Carley ordered, her hands on her hips.

"Just that. Cute. Cuddly." Then Mitch bent to lightly brush his lips over hers and followed Aaron downstairs.

Stunned, Carley stared at Dinah's framed Monet print of water lilies and tried to understand Mitch's comment and his light kiss.


In the van, Jemma stood aside as Hogan entered, bending slightly. "You can stand straight. It's called a high-top."

She flattened against the small closet she'd had designed for fishing gear, and held her breath. Hogan, in small places, was even more intimidating, his shoulders blocking the rest of the small enclosure as he turned. She noted the small flare of his nostrils, that quick agile turn of his head as though sensing something he would keep to himself, locking it there to turn and examine it. His hand opened and gracefully stroked the paneling on the ceiling, an admiring touch. He glanced at the lush captain's chairs, the sprawling dashboard and comfortable accessories, the television, tiny kitchenette, and bathroom. "Nice."

Just an average "nice," after she'd worked until she dropped, using muted jade and cream and soft willow patterns to emphasize her vivid coloring, and softly shaded birch cabinets and woodwork for contrast. How like Hogan to withhold the approval she wanted from a world-class artist.

She forced air into her lungs. She hadn't realized how dynamic Hogan could be in small places, his dark coloring and black sweatshirt a masculine contrast to the softly muted colors. In her lifetime, she'd never been aware of another man like she was of Hogan.

He was always so controlled, covering his emotions, and while she ached to tear that mask away, she also feared what she would find in herself.

"It should be nice—it cost a mint. It's an investment in getting that television series. It has a huge bed. You take the dining table and—Hogan, I want you to move into the bunkhouse, if not the house," she found herself saying. "Old Joe needs company, and you could enjoy Aaron's big-screen television. You don't have one."

He wouldn't, she thought. Hogan preferred quiet and shadows, and the haunting tenderness of that kiss had surprised her—so had his playful pursuit of her. Tonight he hadn't wanted to be near her, and that raised an uncertainty if she'd misunderstood—

His expression tightened, that tiny scar on his cheek deepening. He rubbed it thoughtfully, then said, "I thought you were going to show me your button collection."

"I will. Sit down—here, put this towel under you. You've got mud on your jeans. Would you like some-

thing to drink? Carrot juice or sangria?'' She wanted
Hogan comfortable and agreeable for once; she wanted
to take his perversity and wrap it to her needs—to have
the Kodiak family reunited, to make Carley and Dinah
happy.

"Guess," he returned. "And it's not carrot juice."
She took the wineglasses from an overhead rack, where
they hung upside down. This sangria wine was cheap
and sweet, used when she couldn't sleep and her nerves
were showing. She hated when her nerves showed, when
her shields were down.

After arranging the towel on the seat, he eased into
the cozy booth around her table, his long legs extending
into her path. She stepped over them on her way to the
closet with linens and withdrew a towel, tossing it to
him. He'd seen her button collection before, knew the
ceremony of carefully spreading the towel, so that none
of them would slide and be lost forever. When they were
teens, Mitch had stolen her collection and hidden it, and
Hogan had made him return the old coffee jar.

"Pour this, but don't spill any, will you? The upholstery on this rig cost a fortune," she said as she flipped
on the surround-sound system and Kenny G's smooth
clarinet curled around the paneled interior of her van.
Sprawled in the booth, his arms across the back, Hogan
looked too big and too dangerous . . . and wary and immovable. He poured the wine expertly, his eyes never
leaving hers. Her hand shook as she retrieved the large
flat metal box decorated with flowers from a shelf. Another stealthy look at Hogan told her she needed him in
a better mood. "Would you like something to eat? I
could make sandwiches."

She bent to study the tiny refrigerator and the sliced
turkey and bread she'd tucked away for a private moment away from the volatile Kodiaks. She glanced at

Hogan and decided that what she wanted was worth the effort of playing hostess and serving him, catering to him. If she could find just one weak spot, something he needed, she could barter for what she wanted.

Hogan glanced at the magazines on her bookshelf and the videotapes, all concerning sports and fishing. He nodded as she placed the plates of sandwiches on the table.

After considering where to sit, Jemma decided anywhere would be too close to Hogan—she remembered his hard body beneath hers when she fell from the roof. His big hands had tightened on her hips, a dark, almost savage look in his eyes. Now, he'd drawn that cool shell around him, no doubt expecting her to want something—he was right. She eased into the booth beside him and out of habit, began to eat quickly, hungrily.

She was too aware of him, uneasy with the emotions scurrying through her. She liked being in control of herself, and Hogan had the unique ability to set her off-balance. One look from those dark, solemn eyes, his straight, sooty eyelashes gleaming in the soft overhead light, and her body tingled.

Hogan ate slowly, stopping to sip his wine and study her. After eating one of the two sandwiches she'd prepared for him, Hogan placed half of another onto her empty plate. "Thanks," she said, hurrying to eat the sandwich, as always. "I didn't realize I was so hungry. It will take at least another full month to get the house in shape, and—"

She placed the sandwich on the plate, her eyes filling against her will. She turned to Hogan, who was always so safe. She gripped his hand—it had always been so safe, and now she needed that strength more than ever. "We've been here a month and no word from Carley's attacker. Don't you think he should have sent her some-

thing, shown his hand or something? Tell me he isn't
going to hurt her, Hogan. Please tell me.''

Hogan slid his hand away, his expression grim. ''He
won't. She couldn't be in a better place to be protected.
He'll wait for what he feels is a safe opening, but we're
not going to give it to him.''

''Maybe he forgot about her,'' Jemma offered, pray-
ing that would be true.

''No,'' Hogan answered softly. ''He's just waiting.''

He set their sandwich plates aside and eased the towel
over the table. The casual easy way he said Carley
would be safe curled around Jemma. For just an instant,
she wished his arms would hold her tight. His eyes darkened, and that strange churning, timeless feeling en-
folded her, until she shrugged free. She wasn't certain
what was happening, but whatever the emotion, it was
too powerful to step into.

Then Hogan said slowly, ''Let's look at those buttons.''

# seven

"And these are the Kodiaks'. I really only brought my best collection. The rest are back in my new apartment. It was a real buy, and it's in a good location, too," Jemma said, her voice humming with emotion. Taped to paper, or on a scrap of cloth from where they'd been cut, the neatly stored buttons were carefully removed from the red-velvet lining of a big metal box, black with lush red roses.

She bent over the buttons, intent upon memories, her fingertip circling each one as if it were precious to her. "This is from Carley's birthday dress when she was nine—we'd just known each other a year then. This is from Mitch's blue-flannel shirt—remember? He'd never had a flannel shirt before and at fourteen, he thought he looked pretty handsome, wearing it open over a "Dirty Dogs are Best" T-shirt. Remember how he swaggered, and we all wondered if those jeans were going to fall down? His hair all slicked-back and curling at his nape?"

With a fond smile on her lips and laughter in her gray eyes, Jemma turned to Hogan. "This is Ben's, from an

old work shirt he'd tossed away. Look. I snipped a piece
of the material, too, just old worn flannel, but a remem-
brance of the man I adored. He always gave me the old
shirts before they were discarded, saying the buttons
would scratch the windows when the shirts were just
cleaning rags. But he knew how I loved buttons. He
gave me two of his mother's—a pretty black one and
an ornate brass one. Here they are—I sewed them on a
patch of black velvet so they wouldn't get lost. Dinah
gave me this one . . . it was made from shell, and she
gave me a few of her mother's—Dinah was disowned,
you know, for marrying Ben. But she loved him so much
that she never went back to her family, because they
couldn't accept him, a rough Montana cowboy. She still
loves him desperately, and he loves her.''

Hogan traced the emotions racing across Jemma's expressive face, the angles soft with love. He touched the
wildfire of her hair, felt it cling to the rough calluses of
his hand, a delicate gleaming web as he held his hand a
distance away. She'd always been full of whimsy and
dreams, dancing through life, a romantic when it came
to the Kodiak family. ''You've got a romantic streak,
Jemma. Let it go. There are too many years between
them.''

''No, I won't,'' she stated fiercely. ''I will not, Hogan
Kodiak. Don't ask me to. Dinah says the split was her
fault . . . she realizes now that she pushed Ben too much
at a time when he needed to heal. She says she shouldn't
have wanted to show him how much it didn't make a
difference, that Ben is a man who takes his time healing
and he would have healed if she hadn't gone in that cave
after him. It's that cave thing you Kodiaks are into . . .
it's so maddening. Carley has been in an emotional cave
since that night, and no one is making a move to heal.
Anyone can see you all love each other.''

Hogan flattened his hands on the table, preparing for the path Jemma was certain to take. "Leave it."

"You sound just like Ben. You're so much alike, despite your worldly artist-guy trappings. This white one was from that dress shirt you used to have—Ben was angry with you for tearing the sleeve, and you fought— Oh, Hogan, please make it stop. Please end this."

She was pushing him, her fingers pale and slender upon the back of his hand. Hogan turned his hand, catching hers. The bones within her hand, lying restless beneath the smooth skin, were fragile and enticing. The essence of woman, he thought—capable, strong, and fascinating to him, the nails neatly clipped when once they had been long and tapered. The chameleon, he decided, a woman who had to survive, adjusting for another role. He stroked the back of her hand and slid two fingers down the shape of each finger before looking up at her. "This isn't your family, Jemma. Back off."

"I've made it mine—for Carley's sake," she said firmly as if she'd taken an oath she'd never break.

Hogan didn't like the quick surge of his temper, the way he felt himself coiling to strike back. This was a woman he wanted to make love to, tenderly, with meaning, and yet there were rules—He settled back in the cushioned booth to watch Jemma's eyes widen and her face pale. "Let's talk about your family for a change. Your real one."

"What do you mean?" Her tone trembled enough to make Hogan feel guilty, as if he'd slapped a kitten. Yet the anger and frustration riding him was enough to slash at her, to make her keep her distance—at least from his shadows.

"With ten children, the Delaneys were easy to trace. They worked the green bean and fruit harvest in Oregon, then moved up into Washington state. You and Carley were in the second grade together until your parents moved. Somehow you found the money to take the bus to Seattle, to play with Carley. No doubt Dinah helped you—''

*"You had no right!"* Jemma shoved her hands through her hair, mopped it back from her face, her eyes blazing at him. He admired the dangerous sharpening of her pale taut features, etched by anger. Then she was on her feet, pacing the small length of the van, slapping the cabinets on both sides as she passed. "You just had to do it, didn't you? You had to step into my life."

He'd wanted to know more about her. What drove her to cuddle a dysfunctional family? It had to be more than friendship with Carley. Now, seeing her pain, he regretted the trespass. Hogan hadn't made many mistakes in his lifetime with relationships, or cared enough to feel guilty. He didn't like feeling guilty about hurting Jemma—

But Jemma was a fighter, slugging back at him. She bent to hurriedly search a mound of buttons, pushing them all into a line. She jabbed them one at a time. "Here. You know so much. Meet my family. Mom. Dad. Penny. Sue. Mary Jo. Zoe. Freddie. Timmy. Jeanne. Mack and Laura. Dad''—She shoved the button on the towel—"Dad was a foreman wherever he went. Mom''—She pushed another button, a cheap white plastic worn by many washings.—"Mom struggled every day of her life. They both did with little education and barely enough to feed us all. You'd think there would be love in a big family like that, wouldn't you? There wasn't. My parents were two careless, irresponsible, immature kids all their lives. They moved off one time and forgot me. As kids, we had to protect each other, making certain we were all in that broken-down truck before the folks took off."

She shoved a coat button on the towel. "Freddie's. Dead at fifteen from a fight . . . Mary Jo was sixteen and—" Jemma's voice caught, her eyes filling with tears that she slashed away. "Mary Jo's husband didn't like cinnamon in her apple pie and he was fast with his fists. She died in the hospital. She was just sixteen, too."

Hogan closed his eyes, guilty that he'd struck back at her. He'd laid her open, the pain kept too long beneath the surface. He knew how she felt, pressing it back— "Jemma. Don't."

"*No.* You don't like the nasty details, do you? What's the matter? Don't you like reality? Or do you know the rest—that Mom and Dad and all the rest died when the truck's worn tires finally gave out on that mountain curve." She slashed at the tears running down her cheeks. "The funny part is, they probably didn't miss me. I was with Carley that week. No one even knew there was another child—me. I was just fifteen and on my own by then. Ben and Dinah both gave me money, and I took it because I had to. They knew my family wasn't buying me clothes or taking me to the doctor, and I wasn't telling that I was on my own. Dinah made certain I had good clothes by saying Carley didn't need them, but I knew they were bought for me—I was taller than Carley. When I wasn't here, Ben sent me money every month, and I managed. I owe them both now, and I'm paying them back by doing everything I can to make this family see reason. I knew how to survive and Carley never knew and you're not telling her, Hogan."

She slammed her fist down on the table, tears shimmering in her eyes. Hogan who was more familiar with soothing horses, didn't know how to hold her, what to say—after all, he was a Kodiak without a heart. Vibrating with passion, Jemma hurled on without him, deepening his guilt. "Don't you dare tell Carley. She couldn't bear it, to know about my life, and she's the very best part of mine. There isn't a truer heart in the world, and you know it. I lived for the summer and holidays here. Somehow I managed because I knew how—I'd had plenty of training with careless parents. So there it is. The whole, not so sweet, picture. It isn't debt that keeps me hounding your family—it's love.''

She slammed another fist on the table, jarring the buttons and glaring at him. ''Don't pull that dark closed-in cave look on me. You've got a loving family, Hogan, and it's time you got off your duff and pulled your share.''

Hogan settled back into the booth, forcing his hands open and his temper into the night. ''You can't bring your family back by saving another—the Kodiaks. You're not getting me to move closer to Ben. I had enough back then.''

''You just don't get it, do you? You are my family now, and you are not going to throw a fit over Ben's transferring cows into your name.''

Hogan snared her wrists, holding them as he stood. He hadn't asked anything of Ben, didn't want to owe him. ''*What*?''

''Cows. Cattle. Whatever. His pride wouldn't let him take your money to fix up the house. You should have known he wouldn't go down that easy. He just transferred a good quarter of his herd to your name, so be prepared for the tax statement . . . Oh, no, you're not,'' she said, as Hogan moved toward the door. She flattened her body back against the door, blocking his exit. ''You're not going to Ben and get everyone worked up.''

Hogan's pride tore at him. ''You know, I've had just about enough of you telling me what I'm going to do.''

Jemma closed her eyes and when she opened them,

there were tears shimmering over the soft gray depths. "Please, Hogan. Can't you let it go until we're through this? Until Carley is safe? Ben's pride means everything to him, and he feels he has to pay for the updating of the house and ranch. Let him have his pride, Hogan; you've certainly got as much or more."

Hogan reached out to crush her hair in his fists, lifting her hair away from that fascinating face. No other woman had ever reached deep inside him, and he didn't like it. "Jemma, you're not the guardian angel of the Kodiaks. Take your misplaced maternal needs and—"

*And what?* Begin her own family, take another man as a lover—Hogan was stunned by his desperation to both comfort and claim her.

" 'Misplaced maternal needs?' What about you? You're still trying to shove everyone around, and you haven't cleaned up your own life yet? When are you going to stop being the observer, Hogan? When are you going to move into life and live it?" she whispered. *"And what about the grandchildren?"*

The soft question had the impact of a charging two-thousand-pound bull. When Hogan's thoughts began moving again, he released the living warmth of her hair and pushed his hands down at his sides. "Artists are observers," he repeated, backing slightly. "I like studying lines and textures. I like movement and emotions. I use them in my work, translate them," he admitted, nettled because he felt the need to explain his behavior and because Jemma's uncanny ability to pin down his emotions made him feel too exposed.

"What about your own emotions? What about your own desires and needs and fulfillment? What are they? You may create beautiful work, Hogan, but you're living in a gray zone." She threw out her hands. "I've had enough of the moody-artist bit. You've got to get in the stream of life and live it, Hogan. Not just watch everyone else in their lives.''

Hogan resented the truth tossed at him by a woman who wanted to remake his family and his life. At the moment he felt like sliding into something hot and exciting, and it wasn't the "stream of life." Hogan braced his hips against the counter and folded his arms over his chest. He knew that Jemma was set to argue; the sight of her digging in, all fired up and ready to ignite, fascinated him. He dreaded another cold shower, but couldn't resist prickling her temper. "You're going to be difficult, aren't you? What's this about grandchildren?"

Jemma rubbed her hands over her face, clearly frustrated. "Do I have to explain the nesting urge or biology to you?" Then, too patiently, she said, "Carley, Mitch, Aaron, you, all have the potential to be parents. When you get done playing with Simone D'Arcy, you might want to settle down, get married, and hold your own baby. All of you are way too old not to have thought of that. That makes Ben and Dinah grandparents. You wouldn't want to have the sweet little babies torn apart like we are now, would you? Jeez, you're so exhausting, Hogan. It's like dragging you, step by step, into the living world."

With a tired sigh, Jemma pushed him aside and quickly put her prized buttons away. "I'm beat," she said. "Go home. I don't have any more energy to work on you tonight. You exhaust me."

"What about your life? What about your nesting urges?" he asked, more to defend himself than to know.

She sighed abruptly. "I don't have them. I raised all the children I wanted to when I was only a child."

"That's unfair, isn't it? Living through our lives? What about your own?"

She leveled a dark stare at him. "I've been married. I didn't like it, and, yes, it's fair. Because Carley needs this whole thing resolved, and you're all standing at opposite ends of any healing . . . Now will you leave?"

Hogan wasn't about to be dismissed on Jemma's terms. As she stood to replace the buttons in the cupboard, he studied the graceful line of Jemma's backside, the long legs running into her slender hips. The van's softening light was designed to best suit her, of course, twisting through her hair, igniting it as it swayed across her back. A natural athlete, she moved gracefully and he admired the symmetry of her body, the textures and vivid coloring. Jemma shot through life like a rocket, and this time she'd gone too far. "You started this, now let's finish it."

She looked over her shoulder to him and lifted a gleaming winged eyebrow. "I really wouldn't crowd me tonight, if I were you."

"But your rules say you can crowd me, is that it?" Hogan smoothed the scar on his cheek. He felt energy surge through him as though he were about to begin a fascinating art project. Passion, he decided, Jemma made him feel—did he like it? He wasn't certain, but he wasn't running away now.

She fastened the latch to the cupboard, then turned to face him. "You're fencing with me and you're good at it. I'm not—I'm straight out. This is for Carley, Hogan, and you know it. We're all doing our best."

"Has it ever occurred to you that *you* might be in danger? You, not Carley?"

She considered the thought as she dropped onto a long, lushly padded couch, kicked off her shoes, and placed her legs on the cushions. "Let's leave me out of this. I've been in rough spots before. I survived. Carley has been too vulnerable since that night. Either sit down or get out. You're taking up too much room and you're not sweet . . . Hogan, you don't have to sit here by me.''

He sat on the couch, lifted her legs onto his lap, and gave way to the need to touch her. ''You're not closing me out, Jemma. Let's set the ground rules now, to-night.''

Her eyes drifted closed and she scooted down to relax on the couch, as he began to massage her feet. ''That's cheating.''

''Uh-huh, that from you. It's only a massage, Jemma.'' He stared at the pale narrow foot within his hands, the contrast of male and female stirring a ready passion in him that he did not want to examine. The warmth of her skin prevented him from being the ob-server, at least when he touched her.

''You're not putting me in a better mood . . . Oh! Oh! Do that again.'' Jemma groaned and stretched luxu-riously, arching her foot within Hogan's hands. The un-dulating curves of her body, the light smoothing her breasts and belly, the length of her thighs caused Hogan to want to touch more than her feet. He wanted to pull her beneath him and—

In the next instant, she sat up, tearing her feet away from his grasp. ''I saw that look, all dark and closed-in, the observer look, seeing how I react to what. You're experimenting, Hogan—with me, and I don't like it. Is that what you do for Simone?'' she demanded, her eyes flashing at him like raised steel swords. ''Play with her feet?''

Her temper raised his and he resented the easy over-throw of his control. Simone had taught him many things, but not how to deal with a hot-tempered woman he wanted to hold close and tight and protect. ''She's been my friend for years. There is no need to explain anything to you.''

"Friends. What a nice civilized term. In the newspapers, at the art showings, you look like lovers. She's twined around you tighter than a boa constrictor."

Her condemning tone chafed; he wouldn't explain his comfortable ongoing relationship to Simone through the years. They'd been a match, suited to working a room and promoting his designs. But the man in him wanted to taste the fire burning in Jemma, taste that passion. He bent his head and brushed his open mouth across hers, tasting her breath, that fire within her. While she was dealing with that, eyes opened and stunned, Hogan's fingers traced and absorbed the outline of her lips, the sweep of her cheek.

"I don't like how you see inside people, Hogan," she whispered shakily, leaning away from him. "It's like you're seeing into my bones."

"Is it?" he heard himself ask as he traced the sleek eyebrows that soared at the arch and cruised his thumbs across the sharp line of her cheekbones.

"You're so damned sensual. You even move like a cat—gracefully," she muttered, blinking as he came close for another taste of her. He could feel her body align with his, curves and softness against his angular form—the tempting of textures and scents. He could sense the heat within her, his body gearing up, hardening—He eased his hands to her throat, keeping her still as his mouth traced the sleek warmth of her skin. She trembled, an excitement more powerful than an open seduction. "And we're both tired, riding on edge . . ."

"Is that what it is?" Still close, tasting her soft breath upon his lips, Hogan let one hand rest lightly upon her closed fist, smoothing her nape with his other hand, watching her respond, her eyes darkening, her body softening.

She arched her throat as his thumb skimmed the sensitive cord there, and higher to the underside of her chin and the fragile line of her jaw. She relaxed beneath his touch, her body responding to his hands, her eyes drowsy, and because he was hungry and a hunter releasing his needs, Hogan bent to take, to fuse his mouth to her slightly parted one.

His primitive need to claim her for his own shocked him, even as he was taking, devouring her. He took in the slight resistance, the stiffening of her body, the warring debate of a woman deciding if she liked the taste, the excitement of him.

Jemma's eyes opened close to his. "Are you in this, Hogan? Or are you just observing?"

He almost laughed; he'd been wondering what her breasts would taste like and how hot and tight she would be inside—"What does it feel like?"

"You're watching me—"

"I'm enjoying the sight."

She tried to push him away, her hands spread upon his chest, and Hogan took advantage of the shift of her body, lying over her.

"Get off me!" Suddenly she'd paled, shaking beneath him, her face taut with fury. She looked up at him, her expression shifting between anger and curiosity. Hogan smoothed back her hair from her face, splaying his fingers between the heavy, waving strands. She tried once to buck him off, a quick thrust of her hips against his, and Hogan held her wrists beside her head, enjoying the sight. He had never held a woman against her will, but Jemma was not just any woman. Maybe it was the hunter in him, or the man admiring a fiery woman, or maybe it was because his desire had hitched up a notch when she moved beneath him, but Hogan found himself enjoying the play.

"You look just absolutely wicked and full of yourself, Hogan Kodiak," she muttered, glaring up at him.

"I have the upper hand for the moment anyway. Are you afraid of me?"

She frowned. "Of you? No. I know you're just trying to drive me off course."

"Drive you off course? Is that what I'm doing?" Because he couldn't resist, he placed his lips just where her pulse was pounding in her throat like a trapped bird. The erotic scent of her skin swirled around him, and Hogan tasted her with the tip of his tongue. There was just that quiver in her body, that stiffening, and her breath sucking past his cheek that drove him further. He felt his senses shift, homing in on her, aroused, skin heating against her throat as his fingers pushed hers, laced with them beside her head. He nuzzled the soft area behind her ear, traced her lobe with his lips and bit gently.

"Hogan . . . this won't work," she whispered unevenly, huskily. "Let me up. I've got things to do—"

"Mmm. Running away? You've been doing a lot of that, and you're skittish." He wanted more, he wanted to feel her body smooth against his, twining, warming, those long thighs opening for him—Her cheeks were warm, and that heat made Hogan think of a deeper one as he brushed his lips across her jaw, her forehead, her eyes and cheeks. He trembled, shocked by his need, one hand leaving hers to slide downward, enclosing her breast gently, adoring the sleek shape, the softness that was—

The artist left the man, and Hogan tore away his chambray shirt. Her eyes widened, taking in his chest and still lower. "You'd better just stop it, Hogan Kodiak."

He breathed raggedly, his body aroused, needs pounding at his control. He found humor in the situation: Jemma beneath him, threatening him. That would be Jemma, unafraid of the consequences and not knowing when to pull back. "Or? You like setting the rules, don't you? Take a note, Jemma. I've never liked rules."

She glared at him. "You're so perverse. I've waited to see you smile like that for years, not that cold tight smile that didn't reach your eyes, but a real, open warm smile—and now you're doing just that, and I am not in the mood for playing. I thought you had more control than to try to . . . to get me into bed."

"This is a bed, right? This couch folds out? So I guess I've succeeded, huh?" he asked, unable to stop grinning. He wasn't certain about the lighthearted boyish feeling within him, the sudden shift from arousal to playfulness, but for the moment, he was enjoying Jemma's changing expressions. Clearly, she didn't know how to approach him next and was circling ideas. Jemma, without a plan and acting like a fully charged summer lightning bolt looking for a place to strike, was bewitching.

She licked her lips, and he bent to lick them again. "Hogan!"

He stood up, aware that he wanted much more than playing, his body still singing with sensual tension, and Jemma quickly slid from the couch to fling herself into the driver's captain's chair. She stared out into the night and propped her feet up on the dashboard. "You're playing with me, and I don't like it."

Hogan eased upon the couch, placed his hands behind his head, his feet upon the opposing booth and studied her as she spoke. "You're too much in control of yourself and you're just pushing me because you feel threatened. You're defending some weird idea that I'm taking over your life. Oh, don't snort like that. That's just what

Ben and Aaron do when they're making light of a suggestion, as if men know best—''

Jemma stared at him, crossing her arms over her chest. ''I know what you're thinking, of course. That my marriage went down the tubes because I'm frigid. Because I didn't tear off my clothes, Hogan Kodiak, does not mean I am frigid.''

He smoothed her bottom lip with his thumb, removing it before she could slash it away. ''You're definitely not that, and you do respond to me.''

She brooded on that and in a typical lightning change of her emotions, asked, ''What now?''

He allowed his body to stretch, easing the sensual tension he didn't want and hadn't expected to arise so quickly with Jemma. ''We wait. You can drive home now,'' he added, aware that the dismissal would set her off, and that was something he'd begun to enjoy very much.

''Get out!'' When Jemma would have shoved him out the door, Hogan caught her hand, turned it, and elegantly kissed the back. Taken aback, Jemma blinked up at him, and he forced himself to kiss her forehead when he wanted to sink deep within her body and take—

''If you want to learn how to fly fish, meet me down by the steam tomorrow afternoon. The native cutthroat are biting. The hatches are good.''

She'd shot out a fist to grip his shirt. ''You'll really teach me how to fish? This isn't like the time you told me to meet you at that cemetery to hunt snipes, is it? What's a cutthroat? A fish? What's a hatch?''

''A trout and big fat juicy bugs.''

''I knew it.'' Jemma clutched his shirt in her other fist. ''You're having some kind of sick joke and I'm in a fix. I need to know how to fly fish, Hogan, not catch bugs.''

"Trout like to feed on the hatch. Sometimes they even take a lure disguised as a bug, Jemma," he explained and watched with fascination as her expression followed her thoughts and her face lit up.

"I'll be there. Look—" she said, hurrying to open a closet of new fishing equipment. "I'm stocked up. I spent a fortune on what they said was the top brands. What do you want me to bring? Waders?"

"Yourself."

"Okay, okay, okay. Go home now. Get some sleep. Eat a good breakfast and I'll see you tomorrow for my first lesson. Well? Hurry. Go home."

Hogan folded his arms over his chest. Jemma was back to being pushy, and he enjoyed the excitement lighting her expression. "Now why do I get the feeling that I'm being rushed? That I'm being used?"

"Hogan, you are so exasperating. You're just stalling because you know how anxious I am to learn and get this right. I could make a mint on this deal."

"You've hurt my feelings," he lied, enjoying the sight of Jemma harried and frustrated for a change, reversing their roles.

She stared at him blankly. "You?"

"Uh-huh. You'll have to make me feel much better," he answered, and dipped his head for a kiss.

Ben finished washing the salve from his hands and dried them. He stared out into the night, toward the "needle and thread" natural grass field where the longhorns were grazing. The image of Dinah in her satin robe, the tightly belted sash drawing the material over her breasts, outlining them, had shaken him.

He rubbed his hands over his face. He was almost sixty years old and had set his trail in life; but how he ached for Dinah, wanted to touch her, to feel her close and soft and sweet against him. He leaned his arms over the corral boards, thinking about how sweet she'd been, how she made his mind stop, just looking at her. Then the babies had come along, Aaron and Carley, and everything had been perfect.

He stiffened as a light step sounded behind him; an experienced hunter, Ben knew how to define sounds. Then Dinah's fragrance curled around him, that light feminine scent, reminding him of flowers. When she came beside him in the moonlit night, placing her delicate hands on the weathered old boards, he didn't move, couldn't move away, fearing he'd say the wrong thing, hurting her. He stood there, a man missing a leg, damning his inability to say what was in his heart. He swallowed, a tough rancher more comfortable talking with a horse than a woman he'd always loved. The ring on his chest seemed to burn his skin because he wished he'd never—

"It's a beautiful night, Ben. Is that Jemma's van soaring back to the ranch?"

"It is. She's been holed up with Hogan. Lately the boy is getting to her and she's backing up some, running in the other direction, skittish as a filly with a stallion chasing her. I wondered when he'd have enough of her bossing him around."

Dinah turned to look at him and Ben feared looking down into her face—her beautiful face unchanged all these years. "Do you think this will work, Ben?"

"Damn straight it will." The thought of the stalker putting his hands on Carley made Ben sick.

"Aaron and Mitch can't stay here forever. What will we do when time runs out and he hasn't surfaced? What will we do when they have to go back to their lives?"

Ben knew his sons. "They'll stay until the job is done, and he'll come. He's wanting her, fastened on her, sick with wanting her to himself. Then we'll get him.''

"You're going to kill him, aren't you?" she asked slowly, and he nodded.

Fury boiled in him, and he fought its release. "The damned bastard wants my daughter. How do you expect me to feel?"

Once the release opened slightly, the bitterness deepened and he turned to Dinah, disliking himself even as he attacked her. "Feel sorry for him like you did for me?" He slapped his prosthesis, frustration boiling out of him. "You should have let me bleed to death, Dinah. I've been a half a man since."

She paled, her head rising for a battle as Ben's gaze ripped down the flannel shirt too big for her, her slender legs sheathed in jeans. She looked no older than she had as the bride he'd brought home to this rough country, but this time her eyes weren't filled with hopes and dreams, they were filled with fury, lashing at him. "Well, now, isn't that progress. That's the first time you've put it in words, Ben Kodiak. And you've never been half a man."

"Don't be wearing my clothes, woman," Ben ordered. He felt uncertain now and pride demanded that he strike back. The strength of her words, the certainty of them, had knocked the breath from him. If he backed off, holed up, she might move away. If he pushed, she might push back, because Dinah was strong. "You're a strong woman, Miss Dinah. I admire that. I always have. But I'd purely appreciate you not wearing my clothes."

She tilted her head, and that silky soft pale hair slid on her cheek. "It was there. I wore it. You wouldn't want me to come running after you in my bra, would you?"

Ben tried to think, but his mind was reeling, imagining her in just her bra—"Well, uh . . . I—"

Dinah laughed aloud, her delighted laughter rippling through the night. "You're blushing, Ben. I've embarrassed you. You still can't stand the thought of 'unmentionables,' can you?"

Ben watched Jemma's van skid to stop; the motor died as she leaped onto the ground and slammed the door shut. "That rig cost a pretty penny," he said, wanting to derail Dinah from talking personal.

"Mmm. She can afford it. She's determined to get that television series, and from the looks of it, she's been tangling with Hogan again."

"I'm not teaching her how to fly fish," Ben muttered. "I like my hide in one piece—Why did you come out here to disturb my peace?"

The slender, feminine hand on his arm should have been wearing his ring, Ben thought. She'd come to ask something of him, he saw that in her face, and wished he knew how to ask her forgiveness, "You want something for the boys and Carley. You've got that look. What is it?"

"They're not boys any longer, Ben," she said gently. Dinah studied him for so long and so intently that Ben feared she would see the age and hard times riding him. "It's time to tell Hogan about his mother. Oh, don't look like that, all closed-down and your jaw set as if the words would never come out."

"I'm not good with words, and you know it. Never have been."

She touched the gray in his hair, her eyes soft upon him and setting his nerves quivering with a weakness he'd probably have until his dying day. "You can do so many things, Ben. You have already, and you're afraid for all of us. It's time to let us do our share now, Ben."

Oh, God, he wanted her hand to touch his face, just to feel her warmth against him again, even for a heartbeat. His voice came out strangled, emotions twisting a lariat around his throat. "What do you want?"

"Let them help. Let them do what they want to help you and—"

The word dropped cold and heavy upon him. "Charity. I've never asked for anything from them."

"This is something they want to do, rebuild the Bar K." Dinah straightened her shoulders. "We don't know how long this will last, Ben, and I've got to keep busy, so does Carley. I told her how I had started that Montana jams idea and the garden I loved and—oh, Ben, how I loved gardening. I've been looking forward to it."

He wondered how he could have ever refused her anything, how he could have refused her love. Then he heard himself say, "I never slept with Maxi. I know people talk, but it wasn't—isn't that way."

She smiled impishly. "I know. I never thought that for a minute. You saw a woman in need, one carrying a child, and you gave her a home, and you raised Savanna as best you could. That's you, Ben."

He shook his head, wondering if he was so unappealing to women that she wouldn't think he'd had another woman—which he hadn't, not since the last time he'd made love to Dinah. "How do you know?"

"Oh, I just do. Your cat?" she said lightly, cheerfully, and bent to pet the heavily pregnant female cat obviously in love with Ben, twining around his legs.

"She just likes how the mice taste around here." Ben didn't want Dinah seeing his affection for the cat he'd named after her. He fought bending to pick up the cat, nuzzling her, like he did when the lonesome times came upon him and the need to touch something that wasn't leather, machine, or horse. The cat had been thin and weak, and he'd loved her on first sight. "Cat. Shoo."

"You'll listen to our"—Dinah paused and then

grinned again—''our boys, won't you? When they come
to you? It won't be charity, Ben. They're Kodiaks, the
same as you, with a right to tend land that will be theirs
and our grandchildren's someday.''

''They're not like me,'' he said, hearing the bitter echoes of how he'd yelled at her, shut her out, hurt her.

''You're just doing fine, Ben.'' She patted his cheek,
and Ben cherished the touch of his dreams. The words
were all locked in him like cold stones, and he couldn't
wrest them free, to tell her how sorry he was—

''It's okay if you wear my shirts now and then,'' he
said quietly as she stood looking up at him and that old
sweetness curled around him.

''I know.''

''You know so much, Miss Sass.''

''That I do, cowboy. And there's another thing. Aaron
is out on the roof, sitting up there watching us—oh,
don't turn now. Leave him to me, Ben. Don't start snap-
ping at him and telling him to treat me with respect.
He's angry with me for leaving you; he always has been.
Let him and me work this out without interfering.''

''You're asking too much, lady. The boy doesn't treat
you with respect.''

''Maybe he's right, maybe I should have stayed. But
I didn't. And now is a time to heal. Aaron and I can't
do that with you standing between us, protecting me.
Ben?'' she prompted urgently.

He nodded abruptly, knowing that she was right. Ben
traced Hogan's tractor lights as they circled the old
Holmes barn. The boy was like him and old Aaron, stubborn and hard, clear through.

''He'll be fine, too. Just think about telling him.'' Dinah stood on tiptoe to lightly kiss his cheek, and while
Ben dealt with that, she brushed her lips lightly over his.

# eight

A half hour after her return to the Bar K, Jemma stepped out the window and onto the roof where Aaron was sitting. "Go away. Don't start on me tonight."

"Hold this," she said, handling him the two plates laden with food. She settled beside him and licked her bottom lip, the one that Hogan had nipped gently, surprising her. He was full of surprises and when he'd grinned boyishly, she'd known her heart was flip-flopping loud enough to hear. There wasn't anything like diving into Hogan Kodiak when he was heated up, but she wasn't certain she wanted more. She dragged an old blanket through the window and wrapped it around her. Aaron had always been like a brother; her relationship with Hogan was not the same any more. Hogan moved too quickly, too intently, and had her simmering. She didn't like handing him any control. "This is like old times, isn't it? Cold night, pretty stars, and dark thoughts, right?"

He flicked a dark look at her, a male not wanting his space to be invaded. He handed one plate back to her and glanced at the turkey sandwich, laden with tomato and alfalfa sprouts, then at Jemma. "You're looking all hot and bothered. Another argument with Hogan?"

"He's going to teach me how to fish," she stated airily. Jemma dived into her sandwich, ignoring him, and for a while they ate in silence. Aaron watched his father lead a half-broken mustang around the corral as Dinah watched. "She won't hurt him, Aaron," Jemma said, meaning it.

"He's showing off for her, and she's letting him. He never got over her. When this thing is over, and Carley is safe, Dinah will be off again—big-city woman done with playing country girl." His words were bitter in the Montana night.

"Is that why you never married, because you're afraid you'll get hurt? Or is it because you've never gotten over Savanna?"

"We were kids back then. I'd come home from college and thought I knew everything there was to know. She'd changed overnight, a woman at sixteen. We were too hot for our own good. She broke it off by going out with other guys, and I was ready to move on, too—" He glanced at Jemma, who had just laughed. "Lay off. It's just sometimes I think what might have been, if I had stayed here . . . with her. She's got a thing going with Richard Coleman anyway. You can tell it by looking at them together."

"Well, he's nice. You're not." Jemma's thoughts flew back to Hogan, how he tasted, how he looked her over, arrogant, cocky, with a grin she hadn't expected. The rest of him wasn't as she expected either—he'd been aroused, hard against her. She took a small dried branch from the roof and sailed it into the night, like she wished she could her shaken emotions. She'd expected Hogan to be remote, not playful.

That kiss on the knoll had definitely tasted of male hunger; he'd opened his mouth upon hers, his exotic, mysterious taste had invaded her mouth, holding her head in place like a—she tossed away the primitive illusion of a stallion holding a mare in place, nipping at her. In the van, he'd held her beneath him—

His tenderness was even more earthshaking than his passion. She'd always known that Hogan enjoyed touching, feeling textures and forms shift beneath his fingertips—but she hadn't expected to be stroked or held like that, the gentle press of those long fingers, shaping her breast.

He'd terrified her then, because she hadn't expected the sensual onslaught, the change from intense observer to touching to playful lover. Those long fingers had been so strong, digging slightly into her wrists, Hogan's face too warm against her throat.

*But then he'd be missing Simone and the conveniences of their affair.* A meticulous man, Hogan was not likely to go shopping for one-night stands. "I will not be taking up the slack," she muttered, resenting his need for a comfortable, convenient substitute—herself.

"What?" Aaron asked, not really listening.

"Your brother is a jerk. You and Hogan and Ben and Mitch—all absolute jerks one minute and then like boys the next. You and Ben and Mitch have a certain charm, but Hogan is one hundred percent jerk." She pushed her hands through her hair, an attempt to remove the taut feel of Hogan's big, unrelenting fists in it.

Aaron studied at her. "You're in a good mood tonight. Hogan is laying off Dad, for now anyway, and that can't be easy. They're circling each other now, though, and who knows when that will erupt. It won't be pretty."

As she looked across the small valley, she saw that

every window in Hogan's house was lit. He'd kept himself apart all these years, and now, he'd be lurking there, fighting his shadows. Jemma sucked in the crisp Montana night air and tucked her bare toes beneath the blanket. She'd handle Hogan.

Mitch passed by the open window. "Found Ben's candy-bar stash," Mitch said, stepping out onto the roof and settling beside Jemma. He handed each one a candy bar, then lay back with one arm behind his head to study the stars. "I've been working the irrigation ditches, damming for the overflow onto the fields. Even my butt hurts," he said finally with a long, weary sigh.

Then Carley, dressed in a ragged sweat suit she loved, stepped out onto the roof. Aaron and Mitch both shot out hands to grip her hands until she settled firmly on the roof. She shrugged them away. "Like old times. Wonder what Hogan is doing?"

"Breathing brimstone and fire and cruising that cold box he calls a house like a warlord on the prowl, and along the way he's probably making another million designing jewelry that will sell for outrageous prices. His work will probably rest on every millionairess's silicone bosom," Jemma muttered, more darkly than she had intended. Pictures of Simone D'Arcy preyed on her mind. "Don't tell me D'Arcy's size Cs stuffed into that belly-button-low neckline were real."

"Wow. That was impressive coming from you. You rarely care about necklines unless you're wearing them." Just then Carley snapped, "Stop blowing in my ear, Snake. You're lucky you're not rolling off this roof."

"You'd just have to take care of me," he drawled. Sighing contentedly, he settled back.

"Home sweet home," Aaron murmured dryly. "To think I could actually be in my nice quiet, civilized penthouse and not worry about if a hoof is going to unman me during branding. This place doesn't have a stereo system. I tore my hand to shreds with that putty knife today.''

Carley peered down at Ben and Dinah. ''The folks look okay together, don't they? I wonder how long Dad can manage his illness. He looks so good. I'm glad he's got Savanna here to help him. She's totally dedicated to him. But I'm glad we're all here, too.'' She looked down to Mitch, who had just stretched out his arm, patting his shoulder to indicate a place for her head. ''We're all grown up now, Snake. I'm not a little girl anymore, and I don't need cuddling. Do you think Dad and Mom ever thought anything was wrong after . . . just after that happened? They never knew, did they?''

''No,'' Jemma, Aaron, and Mitch said together. Then when Carley stared off into the night, all of them knew what she was thinking.

''Dad doesn't know that I've had letters from that stalker, does he? He shouldn't have to worry about anything as dirty as that now, not when he's . . . dying,'' Carley whispered raggedly.

''You're not the dirty one, Carley,'' Jemma stated hotly. ''You didn't do anything wrong. This is bringing it all back, isn't it?''

Carley nodded. ''But I want to be here for Dad. He can't know, and Mom would never forgive me.''

''Dammit! For what?'' Mitch erupted, sitting up and glaring at her. ''For being in the wrong place at the wrong time? Jemma's right, you didn't deserve what happened and you can't blame yourself for the rest of your life. And you can't bury yourself in food and sweat clothes.''

''Take it easy, Mitch,'' Jemma warned. To Carley,

she said, "He's just tired, like the rest of us. His snarling will be gone in the morning."

"Stop protecting her from reality, Jemma. It's time she faced the facts and moved on with her life," Mitch said sharply, getting up to leave the trio alone.

"Everyone is going to have to stop running my life," Carley said very quietly. "I can protect myself from Mitch's evil moods. He just likes to torment me, that's all."

But later that night, when the old house had settled, Jemma listened to Carley sob quietly. Without hesitating, Jemma eased from her bed and into Carley's single one. She nudged her hip against Carley's. "We're bigger than we used to be, huh? Or else this bed is smaller."

"I couldn't bear to go through that again, Jemma," Carley whispered shakily. "He made me feel so dirty. I couldn't bear to be held down again like that."

"You know what? I think you're brave. You're putting aside your fears for Ben's sake. Besides that, you paid a bundle for all those self-defense classes and you're really good."

"I can feel him out there—waiting." Carley began to shake and curled away from Jemma.

Jemma rose to lean over her. "Then feel Ben and Hogan and Mitch and Aaron, too. If I were that sicko, I wouldn't want to tangle with any one of them. And hey, what about me? Don't I count? Wasn't I there in every one of those self-defense classes, bruising my butt along with yours? He won't come near you. He'd be a fool to even try."

Carley was quiet for a time, and then she said, "Don't test Hogan too much, Jemma. I saw him watching you, and he's interested. He's never tried to get women, they've just thrown themselves at him. If he decides he wants you, you might not be able to brush him away as lightly as the others. You were playing with them, getting what you wanted and dancing away. Hogan isn't like Aaron or Mitch. My oldest brother has infinite patience when he wants something. You've seen him work with horses.''

Of course, Jemma had seen Hogan's slow, easy style with balking horses, and that worried her. She'd successfully chilled any moves upon her, but Hogan had snared her for a moment in the van and losing that control, fighting her needs and his tenderness, was terrifying. ''I'm not interested. I went into a heavy-duty commitment when I got married and see how that ended?''

Carley's disbelieving ''uh-huh'' kept Jemma awake long into the night.

Hogan ran his finger down Mulvaney's report. The investigator was thorough, but had not been able to reveal new information. Aaron's visit to the sheriff's office proved that there were no strangers in Kodiak, or the surrounding towns, violence was at a minimum—except for Artie Moore's harassment of Savanna. Closely watched now, Artie hadn't been happy with Savanna's protection of his battered wife and children. Slighter and faster than Artie, and schooled in karate, Richard Coleman had quickly taken away the knife held at Savanna's throat. Artie was now under close watch, and Savanna hadn't filed charges—but she would, if Artie came near his children or soon-to-be ex-wife. But eighteen years ago, Artie had been in Florida when Carley was attacked, and he wasn't a likely suspect.

Jackson Reeves had been a classmate, in reform schools and later jails, and protected by his doting mother, the Richmonds' cleaning woman for years. Hogan made a mental note to keeping checking on Jackson.

Merry Reeves, a birdlike, frightened woman and his mother, would lie to protect him.

Hogan glanced at the digital lights of the alarm system mirroring the one at Ben's house, and then at his own. If anything happened to Ben's system, Hogan's would announce it at the Bar K ranch house. The separate alarm system for Hogan's house remained silent. The mini-alarm unit that he carried on his belt when outside was linked into both systems.

After a cold shower, he went to the stuido and touched the modified drawing of his Fire Feathers necklace design. The edges of the feathers seemed to lift and turn and ripple upon the paper. That is how he had felt when Jemma's long curved body moved beneath his, a flow that had excited him, a quiver of flesh showed she wasn't immune to him. He eased down on the Egyptian cotton rug in front of his fire, watching the flames feed upon the wood.

Her half-closed lids had excited a savagery in him that he hadn't expected. As an artist, he'd studied a woman's body. As a man, he'd served his needs and knew the sensuality in a woman's body. In Paris, as a student and away from the restrictions of the Kodiak name, he'd dived into lush, willing, knowledgeable women, feasted upon them. His sexual affair with Simone had ended long ago, and at that time both their needs had been served. Now, just watching Jemma, that quick restless movement of her head, those elegant hands, he found himself reeling in a sensual mist that he'd sooner not experience now.

Or did she call forth the hunter in him, a man needing more than sex, but needing the chase? What were the haunting images that swirled around and in that fiery sunlit hair?

He was already excited by the thought of her, alone

with him, and that fascination was troublesome, because it deepened by the hour.

He ran his fingers across the penciled drawing, letting the sketched feathers flow into his fingers and into that secret creative place reserved for him alone. He saw Jemma, pale and nude, the feather necklaces almost savage around her throat, her vivid hair swirling up and around her head, taken by the wind. Women usually came to him, not that he beckoned. But the novelty of pursuing a woman he'd known from girlhood, changing the dynamics into lovers wouldn't be easy.

He shifted restlessly; he wasn't happy with the knowledge that his body wanted hers; Jemma Delaney's restless, dedicated-to-self-and-money style chafed the peaceful calm that Hogan had forged in his life. He raked his hand through his hair, pushing back the shoulder-length strands, and realized the gesture was that of frustration.

He never allowed himself frustration; he'd had too much of it in his lifetime.

Hogan smiled as the telephone rang. "Hello, Jemma."

The silence at the other end of the line told him that he'd gotten to her again, a game he really enjoyed. Her "Oh, hello," was too offhand. Hogan rolled to his side and studied the flames. He settled back to enjoy nettling Jemma's fast temper, toying with her and listening to the different, telling tones of her voice. "You wanted me?" he asked to set her off, to place her in the position of pursuing him.

The catching sound of her breath caused him to smile. "Jemma?"

"It says in this book that we should be catching rainbow or brown trout, not native cutthroat. Are you sure you know what you're doing? Do I need to go to the bait and tackle shop tomorrow? How big are they? I need one about forty pounds or so.''

"Cutthroat. I like how they fight. Try three pounds, and you don't need to buy anything to start.''

"But I bought all this stuff! That small? I want a really big fish. Hogan, I think we should—''

"Relax, honey. See you tomorrow,'' he drawled and clicked off the portable telephone. The memory of Jemma relaxing beneath his massage, her "oh! oh!'' close enough to the sound of a woman at the peak of her ecstasy was enough to make his jeans uncomfortably tight over his desire. He smiled as the telephone rang again. Playing phone games with women hadn't been in his life, but with Jemma, he was learning new interests. "Yes?''

"You're rude, you know,'' she shot at him.

He imagined how she'd look, all steamed up and sassy. "Why don't you come over here and tell me that?''

After a slight hesitation, Jemma hung up. Hogan rolled to his back, placed his hands behind his head, and smiled. He realized he was looking forward to having Jemma alone, stirring her up and watching her ignite.

*The Kodiaks thought they could protect her, his Celestial Virgin, but they couldn't.* She'd waited for him, buried herself in food and loose clothing, but she was perfect. He was, of course, the only suitable male for her, himself a virgin after all these years of hungering for her. He saw her opening her silk robe for him, allowing him to be the first—

Time was on his side, and he was a patient man. He'd waited since that night—she'd been nothing but thrashing arms and legs and fearful eyes, and she would be his alone.

Of course she was still a virgin, he'd sensed that immediately, reading the innocence on her face. He'd take the prize she'd saved for him. The others weren't virgins, already used, and he'd had to kill them. But Carley would be intact, her body pure. He groaned aloud, his desire rising hard and aching as he smoothed the folded white oriental robe that he intended her to wear that first time. He'd studied the reports of the area's 1880s Celestial Virgins, brought from China to please the prospectors. Almost children, they'd been auctioned and sold, and then when they were no longer pleasing, they had been taken into the mountains to die. Maybe it was true, that the winds coming down the canyons carried their cries—He liked the sound of crying, pleading women . . .

His skill and patience, his years of waiting, would soon be rewarded with the gift of his bride's body. "Only a matter of time. The Kodiaks are too stormy to stay together long, and they'll fly away to their own lives. Then I'll have Carley for my bride."

"Thanks." Hogan took the quart jar of iced lemonade from Dinah with one hand, and with the other sank his post hole digger to rest deep into the rich spring earth. A fence row of posts that needed replacement stretched over the knoll and into the woods. The new grass was pushing through the rich dark earth now and by summer the stalks would be flowing, undulating like green waves in the wind.

Dinah's fine pale hair caught the wind, lifting around her ageless face. "When you're ready to eat, I brought sandwiches for lunch. Jemma's alfalfa-sprout jar seems to be endless. She's determined that we're all going to be quite healthy, despite the fact that she and Carley managed to sneak down to the kitchen around three or so this morning and devour a can of frosting. Carley must have been upset, and Jemma was there for her in a way I can't seem to be. I love Jemma for what she's done for Carley—Jemma has never once failed my daughter. But I know all of you—Jemma, Carley, Aaron, Mitch, you—share some dark secret that has to do with Carley, and none of you are about to tell me."

Dinah had always taken special care to seek him out, trying to draw him closer to the rest, to mend the wound between father and son. He realized that the familiar sight of her, dressed like a girl in jeans and a sweatshirt, her pale hair catching the slight midmorning breeze, caused him to remember how she had been—happy and glowing—before Ben drove her away. He ached for the woman he could not help then.

For the month that they'd been together again, Kodiak battles flew over the house like bullets. Ben spoke guardedly, warily, and then tore from the house when stretched too far. Jemma would run after him, coaxing him back into whatever chore had caused the rift.

Aaron was on edge, torn between the driving need to be in the middle of the stock-market bustle, and an unshielded need to have Savanna. An expert at flirting, Savanna wasn't taking him seriously, and no other woman had treated Aaron so lightly.

Mitch worried about his Chicago teenage toughs, the girls he was trying to get off the streets, the impoverished mothers and the babies who needed proper nourishment. But Mitch was also drained by life, haunted and clearly determined to salvage Carley, who resented his "psychobabble" and "interference in my life."

Carley found joy in Jemma, who was into everyone's lives, ruthless in her goal of mending the Kodiak family's. Over the horizon, Carley and Jemma were busily planting the garden. The garden wasn't small; Jemma's carrot-and-beet crop needed space. Aaron was plowing the field, preparing for the reseeding of the alfalfa field, and Mitch was walking the irrigation ditches, cleaning out the winter debris. Hogan tipped the jar and welcomed the iced lemonade. Ben would likely be checking his herd—newborn calves that needed ear tags—and marking the cattle that needed branding.

"Everyone has been busy with the garden, including Ben. It's actually fun, all of us together, and Jemma determined to rule us all."

Hogan lifted an eyebrow. His father had always said that a vegetable garden was women's work. "Ben is gardening?"

"Ben. Carley is clearly out to exhaust herself, pitting herself against anything that needs doing. When Carley was out there killing herself, pulling out that old board fence, and Jemma was trying to learn how to drive the tractor without hitting anything, Ben just said, 'Oh, hell, may as well see that it's done right.' He hitched up those two draft horses, the Percherons, and an old plow and plowed a huge garden. He was quite the sight to see— made my heart dance a little bit," she said, turning her face to shield a blush. "He let me drive his pickup out here. In the old days, he would have made a fuss."

"He hasn't changed, Dinah," Hogan said quietly and prayed Dinah would not be hurt again by Ben's rawhide temperament. "He won't change," he corrected, wanting to protect her from more pain.

"He's trying," Dinah stated adamantly. "So should you. I think he'd talk to you now, about your mother."

Hogan drank the iced bittersweet lemonade and pushed away hope, a skill he'd perfected. He pushed away fear of the truth and wondered what natural instinct made women want to soften rock-hard hearts.

"Still trying to make us a family, Dinah? It's a little late for that, isn't it?"

"Not for you and him—no. I firmly believe that, Hogan, or I wouldn't be here now. I think he's really, really happy now, with all of his children together. We haven't had time to talk, but I know what this is costing you," she said quietly, the morning sunlight flowing over her ageless, fair beauty. "You're at the supper table every night, taking your place. You're careful that Carley is always with Aaron, Mitch, or Ben before you take time to see to your own needs. I know your business is doing so well, and I wanted to tell you how proud I am of you. You must be working well into the night catching up on your designs and your company. Now you're out here, working on Ben's ranch, when you could be working on your own. It's only a garden and an invitation, Hogan. It's a start."

Dinah looked at Hogan, tall and strong; she remembered the awkward little boy she'd tried to hold and love. She placed her hand along the rugged planes of his face—a man's face. The ache in him chilled her hand. He didn't move away from her touch as he had as a boy, and Dinah closed her eyes, loving Hogan as deeply as her own children. "I want grandchildren, Hogan. I want Aaron's and yours alike, and Mitch's, too. I want Carley to heal and find peace and to become a woman. I want us, as a family, to heal. If we are strong together, we can emotionally meet whatever Carley's stalker tries. I'm not worried about the physical threat, because I know that Carley is well protected. It isn't just protecting Carley, it's giving her a life. As for me—I'm tough, Hogan. I won't let Ben hurt me this time, because now I know that I pushed too hard, and the timing was bad. I only made things worse. You were only a child, Hogan. Just a boy, all big eyes and hurting, and we made it worse with battling at every turn. I'll never forgive myself for that.''

Hogan studied the swaying tops of the willows lining the stream where he would fish later in the day; the clear air echoed with the arguments of long ago. ''Stop blaming yourself, Dinah. Ben is what he is.''

''He needed time to adjust after the accident. Jemma thinks the Kodiaks were the original hide-in-caves clan, apart and licking their bruises, and that everyone needs time to adjust and heal. She's right. It took years to put this in place, long hard years, but now I know the truth. I replayed scene after awful scene, and I was wrong. I insisted when I should have given him time to heal, Hogan. You're a man now, you understand what passes between a man and a woman. I wanted desperately to prove to Ben that his missing limb didn't matter. He wasn't ready. Each time I tried, the scene was worse.'' Her breath caught, and she swallowed, turning her face up to Hogan, her eyes bright. ''You and Ben are so much alike, not willing to accept until you are ready. Open your heart, Hogan. Heal. And never, never think that you are not my child. I love you dearly.''

Dinah straightened, brushed his hair away from his face in a tender gesture that he'd once avoided. ''And I love Ben still. I married another man whom I respected and who I thought would provide a stable environment for my children. But Joseph was dying then, all alone, and love didn't run between us, not like with Ben. We had separate bedrooms, and he never asked for more. Raw from my divorce and feeling like a failure, I needed Joseph's friendship then. But it was Ben who sold Kodiak land to you to set up my temporary employment company. He wanted me to build something of my own. Oh, I was furious at first—him pushing me away, but then I knew that he was doing what he thought was best for all of us. Go to him now, Hogan. Ask your questions, but do it when he isn't feeling raw and a failure. You can read him—ask when the time is ripe.''

By midafternoon, uneasy with his emotions, Hogan had left his work. He now studied the sunlight on the graceful arches of his fly-fishing line, the drops of water flying in a perfect design. The willows bordering the stream were quiet, clear sunlit water sliding over the round rocks. He played the line with his left hand, getting the feel of fishing after years away from it. His reel was old, heavy and familiar, dug from the rubble of fishing equipment haphazardly stored in the barn. Years ago, he'd made the flies from horsehair and whatever else he could find.

There were cutthroat trout in the riffle on the opposite bank, lazing in the shadows of a fallen log. They weren't hungry now, but Hogan enjoyed the sunlight on his back, the flowing, constant beauty of his line, returning to the calm, storing it within him.

He didn't feel like blending metal and rock, and though his business was ongoing, managed by computer and fax, he realized now how badly he had needed to recover who he was, to rest from his struggle to success. Dinah thought it was time, but Hogan didn't sense Ben's willingness to open the past.

Ben had taught Hogan how to fish, to sail the line over the water, working the fly to appeal to the trout— there had been a peace about him then that he'd patiently shared with a small boy. Hogan cast again, too quickly for the line to sail properly, and set his jaw, determined to push away the thought that he'd come back to make his home, his nest. The restlessness in him was for a woman. He could almost inhale Jemma's unique, feminine scent now, feel that smooth skin, her body tremble against his, the taste of her mouth had shocked him . . . rather his need for the taste of her had stunned him.

*He hadn't expected the excitement within him, nor the tenderness.*

A trout took the wet fly beneath the water and Hogan, his thoughts on Jemma, tugged too quickly. The horsehair fly tore from the water, the fish wiser now and retreating back to the riffle.

*Jemma.* He wanted her beside him, filled with life. He wanted to hold her, place his hands on those taut perfect breasts and—Hogan admitted that he was, as Ben would put it, "in season."

Her wary glances only excited him, much to his disgust. He was long past playing boy-chasing-girl games. He disliked watching for her, his senses alert and hungry, yet there had been a certain sense of victory when he'd held her beneath him, holding her still when she would have moved away. Hogan detested men who needed to subdue women, and this discovery within himself was not a pleasant one. The male-female challenge had made him want more. He doubted that Jemma knew or cared about the pleasant intricacies of a civilized sensual relationship.

He settled into his thoughts, casting automatically, letting the hissing sound curl around him, jerking the fly lure back before the trout would take it. He drew nature's colors around him, the gray river rocks beneath the surface of the stream, dark lichen lace swaying on the trees, the snowcapped mountains soaring in the distance. He settled into the sunlight on his bare back, the almost imperceptible sounds of leaves brushing against each other, the stream gently murmuring.

Attuned to nature's sounds, Hogan noted the slight stirring of the brush higher on the embankment. He stretched slightly and used the movement to disguise a stealthy look at the intruder. Jemma had found him, and the knowledge brought a mixture of pleasure and irritation.

The brush crashed behind him, Jemma cried out, and Hogan turned to watch her slide down a small ridge on her backside. She glared at him as he stood on the stream bank, stood up, dusted her backside and tromped through the bushes toward him. Certain that she wasn't hurt, Hogan took a deep steadying breath and returned to casting. The image of the curves beneath her leopard-print sweater and jacket and tight black jeans at once set him on edge.

At his side, she said, "I had to hunt all over to find you. Aaron let me off his horse a while ago when we spotted your Appaloosa. You didn't say where you'd be, and I had to track you down."

Hogan tried to ignore the "caught you" and "track you down" statements. He'd never liked the idea of being caught at anything.

"Don't ignore me, Hogan. Teach me this stuff and then I need to use your office."

"You can use my office equipment, but stay out of my studio," he agreed, taking his time and realizing just how much he might regret any arrangement with Jemma. He tried to ignore her scent, but his senses locked on the warm brush of her breast against his arm as he eased slightly toward her and fought the tug of her body at the same time he enjoyed the touch.

"How do you do that?" she asked, staring at him, obviously fascinated as he cast again.

Hogan scoffed at himself, at the heady sense of attracting a woman's attention—the woman he wanted in his bed. He was showing off, flexing his muscles and skill. "Come here, and I'll teach you."

He loved the excitement and pleasure in her eyes. He'd seen it before, and realized now that her vivid, easily read expressions had always fascinated him.

# nine

Sunlight gleamed on Hogan's dark skin. With his body outlined against the glittering sunlit stream and the grayish green cottonwood trees, he took her breath away. She'd been watching him for a long time before she'd moved closer. She'd never stopped to appreciate the smooth play of muscles across a man's back. She'd never cared about the sensuous slide of gleaming tanned skin in the dying light of day, the breadth of shoulders narrowing down to a lean waist, but now she held her breath, just looking at him. When his jeans had slipped, just that bit, she'd expected a pale strip and found none. Then all that strong length of leg, braced wide upon the river rocks as he cast out into the stream. There was graceful beauty in the way his hand worked the line, a man at ease with life.

Hogan Kodiak was beautiful, black hair covering his nape, his arms surging with strength as he cast, his hand slowly, patiently working the lure as it glided downstream from the riffle. After the cast, the line snapped back out of the water, curved elegantly in the air over his head, and shot the fly upstream. His pose was timeless and devastatingly male.

He was too complete, too cold and controlled, and he had a lover. Worst of all, Hogan could not be enticed or threatened. She'd tried for years to bend him and failed. There was no reason why she should find him exciting, why she should want him to hold and to kiss her, and more.

Hogan looked down at her with a devastating smile. "You don't have the patience for this."

"I can do it," she said, watching him gracefully sail the line into the air, whipping it gently, the lure tantalizing the fish in the stream. "It can't be that hard, and I have to know what I'm doing when Les arrives. I want that television slot. The reruns really pay off. What are we fishing for? Great big browns or rainbows?"

"Cutthroats. Nice try." He lifted an eyebrow, glancing at her as his right hand worked the line. "What do you know about starring in a weekly television show?"

"What have I ever known how to do? I'm a learner, Hogan. I do what I have to do." She caught his scent— he'd bathed in the stream, and the soapy scent blended with another sweeter, fresh one, like that of grass. She wanted to brush that strand of hair away from his forehead, to feel those rugged contours warm and smooth beneath her hands.

"From the looks of that van, you're using yourself as bait. Sooner or later, he's bound to discover that you are about as much sportswoman as I am. Doesn't that worry you, just a little bit?"

"Of course not. I know the pros usually do those shows, but I can pitch the how-to on a beginner's level. We watched those shows and sometimes they explain way over the average person's head. I'm into supply and demand, and fly fishing is a top sport—and by the time he comes in July, you'll have taught me how to fish. I need enough skill to make the sale, Hogan. Then I can pick up as I go along. I've pulled off deals like this before, though not quite as big. All I need is my foot in the door, and I usually come through.''

He cast again, and she watched fascinated as the fly lure whipped above the water and a trout leaped to take it—just as she had risen to Hogan's kiss, his touch, that light trapping of her breast. The trout fought the hook, but with patience, Hogan slowly drew it toward him. He let it fight the length of line, then wound a bit onto his reel, and repeated the process, working the fish closer. When close enough, he lifted the line and the fish, grinning at her. She could have killed him for that boyish grin, the pleasure easing his harsh features. ''Supper,'' he said, crouching to slide the trout onto a line in the water with other fish.

''They're so small, Hogan. I can't make an impression with those. I need a giant one that looks great on a board over a fireplace.'' Jemma's stomach contracted—she liked to eat fish, but didn't like to meet them when they were alive.

Her throat dried, just watching his graceful movements, the flex of his muscles, the smooth skin shifting sleekly over them. She nudged his bottom with her boot. ''What do you say, Hogan? Now's just as good a time as any to start lessons, don't you think?''

''I thought you needed my office, to fax the world and check on your millions.''

''You can be so difficult. You're here now, and so am I. There are fish out there, and they're biting—you just caught one.'' She looked down at the long, flexible rod he'd placed in her hand. ''But this is old. I'll just go get mine—''

''Yes, go get yours,'' he said too easily.

She studied Hogan and knew he'd get away if she

took time to get her equipment. Hogan knew how to fade into the countryside when he wanted. "Okay, okay. Show me. I'll catch a few of the little ones first. And I need a few good shots of me holding a champion fish and some trophy or other in my other hand."

There was just that darkening of his eyes, that tilt of his head as he rose to tower over her. She fought to keep her gaze from lowering to his smooth, gleaming chest, the muscles of his stomach, and the neat indentation of his navel. "Let's start by dropping the orders, shall we?" Hogan asked too softly.

The challenge was there, a man setting down his rules. If she wanted to learn from him, she'd have to note his limits. Jemma resented anyone's rules but her own. "You're the natural candidate, Hogan. An artist usually has that inner eye for the best camera shot. I saw the photos that you sent to Dinah and Carley through the years. But I don't want to actually touch fish, or clean them. They can just hang at the end of the line and we can fake whatever."

His lifted eyebrows said she would have to do both. "Fine," she said unwilling to let him set up barriers to her goals. "I've shucked oysters, I can touch fish. Let's get started. We don't have much time, and the light is dying."

He took the rod and flicked the line over the stream. "It's a seduction, Jemma. You can't ramrod and bully a trout to take your lure."

"They're hungry, aren't they?" she asked, standing closer, peering into the smooth-running stream as he flicked the line and played it with his left hand, letting the current gently take the fly lure.

"Here," Hogan said, stepping back and drawing her in front of him. "Hold the rod like this, and center on where you want the lure to go." His hands fitted hers

to the rod and to the line and remained, his body moving
behind hers, framing her. "Patience, Jemma," he murmured against her ear. "Not too fast and hard. Slowly.
Enjoy the feel of the rod in your hand. Flick it."

His open mouth moved across her cheek, just a brush
of heat, but enough to stun her. While she caught her
breath, decided whether to edge aside or to stay within
the circle of his arms, Hogan's dark gaze traced her body
against his, igniting a heat within her own body.

Unprepared for the tremble, for the awakening she
hadn't expected, Jemma studied his rugged face, the
harsh planes and shadows, the small scar on his cheek.
"How did you get that scar?"

"I fell," he said simply, his expression darkening,
closing into the shadows that were so much a part of
Hogan. "No more questions. Keep that wrist straight,
use your elbow. Get the line wet first."

His hand moved her arm, the motion sensual and
slow, his hand hard and warm upon her skin. There was
that caress of his thumb on her inner wrist, the smooth
stroke of his cheek lying next to hers. Against her back,
his body moved, almost caressing hers as he showed her
how to move her wrist in casting. His breath swept
across her cheek, tangled in her hair, moved the tendrils
against her cheek. There on the stream bank, Hogan held
her forearm with one hand and curved her close against
his body with his other, his hand opening and spanning
her lower stomach as she cast. She couldn't catch her
breath, couldn't move away from him, or set rules—she
simply enjoyed the flow of his body around hers, a natural graceful movement that captivated.

"Feel the drag of the line in the water, pull it slow—
feel it give as it leaves the water—use that energy to let
it snap back and then cast—" The lure hit a tree branch,
the line draped over it. Hogan took the rod, flicking it

expertly, until the lure dropped into the water. "Do it again," he said. "And not as though you're zipping a baseball across home plate."

After forty-five minutes, Jemma turned to Hogan, who was fitting three large trout onto sticks, bracing them over the small fire. He'd stopped talking to her in that low soft way and at one point had glared at her before walking off. "My arm is tired. The line just goes out there and plops into the water. Why aren't they biting? Aren't they hungry? Should we go somewhere else? Where are the big ones?"

In the evening shade, Hogan crouched by the fire, dressed in his T-shirt and unbuttoned flannel shirt. He spread the horse's saddle blanket on the grass and settled down, his back against a log, long legs extended in front of him. With a stalk of grass in his mouth, he appeared to be relaxed. "You've fouled the line. It can only go so far before it's hung up on the reel. You didn't listen . . . you never do, and you don't know how to relax. Bring the rod over here."

Jemma walked to him, and watched him begin to patiently unravel the line looped around the reel. "My new reel isn't supposed to get tangled. The sports guy said so."

"Uh-huh. Next time, when you're reeling in, try to make the line run across your finger like I showed you." Hogan's long graceful fingers continued to work on the line. He handed her a length of straightened line. "Hold this."

She sat on a rock, watching him rewind and straighten the line, working the series of small loops out of it, his head bent over the task. "You're always so careful, so precise. I think I got the hang of it, don't you? I mean those last few casts—I've been thinking that there really is no need to cast out that three or four yards of line—

that just tangles it. Why not just cast it out there without all that getting the line wet, 'feel the energy' stuff?''

Hogan plucked away the willow leaves tangled within the line. "Do you ever relax?"

"Sure." She pressed the dial that lit her wristwatch and knew that the first refrigerator she hit had better be full. "I really need to contact my sales manager and see if she managed to get a deal on that lot of dolls. You'll have to take me back, Hogan. It's dark now."

He placed the pole aside and checked the fish, sizzling now over the fire. "Aaron and Ben will tell them you're with me. They were up on the ridge about a half hour ago, checking on you."

"Oh. We need to hurry, so we can get back to your place before that supplier closes shop in California. I need to—"

"Eat. We're going to relax and have dinner. Or I am. You're invited. Or you can run away. Moon Shadow will take you to Ben's." His black gaze rested upon her, challenging her. "You shouldn't be shy of me, Jemma. We're both adults now, and we've known each other for years. Surely we can have a meal together and share a glass of good wine."

"You're not a relaxing sort of guy," Jemma stated warily, and Hogan grinned again, one of those flashing, boyish grins that could make her heart leap and race. "What wine?"

He lifted a bottle of very expensive white wine and two plastic cups from his saddlebags. "Do you still like lots of butter on your baked potato and sour cream?"

Jemma sipped the wine he'd given her and watched him prod the coals of the small fire to extract two foil-wrapped baked potatoes. He expertly slit and filled them with butter and sour cream. "What is this, Hogan?" she asked, aware that they were very alone and that Hogan wasn't allowing himself to be hurried into leaving.

"This," he said simply, and leaned down to brush his lips against hers. His hand curled around her nape, his thumb caressing the side of her jaw.

She hadn't been touched like that ever—that slow sensual sweep of his hand on hers, his dark eyes asking her a question she didn't want to explore. This was Hogan, and she'd known him for most of her life. "I think we should be going."

"Do you?" His deep voice slid over her like warm butter, and her heart hitched up double time.

"I suppose we could eat that first. Since you've gone to so much trouble," she whispered against his lips. "Do you know what you're doing?"

"Not quite. But I intend to find out." Then he framed her face with his hands and drew her lips close to his warm smooth ones. "You're shivering, Jemma. Cold?"

His expression mocked her, because he could feel the heat of her cheeks on his callused palms. She dug her fingers into the hard, rangy line of his shoulders, anchoring her senses from drifting away into the night. "You're playing games, Hogan."

"I thought you liked games. But then, maybe you just like being in control. That's right, isn't it? You like controlling the relationship—getting what you want, setting the terms, and never letting your carefully selected partner come too close. You're running too hard, Jemma. You're afraid what you'll find when you stop, and you'll have to stop someday. But you don't want to think about that now, do you? You want to think about getting money and making the Kodiaks' lives your own personal playground. You're a woman who needs life and warmth and most likely a good amount of very physical sex."

For a moment, Jemma stared blankly at him. He'd

skipped the usual friendly chitchat and homed right in on "very physical sex." "I'm not repressed sexually, Hogan. You're worse than Mitch, spouting psychology. You like to observe, to take people apart, see their components, but you're not taking me apart, Hogan."

"Aren't I?" he whispered, and gently bit her lip. He eased a space away and watched her; his expression was as dark and sultry as when he'd rested over her in the camper van. "Shall we eat?"

Using one hand as a pivot, Mitch launched himself over the corral gate. He strode to the center of the corral and grabbed the reins of the horse that Carley had been riding. "Reining," the short stop, change position, stop, change directions riding was competition rodeo riding. Originally used as "cutting horses," horses that separated cattle from the herd, reining competition no longer needed cattle to demonstrate their agility and obedience. Carley was good—too good to hide her talent. Tonight, she was using the horse to relieve her tension, sweat gleaming on her moonlit face and the animal's rump. "Stop it. You're wearing out yourself and the animal."

"Sue is a great reiner. She responds perfectly to directions."

Mitch gripped Carley's waist and pulled her from the saddle. She tugged up the sweatpants that were now too loose on her and glared up at him. "You're in an evil mood. Don't ever pull me off a horse again."

With the air of an older brother used to attending his sister's needs, he reached down to find the inner loop of her sweatpants. In jerky motions, he retied the knot tighter. "If you want to kill yourself, that's one thing. But don't abuse that animal."

She hit his chest with both fists, tears streaming down her cheeks, each one like a painful lash in Mitch's heart.

"I've never abused an animal in my life."

"Carley, take it easy." Mitch trapped her arms with his, holding her tight. How many years had he loved her? That first sight of her riding a horse far too spirited and too big for her, her pale hair blowing in the wind as she stood on the horse's bare back, riding him around the arena?

While her silky hair webbed across his cheek, Mitch looked out into the night. He detested the lie that had brought and kept her here, but Carley's stalker had a big advantage—time and invisibility. They'd have to find a way to take away that advantage.

"Jemma's worried about something. She's started talking in her sleep again, and last night, she damned Hogan well and good. Now she's out there with him, and he's in that dark stormy nasty temper again, keeping to himself. They're certain to be fighting, and no telling what Jemma will do."

"Why don't you worry about yourself for a change?" Mitch asked, then he lowered his mouth on Carley's sweet one.

Two heartbeats later, he found himself flat on his back, looking up at the horse and the starlit night. "That's my girl," he said, gingerly easing to stand, and watching Carley's round backside as she stalked toward the house. He kissed the horse. "Ah, old Snake still has it, huh?"

Mitch watched a horse with two riders crossing the field on a path for Hogan's house. "He's doing better than I am. This should be interesting. He's had her on the run, and now the noose is closing."

He kissed the horse again. "But you've got me, babe, and I've got you."

\*      \*      \*

"Oh! Oh! Oh!" Jemma cried out as Hogan massaged her foot. "Oh!" She fell back onto the soft thick rug in front of Hogan's fireplace, a graceful feminine sprawl. "I've got to get back to your office and check my e-mail. Oh! That feels so good, Hogan." She sighed as he began to work on her other foot.

When Hogan had asked her if she wanted to ride back to his house, her pride said no and her lips said yes. Using his office was just an excuse—Jemma wanted to be close to Hogan, and since his horse was the only transportation . . . She'd wanted him holding her close, pressed against her back and legs as they rode. "You look tense," he'd said after she'd used his fax machine, and cursing herself for not resisting, she slid into the relaxing massage he'd offered.

Jemma had never given herself to the luxury of relaxing. Even after a professional massage, she would be tense by the time she walked to her car, her mind separating into a hundred little have-to streets and calculating lucrative buys and sells.

"Mmm." Jemma let Hogan's large, strong hands take away her problems. The small warm fire, the wine Hogan had poured after the first bottle at the stream, and his hands—his marvelous strong hands massaging her feet, her calves, had made her feel limp and floating happily.

She'd known from the moment that she'd seen him lying on that horse blanket with that expensive bottle of wine in his hand that what he offered was too good to pass up. She'd wanted to see Hogan without his defenses, and she'd refilled their glasses several times. She'd always known that Hogan had something unique to offer her and when the time came, she'd take it—the massage was worth her aching casting arm. He'd offered to take her home, but Jemma wanted more of him—that

low soft chuckle that she suspected had been loosened
by wine. Filled with the pleasure of his massaging
hands, she sighed again as he turned her onto her stomach and began massaging the sensitive arches of her feet,
sliding his firm hands over her calves.

Hogan leaned close to her ear. "I could do this a lot
better if you were wearing something less restricting.
Wouldn't you like your back massaged?"

"Hmm?" She allowed herself to drift on the clouds,
pleasantly warm as Hogan's hands slid up to start working on her back. "Oh, Hogan, don't stop. Ohhh!"

That purring, pleasured sound of a woman near the
peak of her riveting climax, jarred him. His hands
paused just over her wiggling bottom, and the need for
Jemma ran through him like a hot stake.

Hogan swallowed and scrubbed his trembling hands
over his face. He'd wanted women before, to serve a
basic need, but Jemma excited him on another level. He
wanted her, but not like this. He'd had his fantasy ride
with her on the saddle in front of him, carrying her to
his lair, her hair blowing back against his face. Hogan
didn't like the primitive needs she drew from him. He'd
needed to claim her, take her to his lair and have her.
He'd set out to see what Jemma was like with all the
tense edges smoothed away, and now he knew—she was
vulnerable to his touch, responding immediately to the
control of his hands—on her feet.

"I'm ready," she murmured sleepily in the manner
of a woman used to giving orders. "Do it."

Hogan allowed himself a smile and lay down beside
her. Jemma was too used to getting what she wanted
from men, and he didn't intend to be one of the crowd.
She lifted her head, peering sleepily at him. "I can't
move, you know. I feel like a limp noodle. You're very
good. I could get you a job at my spa."

"You've had massages before. You're wound too tight, Jemma. Someday all the pieces are going to fly apart." He wondered what she would feel like under him, around him when she did just that. He reached out to stroke her hair, to twine his finger in the silky strands and Jemma's eyes drifted closed.

"Hogan," she whispered sleepily, and he longed for her to touch him, to hold him. The quiet sound of Carlos Nakai's Native American flute played in the background, and for just that instant, his shadows were quiet. Being near her, at her side, gave him peace.

The oddity of seeking warmth from a woman stunned him, even as Jemma sighed and plopped her hand on his chest. It wasn't a loverlike move, but Hogan settled for massaging her palm and fingers, drifting in his thoughts, and examining a peace that he'd never had—Jemma's relaxing quietly beside him, her hand soft and pliable within his.

Taking care not to disturb her, he turned on his side, bracing on one elbow. Lying on her stomach, her arms at her sides and her face turned toward him, Jemma was nothing like the pushy woman who shot through life, dedicating herself to profit. She fascinated him, even drowsing without all that usual fire. He eased aside her hair, found the still taut cords at her nape, and slowly drew his fingers down them. The sensual wave of her body, flowing from the arch of her head, down her shoulders to her hips and legs, startled him. He'd wanted her like this, the barriers down, and now he wanted to make slow, gentle love to her. His unsteady emotions nettled him, the tenderness he was feeling for a woman who had interfered and pushed and fought with him for years.

Jemma could match his dark moods with her own; she could lift his heart and pierce the shadows. He'd mocked a lover's eternal quest for a mate, and now he was faced with his own uncomfortable driving needs.

"You think too much," she murmured sleepily, one eye opening slowly. "I can hear your thoughts humming. What are you thinking about? A new design?"

"Something like that." The design of his life, he thought, smoothing her cheek with his fingertips.

"I can't move," she whispered again, as he massaged her tense shoulders and the slope of her back.

He smiled again and let his hand rest upon her hip for a moment, claiming her softness. In the morning, Jemma would be furious and aware that he'd used wine to relax her. But then, he'd known that she was trying to do the same to him.

"That's beautiful music," she whispered, and sighed deeply. "Are you going to do my back? You could sit on my thighs to get a better angle."

"Can't. Too many clothes." Hogan wanted to do more than kneel over her thighs. He wanted to reach down and lift her hips and touch her where she was dark and scented and made for him. He wanted to be a part of her when she came apart in a fiery storm—He toyed with her hair, the edges feathering across his skin, gleaming brilliantly on the dark rough surface. In his creative mind, he saw her in the wind, dressed in little but a shawl, the fringes gracefully around her pale body. As a man, he saw her wearing nothing at all. The eagerness was there, the hunger and a need he couldn't define.

"Do something, Hogan," she whispered sleepily. "I feel like I've melted. I'm feeling too relaxed—ohh," she crooned as his thumb found a tight spot by her shoulder blade, smoothing the knot gently.

"You should go home. I'll drive you." The admission that he couldn't trust himself with Jemma as she was now, caused Hogan to smile. Maybe a scrap of his honor remained when it came to a woman he respected—he did admire her; she'd struggled against life and stood by those she loved—even if they didn't like her meddling.

"You're not so bad when you look like that," she said, lifting slightly to study him.

Hogan bent to brush her lips with his, to taste the wine on her lips, the softness between them. Jemma's lips lifted slightly to his, an experiment, he thought, answering and questioning his. Her mouth parted slightly, following the contours of his, and Hogan closed his eyes, savoring the unique experience of Jemma delicately exploring him. She reached to smooth his face, to trace the ridges and the scar, and time stood still for that heartbeat as Hogan allowed himself to be studied. She traced his eyebrows and the soothing calm within him spread an ease he hadn't known. He allowed himself to drift beneath those feather-light touches, the scent of her hand a seduction. Had he captured her, or were the roles reversed now and he was under her spell?

A tiny shower of sparks burst from the firewood and Hogan pushed away the disturbing thought. He didn't want to be pushed and maneuvered, and anyone close to Jemma didn't lead an easy life. He studied the very sensual woman dozing at his side. Without her drive-for-success persona, Jemma was warm, feminine, pleasing, soft, and soothing. Hogan saw her as Everywoman, one hand upon a rounded belly, a slight curve to her lips. He saw her running in fields, long legs flashing as she chased a child. He saw her as a fierce, demanding lover—

Her voice was as soothing as her touch, this gentle quiet Jemma he was exploring. "You gave away bits of yourself when you were away all those years, didn't you?"

"Yes," he answered truthfully as a flash of distasteful memories burned him. He'd been the show animal, the Native American model that wealthy women wore on their arms like an expensive fur stole, or a piece of jewelry. The art world was cruel, harsh, but his training as a Kodiak had served him. He'd managed, and he'd survived.

"You want something more now, don't you?" she asked, surprising as the eternal knowing, soft woman, her fingers threading through his hair. Hogan closed his eyes and allowed himself to drift—he'd never allowed a woman to see into him as Jemma was doing now.

"Yes, more. I want more." He wanted what he'd never had—peace.

"You'll have what you want, Hogan. It's just out there, waiting for you." She was dozing now, smoothing his hair, already sliding away into sleep. This was the woman whom Carley loved, who loved back and whose basic nature when she let it be seen, was to comfort and understand.

"What if I said, what I wanted was here—you?" he asked, bending to kiss her, to taste her mouth, to gently suckle her tongue. The taste of her shot to his loins, filling his need painfully.

Her lids fluttered, but didn't open, her smile wry. "You're not playing fair. Wait until I'm awake and not massaged into a limp noodle."

"But I'd lose my advantage then, wouldn't I?" he murmured. "You'd pull back into that demanding, hot-tempered woman, and I'd be left wondering if this warm soft one was a mirage."

"You're sweet-talking me, Hogan," she returned warily. "And I've never been seduced."

"Neither have I." But he already had been . . .

\*　　\*　　\*

At six the next morning, Jemma awoke to the slap on her butt and Hogan's cheerful smile. "Let's go fishing."

She flopped over, drawing the blanket up over her head, and Hogan had chuckled. She groaned as he placed his hands on the bed to bounce it. "Biggest cutthroats you'd ever want in that mountain stream. I'm headed out now, and I'm staying a few days. You can come, but I'm not waiting, city girl."

"Get lost." Her plan to relax Hogan with wine had backfired. She'd wanted to release his secrets and instead she remembered wanting to soothe him, to hold him close all night long. But instead she'd fallen asleep.

"Okay. There just might be a big brown there, waiting for my lure . . . a real trophy catch."

Jemma opened her eyes and knew that Hogan would leave her and she'd never get another chance to learn what he could teach her. She sat up with a groan and realized she was still dressed in her clothes from the day before. She cursed Hogan, jammed on one boot, and hopped along as she put on the other. In a temper, she ripped the blanket off the bed—she was going to sleep after she caught her trophy fish. She grabbed a biscuit, looked at the others in the pan, scraped the butter from the dish onto the top of them, and holding the pan, blanket, and toilet paper, hurried after Hogan. Along the way, she grabbed her jacket from a wall hook and hung it from her head.

Outside in the cold air and predawn light, she staggered and grabbed the back of Hogan's denim jacket. "You know darned well that I want to learn how to fish and camp. But, oh, no, you can't wait until I'm up to it. You have to choose now—You're absolutely perverse. Hogan, I'll pay you a thousand, just to wait until I can take this. Oh, I hate it when you don't talk. I'm dying, Hogan. On my last feet, you coldhearted—"

"Oh, well, yes. We all know I'm a bastard, don't we?"

Jemma grabbed his jacket front with both fists and tried to shake him. "I'm not up to those quick, cold jabs, not now. I can't battle a Kodiak mood when my head feels like ten tons of concrete. *You* were supposed to relax last night, not me."

He glanced at her in the barn, tore off the blanket with a jerk and pushed her arms down into the leopard jacket she'd been carrying. He ripped the zipper up to her throat. "You can ride to Ben's. I'm going camping and fishing. I've already called Aaron. Carley and Dinah are wallpapering in the house for the next few days, and I'm taking time off."

She'd glared up at him from her tangled hair. "Just up and pack off without warning me? *No clean underclothes*? Hogan, I need clean underclothes. I need face cream and shampoo."

He'd shrugged in a typical Hogan gesture, watching her from beneath his Western hat, his expression impassive. He tightened the ropes on the packhorse. "I brought necessities and whatever else you need, you can share mine. Stay or go."

"I hate you, Hogan Kodiak. You know exactly how I feel." She had dragged the blanket around her and struggled for dignity as she tried to mount the saddled mare, and failed. Hogan had reached down to place his open hands on her bottom and lifted her as she struggled to sit in the saddle. With a last look, he rode ahead of her on the narrow trail, leading into the foothills.

To add to her humiliation, Aaron and Ben were seated on their horses watching her follow Hogan.

"Nice day," Ben said, studying her.

She knew she was evil-looking, a tangled, rumpled mess with a headache, and she hated them all and the deer in the meadow and the hawk in the sky. "No, it's not a nice day."

"Are you okay?" Aaron asked her.

"I'm mad," she said, burning a stare at Hogan's expressionless face. "We're going fishing. There had better be the biggest fish ever at the end of the trail, or I'm making his life unbearable. I'm making *your* life unbearable for even being related to him. I am going to learn how to dazzle fish with immature bugs from a hatch if it kills me. And him."

"I'll take care of her," Hogan said quietly, and in the still of the morning, it sounded like a vow. She'd been too angry to note how Ben studied Hogan and how Hogan met that dark, quiet look with his own.

"Well, I guess it's time, then, and you've found what you want," Ben said quietly, reining his horse back. With a nod, he rode off into the dawn sweeping across the pastures.

"I have," Hogan returned quietly.

"You'll pay plenty," Aaron noted with a grin.

Hogan chuckled at that and nudged Moon Shadow back onto the trail.

Her head aching, lashed by the rising dawn sliding between the pine trees, Jemma didn't know what Ben meant, and she didn't care.

"I'm not happy," she called to Hogan, who didn't turn back. "I'm not happy," she called back to Ben and Aaron, and stuffed another buttered biscuit into her mouth. "Coffee, anyone?" she asked the deer grazing in the field. "Orange juice? Granola? A banana?"

She could have killed Hogan when he looked back over his shoulder and grinned. "You wanted it, you got it, Red."

"What's this 'Red' stuff? I'm going to kill you, Hogan. You're a beast!"

# ten

Jemma sighed as she moved stiffly to a patch of thick grass and spread Hogan's bed blanket across it. She eased painfully down on it, whipped the edges of the cloth around her body, and, from her cocoon, glared at Hogan. In another instant, she was on her knees, foraging beneath the blanket and retrieving two rocks, which she hurled into the smooth-flowing stream. "If those hit my trophy fish, wake me up after it's cleaned. That's just what I'd like to do with you, Hogan Kodiak—drown you," she called darkly as Hogan began to unsaddle the horses.

"Don't hold anything back, Red. Go for it," he said mildly.

"Red?" she protested, outraged that Hogan, who had never teased, would grin wickedly at her.

She pushed down the temper that her body was too tired to deliver and settled for a menacing glare at Hogan, who was clearly enjoying her bad mood. "You can hand it out, but you can't take it. Are you ready to go back now?" he asked quietly, studying her intently as if trying to read beneath her temper.

"You could not tear me away from here, no matter how evil you are."

She tossed upon the hard ground, furious with herself for letting Hogan set the terms, for forcing her to run after him. She flipped over to glare up at him as he crouched by her side, smoothing her tangled hair. "You are truly a fascinating woman, Jemma Delaney. Especially when you're wide-open, stormy-hot, nothing held back."

She shook her head, closed her eyes, and firmly drew the blanket over her face, blocking out his sexy smile. Hours later she awoke to a burning-hot mountain sun, stiff muscles, and the sight of Hogan putting away his fishing gear. He turned toward her and held up a stringer of five fat trout. If she hadn't been so dazzled by the sight of him, she could have killed him for the boyish grin, for the pleasure on his face.

Without his shirt, sleek and perfect, pooled in sunlight and with a background of glittering water and pine and juniper trees, Hogan was beautiful. He dipped his hands into the clear water and splashed his face, then crouched to study the water as it drifted through his fingers. Clearly at peace in the rugged mountain clearing, the stream gurgling through it, Hogan seemed more like a man from the Old West than a sophisticated world traveler.

Feeling rumpled and dirty, Jemma flung back the blanket and groaned when she tried to leap to her feet. He watched with interest as she struggled slowly to stand, stretching her aching body. "Need help?" he asked.

"Not yours." She snorted and didn't care what he thought as she grabbed her backside with two hands, walking stiffly to his expensive canvas-and-leather bag. Crouching painfully, she dug into the contents, tossed aside what she didn't need, took out Hogan's clean T-shirt and jeans, and flopped them over her shoulder as she glared at him. Digging into another bag, she tore away a washcloth, towel, and soap. Jamming everything under her arm, she grabbed a flattened-out roll of toilet paper and groaned when she bent to pull a bucket through the stream water. She shot Hogan another dark, warning look, and hobbled slowly off into the Hogan-free privacy she badly needed.

"Feeling better?" he asked when she returned.

"Not a bit," she lied, and ripped a flannel shirt from his pack. She jammed her arms into the sleeves and gingerly rolled them up. "If you're expecting to send me packing, think again. We camped by streams when I was growing up. There wasn't running water in those migrant cabins. I can take care of myself. All I need from you is—oh! Food!" She took the turkey sandwich he'd just handed her and settled down on the grassy bank to devour it.

"I make you nervous, don't I?" Hogan asked, settling down beside her.

"Of course not," she lied, panic skittering up her back and radiating out to her trembling fingers as every cell of her body went on Hogan-alert. He smelled fresh, of juniper and pine, and grass, an intoxicating blend. "But you know what you did last night—you deliberately set out to make me drunk—rather to relax me. For my part, I only wanted to be friendly when I filled your glass That's an old act, Hogan, getting a girl drunk. You were playing with me, seeing just how I'd react. You probably don't even feel bad. Then you forced me to run after you, and how you must have enjoyed the whole nightmare, Hogan Kodiak. I have never in my life ever chased a man anywhere. You should be ashamed of yourself."

"Mmm, I truly am. I wondered what you'd be like, all relaxed, and now I know." He began to work his fingers through her tangled hair. The movements were seductive, calming, and just for a moment, Jemma gave herself to the luxury of Hogan's soothing hands. She wanted to push him away, but decided that she needed a bit of pampering. His hands were marvelous, soothing, and *he deserved to wait on her*. She ate the second sandwich and realized that now her hair was separated into two thick braids, and Hogan's marvelous touch was massaging the taut cords at her nape. She rotated her head, rolled her stiff shoulders, and forgave him just a bit as he sat behind her, his legs running along hers.

He began to massage her stiff back, finding the knots and working them out; the warmth of his thighs along hers helped her strained muscles. He pushed her head down gently; her forehead rested in his hand as his fingers eased the tenseness in her neck. As she began to relax, she decided that each time he touched her, she came more easily into his hands, trusting him to treat her gently.

"You look like a child," he said, close to her ear. "Like you used to. Sweet and wild."

He caused her skin to tingle, her lower stomach to contract, and turned her body into one taut knot. Supremely sexy when he tried, Hogan could be devastating. Clearly, he was interested in her as a woman, and that was terrifying. She could handle him, she thought; she'd always controlled relationships. "Well, those days are long ago. I really needed my face cream, Hogan. You could have at least let me have time to pack what I needed. Sun ages, so does wind."

"Here—" He turned her face, gently smoothing cream into her skin, his fingers slow and relaxing.

She closed her eyes, and realized that she was once

again melting beneath Hogan's ministrations. "More around the eyes."

"Perfect, expressive eyes. Like flashing steel one minute, thunder and lightning the next, and glittering with laughter the next. Mmm." He looked at her critically. "There is just a little line, right there. But it's perfect. You'll age well."

"Only you would dare tell me I am aging. Put some more cream on there and don't tell me about one more line on my face. I miss my makeup," she mumbled, too shy of this new Hogan. His close inspection caused her to turn away. She didn't like anyone seeing too deep, and Hogan knew more than anyone about the shadows that haunted her. His lips drifted along her nape, just a brush of heat that caused her nerves to tense and shiver. In the next moment, his big hands moved slowly down her back, finding the taut muscles and working them.

"None of this is fair," she muttered, surprised by the ease with which her body moved to the flow of his hands. "I'm in pretty good shape, and now even my toes hurt."

"You truly are in good shape and very soft," he returned in a drawl that lifted the hair on her neck. He circled her with his arms, drawing her back against him. He placed his cheek along hers, and murmured, "Deer on the other side of the stream? See?"

His head tilted, urging hers to turn toward the sight, again his body directing hers. "Oh, they are beautiful, Hogan."

"Look below that fallen branch, into the shadows of the stream. Those are big juicy trout, and we're going to catch them."

She tensed and started to rise, eager to learn. "Let's hurry, Hogan, before they get away."

She turned then, to look back at him, and found his face too close and too inviting. His lips brushed hers,

and what she saw in his eyes terrified and enchanted her.
A fish leaped and plopped back into the water. Or was
that her heart leaping, settling into a heavy, excited thud
that rippled throughout her body? "What do you want?"

"You." He tugged her hand, unbalancing her, and she
fell upon him. His hand slid higher, easing beneath the
T-shirt, to close over her bare breast. When she met his
kiss, turned slightly to trap him close and warm against
her, to step into the magic, Hogan leaned back and eased
her over his body. He cupped the back of her head,
drawing her mouth down to taste and to tempt. The heat
growing between them seemed so natural, as if it had
always meant to be, and there was Hogan, his lips soft
upon hers, his tongue suckling hers, and hers tasting
him. The hard rise of his desire against her bare stomach
told her what he wanted, his hands soothing her, lifting
her shirt away.

She'd never been touched like that, nor allowed the
caress, despite marital sex that she'd wanted to end
quickly. She felt her body move against his, flowing into
his hard planes as if she were meant to be with him—
Hogan easily turned her beneath him, a natural movement, his weight settling above her. She managed to lift
her lids, to see his expression—dark, intense, heated—
as he looked down at her. When she moved to cover
herself, his hand drew hers away; his dark eyes were
soft upon her, the tip of his finger touching her lightly
and her breast hardened, aching. "You're beautiful—
perfect. Cream and dark rose . . ."

"Hogan?" she wanted to run, she wanted to—"Oh!"

When his lips closed upon her breast, gently tugging
at her, Jemma almost cried out, her body tensing, a tiny
explosion hitting her lower abdomen. They were on the
sunlit blanket now, Hogan's skin smooth beneath her
touch, his mouth moving upon her, taking her other

breast, caressing her. The gentle bite shocked her, threw her hips hard against his. She shivered, fighting the unexpected desire jolting her, and yet wanting more. Trusting him, giving herself to the floating magic, she held him close, his hair dragging across her skin, tormenting her as he moved lower, a flick of his tongue sensitizing her navel, sending more shock waves through her. She stiffened, protesting and then giving way, as his hands moved within the jeans too large for her, easing them away. His hands moved over her thighs, massaging them, caressing the backs as his mouth pressed low on her stomach. She pushed him away slightly, shivering, fearful of emotions that were flying away from her control. She hadn't trusted, hurrying through marital sex, because it was expected, but Hogan was asking more, his hand cupping her, his fingers incredibly warm and coaxing—

Still trusting him to touch her, she dug her fingers into his shoulders as he held her there, high on that blinding pinnacle, shocking her, and then, flying into the heat and flashes of color, she cried out and melted slowly, slowly back onto the blanket beside Hogan. She thought she heard his chuckle; she didn't care, flopping her hand aside and lying in the aftermath of her riveting pleasure.

He turned her face to his, shaking it gently. "Jemma, open your eyes and look at me."

"I can't. Don't make me do any more today. I can't find my bones—I'm one big warm puddle." Then she turned on her side, wrapped her arm around his body and her leg between his, anchoring him until she could catch her breath and do—do something to him. "Rat," she accused drowsily, drifting pleasantly.

At sunset, she helped drag fir branches to cover the bent young trees that served as a framework for Hogan's sweat house. "You're exhausting me. We've already cast for hours—my arm is falling off, and I didn't catch a thing, and then you had me clean those fish—oh, I'm never, never going to get the feeling of those scales off my hands, and guts—why do fish have to have guts? And so many of them everywhere? Hogan—wet flies, dry flies, hatches, spinners, leaders—it's all too much. Now I have to understand bugs and their life cycles— the almighty hatch and nymphs. There is no way that a fish can be that selective about what he eats. And I do not like looking into a fish's eyes and know that he's my next meal. They are slimy, Hogan.''

Hogan bent to take a quick kiss, one of several that had taken her breath away since he'd touched her so sweetly. When she stopped talking, stunned by the quick, knowing kiss, he grinned and placed his hand on her head, waggling it and then tugged one of her braids. "Fun, huh?"

When she tried to hit him with a branch, he side-stepped, raising his hands. "I give up."

She blinked at the boyish, playful man in front of her. "You've been rotten all day. What's wrong?"

He had frowned, tilting his head to one side and listening intently. "Bear. A big one."

Jemma almost leaped into his arms, and Hogan drew her tight and safe against him. Then his mouth was on hers, not sweet and tender, but demanding, slanting to take her breath away. This wasn't the gentle lover of the afternoon, or the stoic, stormy man she'd always known. This was a man who wanted everything from her, who would demand everything. She fisted his hair, damning him and herself, trying to hold on to reality, when magic was taking her flying. "Are you afraid?" he asked roughly, picking her up in his arms and carrying her toward their bedrolls.

The sunlight glittered between them. Or was it magic?

"I should be afraid. I'm not." This was Hogan, who'd always been safe, whom she had always trusted, and now he was the man she wanted to share her body, to give and to take pleasure. "Are you going to give me one of those marvelous massages?"

He eased her onto the bedroll and stood straight, stretching his arms high. Her body rose slightly, aching for his, and she waited for him to come to her arms. To gather all that powerful body into her keeping—

"Nope," he said. "I'm going to tie flies and try to better match the hatch in this area."

She stared at him, her body humming with the need to be stroked and touched by Hogan's hands. She wanted to feel that wonderful mouth upon her skin—"I suppose that would be the thing to do, since we're up here to teach me about fly fishing and camping, right? Tie flies to match the hatch?"

His grin flashed in the dark. "You don't have the patience for this, Jemma. You want to hurry to the finish line without enjoying the prework."

She struggled to her feet. She'd wanted his hands on her, she'd wanted to kiss him and feed upon him—"Prework?" She regretted the frustration in her voice, but then she'd never been hungry for a man before Hogan.

He lifted his eyebrows. "A good fly fisherman knows how to tie lures. You want to know all that, don't you?"

She knew he'd deliberately jumped subjects, waylaying her, taunting her. Twenty minutes later, Jemma wrapped the blanket around her and sat staring off into the night. "I don't want to talk or think anymore about flytying now. Everything is too tiny and too precise. I just wanted to learn how to fish, not how to build bugs."

"Good, you're thinking now," he said, putting away his supplies and closing his tackle box. "Maybe you'd better rethink this fly fisher woman television-thing."

"I can't. The money is too good. But I may have to put a different spin on it. I've always been able to find a way to get the things I want, Hogan. I was thinking about that reflexology—the massage you did for me. If I got good at that, Les might not notice I was missing the finer points of fly fishing."

"Uh-huh. Find a way around this," Hogan said with a dark edge to his tone, drawing her roughly up and into his arms.

Hogan had never used his strength to hold a woman before, never taken a woman's mouth with raw hunger and need. But then he'd never felt the lash of jealousy before, raised by the thought of Jemma touching another man—Jemma's hands dug into his back, her arms holding him tight, her mouth as hungry as his—

He hadn't needed in his lifetime, really needed, and now, shaken by his desire, Hogan grasped for his control and found Jemma, moving into him, hot and warm and passionate, burning away everything but the need. She wrapped her arms around his shoulder and lifted her mouth to his. "Hogan?"

Hogan eased her away, shaking his head. "I didn't want—Not like this."

She stared at him for a heartbeat, then hit his chest with both fists. "There are just times, Hogan, when contemplation and meticulous patience are not wanted."

Hogan ran his hand across his taut jaw. "You're angry."

"Wrong. I'm good and mad. I'm tired, I ache, and I can't figure out what's in this for me, except a few good massages. Did I ask for 'prework'? Did I? I know the mechanics, Hogan. I know there is something between us. We're adults. I thought we'd get it over with and continue with our lives. I trust you. I know you are a meticulous man in your relationships and not a bed-hopper. It's just something that is on the desktop now, and we're going to have to deal with it and get it out of the way. There is Simone, you know.''

Hogan tensed as though slapped; she'd reminded him of another relationship without the passion and tenderness he'd felt with Jemma. And now Jemma's clinical assessment of adult needs burned him, because that was exactly the basis of his relationship with Simone. ''Just like that? 'Deal with it.' Is that how you think of lovemaking, Jemma-sweetheart? Rush-rush, hurry-hurry, have-to-get-it-over?''

Jemma took a deep steadying breath and looked at the fiercely angry man tearing away his clothes and glaring at her. ''Now, Hogan—''

''You've always been difficult, Jemma. Let's try for a little class, shall we?'' Hogan reached to remove the single small hematite stud in his ear. The gesture was masculine, abrupt, a dismissal of a personal irritant he didn't want, as he flung it into the campfire. The removal of that earring seemed shockingly intimate to Jemma, as though he'd tossed away civilization and the rules between them.

She'd seen Hogan retreat into his shadows when pushed too far—she'd never seen him truly angry, his emotions exposed. The rigid set of his naked, beautiful body spoke of his anger as he turned and walked into the stream. Using soap, Hogan cleansed himself quickly, returning to the grassy bank, to quickly wrap a towel around his hips. He stoked the fire, studying the flames as he crouched beside it, ignoring her.

Then, suddenly finding her in the night, studying her, Hogan said, ''It's your choice. I won't hurt you. I'll treasure what we do, I'll keep you safe, and I'll tend your needs. I want you, Jemma. I want to be in you, by you, over you, under you. I want to feel your body take mine, your heart beat against mine—I want those gates wide-open like they were a moment ago. I won't settle for anything less . . . and I'll be true to you. I ask that you do the same."

The declaration was too tender, too sweet, and tipped her over a frightening edge, asking for a commitment of body and soul that she'd never given anyone. She'd always been in control of relationships—Relationships? She'd been married, a bargain that suited her. Heat burned through her, the need for Hogan wrapped tightly against her, but he was too dangerous, warning bells clanged amid the chatter of chipmunks and birds calling. "I don't know how to do this. Not with meaning. You terrify me, Hogan. You'll always want more. You're too intense."

The fire crackled, sparks arcing off into the night. "You want a business arrangement. I'm not made like that—now, with you. I enjoy textures—your skin against mine . . . scents—your scent is very erotic, Jemma, I'd know it anywhere . . . taste—I want that and the rhythm of your heart beating against mine, that trapped little frantic heart, the dark glitter of your eyes when your body is heating for mine, waiting. I want that wide-open fierce passion, unleashed and just for me."

"You want everything." She feared giving too much of herself; she'd already left pieces of her when her family died.

"I want honesty. In this, you're honest with me. Your body tells me what runs between us."

He'd shaken her deeply, and she struggled to make sense of the melting of her heart, the need to hold him close—"You're cold."

"No, I'm not," he said, standing and taking away the towel. She fought to keep her eyes above his waist and failed as he walked toward her. Her body tightened as unwillingly, she found his arousal, awed by the bold, jutting shape. She shivered, a memory of pain slashing at her—cold marital sex. Hogan would be too thorough and demand too much. He'd forge too deeply, taking a part of her that no one else had reached.

He touched her lips with his fingertips, her cheeks, her lashes, then lifted her hair back from her face, studying her. "Jemma?"

"Yes," she whispered, knowing that she had to have Hogan, to taste him, to feel his body ripple within her keeping. She could do this—enter a relationship, learn how to control her senses—but not just now, not when she ached to hold him tight, and feel his breath sweep across her skin, to have him in her arms . . . To give herself to him, here, without restrictions in the pure, fragrant air seemed as natural as breathing. It seemed as if all the years knowing him as a boy and a man had led to this.

He undressed her carefully, studying her body so intently—the slope of her breast, the indentation of her waist, the reddish nest of curls between her thighs—that she shivered. Unused to being treasured, admired, she folded her arms in front of her and Hogan drew them away. He touched her nipple with a fingertip, his expression darkening as he watched it contract. He skimmed her throat with his thumbs, framed her shoulders with his hands as if measuring her for his body's fit. Then his hands flowed down her, learning her, smoothing the indentation of her waist. His thumbs tracing her hipbones, fingers digging into her hips, his palms hot and hard against her. He lifted her hands, brought them to his lips and suddenly lifted her in his arms, walking out into the stream to bathe her in the chilly water. He quickly soaped her body while she shivered and pushed at him. "Oh! Hogan! Stop!"

"Okay." Then he placed his large hands over her breasts, caressing them. There was that quiet moment, his hands burning her skin, callused palms gentle upon her nipples, his eyes locked with hers, when Jemma forgot they stood in an icy stream.

"I think I'm turning blue," she whispered, and wished she could leap upon him and—

He laughed outright, the first rumble startling her— the first real laughter she'd heard from him. Grinning as she swatted at him, he carried her to the bank and briskly dried her. "Oh! Oh! I'm freezing." Jemma ran for the sleeping bags and scooted into one, drawing it up to her throat and glaring at him. "Hogan, I'm going to make you pay for that."

"I know. I'm looking forward to it." He dried, hurled the towel aside, and walked toward her, a man standing outlined in the moonlight, waiting—"Are you going to let me in there, or not?"

"I should let you freeze." But Jemma knew her needs, and tonight Hogan was definitely on the menu. She flipped back the edge of the sleeping bag and shivered, fearing that he'd take too much, that she'd give too much.

He eased into the sleeping bag and gathered her close against him. The naked impact of his burning skin against hers tore through her, locking heat deep within her. "I won't hurt you," he promised again, and lowered his head for a long, sweet kiss that left her floating.

"Hurry," she whispered, desperate for him now, her body humming, tight with hunger.

Against her mouth, he whispered softly, "I'll treasure this, here with you."

He'd startled her, the words spoken as a romantic vow. The frantic blush rose up her cheeks, and she looked away, shy of him as a gentle lover. In her mind, despite the heat and need of her body, she knew that making love with Hogan would change her life—

In that instant, she knew that Hogan had chosen her for his own, that he'd brought her here to claim her, not to serve a sexual need alone. He'd wanted to forge and deepen the ultimate tie with her—and this moment would bind them in a way she could not ignore—Hogan wanted her quickly this first time, a primitive male need for reassurance from a woman. . . .

"Look at me." She shivered as Hogan eased over her, his hard arousal branding her stomach. He held her hands, roughly nuzzled her breasts, and when she cried out, arching against him, fighting for him, against him, Hogan held her wrists. He lowered his lips to hers, suckling gently, giving her his scent, taking—His hand ran down her thighs, fingers firm upon her, smoothing, easing, and stroking. Against her skin, his was fever-hot. "Don't hold back with me, honey, let yourself fly," he whispered rawly, that smooth control stretching now.

His taut shiver told her that Hogan wasn't certain of his need, of her or himself.

Hesitating, needing to reassure him that she wanted this tumbling river of heat between them, she reached to touch him, to curl her fingers around him, to explore and Hogan groaned slowly, unsteadily, his hips lurching against hers. Yet he held her firmly, carefully, his hands light and erotic upon her skin, touching, brushing, sensitizing. Then she eased him closer, damp and warm and hard against her. The blunt pressure pressing intimately against her, and the gentle, seeking nudge reminded her that Hogan would wait, controlling himself until she was ready.

"Slowly," he whispered unevenly against her breast, his skin burning hers. "You're so tight."

She tried to tell herself this was a simple act—she'd been married after all. But this was Hogan—huge, trembling, his heart racing against hers, his hard body braced above hers. He eased deeper, just there at the beginning, where she was tight and aching, her body clenching, resisting his. "Sweetheart," he murmured, suckling her breast, caressing her as he eased into her full length, drawing up her legs beside his hips until she cradled him.

His kisses were sweet, tender as he lay still upon her, bracing his weight away. "Look, sweetheart. Look how we are together." Hogan's usually low even tone was raw now with emotion.

She'd never played or examined her body during sex; she hadn't really cared, but with Hogan, she wanted to know. The sight terrified and elated her, her body adapting to his more easily as the swift tug of desire caught her, winded her, knocked her resistance aside, and the taut muscles inside her began contracting with pleasure, the starlit night spinning out of her control. "I can't stop, Hogan—I—"

He caught her mouth, the kiss taking her higher, his hand lifting her hips and they moved quickly, perfectly, flying higher into the stormy heat. His body was hers, thighs hard and surging against hers, demanding, pushing, retreating—She flung herself around him, locking him tight to her, keeping him safe as they flew . . . She heard thunder roll and knew it was her heart—she knew it was Hogan's, too, that his strong body fought for release, fighting it, and then pouring into her.

One clear thought sliced through Jemma at that moment—Hogan had come to her with a shocking, primitive need to bond with her. She knew that as surely as she knew her body received his to the hilt, clenched upon him, her arms and legs binding him close. Whatever else they sought from each other would come from this moment—Hogan's claim was eternal, primitive, and binding at a base level they both understood. He was as much hers as she was his, each torn apart at that moment, and when restored, would carry a part of the other—

She knew, deep within her, that Hogan trusted her with his essence and his storms—he needed her in a way he'd shared with no other woman, there on that primitive burning plane.

She reveled in that shocking pulse deep within her, the man upon her, his muscles sliding tautly, rippling beneath his smooth, damp skin, his face harsh above hers, eyes fierce, his jaw clenched as his body quivered and trembled, his hips moving in the aftermath of passion just past. His belly quivered against her, his body easing, his head coming down to rest upon her breast.

Hogan forced the air scented of Jemma and their love-making into his body, his heart still pounding in the aftermath of their shattering, mind-blowing climax. He'd desired her, wanted that sleek curved body flowing with his, but he hadn't expected the tenderness of the taking, the stormy heights that stripped away his control—He shifted, still deep within Jemma, aware that he wanted to linger in a woman's body for the first time. She'd been so tight, quivering around him. She took him slowly, deeply, moistly, and he could feel her clenching life pulse, feel his life and his long-buried needs to make a child. He hadn't expected the deeper needs, to be soothed and held later, to wait until his desire sprung to life again, that taut fit of steel and moist silk. He smoothed Jemma's breast, noted the quiver of soft flesh filling his hand, the still-taut nub etching his palm. He moved his palm, circling the nub, enjoying the play.

In the moonlight, her nipple fascinated him, the aureole an exciting texture—he circled the tiny bumps, noting the difference of color between dark rose nipple and creamy breast, the eternal woman—a lover and a mother, a creator of life and comfort and shelter and passion—Jemma placed her hand over his, her voice drowsy, laced with pleasure, and perfect in its intimacy. "Stop. I know that look. You're creating again."

Hogan smiled—Jemma was shy of him now, and he hadn't expected his instinctive urge to show himself for her inspection; he wanted her to know how he was made for her body, how they would be locked as one. None of that had mattered before, only the need quickly filled. He hadn't meant to go so deep, to hold her so tightly. He hadn't expected the passion heating him, the fever heightened by her soft cries, her nails digging into his skin, and that tiny bite on his shoulders as she pitted herself against her own desire and his. Relaxed now, his body needing a brief rest, Hogan placed his lips over the heavy pulse in her slender throat, eased his hips down to savor her enfolding him, and luxuriously rubbed his chest against her soft breasts, noting the path of her nipples across his. He sighed, settling into Jemma as he would a work he intended to enjoy.

At the Bar K, Carley wrapped her arms around herself. Jemma had gone with Hogan—just like that. Heat ran between them, electric charges easily sensed by the rest of the family. Hogan had never sought out a woman, captured her, and that alone told Carley that Jemma meant more than an outlet for his needs. Carley shivered and studied Mitch beside her. She wiped away a tear. "They'll probably get married and have ten kids. Hogan's got that slow relaxed, nothing-can-stop-him style, and Jemma will be hurrying, and I'll be baby-sitting the

whole lot of baby Kodiaks while he packs her off
again.''

Mitch wrapped his arms around Carley and for once,
feeling alone without Jemma, Carley rested back against
him. ''I don't even want to think about the wedding.
Jemma will drive us nuts.''

''Shh!'' Mitch began to rock her gently, his arms
around her.

''But Mitch, *I'm going to lose my best friend.*''

''You won't lose Jemma, ever. But let me help,''
Mitch whispered gently and bent to kiss her cheek. Carley held very still, then eased away from him. She
couldn't bear being too close to Mitch, to feel the awe-
some heat of his body, sense the strength and desire
humming in it. And none of it made sense—that he
should want her. Mitch's taste in women had run to experienced full-bodied Amazons.

''You want me,'' she stated coldly. ''As a woman?
Why? Don't you realize I'm defective? Everyone else
does.''

For an answer, Mitch took her hand and placed it on
his chest. ''You've always been there.''

Mitch shook his head as Carley ran inside. He knew
that he'd never love another woman, but this one was
difficult to hold.

Jemma must have fallen asleep, wrapped in that soft,
pleasant cloud, drifting between sleep and pleasure,
stroking Hogan's hair, soothed by his lips against her
skin. She looked up at the stars and knew she'd never
be the same, now that she'd given him a part of her soul
and that he had given her something he'd shared with
no one. Then Hogan caressed her breasts and surged
hard and bold within her and she knew that he wanted
more—the second time more hungry than the first,

deeper, more fierce, more demanding—the incredible heat shocking her, devastating her until she cried out, a high, keening sound that carried into the night.

She flung herself upon him when they were through, caught him close, and bit his shoulder to remind him that he was hers. In return, his rugged face nudged her throat, his bite gentle and soothed by the flick of his tongue. He sighed, and to her, the deep, ragged sound said he'd found peace.

She slept heavily, aware of Hogan's solid warmth along her back, spooning her body. He delved gently into her warmth, moistening her, the soft words against her cheek. He shifted her hips gently, positioning her, the gentle prod between her thighs, her body opening for him now, his hand caressing her breast. She moved back against him, sleepily, still hungry, wanting the gentle waves that came more quickly and tossed her gently back into sleep.

She awoke later to dawn and Hogan beginning to enter her, his large hands on her hips lifting her, his mouth hungry, devastating hers. That storm quickly passed, her body quaking too soon and too high as he filled her and again. She dug her fingers into his arms, pushing back at him, bringing him closer, deeper until—just there, she hovered between fierce pleasure and the longing to keep him near, her body clenching his rhythmically, pulling at him. His hand reached low between them, touched her perfectly, and she shot off into heat, crying out again, biting his shoulder. Finished, her body quaking, she pushed him back to find him smiling tenderly down at her, his fingertip strolling over her nose.

"Good morning, Jemma. Sleep well?" he asked in a sexy rumble that would have started her needing again, if she hadn't been so drained.

She managed to wake sometime in midmorning,

aware that Hogan was already fishing. She stretched her body, noted the new ease and unfamiliar aches within it, every muscle perfectly relaxed. Tuned to his surroundings, Hogan turned to her immediately. His smile wiped away her thoughts of how to greet him on the morning after his lovemaking. She simply smiled back and enjoyed the tug of her heart, just looking at him in the morning sun, dressed only in his jeans. "Hungry?" he asked in a tone that sent her senses quivering and heating.

"Starved." She struggled to tug on his shirt before rising from the bedroll and tried to look casual as she made her way to the campfire and coffee. Hogan continued to fish, and she hurried to make a curtain with his blanket, draping it across two limbs. She was just finishing, cleansing her breasts, and noting the heaviness, the small red marks when Hogan looked over the blanket, studying her body closely.

"You're blushing. It suits you." He lifted her wrist, took it to his lips, his eyes solemn over their hands. "I hurt you. I'm sorry."

Unnerved with the intimacy and his tenderness, Jemma grabbed the blanket, wrapping it around herself. "Look. Everything is just fine. I'm fine, really."

He scanned her face, found her shy desire and ran his thumb lightly across her bottom lip. "You look beautiful this morning, sweetheart. All rosy and wild and soft. Like a wild rose in full bloom."

The way Hogan whispered "sweetheart" caused her knees to weaken, her heart to race. The word wasn't smooth, but untested, as if he'd saved it for her.

When he began to kiss her in that slow, soft sweet way, she found her arms locked around his shoulders as he carried her back to the bedroll. Hours later, Jemma awoke, flinging out her hand to find him gone and the

early-afternoon sun burning her face. She struggled to
sit up, brushing her hair from her face and found Hogan
calmly fishing again, the line a graceful arch in the sun.
Groaning as she stood slowly, Jemma ate the lunch he
had prepared, then sat, placing her feet in the cold water.
She cleansed herself again, using soap while Hogan continued fishing. "So much for romance," she muttered,
just as he turned.

Hogan walked swiftly toward her, his black eyes
burning upon her face, tearing down her body—he was
already aroused, his desire thrusting at his jeans, which
he quickly stripped away. "Hogan?"

He terrified her like this—that raw need pouring out
of him, curling around her, setting her body to trembling
and heating—She sucked excitement into her, quivered
with it, eager for the next time his body became hers—
One swift movement of his hand tore away the shirt and
then he lifted her, his hands beneath her hips, entering
her quickly, just as she wanted, the knife edge of desire
hurting her—His desire for her stunned and shocked and
pleasured as she wrapped her arms around him, her fingers locking in his hair to hold his mouth against hers,
demanding, taking, filling her—

The rocketing pleasure took her higher, caught her
there, unprepared and shook her. Hogan, his expression
harsh and forbidding, his great body quaking in her
arms, shook his head. "I shouldn't have done that—"

"Don't say that. It was right." She'd have died if he
hadn't taken her with that riveting, burning passion,
making her feel powerful and all woman. "I wanted
you—I just didn't know we could actually do it—" She
glanced down at his body—"Hogan? Do you ever get
tired?"

He laughed again, a carefree happy sound that curled
around her heart. This time he lifted her high to kiss her

breasts, to nuzzle them gently. There was a tenderness
about him, a reverence for her that surprised and warmed
her and she smoothed his hair, enjoying this new Hogan—her Hogan.

There was nothing sweet about "her Hogan" when
he stood behind her, his hand on her shoulder, claiming
her, and all the Kodiaks stood on the porch studying
them.

Tired, aching, and wildly happy, she leaned back
against him. After three days away, she was certain that
evidence of Hogan's very thorough lovemaking warmed
every part of her body. Her cheeks were still hot from
the moments on the trail down to the Kodiak ranch,
when Hogan had gently pushed her face down on a
warm, sun kissed rock and had lain over her back, lifting
her hips and entering her femininity slowly, loving her
so quickly and thoroughly that she'd barely been able to
stand.

Now—the Kodiak family, the one she loved deeply—
Aaron, Dinah, Carley, Mitch, and Ben were standing on
the porch, and they *knew*.

Certain that she wore one big blush from head to foot,
she leaned back against Hogan. She knew how she
looked—wearing Hogan's big shirt and jeans rolled up
at the cuffs, her hair in wild curls from his wandering
hands, and her body weak from pleasure—Jemma
looked down to the shirt's mismatched buttons and
groaned.

Hogan's arm instantly came around her, drawing her
protectively to his side. "Are you ashamed?" he asked
in a low voice only she could hear.

"No," she whispered back. "But I'm a mess, and you
know it." He let out his breath as if he'd been holding
it, relieved by her answer. Jemma glanced up at him. "I

was right there with you, Hogan. It wasn't a seduction or your fault."

He shook his head, a magnificent man smiling lazily down at her. "Damn, Jemma. I tried."

Ben was the first to break the silence. "Well, it's going to be a long day. Can't stand around here all day. I've got work to do," he said briskly, as though nothing had changed, as though she was still his friend and a part of his family.

Hogan looked down at Jemma, who had turned to look up at him. He'd taken her fiercely, demanded and given, and she'd shattered him—he hadn't expected the emotions between them, the way he adored her body curling against his as she slept. The fierce drive and pleasure of making love to her—and the tenderness later.

He traced her face, softer, warmer now, a woman who had spent three days making love—

Hogan wanted them to see his mark upon her—a primitive need, to mark this woman as his own. It had shocked him at first. He could have told her about the misbuttoned shirt, her rumpled, well-loved appearance, that fascinating, shy blush. But he'd been too busy enjoying the sight.

She was his missing part, finally in place; all else would fall into place after their lovemaking. The thought hurled down from the Montana sun and staked him.

"Come in, Hogan," Jemma said quietly, taking his hand. "I want you to."


Ben watched his son's expression, that wary dark look of a man uncertain about a woman's powers. Ben gripped his bad leg—neither youngster knew the wildfire they held in their hands, how easily it could be destroyed. He took in Aaron's and Mitch's stances, the

hard, knowing looks at Hogan and knew that there
would be an argument, because of Jemma's new rumpled and steamed look. The brothers would have their
say, and so would Carley, and for the first time Hogan
would have to defend himself against them. "Hell to
pay, boy," Ben murmured, but this time he'd stay out
of it. He glanced at Dinah and caught the tear glittering
on her lashes with his fingertip. "They'll be fine,
honey."

"I know, but she was just a little girl only yesterday—
and he was so perfect, that little piece of you." Dinah
rested her head upon Ben's shoulder.

Uneasy with what was expected of him, bringing
home the woman he'd obviously claimed, Hogan met
the stern expressions of his brothers and Carley. They'd
come after him, and he didn't want Jemma to see the
war, because he wasn't backing down, not after he'd
given his heart. Hogan shook his head, gave Jemma a
nice stringer of good-sized trout, kissed her lightly, and
swung up onto his horse. His family would be coming
soon enough, and it wouldn't be pretty.

Jemma held the stringer of fish, stunned that Hogan
could ride away so easily from her; her body still ached
pleasantly from his larger one, and he gave no indication
of what they'd shared. Then she hurled the fish onto the
ground and stood, glaring at him, her hands on her hips.
He rode to his house all straight-backed and Western
and carefree, as if he hadn't placed himself in her keeping more than once.

Ben shook his head. He had his own problems with
Dinah's blue, blue eyes and the unexpected sensual lurch
of his damaged body when he looked at her.

On a road nearby, a driver put away his binoculars,
fearing that the sun would reflect upon the glass surface.
The Kodiaks were hunters, and one flash could pinpoint

the observer. His car wasn't unusual, and passed by this road routinely; he was safe, wrapped anonymously in his everyday passings. Jemma Delaney had serviced Hogan Kodiak; she wore *that* look—her face rosy and excited, her hair tumbling down from where it was knotted on top of her head. Hogan's expression had been grim and wary, until Jemma touched his shoulder and laughed at him—then Hogan had smiled slowly. Hogan Kodiak, lone wolf, had changed. An impure, lowly woman, Jemma didn't matter. Only Carley mattered, the observer's Celestial Virgin. He stroked himself, thinking of how he would tear away her maidenhood and how she would worship him.

# eleven

"You should have left Jemma alone, Hogan. Dammit, she's Carley's best friend, and she doesn't play around," Aaron said, slamming Hogan's front door behind him. Hogan had been daydreaming about how to romance a woman—specifically Jemma— what to say to her, how to give her those softer words telling of his heart.

He'd known without doubt that he was placing his claim, taking Jemma as his woman, his mate. Making love to her burned away all doubt that he had a heart, that warmth could glow within him, that he could be happy. That lock had clicked, and now it was a matter of laying all the components in line, because Jemma was not an easy woman.

Mitch jerked open the door, stepped inside, and crossed his arms. Carley entered the room and glared at Hogan as Mitch said, "I second that. Jemma didn't stand a chance. You hauled her off and she came down from that mountain looking like she'd been steamed and rolled in the bushes. Both of you standing there, glowing like idiots. But you wanted that, didn't you—to get at Ben. He thinks of her as a daughter."

"Ben doesn't come into this." He'd been thinking about Jemma, the way her hair slid through his fingers and webbed across his skin, glistening in the sunlight. The drowsy soft gray of her eyes, her breath on his skin. Hogan blinked, surprised that he was daydreaming about Jemma, talking with her, enjoying the high lift of her chin—

He'd sensed that he was giving not just his body, but his essence to her care. That thought jarred as he met his brothers' glares.

Carley pushed Mitch aside and added her glare. "Jemma is my friend, not some cheap pickup—someone to fill your bed when you feel the need."

"I didn't say she was. Family—welcome to my abode, by the way. Try not to wreck anything costly." He'd had experience with his brothers and sister running him down with fire in their eyes, but back then, it was about Ben.

Aaron had a sizable temper, so did Mitch, but they were nothing compared to Carley, who had a penchant for throwing anything at hand.

For the moment, he was saved by the ringing phone.

Simone's soft French accent purred over the lines. "I've missed you, *cher*. When are you coming to see me?"

Hogan smiled, watching his siblings' out-for-blood expressions as he spoke to Simone. "I'm enjoying myself. I've needed this for a long time."

After a quick necessary discussion about the showing of his new collection in Paris, Hogan ignored Simone's sexual invitation. Jemma had pushed all other women from his mind, his body. That thought nettled as he replaced the phone. "Nice day, isn't it?" he asked his scowling siblings.

Aaron picked up a pencil sketch of Fire Feathers and

studied it. He lifted an eyebrow at Hogan. "You wouldn't be feeding on Jemma? Using her for ideas, would you? This design reminds me of her, instantaneous—burning and yet soft—not your usual sophisticated jet-setter design."

Hogan didn't lie. "She is the inspiration for that design, and others."

"You vampire. I've seen you gather ideas before, harvesting them, taking sights into you and turning them into profit. You're selling her in pieces," Aaron exploded.

"Lay off," Hogan said slowly. He didn't like the image, but it was true. The design was his best, drawn from deep inside him, without thought to marketing what sold, or women's tastes. Fire Feathers seemed to ripple in a sunlit breeze, but they were also boldly tempestuous like a hot summer storm. The emotion in the design had startled him. In contrast, his other work looked good and saleable, but the intensity didn't compare.

He tried to push his unsettled emotions down and return to the routine of his life. The sound of grinding coffee beans tore through the airy, sunlit room, and he ran water into the pot, ignoring his family. He glanced at them and knew he would pay a price before their outrage settled down. Hogan poured the ground beans into the coffeemaker and smiled briefly. Jemma had been worth the payment he was about to feel from his family.

"You're a little old to be collecting notches on your bedpost," Mitch said, and that thought slapped at Hogan. He didn't want Jemma to be in anyone's bed but his. And that thought grated. He intended to keep the pledge that he'd made on the mountain, a vow to a woman he respected.

"Men!" Carley slapped the counter.

"Maybe you need to be reminded of how to treat a lady, Hogan," Aaron offered darkly.

"You? And who else?" Hogan didn't know how to treat Jemma, not when he'd wanted to keep her up on the mountain longer, making love to her. Those three days were the sweetest in his life, and he wasn't certain how they would impact his life. He hadn't expected the passion surging from him with enough power to bruise her wrists; he'd never hurt a woman while making love, never wanted to linger and to play. He gauged Aaron and knew that his brother's ripe temper matched his own. While he didn't like his dark storms and nettling guilt about Jemma, a good brawl might ease the pressure.

One truth ran through him—he'd given her his heart and his vows up there on the mountain.

Aaron met Hogan's narrowed look and stood slowly, matching him for size. "Maybe it is time you got taken down a notch or two, big brother."

Carley scrubbed her hands over her face, her pale straight hair swinging around her face and settling against her flushed cheeks. Her blue eyes sliced at the males, one by one. "Does anyone care how awful it is to live with this much testosterone waiting to show off? Hogan, you've got to keep your hands off Jemma. She's my friend and while she may seem to be experienced, she's not. Her marriage was a nightmare."

"Under all that fast-talking, brassy mouth, she's inexperienced." Mitch said darkly, backing up Carley's appraisal of Jemma. "You took her up there to have her. Not quite a penthouse bedroom, so she came cheap, didn't she?"

That deepened Hogan's anger, because it was true. He should have courted her—given her bouquets and gifts and taken her more gently—but the urgency to have her, to bind them together, had ruled him. He really did not like being at the mercy of his emotions. Now, confronted by his family, he didn't like the "defiler of sweet, innocent thing" label plastered on him.

"She knows what she wants," Hogan said, defending himself. Jemma had wanted him fiercely, but there was that softness in her, too, holding him close and sweet.

"What about good old Simone?" Aaron asked. "You're used to traveling in an amoral set. You took Jemma because you were bored, needed a playmate, and wanted to push Dad."

"Did I? Maybe Ben needs pushing." Feeling surly now and not liking that emotion, Hogan didn't like being the offender, or striking back. In those first years out of Montana, he had been amoral, pairing with women just as careless of what making love should mean. Now he knew the difference, and he didn't like the picture of himself in earlier years, out to devour the world and set it on fire.

"I hope you got it all out of your system, because you're not using her. She's not up to a threesome with Simone D'Arcy." Aaron jabbed a finger into Hogan's chest.

Ben looked down the supper table at his glowering family and at Jemma, who looked as if she could kill anyone who spoke to her. He'd seen his family wearing the same expressions over the years, but they'd never stopped loving one another. Ben took comfort in the love they still shared.

This time, Hogan was in the midst of it, like it or not, and he couldn't play peacemaker when he was obviously the offender.

Dinah's hand moved onto Ben's damaged leg, taking his hand beneath the table. She squeezed his hand gently and he wondered if she could feel the prosthesis, if it offended her. "Well. This is a nice meal, isn't it? Baked chicken, dressing, and a lovely green bean casserole. We'll have the fish Jemma caught tomorrow night. Baked with lemon, I think," Dinah said lightly, trying to make the dinner pleasant.

Ben stared down at the slender pale hand that had somehow inched higher on his lap. He knew he trembled, that his look at Dinah was hot and hungry before shielding it from his children.

That effort was unnecessary. The brood glared at one another and passed the food. Carley slapped a spoonful of dressing on her plate and punched Mitch's shoulder, just because it was there. Ben settled back to enjoy his children and his wife's hand in his. For once, he wasn't at the bottom of the problem. Clearly, his eldest son had stepped over a line.

When the plates were filled, and his children and Jemma were eating slowly in simmering dead silence, sliced by meaningful glares, Ben couldn't resist asking, "Who's behind all of this?"

Hogan leaned back, hooked one arm over the back of his chair and stared at Jemma, not shielding his anger. He rocked back on the chair's legs and studied her. "Here," he said, plopping glittering citrine-and-carnelian earrings onto the table in front of Jemma.

It wasn't the presentation of a lover's gift, rather a challenge. Ben suspected that Hogan had meant to gift Jemma with more romance, but with eyes the color of thunderclouds, she'd been glaring at him across the table.

"Wear them yourself. Simone called here today just after you left. She's in Paris and needed you. She was looking for you. I think she has an itch. Maybe you'd better fly off and—"

"That's enough," Hogan snapped, scowling at her. "What's your problem?"

"You left me with those damn fish to clean and right now, I'd sooner kiss one of them, than you." Jemma stood up, hurled her cloth napkin onto the table, and stalked out of the room and ran up the stairs.

"That is a hot-blooded woman," Ben heard himself say, before he clamped his lips closed and settled for a grin. His son was definitely simmering, Ben thought, appreciating the hot look of a man who didn't know how to handle the woman he'd claimed and who obviously was in a snit. Hogan tried to decide if he should go after her, or let her cool off, or just walk out. Ben had been there enough times to recognize the dark, uncertain look on his son's face.

"Excuse me. Dinner was good. Thank you, Dinah." Hogan got up and stalked after Jemma. The sound of his footsteps tramping up the stairs echoed over the dining table, and Maxi sighed dreamily, placing her hand over her heart.

After Jemma's outraged scream, Hogan's footsteps tramped down the stairs again. This time, on his way outside, he carried a squirming Jemma over his shoulder. One dark look at his family said he intended to keep the argument with Jemma very private.

In the moonlight, Hogan held Jemma's arms to her side, locking his arms around her. "Cool off."

"One woman wasn't enough, was it? Not when she's in Europe and you're needing a—I won't have jewelry you made for another woman—They all know, Hogan. They all know what we did up there—and that you're just bored here and that—" Jemma clenched her lids closed against the burning tears that brimmed and trailed down her cheeks.

"I made the earrings for you this afternoon. The color reminds me of your hair in the sunlight. Are you ashamed of what we did?" He feared her answer.

"I found it entertaining," she said coolly, temper simmering beneath the surface as she licked away a telling tear.

" 'Entertaining?' " He stood, riveted by the meaning of the word. She'd hurt him, pierced his protective shields, ripped him apart.

Since Hogan was holding her arms at her sides, Jemma pushed her face against his chest and dried her tears. She burned him with a dark look. "An entertaining diversion. I haven't had much time to think about it, but I'm certain I can be ready by July. I've been working hard—no time to remember something that didn't matter—you know, phone calls, deals to make. Oh! Hogan, don't you dare try that neck-massaging trick on me!"

He couldn't resist touching her, not when she'd wept for what they'd shared and he was feeling tender and soft and aglow. He bent to gently taste her lips. "Simone hasn't been my lover for years," he whispered against her ear, biting the lobe gently.

"I don't believe you," she blazed and walked back into the house, slamming the front door behind her.

Hogan stood for a long time, staring at the closed door. He wanted to tear it from the hinges and go after Jemma—and what? Prove what an idiot he was? Have his family see that she'd undone his control, laid him open? Unused to the raw emotions jolting him, Hogan locked his boots to the ground and hooked his thumbs into his pockets.

Ben stepped out onto the porch and stood in front of the door as if reading Hogan's emotions. "I've been there, boy. Better give her time to cool off," Ben said.

In her upstairs bedroom, Jemma couldn't resist easing aside the curtain to look down at Hogan. He stood there, looking up at her, his tall body outlined in the silvery moonlight. The tug of his body curled around hers, the memories of his mouth suckling gently, rhythmically at her breast, sent a hot sizzle through her. He looked so lonely outlined in the moonlight, and she ached to hold him tight. Hogan could be sweet, almost boyish, but he was a man of dark, uncertain needs.

Jemma crushed the lace curtain in her fist. Could she trust him? He had a lover who wanted him and yet he had shed Simone easily—for the moment. Hogan was a Kodiak, and that meant he'd want a family, because that need had been bred into him, whether he liked it or not. She hadn't thought of herself as a lover, yet with him, she had made love and enjoyed the hunger and excitement, the image of him moving over her, his face dark and intent as though nothing mattered but what would come between them.

Jemma's hand rose to protectively cover the racing pulse at her throat. He would want too much.

She opened her other hand. The earrings glittered in the dim light, his trademark stamped on a small disk. The gift was symbolic, she knew, marking their time together. She closed her fist over the earrings and brought her hand to her heart. She'd known him for years and yet that sweet gift had shaken her—before his lover Simone had slashed through the tender moment.

Tall and lethal and brooding, Hogan stood waiting for her to come to him. She couldn't, until she knew what moved inside her—the aching tenderness warring with her fears of what Hogan would expect from her—the restrictions and tethers. . . . Jemma slashed away tears with the back of her hand. "Whatever happens, I will not be a fill-in for his lover. But he can be so sweet and tender and if I didn't know that, I'd be just fine.''

Then because she wasn't one to hide in the shadows when her emotions were burning, Jemma shoved open the window. "I love the earrings."

"Why don't you come down here and tell me?" he called back to her.

Because she didn't dare come close to him, to see that grin upon his face—no more than a flash of white in the dark night—Jemma slammed the window down.

He looked up at her and took his hat from his head, sweeping it in front of him as he bowed. Then he straightened, put his hat on his head, and blew her a kiss; he strolled to his pickup and got inside. He backed it up to the house, climbed up on the cab, and gripped the roof, levering himself up. He walked across the roof toward her window. "Are you going to kiss me good night or what?"

Because the move was so atypical of Hogan's contemplative, predictable nature, Jemma opened the window and stared at him. "What are you doing, Hogan Kodiak?"

"Kissing my sweetheart good night—unless you'd rather come to my place. But if you do, you're not coming back tonight."

"You're not going anywhere until I kiss you, are you?"

He stared at her, face harsh and intense in the moonlight, and Jemma found herself reaching for his head, wrapping her fingers in his smooth, crisp hair, and pushing her mouth against his. It wasn't a sweet kiss, but Hogan's hand reached out to cup the back of her head, drawing her into a long, tender kiss.

He leaned back, inhaled roughly as though he wanted to climb into the window and make love to her, and then shook his head—"You're going to need more casting time. Do you want me to help you or not?"

"Not tomorrow." She wanted time to think about this new Hogan, one who smoothed her hair and took her palm to his lips. The gesture was humbling, a proud man yielding a bit to her.

"You're backing off, aren't you? Afraid?"

"Yes. I think we'd both better think about this," she whispered, because Hogan had known her too long, and recently, too well. "You'd better go. Be careful. I wouldn't want you to break that neck before I do it."

He chuckled, the rare sound delighting her, before he crossed the roof and dropped to his pickup bed. Ben crossed to him, and after a brief talk, their rumbling voices too low for Jemma to distinguish, Hogan's sleek truck purred into the night—headed toward town.

Carley came in and plopped full length on the bed. "He's becoming a bit of a Romeo with you. Who would have thought that Hogan could be so romantic? He's headed into town. Aaron is probably already at the Lucky Dollar, brooding about Mom and Dad's romance heating up and Savanna not taking his flirting seriously. Mitch is gone, too. When you get right down to it, they're all boys. Disgusting male showoffs, seeing who can spit the farthest."

Carley's frustration did not cover her love for her family. "And you love them," Jemma murmured, because she knew that Carley's family was her life.

"Desperately. If I could have one wish, it would be that somehow, all of us could find peace as a family. Dysfunctional is a word I know well."

Despite her own tumultuous emotions, Jemma moved to sit by Carley. "You haven't been down to that place—where it happened, have you?"

"No. I thought about it, but there hasn't been time. I haven't had a minute alone, and I need that, to think. I know I have to put it past me, but I just can't.''

"What we need is a break. We've been planting gardens, fighting with Kodiak men, and generally kept like a harem here in the house—doing 'women's work.' ''

Carley lifted an eyebrow. "One of us wasn't. You certainly looked mashed when you turned up this morning.''

"I've been mashed before. I was married, remember? But then it was all very scheduled and clinical, and frankly not that much fun . . . Let's track them down like dogs at the Lucky Dollar. A girl's night out, okay?''

Carley's eyes lit up. "Do you really think it will be okay? I've never been there before. It's all dark and seedy-looking.''

"The question is, do you want to go?" Jemma ached for the experiences Carley had feared to take, her life overshadowed long ago by her attacker. Carley had never dated or played, her nerves skittering when a man came too close.

Aaron placed his beer mug down on the tavern's battered table. "I bought that old Simmons place, all five thousand acres of it, next to Dad's. It's a good investment. I can sell it for a profit, or—Holy—'' he exclaimed, eyes widening as Carley and Jemma walked in the door.

Jemma's hair was piled on top of her head, tendrils curling down around her face and down her nape. With her hair held away from her face by combs, the citrine earrings glittered daintily at her ears. She scanned the dark bar, the three-piece band and a singer whose lusty voice caught the sensual tempo easily in an aching slow song of love gone wrong. Jemma's red sweater and tight jeans and red boots said she'd come to play. She eyed the cowboys lined up against the bar, and they were taking in her long, tall, and hot look.

Carley was smaller, more rounded, compact, dressed in a black sweater and neat slacks, her light blond hair catching the dim neon light. In an unfamiliar setting, she eased back toward Mitch, who had come to wrap his arm around her protectively. He bent to her ear, talking above the loud music, and gently took her into his arms. Carley stood very still, her hands against his chest, her face pale as she looked up at him. He moved slightly, smiling tenderly down at her, and Carley looked away, but her body swayed stiffly to his direction, a safe distance away.

Hogan slowly placed his mug on the table and forgot about convincing Aaron that Dinah wouldn't hurt Ben again, their affection obvious and growing. Hogan looked at the woman who had just this morning demanded as much as he—and now she was obviously ready to romp and stomp with the local playboys. She glanced at him, tossed her head, and looked away, but Hogan had seen that dangerous, wary look.

He pushed away from the table and walked toward her, disliking the anger and jealousy riding him. This wasn't sweet, innocent Jemma, but a woman on the prowl—the chameleon changing as it suited her. She was out to prove that she could do as she liked—without the confinements of a relationship with him.

He'd never coerced a woman into fidelity, but he wasn't having another man's hands on her while she looked like steam heat, her face carefully made up, her lipstick glossy and waiting. She was still burning about Simone's call, but Hogan wasn't letting that come between them. "You've had a long day, haven't you? Seems like just this morning you were groaning about getting up before dawn."

She crossed her arms and ignored him, tapping her boot to the music. Then she flicked a long, lazy look at him. "Maybe it was who I was with."

Hogan couldn't resist smiling. Jemma knew how to handle herself in flirtatious situations; she controlled them and eased away before her target knew what hit him. But she hadn't gotten away; Hogan had staked a very vital claim that he intended to explore with her. He flicked the dangling citrine-and-carnelian earrings, studying the glitter reflected upon her smooth jaw. "Red, we both know you like me."

"Correction. I tolerate you. I make allowances for your arrogance, your dark moods, whatever." She lifted one sleek eyebrow, eyeing him haughtily as though he was a stranger she was putting in place—Jemma was very good when she was cool and cutting. But then, Hogan had seen the other side of her, all glittering with anger, soft with desire, and Carley was proof that Jemma loved without reservation—when she gave her heart.

He couldn't resist laughing, enjoying her reluctance to admit she liked him. He strolled a finger down her throat and watched her tense, dark heat flashing up at him. "This is a little low-class for you, isn't it? It hardly rates with Cannes."

"I'm just a country boy at heart. Are you going to dance with me, or am I going to have to carry you out of here?" He loved challenging Jemma—she responded with fire and storms, igniting easily—everything was right out there, bright as sunlight, with him, her emotions easily read.

Her eyes widened at that threat, because Hogan was always controlled. Yet he'd already carried her out of the house and climbed up on the roof to kiss her. Both uncharacteristic actions told her that he would carry her out now.

"I guess one dance wouldn't hurt. But don't think you're going to do more than that." A moment later, when he had folded her close against him and was swaying to the music, Jemma leaned back to look up at him. "You're aroused," she stated flatly.

"You do that to me. I'm afraid that's a constant state when you're around." He drew her closer, that softness he had to have, his body humming with desire. Then he gave himself to the sheer pleasure of her body moving with his, and wondered how a man who had never thought about sweethearts and tenderness could feel so fine with his arms around one special woman.

"Any woman would do that to you. I think you're easy, and I may have been. But I am not going home with you tonight, Mr. Hogan Kodiak."

"Maybe," he said, giving her a fighting chance, because he intended to have her in his bed all night, waking up to her. Hogan smoothed her back, nuzzled his cheek against hers, and let himself drift in the slow music and the warm, soft woman in his arms. She eased the harsh storms within him, kept them at bay. She was tough, too, determined to succeed, but beneath that, she was pure, sweet-soft, hot-blooded woman—everything up front with him. "Carley needed this. You probably had to browbeat her into it, but it was right. She needs to start life, and, from the looks of it, Mitch is ready to help."

He studied his sister, her life trapped back in the moment of the attack. Carley moved stiffly, wary of the man holding her body. Mitch's expression was tender, as if he'd dreamed of holding her that way.

"I love her," Jemma said. "But you have no idea what a pain she can be when dragging her into a new situation. She shakes, Hogan. The fear in her eyes is worse. I hate the man who did this to her. I didn't know if it was the right thing, coming into town without one of you, but I just had to get her out where she could feel life.''

"We'll get him.''

"We will. I believe that with all my heart,'' Jemma said firmly. Then she eased closer, and Hogan placed his cheek against her soft vibrant hair, letting it settle in a caress against his skin. He eased into the new emotions within him, the softer ones she had brought him, and gathered Jemma closer.

Across the bar, in a shadowy corner, a man sat studying the Kodiaks and that witch, Jemma. She was pushing his Celestial Virgin into that Chicago lowlife's bed, and she'd have to pay. In the dim light, Carley looked up at Mitch, her soft smile proving her enjoyment of the slow easy dance, their bodies barely moving.

The man's fist hit the table, jarring the glass he'd just emptied. Carley was his, and he'd send her a warning to remind her.

He'd deal with the Kodiaks, too, for coming between him and his Celestial Virgin. Then he'd show her the caves where the Chinese women had serviced their masters . . . just as Carley would tend him.

Aaron braced himself above Savanna, his body taut and slick with sweat, racked with the sexual explosion that had just passed. Savanna hadn't asked about his dark mood; she'd opened the door to her apartment and when he was inside, she'd silently stripped away the dark red satin robe, letting it pool to her feet. Naked and slender, she'd turned to him. As teenagers, they'd been lovers, bodies burning, but now her slender body, her sleek black hair spilling over her softly curved body was more sensual, more arousing. Aaron had carried her to the bedroom, and they'd made love silently, hungrily. Now her hair lay in glossy stripes across the black-satin pillowcase. She smiled softly and traced his mouth. ''Better?''

His body eased, but not his emotions, Aaron slid away, lying on his back beside her on the black satin sheet.

Savanna smiled and patted his chest. ''You'll get over whatever it is. Just another Kodiak moment, or rather war.''

He'd known her all her lifetime. She knew him as well, knew that he enjoyed women. Savanna had never pushed him; she'd always listened and knew exactly how the stormy family's dynamics affected each member. She was the only woman he could talk to honestly, skipping the bull. ''Dad is going down for the count, looking at Mom. She's not going to stay past the danger to Carley. Mom is pure city.''

''Give her credit, Aaron.'' Savanna rose out of the bed they had thoroughly mussed and pulled on her robe. She smoothed her long hair over her shoulder, and it gleamed down to her hips, swaying as she walked out of the bedroom.

Aaron lay there, aware that Savanna was the only woman who ever walked away from him. Irritated by Hogan, by Ben and Dinah, by Carley fighting life and Mitch determined to root her out into a life, Aaron jerked on his jeans and followed Savanna. ''Coffee at this hour?'' he asked when he found her making coffee in the small kitchenette.

''It looks like a long night, and I have to open the clinic at six. Richard takes care to see that his mother gets her medication and is comfortable before he leaves the house. It's a convenient arrangement for me—I get time off in the middle of the day to catch up on shopping and whatever. May as well drink coffee now and save time.'' Savanna's actions said she could take or leave him, and her light treatment irritated. ''Help yourself to whatever you want,'' she said. ''I'm taking a shower.''

''Savanna—do you sleep with Richard?'' Aaron had to ask and disliked the jealousy rising within him. There was something about the two of them, their heads together, an intimacy that Aaron could not define—

Her answer was smooth and thoughtful, a woman who knew her mind and made her own decisions, blaming no one for her fate. ''He hasn't asked. But I've had men. I'm not the Celestial Virgin you dreamed of as a boy, Aaron. You were my first, but not my last. I enjoy my body, and I have needs, just like you, Aaron. And I want a home with children and everything that comes with it. The way I see it is I'm just spending time until the right man comes along, and then there won't be anyone else but him. I'm just culling them out for now, seeing what fits right.''

That winded Aaron—the thought of Savanna holding another man, wearing his wedding ring, bearing his child. He didn't like the picture.

Savanna smiled at him as though reading his thoughts. ''We're not getting any younger, Aaron. You've been married, and it didn't work, and you've been engaged, and that didn't work, either. You might end up marrying some sweet young thing—eventually, but I want a man who is mine, who I can tend to in the good times and the bad, and when I find him, I'm never looking back or at another man. He'll be everything to me. Ben gave me an example of a man who is faithful and kind and generous. I think Hogan is like that, deep down, but he isn't interested in me. Mitch is that way, too, and he'll be a wonderful husband and father, but it isn't there between us. Someday I'll find who I want, and he'll just fit, and that will be it . . . click, like that.''

She patted his cheek and walked toward the bathroom, already stripping away her robe. Aaron tried to push down the nettling fact that he didn't meet her standards for a husband. That was fine—he wasn't in a marrying mood anyway, not after a divorce and escaping the charade of a bloodless society wedding. But the label ''cull'' scraped him raw.

Minutes later, Aaron stepped into the steaming shower and gathered Savanna to him, his body ripe with desire. ''You said to help myself to anything—I am.''

She laughed huskily, and found him with her hand. ''You're awfully good at that,'' Aaron said with a long slow groan.

Savanna smiled slowly, knowingly, sleek and feminine in the stream of water and steam and sank to her knees. And then Aaron forgot everything—

In the morning, he awoke to an empty bed and the unsettled sense that he wasn't all that appealing to Savanna. She'd made it plain that she'd had other lovers since they were teenagers, and the thought burned in him. For a man who enjoyed women, he didn't like the feeling that Savanna could take or leave him. He really didn't like that waiting for a perfect husband remark, or the exclusion from the perfect-male class. He didn't like feeling like a ''cull'' from the marriageable-males shelf.

# twelve

Jemma slept with childlike innocence. Hogan lay still, enjoying her awakening in his arms, absorbing the fit of her curved body against his—yin and yang. He'd been a solitary man, protecting his private life. He was surprised that he enjoyed sharing the first quiet moments of the day, cuddling Jemma, watching the dawn slowly touch her face.

He ran his hand over the jut of her hip, a woman's narrow waist contrasting the curve of her hips—a woman's hips made for passion and for bringing life into the world. Natural and almost fawnlike in sleep, Jemma's body seemed poised to spring into action.

He realized he was smiling softly, floating in gentle pleasure and harmony that he'd never experienced. He hadn't suspected that this on-the-go, pushy woman could be so delectable when she slept. Her hair slid on his shoulder, tips prickling his skin just enough to be exciting.

He eased closer to the soft nudge of her breast against his side—her nipple hardening slightly with the friction. He shifted his thigh to enjoy the slender one tangled with his, to feel the nestled heat of her womanhood burn his skin. He inhaled her scent, blended with their lovemaking, and opened his palm upon her bottom; an unfamiliar emotion sawed through him—that of a man who wanted to keep and hold a woman as his own. To bind her to him, so that she wouldn't fly away. He realized that his fingertips were digging slightly into the softness.

That softness tensed, as Jemma lifted, bumped his chin and braced her elbow against his chest; she pushed her wildly tangled hair away from her eyes. Hogan raised his lips to the strand sliding across them; he let his body awaken to the tantalizing, erotic movement of her body and hair moving over his skin. He smiled, hearing the echo of her laughter as he'd tossed her upon his bed, where she should be every night. Playfully wrestling, testing each other led to frantic hurried lovemaking that slowed and lingered and explored.

"I'm dead," Jemma announced desperately, sleep clinging to her voice. "I have conference calls scheduled for nine this morning, and it's already eight—besides that, I'll probably have to protect you from Carley— she's pretty angry with you, and so are the rest." Jemma rolled over him on her way to the bathroom and Hogan grunted, her knee coming too close to his already hardening body.

"Why should they be angry? Because you're here with me?" He wasn't keeping away from Jemma. His need for her was greater than his pride. He grabbed her ankle and tugged her back to him.

Sprawled beneath Hogan's body, she glared up at him. "You're holding my wrists, Hogan, and you look like a thundercloud. Goodness, you can be so intense. I've got a big deal going down this morning."

After a night of lovemaking, Hogan had come in second to making money. He wanted more—and he wanted to serve Jemma breakfast in bed. He'd had a plan, a romantic one, and typically, she'd sliced through it with her money-sword. His attempt to explore Jemma and himself, and enjoy the day with her, was dying before it began. "They'll call back."

Her eyes had that steely glint that meant Jemma was determined to have her way. "I never miss a call that will get me a profit like this one, Hogan. Let go."

"Never?" Hogan studied her, this woman that could evoke tenderness and romantic fantasies within him, a woman who fascinated and delighted him, and decided he could settle for passion. The sensual challenge was too much to resist. He eased Jemma to straddle him, fitting her heat above to his arousal and watched her eyes darken. He took her mouth, kissing her with all the emotion in him, hiding nothing, and while Jemma met him hungrily, he eased slightly into her.

In their time on the mountain and last night, Jemma was a traditional lover, learning quickly to meet his rhythm, but this new position—her dominance shocked her. He wondered how she would react and couldn't help smiling at her stunned expression. "Hogan—I'm not certain—oh! Oh! Hogan!"

"What were you saying about business?" he asked before the firestorm hit him. He guided her hips into the rhythm, pulled her knees up tight to his thighs, and spun out of control.

When she slumped upon him, her heart racing with his, Hogan couldn't resist teasing her. "Time to go, Jemma. All that money is just waiting for you."

"I can't move. I'm still seeing red stars. Hogan, a designer who can produce good garments is hard to find. No one does modesty panels like Cecilia."

"What's a modesty panel?" He sucked in his breath

as Jemma's body quivered, the remnants of her climax fading.

She went into herself, taking in the last pleasure, and relaxed. "You walk around naked. Modesty isn't something you'd know about . . . A modesty panel is a strip of cloth beneath the buttons. When a woman's blouse gaps, that extra cloth panel hides her bra—You rat. I'm not going to comment on your sizable, nonstop, more than adequate, athletic equipment—you're too full of yourself already."

He heard himself laugh, and wondered when a woman had ever spoken to him, moved him like Jemma could. He smoothed her trembling body, still filled with his, and flicked her earlobe with his tongue. He smiled as she groaned and shivered against him; a man had his pride after all. "Do I understand that you would rather be here with me, than punching cash register buttons and stuffing your bank account?"

"You're teasing me. I don't know if I like it."

"What are you going to do about it?" he asked, challenged by her and filled with anticipation.

When Jemma looked at him, her expression was tender, her hand smoothing his jaw. And later he would think how that quiet, intent look—that contented and well pleasured look could be more dangerous than her sultry one. . . .

All in all, it was a good way to start the day, Hogan thought later as he sat with his bare feet propped up on the wooden rail of his sprawling porch. In the distance, the Crazy Mountains surged into the blue sky, wrapping peace around Hogan. He sipped orange juice, inhaled the fresh midmorning air, and examined the glow within him. Harmony in his emotions was a surprise and Hogan

picked through the elements and they all led to Jemma—
she'd changed him, eased him.

Taking care of a woman's sexual needs was one
thing—Hogan had always been very careful in that respect. But his lingering enjoyment of Jemma and the
unfamiliar need to provide for her was new and tenuous.
Hogan smoothed the rough earth-tone texture of the pottery mug he'd created while high on designing the Kodiak Design trademark.

*Jemma.* He enjoyed watching Jemma rush out the
door, flustered and still warm from making love with
him. The gentle sway and bob of her breasts said she'd
forgotten that lacy bra that was crushed somewhere at
the foot of his rumpled bed. He'd never felt the need to
keep a woman in his bed all night, to make breakfast
while she was taking a shower.

He'd never stood by the door for a woman as he had
Jemma—she rushed out, handing her a mug of peppermint tea and bacon wrapped in whole-wheat toast. Not
a fan of beef or pork, Jemma looked at the food grate-
fully, grabbed it and stopped. She looked at him, and
Hogan's breath caught as a blush moved up her cheeks.

"I've got to go to Ben's—my file on this deal is
there." She stood on tiptoe to kiss his cheek. "Thanks
for the breakfast. You're not so bad," she whispered,
leaving him with the scent of her freshly bathed body
and that soft, sweet kiss upon his scarred cheek.

Hogan sipped his coffee, then traced the scar with his
fingertip as he viewed the Bar K; Ben was down in the
pasture, replacing a salt block. The bright day settled
over the lush fields and the grazing cattle, a peaceful
day. *Peace.* Hogan wondered at the peace he found with
Jemma, at the peace that eluded him.

Hogan didn't know what he would find with Jemma,
but he did want the answers Ben could give him. Every-

one else had gone into town, and there wouldn't be interruptions, nor interference in his need for the truth. Dinah had said Ben was ready now—

A half hour later, Hogan swung down from Moon Shadow and walked to where Ben stood next to his battered pickup. He watched Hogan walk toward him, and then turned to continue studying his cattle, calves frisking in the field. Hogan joined him and shared the view. Father and son knew how to share silence, but not their lives.

"Coffee?" Hogan asked, noting a hawk's soaring flight across the sky, its swift dive to take a field mouse. He hadn't made an attempt to meet Ben halfway, and each had stubbornly dug into his own life's path.

The thing about waking up with a passionate woman who fascinated him, Hogan thought darkly, was that it left a man in an unsteady, emotional mood—too drained and body-pleasured to think straight. One wrong word between Ben and him would ignite old wounds, but for the moment, both were enjoying the meadowlark's trill and the sense of peace and harmony rarely experienced by either man.

Ben nodded, and Hogan handed him a thermos that hung from his saddlebag. Ben reached into the seat of his pickup and handed Hogan another thermos. "Trade you."

"Carrot juice?"

"I'm going to turn orange," Ben grumbled, opening the thermos to pour the juice onto the ground. "I'm hoping Jemma will run out of the store-bought carrots. She must have planted an acre of them in the garden. I've been thinking about hiring Winnie Manfred's rabbits one night and clearing out the whole mess." He poured coffee into the thermos cup with a long, satisfied sigh.

"Think of the carrots that died for Jemma," Hogan found himself saying and wondered where the closest natural-foods market was. If he wanted Jemma in his home, he'd better learn how to feed her. He had the contented sense of settling into a relationship that he intended to enjoy—and work at, if need be. With Jemma, he enjoyed giving, and he enjoyed taking. Did he know how to care for her? How to say the right things? To be there when she needed him?

"You'll take care of the girl. You're worried about that now, because you think your heart is a cold lump, no more than an empty hole. But you'll warm to the idea—maybe you already have." Staring at the rugged Crazy Mountains, Ben spoke as if he were remembering his own emotions when first seeing Dinah. "Jemma said I should tell you about your mother. She said I'd been cruel not to. She's a pushy thing, sweet and sassy one minute, and the next coming on like a bulldozer, ramming it down my throat that maybe you and I still have a chance."

"I didn't send her after you, Ben. You do what you want." Hogan didn't want Jemma battling for him, entering his dark corners. The wall had been between Ben and him for years; he didn't expect it would come down easily.

"I want my grandkids swinging in the front yard and my wife—I want my wife wearing my wedding ring and this time, by God, I'll make her a husband, if she'll have me. Or what's left of me." The statement came so harsh and deeply emotional that Hogan studied Ben. Ben's face was hard, but his hand trembled as he rubbed his cheek. "Jemma got me one of those new battery-operated shavers, so I wouldn't look so woolly during the day—if Dinah came to see me. She does that sometimes, brings me lunch. She's a giving, sweet woman—always was."

Ben inhaled and glanced at his son. "But you want to know about your real mother and here's the short and sweet—You're all mine. I was just seventeen when I met her in that camas field up in the mountains. She was a pretty little maiden, part-Kootenai, part-white, and real pretty. Real pretty," Ben repeated, as though going back through the years. "She felt things in her—like you do—earth and wind and trees moving in her. She liked to touch and take things into her that way, studying them, making them a part of her. She could draw, too."

Hogan swallowed and remembered the field where Ben had taken him to play as a child. His mother was Kootenai—a sense of wonder and belonging began to curl around him. *His mother.* "By Willow Creek?"

"That was her name—Willow. I couldn't say the other Indian name. She was a half-blood, raised by her mother. Old Susan hated men, especially white men, and there I was, a blue-eyed, blond white man courting her daughter. Your grandfather Aaron would have had them run out of town, if he'd known. In those days, he had the power to do most anything. Then out of the blue, Willow sent me a note by carrier pigeon—she was really good with birds and animals, just like you, and could she ride a pony . . ."

Ben looked toward the foothills, his voice soft and uneven as he threaded through the past. "Well, by the time I met her in the rough cabin we'd made up in the mountains by that clearing at Willow Creek—to be together—she was already in childbirth, needing help, and something was wrong."

Ben's voice caught, and then he was silent for a time, taking another sip of coffee. "I didn't even know you were coming—I guess she feared for me, too—Old

Aaron had already taken a belt to me for—well, for a lot of things. Her mother had secretly given her herbs to miscarry, because she didn't want another white child in the family, and because Willow wouldn't harm you on her own. Willow used her last strength to protect you. She knew her mother would most likely give you away at birth. She got Joe Blue Sky to help her to that cabin.''

Hogan couldn't move, his heart pounding so hard in his chest that he couldn't breathe, couldn't swallow. A chasm of pain opened and swallowed him. He looked at Ben, hated him, for keeping his mother away from him. ''But you didn't marry her. You couldn't lower yourself, could you? A rich rancher's son and a—''

Ben swallowed roughly. ''I would have had a minister marry us, but Willow said a ceremony between us was what she wanted. That's what we did, under a new moon. She knew old Aaron would cut at me—and he did later, when he found out, mad as blue blazes, but it didn't matter. I tried to convince her that I'd leave, go anywhere to be with her. Hell, I was so green, I didn't know the signs, and I was a cattleman, bred and true. I didn't even know she was pregnant. There was no time to take her down the mountain to see a doctor—old Doc Coleman wouldn't haven't treated her right anyway— you remember how he was, that bigot. She was too weak, a poor little pitiful girl, giving birth to my baby, my first son. I knew about calving and Joe knew about herbs, and between us, I think we eased her. Then you came out with a howl and a mop of black hair, and you were mine—my son, hungry as a bear after a winter sleep. Willow faded out of life, but not before she made me promise—''

Hogan slammed his fist onto the pickup's hood, the metallic sound echoing violently in the quiet country morning. "You were afraid to bring your bastard home—''

"I took you to Old Susan's first. Not because I didn't want you, but it seemed a woman might want a grand-baby from her daughter—and Willow was gone. I didn't know anything about babies or women, and I wanted my son to know a woman's softness. She slammed the door on us and left town—by the way Old Susan died years ago—so I brought home my son. I left no doubt in anyone's mind that you were mine, a part of me. I didn't know how to handle the woman part, how to tell you how sweet and caring she was—even as she died, she thought of you and of me. I didn't know how to tell you in words. But you were mine.''

"You cold son of a bitch—'' Hogan's body was taut with the need to hit Ben, to make him pay for a lifetime of uncertainties and pain.

"I knew you'd take it hard. I should have told you right away, but you seemed so complete and strong. I was too young, too, but that's no excuse for being a poor father. I'd been brought up to think that we had jobs to do—mine was to provide food and shelter for you, yours was to grow up. I buried her up there, where we'd been happy and where she wanted to lie. I promised to take care of her uncle, Joe Blue Sky, and I took you home. You were mine. My fine son.''

Anger slashed at Hogan, his hands shaking as he poured coffee and downed the hot fluid quickly, wel-coming the burn. "That's a simple story. You could have told me that long ago.''

"I was a boy when you were born. I had a crazy dying father, a twelve-thousand-acre ranch to run, horses to break, a baby son, and the whole works depended on me. Old Aaron had left his hard mark in me, but I take the blame. I didn't know how to tell you that I—I loved you, to say the right words.''

"Did you love her? Or did you use her?" Hogan needed to take the knowledge inside him and weave it into sense. He'd lost a lifetime of knowing—

"Hell, yes, I loved her. My first sweetheart will always be with me—I see her every time I look at you."

"You didn't look at me that much." Hogan's statement was as brutal as he felt.

Ben stared off into the Crazy Mountains to that high moist meadow where he'd first met Willow digging camas roots in the old Indian way. "I didn't know how to deal with the hole inside me, with losing the one piece of sunlight I'd had in my lifetime. And there you stood, a reminder of Willow, and how I should have done better by her.''

Hogan was startled by the deep emotion in his father's rough voice. In his lifetime, Hogan could not remember Ben speaking as frankly about love. "Old Aaron must have liked that, an Indian grandson. Black hair and black eyes in a blue-eyed, blond family."

Ben's smile was wry. "Not much. You did stand out in the crowd. A nice straight, tall strong boy—solid, good judgment, and a heart that was kinder than old Aaron's or mine. Animals sensed that about you, even when you were a pup, and they'd come to you. Made him mad as hell to see a foal tagging after you when it wouldn't come to him for an apple. But there wasn't anything he could do about it. He was already sick—I think his hatred of everything and everyone ate him to death. He needed me to take care of him, and I'd have left if he'd made me choose between my son and the Bar K.''

He paused and looked off again toward the foothill clearing at Willow Creek. "*Her name was Willow*. She's buried by the big pine she loved near the cabin. Our initials are on the tree. She liked to draw—I used to bring her pencils and sketch pads,'' Ben said softly. ''I was married in my heart, and how she looked that day, as my little bride when we gave our vows, and when she gave me my son—''

His voice died, washed away by emotions as though he'd spent all his energy on revealing something he'd kept locked in his heart for too long. Ben's usual hard expression eased, and he suddenly looked old and worn—''When she laughed, it was like sunshine. It filled me.''

Hogan rubbed his hands over his face. Ben spoke tenderly of a woman Hogan had never known, a woman who had been kept from him. He'd been missing a part of his life and now it sliced through him, cutting at memories. He realized he knew how Ben had felt, because Jemma had filled him—he hadn't expected to understand Ben and yet he did. ''Why tell me now?''

''Because it's time you knew. Because you've got a woman in your heart now—a good woman—and they make a difference in what a man understands. But most of all, you're hard as rock, Hogan. Maybe you needed that to survive. Cold inside like me, and that was a gift I handed down to you from old Aaron. But you've got more heart than my father or me, and you've got a chance to be happy. And since I'm a selfish bastard, I want you for my son, and I want to hold your babies in my arms.''

Hogan stared at the man he'd hated and loved and respected and fought. He tucked the hot, fast bitter words behind his lips. His heart was already sailing up the mountain to the woman who was his mother—''You'll see to Carley?''

''He'll have to go through us first, that's Aaron and

Mitch and Dinah, too. Take your time. He's not getting Carley.'' Ben watched his son stride to his horse and mount, riding toward the mountain and his mother. "I love you, boy. God bless.''

In the clearing in the foothills, near Willow Creek, the pine-tree bark had been stripped away, a lace of litchen moss covering the scarred wood, the heart with B + W K. *Ben and Willow Kodiak . . .*

Hogan went down to his knees, carefully easing away the pine needles and twigs that covered his mother's grave. River rocks, worn smooth and round covered the small rectangular area. Hogan looked up to the cathedral of tall lodgepole pines and junipers to the blue sky beyond the branches. Ben must have carried the rocks there, because there were no stones matching their pink-and-gray color in Willow Creek. "Hello, Mother. I'm your son,'' he said unevenly, his heart filling with emotions.

He studied the old heart. "Ben and Willow Kodiak.'' *"I was married in my heart, and how she looked that day, as my little bride when we gave our vows, and when she gave me my son—''*

"B and W Kodiak.'' In the spring air, Hogan's voice was distant, not a part of him. Hogan swallowed, blinded by flashes of when Ben had brought him here to plant flower bulbs. Hogan swept his open hand across the smooth stones. He sat back, bent a knee, and placed his arm across it. Resting his chin on his forearm, Hogan tried to see her in his mind.

Three hours later, he crouched by Willow Creek, sipping water from his hands. "Aaron, you make enough noise to scare all the game off the mountain. I've been watching you come up the mountain. If Carley's stalker wanted to pick you off, it would be easy enough and make one less of us to protect her.''

Aaron crouched beside Hogan and drank from his hands as Hogan had done. ''Good water. Pure,'' Aaron noted, and turned to closely study his brother. ''How goes it?''

When Hogan was silent, watching a curled, golden willow leaf drift on the small stream, Aaron said, ''Dad told us. He said you'd be here, making your peace.''

''Peace?'' Bitterness surged in Hogan, and he stood abruptly, meeting Aaron's guarded study. His brother was the same height and build, Kodiak bones running beneath that fairer skin, Aaron's eyes as blue as the sky, as penetrating as Ben's—a perfect match to Hogan's darker features.

''Do you hate me?'' Aaron asked baldly.

''Not a bit. I changed your diapers, remember?''

''The old man is holed up with a bottle. Just like the old days when he lost that leg. If I were to make a guess, I'd say he's thinking that he deserved to lose that leg, and that he doesn't deserve Dinah.''

''Maybe.'' Hogan couldn't spare time thinking about Ben now, not the man who had kept his birth mother in the shadows. He'd felt like a bastard all of his life, an outsider to the Kodiak blond, blue-eyed family, and now he was dealing with who he was—Willow's son. He walked to the cabin, broken and rotted, the roof caved in by time and weather. His hands were raw and torn, used roughly to tear away the brush, to find what he could of his mother.

Aaron stood beside him, studying the remnants of the small log cabin and then Hogan. ''You look like hell, a dead tie with Dad. He's looks like the whole world fell on him.''

''Hadn't you better be getting back?'' Hogan didn't

want his fair-haired brother tangled in his pain, to see
the dark fury and hurt inside him.

"Hell, no." Aaron walked to the packhorse, and began to toss camping gear to the ground. "You're not
sending me back into that pit of worked-up females,
Mitch's psychology manure, and Ben's black moods.
When I left, Mom was threatening to take an ax to the
door Ben had locked and Jemma was brewing up another jug of carrot juice. Carley was shivering in the
shadows and not listening to anything I had to say to
comfort her. Here—''

Aaron tossed an ax to Hogan, who caught it easily.
"I took that ax before Mom found it, because your sweet
self went to so much work to restore those doors. At the
going rates you charge as an artist, those fine master-
pieces are probably worth over twenty thousand
apiece.''

Hogan, unable to say what was right to Aaron—that
Aaron remained his brother, and was in his heart. Re-
acting to his emotions, wishing he could tear away the
pain, Hogan threw the ax in a rotation at a tree twenty
feet away; the blade sank solidly into the wood with an
echoing whack.

"Good toss. I guess your pampered artist hands aren't
that weak." Aaron tossed Hogan leather gloves and a
rifle, then a gun belt and a revolver. "You forgot a few
things you might need up here.''

"Get away," Hogan said quietly, needing to sink into
his thoughts, to deal with emotions he'd shielded all his
life.

"You sound like the old man. Act like him, too. From
the way you jumped Jemma, making certain you'd put
your brand on her, I'd say that matches exactly what I
heard about Dad shooing Mom down the wedding chute.
She never knew what hit her, but she's a lot sweeter

than Jemma . . . I'll leave when I'm ready, bro,'' Aaron returned evenly, meeting Hogan's dark look.

Aaron watched a mule doe water at the stream. ''You stuck when the going was rough all those years ago. You were there, taking it from Ben. You stuck by Mom, and Carley and me. We depended on you and you were there . . . Lighten up, Hogan. All I did was bring beer and food. No women, and you'd better be grateful that I didn't. They're out to make us a lovely, civilized family. Mitch has all those psychology degrees, and he can handle it. In fact, I think Mitch is really into this female bonding thing, studying the dynamics. Dad can handle himself, but I'm defenseless as a baby. Let me enjoy my time away from the house.''

Aaron's discomfort was probably a ploy, but for once Hogan didn't state the obvious. He loved his brother deeply, always had. Hogan almost smiled, remembering the time he took Aaron into the woods to build a clubhouse far away from the stormy Kodiak ranch house. Aaron had been torn between his battling mother and father, and fighting pride and tears.

''Aaron, I want you to meet my mother,'' Hogan said. ''She's right over there.''

''They met in that camas field,'' Aaron stated softly, looking out into the small moist meadow, the camas stalks promising blue flowers.

In his mind, Hogan saw his father, a woman-shy, lanky cowboy, trying to talk with a black-haired girl in the meadow. Hogan's emotions trembled within him, the new knowledge opening up visions he'd never expected. ''He said she liked to draw, to feel. Willow was her name.''

Aaron nodded slowly, studying Hogan. ''I'd like to meet her.''

''He loved her.'' Hogan inhaled the mountain air and

let peace fill him. "He loves Dinah, too."

They stood apart, studying each other—boys who had become men with love running between them. "You ever tell anyone you loved them, Hogan?"

"No one but Carley, and she needed to hear it back then."

"I'm thinking that if I have kids, I'm going to tell them that every chance I get," Aaron stated firmly. "Now introduce me to your mother."

In the morning, Hogan's head throbbed, and a boot was prodding his backside. Aaron yelled, cursing as a bucket of cold water splashed in his face. Hogan sucked in his breath as the other half of the water in the bucket was dashed into his face.

"I'm here and I'm ready to fish," Jemma announced cheerfully. "It's already eight o'clock, and boy, are they biting!"

Hogan stifled a groan and sat up on his bedroll; his head threatened to roll back down to the bedroll—he held it tightly. Aaron was hopping and cursing, his bare feet hitting rock and pinecones—the reflexology lesson last night had required the use of his own feet. A radio blared rock music, crashing through Hogan's skull and Jemma turned up the volume. "Just trying to find the fishing report."

"Get the hell out of here! Men need peace and quiet and not screaming women," Aaron yelled, as Hogan struggled to stand, bracing one hand against a tree. He had a distant memory of Ben yelling the same thing at Dinah.

"This isn't your old clubhouse marked Men Only. This is a whole big mountain, and there aren't any signs telling me to keep me away," Jemma shot back, her hands on her hips and fire in her eyes.

"I'll make one," Hogan stated through his parched throat. A strip of sunlight speared through the pine trees and caught the back of his brain. He braced his hand against a tree and tried to glare at Jemma, who looked as though she'd explode. "You're not mad, are you, Red?"

She threw up her hands. "Oh, gee whiz, why should I be mad? Can't you take a little payback? I had a morning I didn't feel so good, either. But did you have mercy? Oh, no. Not you. Stop calling me 'Red.' I don't like it, and there's a little more volume I can get out of this radio."

Despite his hangover, Hogan couldn't help but notice how fine she looked in a snit, wearing cut-off jeans, a tight yellow tube band across her breasts covered by one of his shirts, knotted at the waist. He took in those long, long legs and stopped at the orange canvas shoes. The colors hurt his eyes, jarred his artist senses. Yellow and orange usually meant Jemma was on the warpath and he'd experienced enough of her temper to know that the gloves were off.

In contrast to the jangling warning bells in his head, he wanted to hold her, to kiss her, and lay her down beneath him. The thoughts weren't sweet, just pure hunger unleashed and devastating. He shifted, uncomfortable with his tight, burgeoning body, his arousal thrusting at his jeans. "I don't know. Why are you mad? Did the modesty panel blouse deal fall through?"

Faced with an angry woman, a hangover, and a cursing brother, Hogan took the safest path and walked to the creek to soothe his parched throat. He drank, and Aaron lay facedown beside him, cupping cold water onto his face. Hogan lifted a heavy, aching lid and eyed Aaron. "You led her here."

"Did not. But if she's on this mountain, I want off."

Aaron stared down at the toothpaste and toothbrush she'd flung at him. "Where's the floss, Mother?"

"Go to hell."

Hogan turned to look up at Jemma, no small matter as she was outlined in the blinding sunlight. "Will you go home?" he demanded, rather than asked.

"I'm here to fish. You said you'd teach me. I've got a schedule, you know——"

Jemma screamed as Hogan wrapped his hand around her ankle and tumbled her into the creek. "Cool off."

Aaron began laughing, then studied Jemma tromping out of the creek. "Hogan," he said in an aside as they sat brushing their teeth and watching her, "there's not a trout in that little creek. Bait fish, maybe."

"I know." Hogan stood up, feeling good enough to grin at her. "But she looks so fine when she's casting."

"Ah, the artist speaks." Aaron's tone was that of a man understanding another's admiration of women's bodies.

"Uh-huh. Something like that." Hogan stood back as Jemma tromped past him, her shoes squishing. He had the odd sense that he needed her to hold him, to soothe him, past the sensual need of their bodies, and that thought terrified him.

"Oh, man, she's tromping over our camp and calling us pigs—takes me back, but I really hate being called a pig. I'm getting the hell out of Dodge——" Aaron's expression was a Western one that said he wasn't staying anywhere near Jemma and her current mood. He grinned at Hogan. "She's tracked you down like a dog, man. You've already been bagged and don't know it yet."

"We're just sorting out the rules," Hogan began carefully, wary about his brother reading him so well.

"She doesn't have 'em," Aaron returned cheerfully. "You're just wide-open for the kill."

Hogan studied the tiny weathered cabin, the distant snowcapped mountains and the stream and the woman. "I'll take care of her."

"Never a doubt in my mind," Aaron said, swinging up onto his saddled horse. "I'll tell Joe Blue Sky you'll be wanting to talk with him."

*Killing the old man was so easy*, the murderer thought as he tucked Joe Blue Sky's heart medicine pills back into the dead man's pocket. It had been so easy to fake car trouble on the country road that Joe took to visit his cousins. Once Joe stopped, the killer had only to excite the old man and keep the pills from him. While Joe was gasping for life, his heart bursting into pieces, the killer told him what he would do to Carley and the Kodiak family—just to enjoy the panic in the old man's cloudy, pain-racked eyes.

Joe Blue Sky's killer patted the old man's flannel pocket, the medicine bottle safely inside where it would be found.

"It will be ruled a natural death, Joe. Too bad you couldn't get your medicine when you needed it. But the Kodiaks will know. They'll know that Carley is mine and that I am displeased. They'll take this as a warning."

He studied Hogan Kodiak's house, outlined against the bright Montana sky, big windows catching the sun and hurling a challenge at him. Hogan was the worst—not read easily, wary enough to stand back and separate himself from his emotions.

Then there was Aaron—a smooth-talking ladies' man. He'd always had everything—charm, talent, looks, an all-American golden boy.

*Mitch.* He'd dare to take Carley into his arms, to touch her virgin body. Dared to look at her beautiful pure blue eyes. With his Chicago street and gang background, his death could easily look like the result of his interference as a social worker—

Jealousy rose and flamed within the murderer, his fists clenching as he stared at the remodeled contemporary house. Hogan was too talented, rising from nothing, a bastard making a fortune without half trying. Women clustered to his dark brooding looks, and Carley loved him. He was too strong, too complete, and invulnerable. But he wasn't, not really, not when a superior intelligence wanted to defeat him, hurt him. Hogan had come back to make a statement to Ben and Hogan's house was a monument stuck in his father's face.

The killer knew he had time on his side; sooner or later, he'd have Carley.

He returned to his pickup, slipped the coil wire back onto the distributor cap and closed the hood. He wiped his grease-covered hands on a rag, tossed it into the brush, and briefly saluted Joe Blue Sky's body.

# thirteen

"Hold still." Hogan tried to work free the lure tangled in Jemma's hair, pushed up onto the top of her head. She squirmed, twisting the horsehair hackle lure deeper into the thick, fiery strands. Hogan couldn't resist the pleasure of running his thumb over the warm sleek strand, a vivid contrast to his dark skin. Holding the lure safely away from her face and scalp, he worked it from her hair. The pleasant bumping of her body against his was an added bonus.

He swatted her bottom lightly, not to hurt or remind her to stand still, but because the playful familiarity pleased him. Wanting more of that light feeling, he bent suddenly to growl and nuzzle her throat, and grinned when she squealed in surprise. The play was a first for Hogan and he'd stunned himself—and her. He loved stunning the woman who had pushed him into desperation.

"You rat. I've got to learn how to do this, and it's impossible when you're standing there grinning," she said for the tenth time, temper quivering in the sunlit morning air.

"Shh." He ran his fingers down the taut cords on her nape, and massaged lightly. She relaxed momentarily, issuing a long sigh of pleasure, then pulled away. "Don't try that on me. I'm not turning into a pool of jelly before I've told you just what I think of you, and I'm getting that list in order now."

Hogan tossed the nymph lure and line away and Jemma grabbed his wrist, turning his damaged palm up to her inspection. Almost pale as silver in the dappled sunlight, her eyes shot to his. She frowned, her voice husky. "How did you do this?"

Before Aaron had come, Hogan had wanted to see where his mother had lived and been happy. He'd hoped for a glimpse of her, and there was none. He glanced at the tiny cabin, the brush torn away, new timber replacing the old. His brother had worked easily at his side, as he'd always done, complaining occasionally about his posh office and missing the sweet young things that supplied his morning coffee. But he'd stayed and they'd cut trees the old way, taking turns, chopping a big wedge from the trunk. After hacking away the branches, they'd each taken an end, hefting the log to their shoulders and carried it to the cabin.

"You and Aaron, I suppose," Jemma said. "I'll have to talk to him. He can't just—Swaggering . . . concrete heads . . . Come on. I brought a first-aid kit, and you're going to let me take care of those hands. Hogan, you're a talented artist and you've abused your hands. This family really needs me." Careless of her expensive equipment, Jemma tossed it to a grassy bank and grabbed Hogan's jeans waistband, tugging him toward the small camp.

He looked down at the slender, efficient hand, the knuckles brushing his bare stomach. He didn't like comparison of himself to a fish being reeled in as the catch.

His instincts told him that he should be in control, but with Jemma, the balance of female-male roles never seemed safe. "Let go. Jemma, let go. Don't you have better things to do? Run down some potential backer and put a few more thousand in your piggy bank?"

She turned to him, hands on hips, eyes flashing. "I always do what has to be done, the same as you. Why would you expect less from me? I'm here for the duration, chum."

Hogan caught the glitter of tears on her lashes before she turned from him. He turned her gently to him, lifting her chin with his fingertip. "What's wrong?"

She shoved his hand away, then caught it, turning the abused palm upward. "That's what's wrong. You hold everything in—"

She sucked in her breath when he bent to brush his lips across hers. "Oh, no. Not that. You want to distract me, and you're not doing it. You just let me put some salve on those hands—"

"You're relentless." But Hogan wanted her touch, he needed that warmth and vibrant life wrapped around him.

"The cabin doesn't have a door or a roof," she noted, cleansing his hands carefully, her hair gleaming in the shadows. "You came up here to brood and it seems my lot to take care of you, because no one else will bother to tell me anything about fishing. They just look scared and pale and hurry away to hide."

"Now I wonder why they would do that. The hardware for the door and shutters is still there." Hogan watched Jemma squeeze ointment onto his torn hands, carefully working it in with her fingertips. "Why are you doing this?"

When they lifted to his, her eyes were bright. "Because I know your hands aren't the only shredded places in you now. You've always stood beside everyone else, Hogan. Don't you think it's time you let us stand by you?"

He swallowed the emotion clogging his throat, and looked away to his mother's grave, the weeds torn away. Her hands gentle upon his face, Jemma turned him back to her. She traced his eyebrows with her thumbs and her touch reached inside him, soothing that black churning torment. "Let me help, Hogan. I want to."

"You're not going to stop anyway," he said, feeling condemned and not quite so alone. A painful emotional fist slammed into his midsection as he looked at the cabin Ben and Willow had shared.

She stood on tiptoe and kissed his cheek. "You just sit down here." Jemma eased him down beside a tree and settled behind him. She wrapped her arms around his back and her legs around his thighs, placing her cheek on his bare back. She turned to kiss his back occasionally, then replaced her cheek against him.

Hogan sucked in his breath as she began to rock him gently, and unused to being held, asked cautiously, "Are you trying to cuddle me? Is this something you got in a therapy class?"

"Yep. I always wanted to, but you were always so big and tough and cold-looking. I knew you were hurting, Hogan, but you never failed Aaron or Carley. If Carley hadn't had you back then, proving that men could be gentle and honest and safe, I don't know what would have happened to her. Ben didn't show that softness, the way you did. He wouldn't have a cat in the house, and you smuggled in a kitten for her every night and put it out in the morning before Ben knew. You've been there through the years for everyone, seeing after them, worrying about their lives, when you need now to look after whatever troubles you—"

"I'm a little bit big to cuddle." Hogan closed his eyes and gave himself to her gentle rocking, her body enfolding his. He caressed her ankles, and, for once, the orange shoes in his lap didn't jar his esthetic sense. "You're going to want something major for this, aren't you?"

She gently circled his temples with her fingertips. "Yes, I am. I want you to sit still and enjoy the birds chirping and the stream gurgling—"

"And then what? An examination of my relationship to Ben?" he asked, wary of her.

"Nope. Just this." She smoothed his hair back from his face, toyed with it, and Hogan fought a sigh of pleasure. Just as he was settling into the softness of her breasts, easing his back against her, she asked, "Better?"

When he nodded, wondering how this woman could charge into his shadows and ease his pain, Jemma squirmed free and hurried to her bedroll. She brought it back and placed it carefully in front of him, unrolling it. When Hogan could tear his gaze away from the shifting feminine flesh surging over the yellow tube top, he hooked a finger into the crevice between her breasts and tugged lightly. "Is this an invitation?"

He wanted her desperately, to soothe his tangled emotions, to bury himself so deep in her that—

"Hardly. Stop that now, Hogan—you're leering. Wait until you see what Ben sent. I wanted you in the right mood before—" With her expression alight, Jemma handed Hogan battered, old sketchbooks. "They were hers. He wanted you to have them. They were up in the attic all the time. I picked that camelback trunk's lock when I was fifteen and asked Ben who drew the pictures. He said his 'first sweetheart,' and I asked for them now. I thought you'd want to—" Jemma studied Hogan and eased to sit by him, her arm looped around his shoulders, leaning close to him.

The pages were yellowed with age, but Ben's face was there—younger, softer, and definitely a boy in love. Willow had sketched him as a leggy, happy youth, showing off for his girl with his lariat, jumping in and out of the loop. Another sketch was that of a girl, dressed in a fringed shift, standing beside Ben in a shaft of moonlight, their hands linked. Hogan forced air into his lungs, his chest filling with pain—*his mother*. He studied the sketches of mountains and flowers, and the camas meadow, filled with flowers—and the small gold ring that lay in Jemma's open palm. "This was hers, a gift from Ben. For their wedding, she made him a doe-skin shirt, and he wants you to have that, too. It's beaded and—oh, Hogan, you look so—"

Overcome, he rubbed his face, memories of Ben carrying him on his shoulders, rocking him in the night, slashing at him.

Jemma took his hand and placed the small ring on the tip of his little finger and stroked his hair. "In their hearts, they were married. He knew how he treated you was wrong, but he didn't know how to—He was just a boy, Hogan, and faced with survival and a newborn son. I think for a time, he blamed you for taking her life—"

She caught Hogan's arm as he started to rise. "Oh, no you're not. You're not running away now, not after you've come so far. He said you were named after your great-grandfather on Ben's mother's side—an Irishman named Hogan. When Ben was only a boy, she died of overwork and Aaron's harshness. He wanted you to have a part of her and the sunlight old Aaron couldn't spare. That old camelback trunk has more of your mother's things. Ben said that he always wanted to go to Ireland to seek out her relatives, but he never did. He said you'd probably 'get the job done.' ''

She leaned her head against Hogan's shoulder, and he shot an arm around her, keeping her close, an anchor when his life was spinning around him. He circled the stunning new emotions of who he was and the explanation of the link between himself and Joe Blue Sky, his uncle. Now that Ben had relented, Joe would tell him about Willow, what she was like, how she felt about Ben. All the pieces came spinning together, winding Hogan and tightening his throat.

Filled with emotion, Hogan grabbed Jemma's wrist and tugged her into his lap. He held her tight, his face pressed against her throat, her arms wrapped around him, her fingers soothing his hair. He gripped the small ring in his fist, held Jemma and wondered when the world had ever been right. "You just don't give up, do you?"

"Not when the merchandise is worth fighting for— mmm!" Jemma pushed at Hogan's shoulders as he took her face in his hands, taking her mouth without tenderness. Her widened eyes, that flash of fear, told him that he'd surprised and hurt her.

Unable to tell her of his need, damning himself for hurting her, Hogan looked away to a raven, gleaming blue black in the sun.

"Oh, no, you don't! You're not going inside yourself again. Not when those beautiful eyes are so sad and lonely." Jemma pushed him away, rose lithely to her feet, her back turned to him, her arms hugging her body. The sunlight shooting through the fir and spruce trees framed her slender body, and Hogan knew her emotions tore at her. He rose slowly, his thumb smoothing the little ring on his finger and walked to stand behind her.

She edged away from him, as though she couldn't

bear to have anyone near her. "You haven't anything to do with what I'm feeling now. I'm not frigid with you, am I? Oh, no, you've got great hands, through you've tried to butcher them."

"If I touch you too suddenly, you get that panicked look—I want to know why. That day I hauled you out of the ranch house over my shoulder, there was just that moment of fear before you started calling me names— not pretty names, by the way."

"You don't give up either, do you?" she demanded bitterly. She spun to him, eyes bright with tears, body rigid and shaking.

"Come here." Hogan tugged her into his arms and held her tight, pushing her damp face into the shelter of his throat and shoulder. He smoothed her hair, found her scalp and gently rubbed as she locked her arms around him.

Her body shook as she fought the sobs tearing out of her. "It was a real mess, my brothers and sisters—immature, selfish parents—There are parents with large families, who love and care for them. Mine just didn't care."

He held her close and safe against him, wishing he could do more than give her soft words and after a time, she quieted. "When I was visiting here, that mechanic in town caught me at the garage—he's still working there, leering as always. Carley was with Ben at the feedstore, and you'd come back to check on me. Rather you were disgusted that you had to check on me—the pest, the bane of the Sasquatches' lives. I had to have that new brand of candy bar. You don't remember that, do you?"

Hogan fought through the years, seeing a frightened little leggy girl backed up against the dirty walls, Jackson Reeves sneering down at her.

"That was when I knew what men were supposed to be. You said, 'Go find Ben, little girl, and tell him I'll be a little late.' You spoke so softly, ice ran up my spine. I told Ben that Jackson had frightened me, and you'd be late, and I saw terrifying anger in his expression. 'Come here, little girl,' he said just as softly as you had. 'It's about time we bought you a pretty blue ribbon for that red hair. And Hogan will be along in a little bit.' I was shocked—Ben had always complained about spending money foolishly. But then, he held my hand, put his arm around me, and wiped away my tears. 'You didn't do anything wrong, honey,' he said."

She lifted her cheek to Hogan's, shuddering in the aftermath of long repressed emotion. "*I didn't do anything wrong*. All those years, all those dirty situations when I was growing up, I thought I had. And I see Carley trapped in the same nightmare. I love her—she's my sister, really. One I can protect. I watched you and your brothers and Ben more closely after that, and I saw this really beautiful thing—I thought of you as the Knights of the Round Table. Despite all the furious wars between you, all of the Kodiaks really cared about each other. They care now."

"Maybe." Hogan wasn't certain of his emotions, scrubbed raw by Ben's too-late revelation of Willow.

Jemma shoved free and Hogan admired the way she pushed herself back into one Jemma-piece. He wondered how many times she'd had to do that, pulling herself together and putting up her shields. She turned to him, pale and clearly battling for control. "There. You know your mother now—in your heart. I've had a nice little cry. What's next?"

She straightened her shoulders and pushed back her hair, looking at the small cabin—Jemma–in flight, ready to take on anything to push away her past. "What's next? A roof? How are we going to do that without a lumberyard nearby? Hogan, I think that—''

He traced her still-damp cheek with his fingertip. Jemma's energy was throbbing between them, and he wondered at her strength to go on as she had. She'd battled to survive and collected her buttons, keeping those she loved close. "Ease up, sweetheart. Take it easy—stop running. There is just you and me and nothing to do, but rest and heal.''

She threw out her hands, shaking with emotion, her eyes swollen from tears. "I don't know how,'' she cried helplessly.

"Well, that's what I'm for,'' Hogan murmured, and drew her into his arms. He was just settling in for a deep, exotic taste of Jemma when she tensed and exploded out of his arms. "Jemma, come back here.''

She dug into her jeans. "I forgot. Here—'' She took the small ring from his finger and slipped a gold chain through it. She eased it over his head, and when it lay gleaming on his chest, she patted it. "There. Courtesy of Ben. He's started wearing his wedding ring again. He doesn't need the chain.''

When Hogan inhaled, shaken by emotion, and looked up at the spruce limbs filtering the sunlight, Jemma held his face and brought it down to hers. The tiny, gentle kisses she trailed all over his face left Hogan a little woozy and uncertain. He wanted to push her away, to shield himself, and yet he couldn't move, his hands locked to her waist. "You big lug,'' Jemma whispered softly, sliding into his arms and resting her head upon his shoulder.

Hogan stood for a long time, wrapped in a shaft of sunlight, the knowledge of who his mother was, who he was, and the soft, soft woman in his arms. He filled his hands with her hair, absorbing the silky warmth as he gathered her closer.

"What's that sound?" Jemma asked, tilting her head.

"The wind sweeping down from Crazy Mountains. One of the old legends says it's the sound of the Celestial Virgins crying."

She nestled against him. "That's so sad, Hogan. Do you really think that old legend is true—that they took the Chinese women into the mountains? When they were of no more use?"

"Most of the mines are up north and there were Chinese in Fort Benton, but there were only a few prospectors here. But it is possible. Back then, the Chinese were used, discarded, and memory of them erased."

Jemma's smile curled against skin. "But you young studs liked to believe in that legend, in rescuing those Celestial Virgins. I heard you talking about it too many times."

"Jemma, dear heart. If the most beautiful Celestial Virgin strolled out of the woods right now, buck-naked and begging for me, I wouldn't look at her. I'm too busy looking at you."

Jemma's eyes widened, then she grinned and leaped up on him, circling his hips with her legs. "Liar."

With his hands supporting Jemma's soft bottom, her heat burning his stomach, and her tiny butterfly kisses cruising over his face, Hogan let himself float.

Aaron levered himself away from Savanna's welcoming, moist body, his heart still pounding after a fierce coupling. "What do you mean, I'm not suitable husband material?" he asked roughly.

Savanna smiled that pleasured feminine way, her voice lazy in the afternoon shadows of her bedroom. "You're not going to settle down, Aaron. I want children and a home and a husband who isn't drooling over other women.''

Aaron shoved himself to his feet. ''Richard Coleman?''

''You idiot.'' Her words had an unexpected edge, surprising him. Savanna came to her feet, her long sleek black hair swaying around her slender body. ''You absolute idiot. I've got to get back to the clinic. I think it's best if you don't come around anymore.''

''I'll be around,'' Aaron said, meaning it. He didn't like Savanna's ability to set him aside, to move on with her plans for that husband and kids. ''I like kids,'' he muttered after she'd closed the bathroom door behind her.

Aaron pushed open the door and stepped into the steamy shower with Savanna. ''Exactly what is wrong with me? I haven't looked at another woman since I've come back.''

''Do my back, will you?'' Savanna turned and lifted her hair. ''It's called a bit more than sex, lover. I want a man with staying power. I'm going to be an old hag one day, and I want to know that he won't move on then, or when I'm pregnant with his baby—''

Aaron turned her roughly and when Savanna frowned at him, he dropped his hands. ''You think that's what I'd do?'' he demanded.

''Maybe. I have to be sure, and when I meet him, I'll know. Just like that. Something in me will go click, and that's what I want.''

''So I don't make you go 'click'?'' Aaron caressed her wet full breasts. Without her clothing, Savanna was even more delicious—

''Not like that, lover. But in other ways, you know you do. It's the relationship, Aaron. We don't really have one. Sex is just the frosting. I want the cake.''

An hour later, Aaron stormed into the house and slammed the door. He'd never had a relationship with a woman beyond the sex. But Savanna was worth any effort. He was revved, the way he felt with a new account that he did not intend to lose. She not only challenged him, she excited him in a way no other woman had. Just watching her pleased him, the simplest movement of her hands fascinated him.

If Savanna found him lacking as a potential husband and father, he'd change her mind. Savanna was a sticking-long-term kind of woman, a novelty to him— and no other man was putting his ring on her finger. Aaron had found what he wanted—all he had to do was make himself appealing to her. "Carley," he called, "where are Jemma's men and women's relationship books?"

The old house stood quietly in the Montana sun, a contrast to the blazing battles and life in the past month. Aaron let the house's memories seep into him—how it might have been if Dinah hadn't left . . . After a minute, Ben's bedroom door opened slowly and he leaned against the door. Aaron recognized the look of a man who had just left a woman's arms. With his shirt hastily thrown on, and the right leg of his jeans dangling empty, Ben looked dazed and woozy. His voice had that deep lazy tone of a man who'd been thoroughly satisfied. "Carley and Mitch aren't here. He took her to visit old Mrs. Coleman."

"Who's that, Ben?" Dinah asked from inside the bedroom, her voice soft and sultry, a feminine match to Ben's.

"It's our son," Ben answered, meeting Aaron's dark look evenly. "I started wearing my wedding ring again, son. I never stopped loving your mother."

Aaron swallowed back the fear that once again everything would be torn apart. Dinah would tear Ben apart, and the yelling would start, hurting everyone. Resisting the bitter accusations tearing through his mind and the painful memories, he turned and walked out the door.

In the roofless cabin, smoke and ashes drifted up to the starlit sky. Hogan sat with his back against the log wall, legs extended, studying the small fire. He listened to the stream running in the distance, the night breeze whispering through the branches of the tree over his mother's grave. "Willow was her name," he mouthed, taking care not to wake Jemma, sleeping at his side. He glanced at the makeshift door Jemma had insisted upon. The door was silly and weak, easily pushed aside, yet he'd fashioned it for her—to make her feel safe. He hadn't told her that it wouldn't stop a jackrabbit, much less a bear.

But the enclosure silenced the eerie howling, the wind blowing down from the rugged, jutting stone peaks of the Crazy Mountains. Jemma couldn't bear to think of the women—suffering, lost souls who could never rest until their bones were returned to China.

Jemma slept restlessly. She flopped her arm across his jeans-clad thighs, and he circled her slender wrist with his fingers, amazed at how such a strong woman could be so delicately made. She mumbled, and Hogan reached his other hand to smooth her hair; with a sigh, Jemma slid back into sleep.

Hogan's shadows had eased, but he knew that they would return. For the moment, he let the sound of Jemma's breathing, her slender wrist claimed by his hand, the warmth of her hair flowing between his fingers, calm him. He eased aside the hair shielding her face, ran his thumb down her cheekbone and jaw and studied the shadowy spikes created by her lashes upon her cheeks. His hand tightened on her wrist. He knew what drove her to push and shove, her desperate need for money, and why—just then, when he would reach for her too suddenly, fear would flicker in those smoky gray eyes.

She'd torn away his shadows, refusing to let go, challenging him when he would have turned away. When they made love, each time was more—giving and taking, the pleasure sweeter.

Jackson Reeves would have had her that day, a little girl against his brutality. Jackson was a definite possibility for Carley's attacker.

Hogan forced thoughts of Jackson away, stroked Jemma's wrist, and found her slow, sleeping pulse and pulled peace into him. *Willow. Her name was Willow.*

Images and shapes moved softly within him, and he knew that Jemma had torn at his shadows. He listened to his heart, to the life within it, all the pieces filled with life. Colors came moving into shapes, concepts blending with the flow of horses and the land, with rocks, hidden and yet so clear, an insight into nature and man, given to him from his mother.

Jemma awoke to the scent of wildflowers scattered across her sleeping bag and Hogan stripping away his jeans. He stood in the shaft of moonlight piercing the open roof, a tall shadowy man with broad shoulders, lean body, and long, powerful legs. His gleaming eyes found hers and instinctively, she knew of his desperation, that need to lock his body to hers as he had during the day. The excitement of Hogan's primitive need tore away sleep and fatigue, tore away her own drained emotions.

He had taken her gently, soothing her and giving her pleasure without the wild storms, but now they rode him, and he'd called her from sleep to ride with him there in his shadows, matching him. She had to meet Hogan, a fierce and gentle lover, on equal terms, not letting him take her easily.

The flowers were symbolic, a man giving a present to a woman he wanted, and she gripped a mountain daisy in her hand as she pushed away the sleeping bag and stood, wearing only his T-shirt and her briefs.

Earlier, they'd been tender lovers, soothing the dark rivers within them, but now came the fierce cleansing they both needed. She faced him, unafraid of walking into his storms and shadows. Bracing herself, Jemma knew that words weren't needed. He'd come to her, and she'd take him on her terms.

Taking care, she wove the long daisy stalk into Hogan's hair, fashioning a small braid along his face. Hogan studied her face, swept her hair back from it. Then his other hand found the elastic in her briefs, traced it around her leg and stroked her gently, that deep dark moist feminine softness. She thought her legs would give way; she gripped the small ring resting on his chest, binding him to her, her fist upon the hard proud beat of his heart.

To keep herself from melting into the wonderful stroking of his hand, Jemma gripped his arm, took strength from the rippling hard muscles, and locked her gaze with Hogan's dark, heated one. His features were harsh in that shaft of moonlight, eyes glowing in the deep-set shadows. She inhaled sharply as his fist wrapped in the fine cloth and tore it slowly, as he watched her reaction, almost testing her to see if she could meet his challenge and his need—the testing of a woman by the man who had sought her.

The silky wad of her briefs sailed into the smoldering fire, sparks igniting and ashes floating upward with the smoke. Through the elemental pounding of her desire, she understood the ceremony. Hogan would do more than make love with her; he wanted her to know that she was a part of him, deep down where no one else had reached.

Jemma gloried in that, lifted her head, and sucked in her breath when he edged the hem of the T-shirt slowly upward, then lifted it away. Hogan wanted nothing between them, no shadows, no memories, just the night and each other. She wanted the same, proud of the desire in his expression as he looked down her body, that honed taut masculine look she loved—or did she love the man? In her heart, she knew whatever happened now would be binding to them both, forging them together in a way not easily broken—

His large hands smoothed her body, following the curves and indentations, the softness of her belly, the soft fragrant nest of reddish curls between her legs. He inhaled shakily, nostrils flaring as his hands flowed to her breasts, covering them. She could feel his heavy arousal jutting against her, demanding to fill her. Heat poured from Hogan, flowing into her body, as he smoothed her back, caressed her bottom, his body gently nudging the entrance to hers.

She eagerly met his demanding, seeking mouth, shivered as he lifted her easily, suckling one breast and then the other. The laving of his tongue and the gentle bites jolted her lower body, tightening it, and then Hogan eased her down to the bedroll. His hands were trembling now, flowing over her as hers were smoothing his body. Muscles surged in his thighs, his breath harsh and unsteady as it swept across her breasts, his mouth open and hot upon her. She found him with her thighs parted, and allowed him entrance.

He filled her instantly, withdrawing only to return, his hands going under her hips, lifting her, her arms tight around him. Pleasure tempered with hunger and primitive needs drove them deeper, skin against damp skin, kisses so hot they branded, heartbeats racing against the ultimate pleasure, fingers digging deep, locking them together in the flow toward fire—

She cried out, and again, Hogan's rough shout echoing in the small moonlit cabin as pleasure riveting them on that edge, bodies becoming one, burning away all else.

When Jemma surfaced, there amid the flowers he'd given her, she gathered Hogan closer, because she knew they'd love again and from his taut, still-throbbing body, she knew it would be soon. They'd found not only heat within each other, but another part of the whole. Lying beneath Hogan's pleasant weight, stroked lazily by his hands, his uneven breath upon her damp skin, she knew she'd never be the same. She knew that her life centered on this man, and, whatever else happened, he would be true to this moment.

The second time, he loved her tenderly and slowly, and when finally he drew her to his side, to rest upon his shoulder, bodies entwined, Jemma drifted pleasantly . . . she'd come home—"What's that sound?" she whispered drowsily, aware that Hogan's body had tensed around hers, his hand had stopped sifting through her hair.

Then his fingers found her scalp, soothing her. "Only an owl. Just an owl in the night. Go to sleep."

"What was that Old Joe Blue Sky used to say about the owl hooting like that?"

"Just an old superstition. Shh. Sleep."

As he gathered her closer, she wondered about the

incredible sadness in his voice. "Hogan, tell me what Old Joe said about the owl."

Hogan inhaled slowly. "He said someone would die— that the owl was coming for an earth spirit."

# fourteen

June lay softly upon the Montana morning, the Crazy Mountains rising over the pastures and the foothills. Old Joe Blue Sky had been found along the road, his heart given out, and Hogan would miss him. Hogan knew now why Joe's stares at him seemed so familiar. His uncle—Willow's half brother—would never tell him about her.

But Hogan had found an ease with Jemma, and though he'd miss Joe and always wonder about his mother, life with Jemma didn't allow much time for grieving. The peaceful scene matched Hogan's emotions as he sat outside on his front porch, overlooking Ben Kodiak's ranch. Jared Morgan, Hogan's second-in-command, was on the speaker phone in New York. "Get those very expensive Italian loafers off my desk, Jared," Hogan said, smiling as he heard the rustle of papers.

"Your sixth sense is uncanny," Jared grumbled as a chair creaked. "These sketches aren't your usual. The Fire Feathers pieces will require the right woman to wear them—a special woman. That vibrant style will overpower a good percentage of our faithful buyers. It's very—primitive, like . . ."

"Like fire and wind riffling a passionate woman with red hair?" Hogan asked, and grinned when Jared let out a low whistle.

"A pagan goddess. I've been looking for a woman like that all my life. You find one, and you let me know."

Hogan chuckled and realized that the happy sound ran clear through him. He rolled his shoulders and stretched, contented for the first time in years. "Fat chance. She's mine and she's certified, one-hundred-percent pagan goddess. Go ahead with the marketing—"

"Can't tear yourself away from Montana? You usually like to be in the middle of things."

"I am." Hogan knew at any moment the Kodiaks could explode, and it would be hell pulling them back together—but they would, to defend Carley. The attacker was taking his time, and Carley was certain to find that Ben was in perfect health. Jemma would stand to lose a friend she loved. "Just fax me the discussion from marketing. I'll input from here. I'm considering a citrine pendant for Fire Feathers, but it's only a thought now."

"Wow. That will be a necklace for a goddess-type with enough color and personality to carry it. Do you want Simone sent a copy of this? You usually do. She's been asking about you."

"No. I'll tend to Simone myself. On second thought, send her a copy." Hogan wanted his former lover and long-term friend to be prepared for his call; she'd know by his new work that his life had changed. They would remain friends, but he didn't want Jemma upset by Simone's careless endearments. He wanted no doubt in Jemma's mind that he was taking his vow to be true seriously. He clicked off the line, took a satisfying sip of his morning peppermint tea, and placed the mug be-

side Jemma's. He liked the look of the two pottery cups
sitting together, as if they were meant to be and would
be every morning of their lives. However, if his brothers
discovered he was having morning peppermint tea—preparing and serving it to Jemma—he'd never recover
from their teasing.

With a sigh, Hogan picked up his old tackle box;
Jemma had destroyed its neat order and now lures, leaders, sinkers, and line were one colorful tangle. He began
to work free the mess and thought about how she looked,
casting her line and grumbling—and how she'd thrown
down her pole and how he'd thrown down his. After a
toe-to-toe argument about nymphs, wet and dry flies and
women who were too pushy and impatient, Jemma had
stalked off. Hogan had tackled her in a bed of wildflowers and—

They had a date for Saturday night. Asking a woman
for a date had been a novelty for Hogan, leaving him
excited. Jemma had flushed, looking away, because she
knew that he was taking their relationship to another
level. Just an old-fashioned date—taking his best girl to
dinner and a dance—and he was looking forward to
courting her. In the two weeks since he'd learned about
his mother, and Jemma had met him in that cabin, Hogan
knew another woman would never touch him inside like
that—never fit his body so perfectly. He ran his hand
over the small ring on his chest. For the first time in
Hogan's life, he had a sense of place and home, as if he
belonged.

Across the small valley, beyond the pastures of grazing cattle and horses, Ben was helping Dinah carry groceries; from the stance of their bodies, they were
arguing. Their arguments had a different tempo now, not
the hard, biting slashing, but more the sorting out of a
couple who had just found each other. Hogan suspected

that Ben liked to balk, just to get Dinah's full attention.

Aaron had been working a yearling in the corral, and when Savanna left the house after a visit with Maxi, he stopped. With one hand, he vaulted over the gate. A twirl of his lasso caught Savanna and Aaron slowly pulled her to him. He kissed her, and she stepped back, freeing herself of the lasso. She shoved her hands against his chest and stalked toward her compact car. When it shot away from the ranch yard, Aaron threw down his Western hat and swung up on the bare back of a good, fast quarter horse mare. The mare sailed over the fence and by taking the pasture route, Aaron would catch Savanna before she hit the main highway.

"Aaron, you'd better step back and give the lady time to think." Hogan knew that with Jemma, he wouldn't follow his own advice; he intended to build a stable relationship with a fast-moving, fast-talking, volatile woman. He placed all the mangled lures in a neat row, shaking his head at the bent hackles. Jemma didn't take time to replace them in the small protective sections of his tackle box. His office looked like a tornado had hit it, and somewhere in the house was a pair of lost shorts, rolled into a ball in his haste to bed her.

Jemma was using his office this morning, bargaining with a florist chain over specialty rocks cut with the names of herbs. The great modesty-panel-blouse war still raged. The manufacturer had upped the price tag, and as a middleman—woman, Hogan corrected, still a little off-balance from lovemaking on the kitchen table— Jemma didn't want her cut lowered. Hogan planned to take her riding that afternoon, just to watch her backside bounce in the saddle, that shimmering flow to her breasts and the high color on her cheeks. He grinned and wondered if he remembered how to trick ride and show off a bit—

Jemma crashed out the front door and stalked the length of the porch, tangling her bare feet in the line Hogan had let drop beside his chair. She hopped free on one foot and glared at him. "Don't just sit there grinning. I'm having a bad day."

"You felt pretty good an hour ago." He reached out to smooth her bare thigh and slide his fingers beneath the fringes of her jean cutoffs. She still wore that hot, wild, flushed look that could set him off in a heartbeat.

"Oh, yes, well, that little kitchen-table incident. You really shouldn't walk around naked, Hogan. I just came over here this morning to use your office—and there you were, strolling around buck-naked and fresh from your shower. You had water beads on your shoulders and that hoop in your ear and that raw, untamed sultry look that just makes me want to take you down. There's so much of you that no woman could—"

Hogan studied Jemma stalking across the front porch, sunlight creating a fiery halo around her hair, her body taut and her sassy mouth burning the morning air. She moved him in a way he could not yet fathom to the fullest, but he knew that he wanted a home and a family of his own. Perhaps the natural urge to make his mark, to carry on his blood had drawn him home, but Jemma had given him an understanding that was far beyond the hard, fast lock of their bodies. She'd given him tenderness. He cherished that silly little daisy she'd woven in his hair that night he'd come to her. Flat and dried, it was tucked safe in his wallet, where he could pull it out in the quiet moments and think back to what he considered his wedding night.

"I want you to think about moving in with me," he said very carefully. Jemma was still nervous around him. While Jemma had kept close to Carley, she'd never really shared her life, nor had he. He wanted to prove to her that they had a lasting, comfortable, and growing relationship—and he wanted to romance the lady he had chosen.

Hogan wasn't certain that he had romantic qualities, but he would try—because Jemma deserved everything he could give.

He sensed Jemma emotionally backing away, as she walked to the big pots of herbs and crouched to run her hand across the chives. She'd made changes in his house, and while they were unfamiliar and feminine, he liked the softer elements of plants and herbs, bringing the natural world inside his home.

Jemma stood and turned to him, her face pale and serious. "I'm here quite a bit, Hogan. There's no need for me to move in."

"I want to wake up to you in my bed every morning." The statement was too bald in the morning air, and Hogan wondered how Jemma would react. "I have never stayed with any other woman all night, sweetheart."

Frustration wrapped around Hogan like a cloak as Jemma took her time, breaking a fragrant lacy leaf from a scented geranium stalk. She drew it beneath her nose, watching him. "I've been married, Hogan. I gave everything, and it didn't work. I tried to be something I'm not."

"Have I asked you to be anyone but who you are?"

"I felt cramped and contained—stifled. I like to travel, to move around a lot, and you're so scheduled, so intense. You'll need a woman who can support your talent, play the hostess. I like to be out there, wrangling for myself. There's all sorts of obligations when you live with someone. I've got a lot of things going at the same time and you—"

Hogan inhaled slowly. "You're evading the real is-sue. I'm getting the picture that I might be boring.''

"You know you're not, and you're just wanting to brood. You're not happy unless you can brood, Hogan. All of you Kodiaks are that way. I've come to accept that that's your level of happiness—brooding.'' Jemma smoothed his shoulder. "I have to be with Carley until this is over, Hogan. I'd never forgive myself if he came for her one night and again I wasn't there for her. You know that my feelings for you are unique, but—''

Hogan wrapped his hand around her wrist. He intended to keep her; she'd already taken his heart. "I'll wait. We'll finish any danger to Carley, and then I'm coming for you.''

"You're not done hating Ben. I don't want to be a part of that. I don't want to know that while you're making love to me, you're hating a man I respect—that you could hurt him.''

"You're making excuses and putting Ben between us.'' Hogan wasn't letting anyone else do his resolves for him. "You're setting conditions—terms, aren't you? My relationship with Ben hasn't stood between us so far.''

"It might. I'd be stuck between the two of you, men I respect and—men I like—hacking away at each other.''

" 'Like?' '' He picked up the word, cradled it close to his heart, and hoped that Jemma meant more. She tried to tug her wrist away, but Hogan held her still, using little force. Her hand turned, caught his tightly.

"I thought marriage would work the first time, but after we were together, it was as if I couldn't breathe— so much was expected of me. I really did not like the confinement. We'd fight all the time—look at you, you can't stand me using your things—''

"Jemma. You have a tackle box filled with high-priced lures. Because I catch trout does not mean my lures are better than yours. There are things we wouldn't share. But I think we've got enough working on our side."

"You can think, that's the problem. I can't think when I'm around you. One hot dark look from you and I start—" She caught herself and ran her hand across the knotted T-shirt on her stomach. "My ulcer is acting up. Hogan, what am I going to do about getting those blouses? I could lose a fortune. Here's the deal—" She launched into animated, fast story about a temperamental designer and a good manufacturer she could lose. "Ordinarily, I'd be wining and dining, but I don't want to leave Carley now. And I'm doing so well with my fly fishing, don't you think? I mean Les is certain to be impressed."

Hogan wanted to keep on track while Jemma was escaping, freewheeling through her profit margins. He needed a little reassurance, and stopped her hands toying with his hair—"Let's get back to where you start—start what with me?"

"Stop pushing. You are so intense. I start . . . simmering, ok?" She tugged the braid she had just done beside his face. "You're grinning, you arrogant piece of—That's what you wanted to hear, wasn't it?"

"I wanted to hear something else, but that will do." Hogan didn't want to think about Jemma cornering Les Parkins for the television pilot, and tried to subdue the jealousy skittering up his nape. He had definite plans to have Jemma move in with him, to share his life with her, not just a fast coupling between the other Kodiak's problems. He put the tackle box aside, then found a horsehair lure that Joe had helped him make years ago. The memories curled around him, an uncle he'd never known had died, found along the roadside. Now he'd never know what Joe could tell him, but he understood the looks they'd shared, the tangling of blood and of a woman who bonded them together. Who bound them to Ben.

She moved away from him, and Hogan knew she was closing doors that he wasn't ready to be have shut. "What's the real reason, past all this manure?"

She hesitated, then turned to him, tears in her eyes. "Deep down, you're a family man, Hogan. You love children. Someday, you should have someone who wants children, too. I don't. I've put in my time of changing diapers and midnight feedings, and terrified one of my brothers or sisters would die of the flu or a cold—I don't want children, Hogan. I helped my mother through childbirth, I've fed and washed diapers and toted babies on my hip when I was no more than a baby myself. That means regular meals, laundry, and colic. I've been through that nightmare."

"I haven't asked for children, Jemma. I just want you." But he wanted children, deep down inside, as she had said. Life flowing on, like the salmon coming back to its origins to spawn, a little piece of himself to hold and know that life would go on—but he could do without that need, if he had Jemma.

"It would always be there in your eyes—the way you look at children, play with them, and I'm not the woman for that, Hogan." Jemma's tears shimmered in the sunlight, her hand trembling as she slashed them away. "I don't know if I have maternal instincts—my mother certainly didn't. The whole thing is wrong, Hogan. You'll see that, sooner or later, and I'd hate myself. I'd see that need every time you held someone else's child."

"Come here." He wanted to hold her, to give her comfort, to take away those early painful memories. If he got up and went to her, Jemma would balk. If she came to him, there was just a chance—

Jemma slashed away her hair and glared at him, fighting her past and the link between them that was more than the locking of their bodies. "I'm in a fix, Hogan. The least you can do is listen. I stand to lose a fortune."

"I'll listen. Come here." He wasn't pushing her, forcing her into anything. Would she trust him to hold her now, while she was fighting herself and her past?

The intricacies of dealing with a woman he wanted fascinated Hogan. He wasn't certain that she would stay or leave. A little trickle of fear shot up his spine. Handling Jemma's fast-moving emotions was a real challenge. If he moved too slowly, he was in trouble—too fast, and he'd step in the proverbial cow pile.

She came to him and let herself be drawn down onto his lap. Hogan kissed her damp cheeks, and she leaned back against him, momentarily drained by her emotions. Hogan relaxed, settling into the unfamiliar peace she gave him, gathering her closer before she started wiggling to be free and running into her world of bargains. "You're getting the blouses—the bosoms of the world will be covered from the horror of button-gap."

She turned to him, her hair flying out around her face like a firestorm. "What?"

"The designer likes my work. I agreed to design a small logo for her. It's a tradeoff. The carved herb stones are headed for a warehouse. You've got the exclusive on them."

"*What?*"

Hogan smiled, a little heady with his success—presenting the woman he wanted with her desires. He stroked her thigh, enjoying the slender feminine strength, the leggy shape that ran up into—

He bent to kiss her parted lips, and Jemma eased back,

her eyes smoky gray. "Let me get this straight. You entered my business deals."

He nodded, feeling good about helping her. "You've been talking about how much you wanted both deals. I just added a little weight to your bargaining table."

"Did you really? Did I ask you to interfere? To help me?"

Hogan frowned, trying to understand where he had erred—her furious expression did not bode well. "Jemma, I was trying to help."

"*Did I ask you to fix things for me?*" She bolted off his lap and stalked down his porch stairs. She gripped the reins of the saddled horse she'd used to ride to him and then retied them on the hitching post. "You are so dense, Hogan Kodiak. I do my own deals, got it? You were just supposed to listen, not try to fix anything. *Did I ask for your help*?"

Hogan inhaled slowly, feeling as if he'd been broadsided. The intricacies of pleasing Jemma had escaped him. "Next time, I'll just ask if you need my help, honey," he muttered, and wondered where the beautiful morning had gone wrong. She slammed into the house, and he was fast learning that life with the woman he wanted was not a clearly marked trail.

"Hogan!" He closed his eyes and wondered if he'd waded into another taboo-land as Jemma eased out of the front door, carrying a large painting.

"I was looking for more fly-tying supplies in the closet and—This is Carley on that night she was attacked. This is why you don't paint anymore. You see her horror in your mind," Jemma said quietly, studying the painting that Hogan had been unable to throw away.

He looked away from Carley's large haunted eyes, the shadows around her girlish face, her mouth parted in a silent scream that had echoed in Hogan for years. In the distant pasture, he found Carley–the woman in the field, racing from Mitch, and when he caught her, he held her high in his arms. Mitch twirled her around, then slipped her down to kiss her. Hogan rubbed the ache in his chest. "That's how she should have been years ago—happy."

Jemma placed Carley's portrait against the wall and came to stand beside him, her hand on his shoulder. "She's lost weight, and she's gorgeous with that new haircut."

"Thanks to you helping her."

"She's just awakening, thanks to Mitch's patience. When I first met her, I thought she was an angel with that pale hair and blue eyes. Then, with that so-innocent face, she lied to the teacher about something I'd done, protecting me—she still crosses her fingers behind her back when telling fibs—and I knew I'd love her forever. Look at them, Hogan. They're in love, and Carley doesn't know it," Jemma whispered.

He remembered when Mitch had first come to the Bar K, a sassy-mouthed, bitter street kid. Then Carley had given him an extra portion of chocolate cake heaped with ice cream, and Mitch had probably loved her from that moment. When Carley nursed his bruised hands, cleansing them and applying ointment, Mitch had lost his heart. He'd hidden that love for years, and now it was blooming—

"All my kids are growing up," Hogan mourned quietly, and drew Jemma into his lap again, needing her comfort. He placed his chin upon her head as they watched Carley break free and run from Mitch—their happy shouts carried across the pasture. For once, everything in the Kodiak family was as it should be—

"You came through for them, Hogan. You were a parent at an early age, too, and almost a parent to Ben when he was drinking after Dinah left. Where is this all going to end, Hogan?'' Jemma asked, smoothing his shoulder. The caress was still new to him, and he remembered an old scarred tomcat who leaned into petting as if he couldn't get enough.

"The right way. Sooner or later, we'll get whoever has been threatening her, but she needs to tell Ben and Dinah. It's all going to come out." Hogan had spoken to Aaron and Mitch about the need to expose the family's deep secrets.

He'd missed years of knowing who he was, because Ben hadn't revealed Hogan's mother—he knew the damage secrets and lies could do.

"Carley can't bear to tell them what happened that night. Don't ruin it now, Hogan. It's been so long since everyone was happy—if they ever were." Jemma smoothed his hair, twined it through her fingers, and Hogan leaned slightly into her touch, noting how she soothed the raw edges within him.

"You're always so practical. I know everything needs to come out, but it's just so nice now. Can't we let everyone be happy for just a bit more?"

With a sigh, Hogan let the heady peace overrule his sense that disaster loomed too close to the Kodiak family. He stroked Jemma's back and held her close. When she suddenly sat up, Hogan jerked back to safeguard his chin. From experience, he knew that Jemma's head, elbows, and knees were all potential weapons. She looked at him, her expression vividly alive. "I'll pose for you. You can paint me."

He snorted at that and studied the sun catching the varied shades in her hair. "You can't sit still long enough."

Jemma wiggled her eyebrows, leering at him. "Who said anything about sitting?"

\*   \*   \*

Mrs. Coleman was a birdlike shadow of a woman, confined to her wheelchair, an afghan covering her legs. She seemed more like a piece of furniture in the small cluttered parlor laden with keepsakes and doilies. "I'm so glad you came, girls. Goodness, it's hot for the second week of June," she said cheerfully, pouring tea into elegant china cups. "Richard, would you please get the tea cozy? We mustn't serve our lovely guests tepid tea. Goodness, Carley, but you're looking rosy. Jemma was always quite colorful, but you've blossomed into a beautiful young lady."

Jemma had just caught Mitch and Carley kissing in a closet, and Carley still wore that dazed, floating-in-heaven look. From the look of Mitch, he was steaming nicely and quite in love.

Mrs. Coleman glanced at the kitchen door, closing behind Richard, and leaned close to whisper to Jemma and Carley. "He's just like his father. He may seem sweet, but underneath he's a monster. He makes me take medicine that—"

Jemma met Carley's look. During their visits with her, Mrs. Coleman had seemed disoriented, confusing her son with his militant, demanding father.

"What was that you were saying, Mother?" Richard asked as he came back into the room.

"Oh, dear," Mrs. Coleman's hands trembled. "Only that I'm so tired, dear and that you're taking such good care of me. Maybe the girls would like to help me to my room."

Richard's thin face warmed in the dim light, filtered by the lace curtains at the window. "I will, Mother. It's time for your medicine anyway."

"Girls, you will take that box of old clothing and mend it? Before donating it to the church thrift shop? I'd appreciate that so much. I used to—"

"Come along, Mother," Richard said.

When Richard wheeled his mother away, Carley shook her head. "That's so sad. She was always so nice. She's lucky to have Richard. He's taking good care of her. But she says things like that when he's out of the room."

Through the lacy curtains, Jemma glanced at Hogan. He leaned against his pickup and waited for them as if he'd wait forever. Richard's two big Rottweilers didn't like the tall stranger; the dogs raising a furious row, pacing back and forth in their pens.

Jemma ached for Hogan's loss, for an uncle he'd never really known and for the mother he'd just discovered. She knew that she made him happy, and that he did not like the thought of her coddling a television producer—He'd stunned her, a man who had never spent all night with another woman, and who wanted her to live with him.

Hogan was, at his roots, an old-fashioned man, and Jemma knew that he wanted a commitment from her—she knew he was taking his time, that slow careful way he handled his life, and he wanted her. One dark sizzling look could take away her breath and make her skin tighten.

Richard came back into the room and frowned at the barking, furious dogs outside. "I should go quiet them. They are so excitable. Vicious dogs, but I need them for security."

He smiled at Carley and Jemma. "Would you like to see my collections? I built a room onto the back—quite the place, really. Perfect controlled humidity and quite the display of everything I've collected over the years."

"We'd love that, Richard," Carley said. "Wouldn't we, Jemma?"

Jemma shot a lingering, aching glance at Hogan and

watched as he walked to the penned dogs. He crouched and starting talking quietly with them. Hogan had a gentling way with animals, just as he did with her. The dogs quieted and Richard peered out the window. "How nice. Hogan always did have a way with animals."

Then he smiled, adjusted his thick glasses, and led them to the back of the house and into a huge, well-lighted room, layered with collections of butterflies, World War II memorabilia, stamps, and a carved jade collection. He leaned close to Carley as she studied a glass-enclosed display of opulent jewelry. "I still have the ring you gave me."

"You should wear it," Richard said briskly, and continued his tour of each collection. "Come back when you like. I'll let you try these pieces on—Jemma, you, too. Beautiful jewelry should be worn, but I've never—" He looked down at Carley and smiled. "I'm glad you've come back."

"I'm glad, too," Carley returned, and stood on tiptoe to kiss his cheek.

"I'm trying to pinpoint what is different about you," Richard said, running his hand across Carley's short boy cut. "It's not only the haircut. But you seem more alive, almost glowing. Carley, you've lost weight just since you've been here. Are you feeling all right?"

"I'm fine. Ranch work, you know. I'm riding again. Dad's got a great reiner. Richard, do you think Dad is okay—I mean feeling okay? Not sick or anything?"

"He's never come to me for a checkup, but just seeing him, I'd say he's the same as ever." Richard looked at her more closely. "Is there something else here that's changed you—are you certain you don't need to come in for an exam?"

"Maybe." She blushed and glanced at Jemma, who

knew that Carley had been thinking about lovemaking with Mitch.

When Jemma and Carley left the Coleman house, Mrs. Coleman peered down from the second-story window of the large, ornate house, giant ferns swaying gently on the porch. "Poor thing," Carley murmured. "Richard says she imagines the worst things. He's changing her medication."

But sitting next to Hogan, Jemma noted his silence, the hard set of his jaw. "Hogan?"

He smiled briefly, glanced at Carley, and placed Jemma's hand upon his hard thigh, his hand over hers. But he'd closed her away. Because she suspected Hogan was still mourning his mother and Joe Blue Sky, she raised her arm to the back of his seat and stroked his crisp blue-black hair. She sensed that he liked petting, though he'd never ask her to caress him. Experimenting, she eased her fingers down to his scalp and massaged as he had done to her. Hogan's dark eyes slid to hers, heat sizzling between them. "Stop that."

She flicked the tiny earring, and Hogan's expression softened; he reacted so nicely to play. He reached out his arm, circled her shoulders, and drew her against him, and Jemma glanced curiously at him. "Nope, never drove with my girl tight against me, either," he said.

Hogan could make her feel so wound-up, so young and waiting for the world to spin off its axis. Jemma looked at Carley, uncertain of how her best friend would react.

"I'm glad," Carley whispered. Just that, a simple blessing from a friend Jemma loved with all her heart, filled her with sunshine. She took Carley's hand and held it, because she was never letting her go—her best friend, an almost-sister.

\*     \*     \*

While the bumblebees hovered over the alfalfa blooms and the third week of June simmered on the huge bales of hay, Mitch's beautiful mouth curved as Carley drew the blade of grass around it. They'd just finished swimming—she fully dressed in a blouse and cutoff jean shorts, and he in his jeans. "Snake" had become a part of her life, and lying beside him in the hot June sun, she wondered about—Just there where his stomach flattened and ran into his sagging, wet jeans, and above his thighs. She wanted to touch him—when he tensed, she looked at him and blushed.

"Carley," he whispered, bringing her face down for a long sweet kiss.

"Do you want me?" she asked against his lips. How long had he been inside her heart? How long had she wanted this very gentle man? The light summer breeze moved through the willow branches above them as it always had—and Mitch was the same and yet different.

Mitch eased away, his hands trembling as they smoothed her face. "I've always loved you, Carley, right from that first moment. There's never been anyone for me, but you. When we make love, it will be with all my heart and soul."

"I saw your face that night—you were the first one there, and I never wanted you to see me again like that. I'll never forget how you looked as though you'd stepped into hell and were helpless to—"

"Shh. Are you afraid for me to look at you now?"

She lay down beside him as she had always done, her head resting on his shoulder. "No, and I want you. Now."

"Angel, nothing is going to happen to you. This ugliness will all be behind you soon. You're protected here and—"

She raised up and placed her hand over his lips. "You

beautiful man. My wanting you has nothing to do with fearing that my life will end before I've had the great Mitch-experience. Would you? Mitch, what if I—I mean, what if I get scared at the last minute and—''

''We'll stop.'' He made it sound so casual, leaving her to make choices, not forcing her.

But Mitch was already kissing her gently, drawing her closer there on the sunlit bank with the stream rolling by. His body trembled, and through her excitement, Carley knew that he leashed his needs for her. He'd been her brother and tormentor, he'd been her friend, and now he would be her lover. As she knew he would, Mitch was careful to use protection.

Later, lying shattered by the intensity of Mitch's gentleness, the way he insisted on cleansing her, Carley smiled. Floating in the aftermath of Mitch's care, she knew that their lovemaking wouldn't always be this way—that Mitch had been very careful with her this first time. She lazily smoothed his scarred back. She knew so little about him before he came to them; she knew the man that he was now, the tender loving man, taking care of her, teaching her how to move against him gently—always gently and asking, never forcing, even when his passion rode him. ''We didn't stop. You didn't have time to take off your shirt.''

Mitch tugged her hair. ''Proud of yourself, aren't you?''

''Umm. Very.''

Mitch's expression suddenly changed. He solemnly opened his hand over her soft belly, where babies could nestle and grow; his hopes were in his eyes. ''Someday I want—''

She placed her hand over his. ''I know. So do I.''

# fifteen

Jemma recognized Carley's dreamy expression when she came into one bedroom; the aftermath of Hogan's lovemaking left Jemma looking just that way. The lace curtains fluttered at the window; she drew them away to look at the three men squatting on bent knees in a circle near the barn. Hogan and Aaron's Western hats were all tipped at the back of their heads and Mitch's black waves gleamed in the sun. Ben leaned against the corral.

"I wonder what school teaches that?" she asked, as Carley came to stand by her side after a long, long time soaking in the bathroom. Carley's unmistakable rosy look hadn't dimmed, her blue eyes the color of cornflowers.

"The same one that teaches them how to spit, pee, and use their pocketknives to clean their fingernails, clean fish, and then cut cheese. The primitive male-bonding-ritual school," Carley answered, drawing back the curtains to study the men.

The tinkling of Dinah's new wind chimes floated up to them. Jemma put her arm around Carley's shoulders, and Carley placed her arm around Jemma's waist. "It's a good time, isn't it?" Jemma asked as they stood and rocked together. "What do you suppose they're talking about?"

"Soap operas. Dad is really into them—Aaron, too. Hogan has been too busy with you and Mitch—" Her breath caught and with her face aglow, she smiled up at Jemma. "Mitch is—"

"Mitch. He's always loved you."

"I can't believe it," Carley whispered in awe. "He wants to marry me. He wants children. He wants me to take my time and decide what I want. He'll live anywhere, but I think Montana is where I belong. He's got so much to offer, though. You've heard how he talks about the kids he's helping. I don't know that he can find that fulfillment in a rural area."

Jemma ruffled Carley's short damp hair. "He's waited a long time for you. It will work out."

"He's really a lot stronger than he looks. I mean, physically. He was just letting me toss him all those times. I think it was to boost my confidence."

"Men have so many delicate little hangups."

In the setting sun, the four men were grim. "Something set him off," Hogan said.

Aaron's voice was dark and deadly. "I had to take Artie Moore behind the clinic yesterday and sort things out. He came after Savanna for helping his wife. I got in trouble, too, with Savanna. She said she could handle it herself and blistered my backside. She had his grubby hand prints on her white uniform, and he'd torn away one sleeve, and she still expected me to stay out of it. If it's Artie who sent these—"

He flopped the envelope onto the dirt, and glossy pictures of Carley slithered out. "It could have been any photo shop in Seattle—he just had them forwarded here.

He probably gave them an alias that can't be traced."

"I thought we'd have to draw him out, but now I don't think so," Ben noted.

"Jackson Reeves is on the list, but he's obvious. He hasn't been out of town, but he could have had someone do it for him in Seattle." Hogan's stomach churned at the thought of Jackson touching Carley, then he looked up to meet the fury in Mitch's taut expression. "We'll get him, Mitch. It's just a waiting game now. He'll make a mistake and we'll be there."

Hogan knew that Mitch was in real danger of being taken down, rawhide style. "Supper will be ready soon. Ben, how about looking at that yearling I just bought?"

Ben eyed Mitch, who wasn't looking away. "I suppose you've got the wedding ring all picked out and haven't even asked her old man."

Mitch came up straight and tall, facing the man who had saved and raised him, whom he respected and loved. "We'll do that together, Carley and me, if she'll have me. But I'd like your blessing, Dad, because it means a lot to both of us."

"Huh," Ben said, his hard face shifting into emotion. "You'll be taking my little girl away from me."

"Think of it this way, Ben," Aaron said, and rose to his feet. "It's not like we're getting a stranger who can't handle his share of castrating calves."

Ben frowned at Mitch. "Castrating gets to be a real art."

"Ouch," Aaron said. "I'm going to see if I can find something to eat."

"You wash up," Ben said out of habit, though Aaron was long past the reminder age. Then Ben looked at Mitch, keeping the father-to-son relationship the same as always. "You, too."

In the pasture with Hogan, Ben watched the Appaloosa yearling race along the fence, tail high. "You're all leaving me. All grown-up and not needing whatever little I could give you."

"Carley will always be yours, and I have a hunch Aaron might stay. Savanna isn't going anywhere."

Ben turned to Hogan. "But not you. You'll pick up when this is done and go your own way. You're a hard ride, son. Like me. I suppose you're taking Jemma, if she'll have you."

"She hasn't made up her mind. I'm working on that; but she'll come back here. She won't forget you."

Ben swallowed harshly. "Skinny little thing, all eyes and jumping if you reached toward her too fast."

"I know. But you gave her something. She loves you, too." Hogan knew too well the fear leaping in Jemma's eyes. Her background led her to other fears, that of not having enough, never enough. He wondered if he could hold wind and fire and the heart of a woman badly scarred by other men.

Ben nodded slowly. "Well, the yearling is a good choice. That old barn cat had her kittens. You may as well take one home for your barn—or for Jemma. Women like little things like that. Your opinions matter. The other children listen to you. When did you become so wise, Hogan? When did you become a man that holds this family together? Did I take so much away from you? Your childhood?"

"I'm working through it, Ben." Hogan wondered at the changing relationship between his father and himself; they both loved the same people. Jemma had made a difference; she'd made him see Ben as a man who loved a woman and wanted the best for her—but Ben didn't consider a one-legged man the best. "You ought to take Dinah dancing. She used to love that."

"Hell, I can't—" Ben hit his leg.

"All you have to do is to hold her, and you've been doing a bit of that lately. Take it easy with her, Ben. She's got stars in her eyes and a tender heart."

"I'm trying. That's all I can do. Oh, hell, there's Jemma shaking her finger at Aaron and laying him out and, God help us, she's just spotted us." Ben turned, braced his arms on the corral, and rested his chin on them. "Make her go away. That look always means trouble. She just digs in and keeps hammering."

"Are you asking?" Hogan couldn't help smiling at Ben, who had the drawn-in, hunkered-down look of a man about to be jumped and fried.

"I'm begging," Ben admitted roughly. "*Please*."

Hogan turned and leaned back against the corral and watched Jemma stalk toward him. Her wild red hair flew out from her face; her breasts were outlined in the T-shirt, her hips swaying in her tight jeans. Her long legs, decked out in knee-high red boots, were eating the space between them. "I think I'm going for Appaloosas. Just a small herd, and maybe a few sheep," he said to Ben.

"Willow wanted sheep—she wanted to weave. Rambouillet, I think. Sheep would be practical in that stretch of high ground. Old Aaron wouldn't allow them, but they're practical—they keep down the weeds. You can run them on my land . . . you're wanting to grow things, boy. Could be you're in a family mood. That fireball won't make life easy—"

Ben closed his eyes and shuddered as Jemma called, "You can't hide out here. I want to talk with the both of you."

In the distance, Aaron took off his Stetson and slapped it on his thigh, a gesture that said he was simmering after Savanna's attack on him. He stalked off into the house, and Hogan tipped back his hat to watch Jemma come to stand in front of him. She tapped Ben on the shoulder. "You can turn around. I want to talk to you."

"I'm busy. The boy and I are talking about important things—cattle and such." But he turned and slid a silent plea to Hogan.

"What's on your mind, sweetheart? Did you come after your present?" Hogan asked, enjoying the thunder and lightning in Jemma's glare. He reached out to trail a finger down her cheek, then bent to steal a quick kiss.

For a moment, she stared blankly at him, her mouth still open. He placed a fingertip beneath her chin and lifted it, closing her lips. Clearly struggling to get back to her current warpath, Jemma asked, "What present?"

Hogan slipped the buttons made from horn into her hand and bent to pluck a daisy, tucking it in her hair. Pleased that she wore his earrings, Hogan eased her hair back from her ears and studied her. "Well? No, I didn't kill Bambi's daddy. Deer naturally lose their antlers."

She looked at the six horn buttons in her hand, thin layers of horn, each with four tiny holes. "I . . . thank you."

"I thought when you had time, we might drive down to Big Timber and check out the health-food stores. You could help me stock my kitchen. By the way, when are you making that next batch of carrot juice? Could you make extra for me?"

She continued staring blankly at him, and Hogan smiled innocently. "What did you want to talk to us about, honey?"

Jemma shook her head as if clearing it and rewinding herself. "Ben. Hogan. I want to make certain that you won't jump Mitch. He's asked Carley to marry him. He loves her, and she loves him. I don't want any trouble. No feuding, no tempers, no brawls or threats. He'll take care of her, and you won't be losing a daughter, Ben. You'll be gaining a son you already have."

"I don't know what you're talking about. I've been expecting that for years. Why would we want to jump him?" Hogan stealthily nudged Ben.

"Mitch is a fine boy. I couldn't have picked a better match," Ben said firmly.

Jemma looked from father to son and back again. "You're sure? After what happened to Hogan, I—"

"Fine with me," Hogan said, looping his arm around her shoulders and starting to walk toward the house.

"We ought to have the wedding right here. Dinah would like all the hoopla," Ben said.

"Don't say anything about a wedding. That would terrorize Carley, right now. She's just adjusting to the idea that Mitch has always loved her. I'll handle any wedding plans—"

"That's what I'm afraid of. You'll kill us all," Ben muttered.

"What was that?" Jemma frowned at Hogan and then at Ben. "I don't know about you two. I'm not certain I trust you."

"Everything is going to be just fine," Hogan said. He drew her closer to enjoy the pleasant bump of her breast and hip against him as they walked. "Why don't you put your arm around my waist, or is this a nonequal man-woman sort of thing?"

"What's Carley doing?" Mitch asked after supper. His mind wasn't on winning the arm wrestling with Hogan, but rather on the woman he loved.

"Upstairs. For some reason, she wants to be alone. She's avoiding Jemma, who wants to know everything." Aware of the blush on Carley's cheeks, of the shy warm way she looked at Mitch, Hogan met Mitch's look as their hands locked and muscles strained against each other, elbows on the kitchen table.

"I thought artists were supposed to be weak, and beg for mercy," Mitch said, grunting as Hogan pinned his hand to the table. Mitch tossed a quarter onto the table. "Two out of three."

Hogan glanced at Jemma and Dinah, who were preparing carrots for the great juicing. Maxi was taking sugar cookies out of the oven, and Aaron grabbed several. "I thought you might want to go driving with Savanna and me tomorrow," Aaron was saying to Maxi.

She elbowed him aside and placed the cookie sheet on the counter. "You're not sidling up to me, Mr. Aaron. My daughter can make up her own mind about you."

"But Maxi, you've always been my girl," Aaron said. He snatched another cookie and tossed it to Ben, who leaned against the doorframe, watching the arm-wrestling contests.

Ben ate the cookie slowly and studied the match as Hogan took Mitch, two out of three. "You've been working on something other than your jewelry. I'll take some of that," Ben said quietly. "Unless you think you're not up to it."

"Bet," Hogan said, testing his grip against Ben's. The lock of their hands was unfamiliar, grown son to a hardworking father; the lock of their eyes said their lives were changing, a river of hard times lay between them, and both had terms to be met.

"Dollar." Ben pushed Hogan's hand enough to let him know he wasn't easy.

"I win, and you take back the ownership of those cattle."

By the kitchen counter, Aaron and Mitch turned to look at the two men.

"Like I said, you're a hard man. You're going to make me eat those years and a bit of my pride, aren't you, boy?'' Ben asked, as they gripped in earnest now, broad callused palms meeting squarely, free hands locked on their thighs for leverage.

"Uh-huh. Seems fair to me." Hogan increased the pressure, and Ben met it.

Dinah and Jemma came to watch. "Stop it," Jemma ordered coldly, her eyes slashing at him. "Hogan, you stop it now."

"Hush!" Ben shot back, sweating now with the effort of keeping his hand upright and not pinned to the table.

"Back off," Hogan said, finding that Ben wasn't an easy man to take down. Years of ranch work had earned him more muscle than a man of his age—

"This isn't a game, it's a duel," Jemma muttered, folding her arms in front of her, her nails digging into her arms.

"Stop it, Ben. She's right—it's too serious," Dinah said.

"Leave it," Ben ordered curtly and Dinah's expression hardened.

"I'm done taking your orders to leave you alone, Ben Kodiak." Then without warning, Dinah grabbed Ben's face and kissed him hard. She kissed his ear and then stood behind him, her hands resting on his chest. She winked at Hogan.

While Ben was dealing with his head resting against Dinah's breasts, Hogan immediately pinned Ben's hand. "I'll have the sale papers to you in the morning."

"He wants to do this, Ben," Dinah said quietly, stroking Ben's hair. "I think you should let this go."

"Women think different. Two out of three?" Ben asked and Hogan nodded. He realized that Ben's pride wouldn't go down easy, but there was something in Ben's eyes now that caught Hogan, disarming him. The pride in Ben's expression was for his son.

After Hogan won the next match, Ben sat back in the kitchen chair and nodded. Then he stood and took Dinah's hand. "Hogan tells me that I should be dancing with you. Why don't we put on those old Glenn Miller records in the living room and do that now?"

"Where's Carley?" Mitch asked again as Ben held Dinah close and they swayed to the big band sounds.

A thundering blast from upstairs answered the question. Carley was already halfway down the stairway before Hogan took the first step. She pushed his chest with her hand. "Get out of my way."

"Are you all right?" The shot had terrified him. If he'd missed any security upstairs and—

Carley pushed him aside and tromped down the stairs. "Someone will have to fix the roof before the next rain. I shot that old buffalo gun straight through it . . . because I didn't want to shoot any liars down here."

She glared at Jemma. "*My best friend.* A liar. I thought I could trust you. Dad is sick, is he? I just found a copy of his last medical exam in Big Timber. He's missing one leg, but other than that, he's as healthy as I am. Maybe more."

Dinah inhaled sharply, the sound slashing through the room, and Carley turned to her mother. "Was I so pitiful and dumb that you had to get Dad to agree to this lie? It's Jemma's fault, isn't it? She's always the one with ideas, and most of them without a bit of sense."

"Carley—" Jemma began, her tone shattered. Hogan took one look at her stricken, pale face and drew her close against him.

Carley slashed down her hand. "I'm running this show. Shut up. All of you were in on it, weren't you? All of you knew that I was being stalked, and all of you stopped your lives to come here. And I've trusted you all with my life."

She slammed her fist into Mitch's midsection, and he didn't blink, his features taut and pale. "I trusted you," she said, her voice vibrating with passion. "I trusted you completely."

"Honey—" Mitch stopped when Carley glared at him, her usually cheerful expression livid with rage.

Hogan saw the family he loved, tearing in pieces, Carley wounded and slashing at the tenuous bonds. Jemma was shaking badly now, tense within the circle of his arm. Ben and Dinah were rigid and pale; looking helpless and worried, Aaron and Mitch were clearly gripped by Carley's stormy emotions. "That's enough, Carley."

"No, it's not. Not nearly enough." Carley's tears were trailing down her pale cheeks, dripping onto her T-shirt and spotting the dark blue fabric.

Jemma moved from Hogan's protective arm around her waist and started toward Carley, to hold her as she always had. Hogan caught Carley's open hand as it shot toward Jemma's face. "No."

"Let her." Jemma pushed free of Hogan's protection. "Hit me, I don't care. Nothing could compare to losing you. I'd rather anything happened to me, than to have you hurt again. He's been waiting since that night— don't you think I've lived every minute of it with you, every night when you cried out? It has to stop, Carley. Hogan can't paint anymore, because he sees your face as it was that night—eyes open, rounded, your mouth bruised. *It's got to end.* The guy is lurking around here, making threats, and Hogan and Ben and Mitch and Aaron are the best protection you've got—This was the safest place for you."

"The safest place for me is away from you all," Carley said darkly, her voice vibrating with emotions. "You came here, you got Hogan and everyone else in my family and—"

"You want to hit me, fine. Do it. But you were trapped in that night eighteen years ago and—"

"*Dammit, what night eighteen years ago?*" Ben demanded, and the entire room seemed to quiver and stop in time as the younger adults looked at each other.

Dinah took Ben's hand. "What happened eighteen years ago?" she asked softly, fearfully. "I want to know. Something changed Carley—*what happened*?"

"Mother, you didn't know, did you? That was our little secret, the girls and the boys." In blistering detail, lashing out with all the pain in her, Carley told what the attacker had said to her.

Their expressions stricken, Ben and Dinah sank to the couch, and Mitch jerked Carley back from the door she had just opened. "You're not going anywhere."

"I am, and not with you."

"I'll take you," Hogan said, after smoothing Jemma's taut back. Secrets kept too long hurled around the room, and there was nothing he could do to hold them back. Jemma looked as if she were crumbling and Ben stared vacantly into space. Dinah's eyes held tears, Aaron looked off into the night, and Mitch never stopped looking at Carley.

"I want her out of this house, now," Carley stated, glaring at Jemma. "*Or I'll never set foot in it again.*"

Hogan took Jemma's cold, shaking hand and placed his keys in her fist. He wanted to hold her in his arms, to protect her, but she wanted this finished. Jemma wanted the Kodiaks salvaged, and at the moment, he believed that, too. "You be at my place when I get there. Stay put. Aaron—Mitch, make certain she's okay."

"I'll stay with her." In the dim light, Aaron's face looked as aged and haunted as Ben's.

"You're protecting her. Sending her away, so she won't have to face what she's done." Carley was taut with rage, sending an antique glass lamp onto the floor, shattering it. "She's got you all wrapped around her finger, all dancing to her tune and telling me lies. My family, my *fine, loving* family, doesn't think that I can handle my life."

"That's enough, Carley," Hogan said, wrapping his hand around her upper arm and tugging her toward the door. "We'll talk about it outside."

But Carley was running toward a fast horse and when Hogan leaped from the front porch to follow her, Aaron called his name. "Here. If he's out there—"

Hogan caught the heavy automatic Beretta and jammed it into his belt. He glanced at Jemma, took a hard, fast kiss and said, "You're not running away. I'll come after you, if you do. Stay at my house, in my bed, and you'd better be there when I get home."

He didn't wait for her consent, there was no time; Carley was already racing across the pasture. Hogan caught a fast horse, a gelding named Pete. Wrapping his hands in Pete's mane, he sailed over the fence as Carley had. Carley was bent low in the moonlight, riding bareback across the moonlit stretch toward the stream where she'd been attacked. By the time he got there, Carley was running toward the spot in the bushes.

Hogan came up softly behind her. "Carley?"

She was shaking, staring at the spot where she'd been pinned and threatened and where her life had stopped. "I hate myself," she whispered, violence in the hushed tone. "I'm weak, and I'm pitiful."

He wanted to hold her, to tell her that she was the beautiful sister he'd always loved, but Carley wasn't listening now—she was tearing herself into shreds. "You're not. You're Carley."

She pivoted to him, her body rigid, tears streaking her pale moonlit face. "Why are you always at the wrong place, saying the right things? Haven't you had enough? You're probably the only one in this whole situation who knew that I should be told . . . that Mom and Dad should have been told years ago. You told me that— that they should know. How many times was it? There was pain in you then, and now I know—''

She fell into the bushes, lying on her back, arms at her sides, shaking as she relived the attack.

Hogan jerked her to her feet and held her a distance away from him. He shook her, willing her to understand, to come back from the evil place she'd been. ''Stop that. Do you want to give him more power? He's already done enough.''

*''I hate Jemma. She did this.''*

''She loves you, Carley. More than herself. She knew what would happen if Ben and Dinah weren't told—how she could be hated by them both, and yet for you, she kept a lie alive.'' Then Hogan released his sister and stepped back. She had to stand on her own, and she couldn't if everyone continued to protect her. She had her pride, too, and Hogan prayed that she could deal with what he would tell her. ''He's dangerous, Carley. He's probably a serial killer, and I think he murdered my uncle—''

''Joe Blue Sky? But—''

''There was motor oil on the rag near Joe's body. The rag hadn't been there long—it wasn't weathered. The oil did not match that of Joe's pickup.''

''That lovely old man? Who would want to kill him? What monster would kill him?'' she corrected, her eyes wide, filling with horror.

Hogan studied her, gauging her strength now. ''There's more. Do you want to know or not?''

He'd banked on her Kodiak blood, that fearless blood that matched his, and when Carley nodded and held his hand, he said, "Remember old Doc Medford, the dentist? His house and lab burned."

"I know, but what does that have to do with—"

Hogan inhaled and wished he didn't have to tell Carley—but there had been enough secrets around her. She needed the truth. "There were unusual bite marks on the women he murdered. Bite marks are traceable now to dental work. Those women were supposed to be—very sweet and untouched—"

"Virgins?" Carley supplied shakily. "Like me? Like I was?" she corrected with a blush.

Hogan brought her trembling body against his, wanting to protect her as he always had. But he had to go on with the truth, or Carley's healing couldn't begin. "Yes. But they weren't virgins. I think he was angry to discover that and killed them in a rage. Those dental records could have proven him guilty."

"He bit me that night—He likes to hurt." Carley wrapped her arms around Hogan, holding him tight. "How awful. That's why I was never left alone, why you and Mitch and Dad and Aaron—"

"And Jemma, too. Try to understand, Carley. She loves you. She knew you wouldn't leave Seattle for your own safety."

"She did my thinking for me. I can't forgive that easily."

"She was trying to protect you, maybe a little too much. But you've changed." He held her back from him, looking down her small curved frame. "For one thing, you've lost weight, and you've been holding your own with Jemma, not letting her push you around. Your one handicap is that you have a family of powerful people around you with their own scars. That's why they want to protect you—because they love you and don't want you to be where they've been—"

"Mitch?"

Hogan prayed that what he was doing was right. "You should ask him about the scars on his back."

Carley shook her head, the short boy cut making her face look more feminine than the longer style. "He won't tell me. I've tried."

"I think he will now."

Carley was quiet, looking away into the rolling pastures. "What about Jemma? I know she hasn't had an easy life, but she's always seemed so strong."

"She made herself that way. She's fought a long time, and she's done her best for everyone else. I want to help her now."

"She had bruises on her face one day—when she was married. 'I'll take care of it,' she said, and then she was divorced. I don't know what she went through. She wouldn't talk about it. Looking back, Jemma never told me anything she didn't want me to know. That's one-sided, isn't it?"

Carley wasn't asking questions; she was trying to unravel and rebalance a lifetime relationship. Hogan let her deal with that, dropping painfully into the realization that Jemma had been in an abusive marriage. The thought startled him; he hadn't thought of Jemma as a woman who would allow that.

Rage began to curl through him, and he slowly slammed the door on it. At the moment, he was trying to get through to Carley to trust the people who loved her, and Jemma hadn't trusted him. He pushed away that sliver of pain and concentrated on getting through to Carley.

In the moonlight, Carley's face was stark with pain. "You're saying that everyone has had pain and that they're working to heal. I don't know if I can do that."

When Carley snuggled closer, Hogan knew that she

would weigh her emotions. "Jemma is staying with me. She's not going anywhere until this is over. I think it will be soon."

Carley pushed free of him and walked to the stream bank. She threw rocks into the stream for a long time, skipping them. Hogan came to stand beside her, tossing rocks as she was. He wanted her to know that he'd always feel the same about her—no matter what she decided about Jemma, or her family. When she sat on the bank, he sat beside her, and together they watched the moonlight caress the stream. "Cutthroat," she said, noting the fish that had hurled itself out of the water.

"Big brown trout—five pounds," he corrected, and could almost imagine Jemma running for her high-priced, designer pole. "You do your thinking, Carley. Take your time."

"Okay." She turned to him. "Everyone else knows this, but me, right? Jemma?"

Hogan shook his head. "No. The Kodiaks have vigilante blood. I didn't want a free-for-all, before the killer shows his hand. He meant to send a message to us— that he was a threat. I want it to appear that we didn't get the message, and he's just sent another in Ben's mailbox—a picture of you in Seattle and a new bra."

He waited to see the fear in Carley's expression, but instead she locked her jaw and narrowed her eyes—she wanted to fight, and that was good. He handed a truth to her, and hoped it would help strengthen her. "I didn't think Jemma could handle it. She would, if she had to, though. I wanted to protect her, and they are only suspicions. I have nothing really to go on. I think he's getting restless, and he's stirred up. I think he'll probably make a move soon. I didn't want Jemma to go off half-cocked and set him off. I think we should sit tight."

"But you thought that I should know, or you wouldn't

have told me. You think that I can handle this, don't you?'' Carley's tone said that knowledge had helped her self-confidence, and Hogan nodded. She inhaled the sweet night air, scented of cut grass, and said quietly, ''I'm ready to take a long ride now, an easy one, to air out. I suppose I'm stuck with you, my Knight of the Round Table, right?''

He smiled at the memory she'd dredged up from her childhood. Carley's emotions were churning now, but she knew what was sensible and right. ''Let's ride back and saddle up, and I'll take you up to meet my mother. There's nothing like a moonlight ride in the foothills to straighten things out. I've been thinking I'd like to roof that old cabin up there, if you'll help me. It's just a tiny thing, and we can use the leftovers in the barn. We'd take packhorses.''

''I'd like that—away from here and working to re-build something that means so much to you . . . One thing, Hogan. I'm still mad at Jemma. I don't promise anything where she's concerned. You're half in love with her, and I don't want to lose my brother, too.''

''You won't, but it's more than half, Carley. I'm thinking about romancing her.''

''Whoa. Romance. That's a big old-fashioned one for my cool-headed, logical, socialite brother, isn't it? But no more, Hogan. I don't want to even think about Jemma now.''

In Hogan's living room, Jemma looked up from her sewing as she had for a thousand times, watching for his return after two days and nights away with Carley. Hogan was perfectly right, taking Carley into the foot-hills and giving the Kodiak family time to recover and prepare. It was almost July, and in the two and a half months since the Kodiaks had all come together, Jemma had lost a friend she adored; Carley would never forgive her. Jemma knew that in Carley's place she would feel the same—

Jemma saw Hogan riding toward his house and pushed away the fabric, almost upsetting the sewing machine cabinet as she stood, her hand over her heart. In the distance, he looked so tired and lonely, as if all the world sat upon his shoulders. She lifted her hand to her mouth, smothering the cry that tore out of her. He was certain to tell her that Carley hated her, and wanted her out of the country, away from the Kodiaks. He was certain to tell her that he didn't want to see her again, either. Jemma dashed away the burning tears and hurried out to the front porch, wanting to run to him, and fearing if she did, she'd learn that much faster that she was exiled from the family she loved.

*Hogan.* The weary set of his shoulders, the way he sat in the saddle, told her those two days hadn't been easy with Carley. Hogan would always do the right thing for his family, no matter what it cost him. He'd always hold them together, though he was still battling his shadows.

*And she loved Hogan.* Two days and nights of waiting and hoping that he'd be safe, that he'd come back to hold her against him in that special way—She'd missed him every moment, her heart aching for the sight of him. Jemma placed her fist over the pain in her chest—

She glanced at Aaron's expensive Land Cruiser sliding from the shadows of Hogan's barn and prowling down to meet him. Aaron had been with her, but he was anxious to see Savanna, and he was carrying a solitaire engagement ring he'd ordered from a New York jeweler's.

Just then Jemma's gold van hurled down the road from Ben's, bypassing the Land Cruiser and Hogan's horse. It squalled to a stop in front of Hogan's house and Carley began throwing out Jemma's vivid clothing and anything else she'd moved into the Kodiak house. The carrot juicer landed on top of the clutter.

Jemma gripped the porch's railing, her knuckles white; a part of her life, her soul, was tearing free and leaving a big, bleeding hole. She'd loved Carley for most of her life, adored her, and now her taut anger whipped at Jemma. Carley had every right to be angry and Jemma should have listened to Hogan's warnings. The cold stare Carley shot at her hurt more than words. The tinkling of the wind chimes sounded like the pieces of Jemma's heart falling at her feet. She knew her expression begged for forgiveness, and she didn't care. Then Carley turned stiffly and marched down to Aaron's silver Land Cruiser. She got in and slammed the door, the sound echoing in Jemma's heart. She'd lost her best friend, a sister—and more than likely, the entire Kodiak family . . .

# sixteen

Jemma ran out to meet Hogan, searched his weary face, and found no hope for Carley's forgiveness. Jemma couldn't bear to touch him, afraid that he would shove her away; she'd crumple into the dirt if Hogan turned away from her now. "Thank you," Jemma whispered, not shielding her tears from him.

"It will take a while. Carley isn't in a forgiving mood." He bent down from the saddle and eased her tousled hair away from her face, his dark eyes searching her face. "You haven't slept."

She didn't care that her face was stripped of cosmetics or that she'd made no effort to hide her swollen lids. In her lifetime no one but Hogan had mattered as much as Carley.

She couldn't tell from Hogan's expression if she was losing him, too. Would he tell her to leave? Would he forget their beautiful lovemaking? "I don't blame her. I should have listened to you, Hogan. But just this one time, all of your family was getting along and—"

Hogan swung down from his horse. His slow movements were those of a redundant weary man, carrying a heavy burden. He stood there, long legs sheathed in worn chaps and looked down at her. "You wanted the best for us. We're just not perfect, honey."

"To me, you are. Are you going to just stand there, or are you going to hold me?" she asked baldly, freezing in the warm June sunlight and terrified that she had lost him, too.

Hogan stripped away his leather glove and placed his hand on her cheek, his expression tender. "Take it easy. We'll work through this. She'll burn it off, but you've got to let her grow, honey. She can't do that with you protecting and making everything smooth for her. Let her fight her own fights."

He watched the white rumps of antelope jog across a pasture of timothy and "needle and thread" grass. "Don't think the burden is just yours. We all were that way from the time she was little. We were all in on getting her here. She didn't like us doing her thinking. Right now, she's fighting her way free of being the baby, and that's a hard task with us."

"Oh, Hogan!" Unable to control the grief inside her, Jemma threw herself against him, locked her arms tight around his lean, safe body. She'd always held her pain, but Hogan was so much a part of her life, in the air she breathed, and she had to hold on to the remnants as long as she could. Another Jemma, one filled with pride and independence, would have lifted her head and walked away, no matter how much it hurt—but not Jemma-now. She needed Hogan too much.

"Shh. Carley is sensible. She'll make the right decisions. It's up to her. We'd all better be prepared to let her do her own thinking from now on. It's my fault—I should have known. She's a Kodiak, and stubborn." Hogan's voice curled around her, deep and rich, and his hand stroked her hair as he rocked her against his body. "I'm glad you're still here."

She pushed her face into the safe cove of his throat. "Where else would I be?"

"Flying off somewhere. Hunting the great bargains, taking care of profit margins ... *Did you sleep in my bed?*" His body trembled, surprising her.

Hogan's deep, uneven tone said that was important to him, where she slept. She used his shirt collar to dry her eyes. "If you're wanting to know if I missed you—yes, terribly, but there wasn't much sleep. You don't look any better than I do. I won't go to Ben's, since Carley doesn't want me there. I'm losing the only family I've ever really had, Hogan. Am I going to lose you, too?"

Hogan tipped her face up for a long, hungry kiss. "Does that feel like you're losing me?"

She traced his beautiful mouth and gave him another light kiss that told him he ran gently through her heart. "She's your sister, and I've hurt her terribly. She'll probably never forgive me. I should pack up and leave well enough alone—"

"You're not going anywhere," Hogan stated roughly, and eased away from her. He slapped the horse's rump and it turned, cantering back to Ben's ranch. Hogan stepped into her van and returned with an expensive sheet, which he flipped open on the ground. He began dumping her clothes into it, then tied the four corners together. He looked at Jemma then slammed the van's door, as if making his point.

Jemma couldn't move, for on the ground was a framed picture of Carley and her, the glass broken. She picked it up carefully, and ran her fingertips over the young, happy faces grinning at the camera. While Hogan carried her belongings into the house, she stood for a long time in the late June day in Montana's Big Sky country. She wondered how it could have all been so beautiful—her adopted family, Carley, an almost-sister. She folded the picture close to her heart and let her tears flow. Then Hogan's strong arms were picking her up and carrying her into his house.

Locked tight in his arms, Jemma wasn't letting go. Hogan carried her into his bedroom and laid her down. His slow, simmering look took in how she lay on his bed, his eyes darkening as if she was where she belonged. He eased to the side of the bed, sitting wearily to draw off his boots. "You stay put," he said again, reminding her of his order that night at Ben's.

While he showered, Jemma shivered and prepared for Hogan's concise bottom line, ordering her out of the Kodiak lives. She hugged herself and wished she could go back in time.

After his shower, Hogan returned to lie beside her, easing her close against him—filling her with familiar scents—that dark mystical Hogan-scent, soap and man. He rocked her gently and stroked her back. She realized her fingers were digging into his shoulders, her face pressed hard against his throat. She knew without looking that his expression was grim, that she'd torn his family apart. Hogan's slow deep breathing told her that he had drifted into sleep. She tried to move apart, to draw a sheet over his long, nude body, but his arm tightened, drawing her back against him. Jemma wanted to be close to him, just this one last time. "I want to undress," she whispered.

Hogan's eyes drifted open, and his arm relaxed. He watched her as she drew the sheer curtains, blocking out the day and the harsh reality of what would come— when Hogan sent her away. When she curled against him, naked flesh against his, drawing the sheet over them, Hogan sighed and gathered her back against him. He slept deeply, instantly, as if he was waiting for her to return and now was at ease.

She awoke to find Hogan moving over her, entering her, filling her gently as though locking his body with hers was a reassurance that he needed her. She opened to him, gave herself without reservation, meeting his easy, tender kisses with her own, drifting deeper into their lovemaking without the desperation of other times. He made love to her gently, almost as if they were sharing a warm ocean wave, rocking upon her, allowing her to adjust to the slow tempo, to spill over into a warm golden cloud and float back to earth with Hogan close and tight upon her. She sighed and met his last gentle kiss, not wanting him to shift away, but to stay with her, in her, keeping him as close as she could. She stroked his back and hips and soothed his hair, loving him, aching for him, until sleep crept warmly, safely upon her.

Mitch leaned against the barn stall and pushed his hands in his back pockets. After her return, Carley's assault on him hadn't taken long. She was tramping back and forth in the airy barn, her short hair gleaming palely in the dim light. She stopped to hitch up jeans that had gotten too large for her, since she'd lost more weight, and planted her feet on the barn's dirt floor. "I want to know about you, Mitch. You know everything about me, and I haven't a clue about you. Is that fair?"

He looked away to the calves frisking in the field. He didn't want to spread his dark life on hers, his angel.

Carley's hand shot to his jaw, turning him back to her. "You'll tell me."

"Or?" he asked, resenting being pushed into corners. As a child, he'd been shoved into too many and locked into them, too.

"I'll have to think about the 'or.' I feel stripped, Mitch. I feel as if everyone knows everything about me—right down to my bones—and I haven't a clue as to what they're about. I know Aaron's reconsidering how he wants to live the rest of his life. I know Mom and Dad will probably remarry. I know that Hogan is watching and caring for all of us, and that he's in love with Jemma. I know that Jemma—well, I'm mad at her now, so never mind about her. What about you? What about the scars on your back, and worse yet, inside you?"

Mitch jerked his jaw away from her hand. "There are some things better left alone."

"Oh, great. It's really true then, what Jemma says, that we all have caves and we sink back into them when someone comes too close. You just closed up on me. Well, you mean enough to me to get very personal, very close. So what if someday I want children with you and something from the past comes between us. No, I want to know and understand everything right now. There's a part of you in that boy, Jimmy—the one you're worried about in Chicago—isn't there?"

Mitch thought of Jimmy, too scared now that his protector was in Montana and too many miles from help. Mitch had done what he could for Jimmy, temporarily placing him with a good couple. As a boy, Mitch hadn't had protection—until Ben had caught and adopted him. He wasn't about to explain to Carley—and then he did, in short fast bursts that he'd never told anyone. "My mother gifted me with those scars. The cord of an iron isn't exactly friendly, nor were her boyfriends. It isn't sweet is it? Neither was living without food, eating garbage from cans, and all the rest."

"That's why you help the inner-city kids, why you

stayed in Chicago, when you loved it here,'' Carley whispered shakily. ''For them.''

''For me,'' he corrected. ''I had to. That's what I'm about, Carley. Why I need to help those kids. I'll be going back in and—''

''And coming out in pieces,'' she finished, wrapping her arms around him. ''I can't bear that, how you looked when I first saw you—like your soul had been torn away.''

''I can manage. Can you?'' Would she still care for him when he started bringing the children into his life, as he wanted—as he needed—to do? Or would she turn away?

Her arms tightened. ''I love you, Mitch. What happened to you is horrible, and I can't even imagine—But you're you, the kindest man I know. After this is over, and it's safe for Jimmy, you bring him here. To heal, just as you did.''

He swallowed, his throat too tight with emotion to speak. Instead he gathered her closer and buried his tears in her hair.

At sundown, Hogan awoke to a black kitten curling on his chest, settling down to sleep. After petting the purring kitten and coming fully, instantly awake with the fear that Jemma had left him, Hogan found her cuddled against him. He lay still with the purring kitten in one hand and his love in his other arm. Sunset eased through the curtains, and he relaxed. Carley's taut emotions had taken their toll, but he was home now—with Jemma next to him. A lifetime of shadows eased as she lay beside him, and he intended to keep her there, and to see her happy. All the missing pieces seemed to be together now, with her breathing quietly beside him. After a time, Hogan eased from the soft tangle of Jemma's body, and placed the kitten near her. The kitten snuggled down to sleep, apparently used to sharing his bed with Jemma.

Hogan padded into his living room; he frowned at the bundle of Jemma's things, reminding him of how she'd looked when he'd returned—all in pieces, bright, glittering, tear-streaked trembling, pale pieces, fear of rejection and pain in her wide gray eyes. She'd felt so frail in his arms, and he'd wondered when she'd eaten last. Dealing with her own pain, his half sister had been brutal, casting Jemma out of the house. Carley's Kodiak blood wanted revenge, but Hogan prayed that she would gradually recognize Jemma's good intentions to protect her.

Hogan wanted no doubt in Jemma's mind where she belonged, and he picked up the bundle and carried it into the bedroom. He plopped it on the bed and Jemma awoke, flaying her arms and legs amid the tangled sheet. She pushed herself upright and blinked owlishly at him. "What are you doing?"

He forced himself to ignore the sheet sliding down Jemma's bare, gleaming shoulders, and the nipple budding against the cloth. He wanted her to know that her place was with him, no matter what happened. He tore open the knotted bundle and began sorting her clothes and cosmetics. He jerked open a dresser drawer and pushed her underclothes in with his, smiling at the tangled mess of black silk boxer shorts and lacy feminine underwear. He shoved the door shut and jerked open the closet door, taking down hangers and stuffing her clothes onto them—he slapped her folded jeans onto the top shelf, next to his, and tossed her colorful assortment of shoes and boots onto his. Gathering an armful of her cosmetics, cleansers, and creams, he walked into the bathroom and plopped them down next to his things. He

studied the less than artful arrangement, and nodded—
he intended to leave no doubt as to whom she belonged
with every day and night.

Hogan turned abruptly, ready to lay down the law,
and bumped into Jemma's soft body, clad now in a
short, ruffled, rosebud-sprinkled cotton nightie she'd for-
aged from the bundle. "You're staying with me," he
said, shaken at how sweet and young she looked.

She pushed her hair back from her face, her expression that of a woman who had been well loved and who
couldn't balance her worlds at the moment. "You're upset, Hogan. You're very emotional now and not quite
yourself—calm, dissecting the causes and repercussions.
I don't want to do more damage by staying here—"

"I'm just peachy." Days of dealing with Carley's unsettled emotions and returning to find Jemma in pieces
had taken their toll. Jemma's only fault—shared with
his family—was that she loved Carley too deeply. She
hadn't trusted him enough to tell him of her marriage.
In his passion, he'd held her too tightly—he'd bruised
her wrists . . . He was no better than the man who had
hurt her—Oh, well, hell, he'd never been in love before,
nor so vulnerable. Of course, he was emotional, Hogan
thought, disgusted with his unshielded mood. He shoul-
dered past her, jerked a pair of shorts from the tangled
drawer, and tugged them on. He wanted to give her soft
words and not orders, and he was ruining any chance—
He pulled her close to him and kissed her with the
hunger and desperation riding him. "Stay with me—
please."

Then because he knew that Jemma was a woman who
made up her own mind, he left her with a softer kiss
and escaped to the kitchen; if he'd stayed, he would have
wanted her in bed, and in the long run, he wanted more
than that from Jemma. In the middle of the gleaming

kitchen, he stopped and slowly took in the changes. The carrot juicer stood next to the bread maker and there were four loaves of bread, uncut and waiting on the chopping block, his first pottery efforts with matching lids were lined up on the counter—An old glass churn sat on the table, next to a cookbook.

From the doorway, Jemma was too quiet. "I bought a cow. Aaron taught me how to milk. I wanted to learn how to make butter. There's wonderful things you can do with buttermilk, you know, and she was so sweet— a little brown cow with beautiful big brown eyes, and small dainty horns. Orchid is supposed to be a good cream cow—I thought the kitten needed cream, don't you?"

"You bought a Brown Swiss." Reeling with the knowledge that Jemma had settled into his house without a royal fight, Hogan slowly opened the double-wide refrigerator door to find three glass gallons of carrot juice. "You've been busy."

Because his world had shifted suddenly, he took one of the gallons and poured two glasses, quickly downing his.

"I couldn't sleep. Making juice is therapeutic, but it didn't help. I'd just lost my best friend, and more than likely, you." Jemma held her glass like a lifeline, her expression wary as if waiting for him to lash out at her. He could no more do that for loving Carley, than he could hurt the kitten. Looking away from him, she rushed on nervously. "Butter isn't difficult to make, if you let it come to room temperature. Ben told me how. You just have to let the cream settle and then skim it off—"

"I know. You're not losing me, Jemma. I'm here for the long run, no matter what." Hogan looked steadily at her and saw that only time would make her believe him. She eased back from his outstretched hand, and that hurt him. He wanted her to trust him, to know that he'd always be with her.

"I've made a few changes," she began hesitantly, as Hogan began to slice bread. He placed a skillet on the stove and with the ease of a man who had tended himself, opened the refrigerator to scan its contents. He withdrew a big bowl of brown eggs and looked at Jemma.

Her expression was both wary and pleading. "Fresh. From my—our chickens. Aaron made a makeshift coop. He said you'd have to make something better. He was getting a little disgusted with me at that point. He kept talking about how he liked fried chicken—Hogan, he's not frying my chickens."

Hogan smiled, a bit woozy with the idea of Jemma settling so comfortably into his home. No wonder Aaron had hurried to meet him earlier; Jemma probably had him running full steam day and night.

"I like canisters. I found some of your pots—you do such lovely work. I would never have that patience. I tried it once, and the clay shot all over the wheel," Jemma said, as he scrambled the eggs, and she toasted the bread, slathering butter on it. She stood awkwardly as Hogan filled their plates and sat.

He couldn't bear the uncertainly on her face and reached to pull her down onto his lap. "We'll get through this, sweetheart. All of us, together. Stop worrying."

She looked down at her folded hands, and shook her head. "I wouldn't blame Carley for never wanting to see me again."

"Take it easy, Jemma. Healing takes time." Hogan began to feed her, and then licked the butter from her lips. "Okay?"

He wanted to ask her about her marriage—why she

didn't trust him, and decided to wait for another time. After eating, Hogan sat back and toyed with her hair. "You do whatever you want with the house. Just stay. Stay with me."

"I've already have made a few changes—" Then Jemma was on her feet hurrying into the living room, and with the resigned sigh of a man trying to find reality, Hogan followed. After one good look at the living room, he reached for his hat and slapped it on his head. He needed the reassurance that this was his home and that was his woman standing in front of the big windows, her curved body outlined in the setting sun. One hand rested on a new sewing machine, heavily studded with gadgets. "I didn't know you sewed," Hogan murmured, reeling at just what Jemma could do. . . .

"Savanna and Richard brought it out. She says she didn't like sewing after trying it, and the machine is way too fancy and expensive to waste—so I got a bargain. I used to make my clothes and sometimes remake them from thrift shops."

Hogan tested the light chambray material, noted the too-large sleeves and hoped—"What are you making?"

"A shirt—for you. To go with the horn buttons. You'll have to come up with an earring that matches."

"Did you miss me, then?" The question tore out of him—he had to know.

"You know I did. It was all I could do, not to come up there, and for once, I knew I'd better not push. You and Carley aren't the pushing kind. What did she say about me, Hogan?"

He shook his head; he wouldn't betray his sister's trust, though he thought Carley would one day accept Jemma on different and more equal terms. Jemma turned suddenly, and asked too brightly, "What do you think about old Jubal's horns? Right there, I mean? Ben sent them over because he was afraid that Carley might decide to shoot at the roof again—they were in the attic. Dinah called and begged me to take them. They'd be great at Christmastime, all decorated with red balls and mistletoe. Do you mind?''

"Nope." Hogan looked at the sprawling horns over a rambling display of tropical plants. He couldn't resist taking off his hat and sailing it across the room. The hat caught and swung from the tip of one horn. "I always wondered if I could do that.''

Jemma smiled tentatively at him, and he sensed her easing a bit. Because he was feeling good, Hogan swept her into his arms and tangoed her into his office. "Show me what else you've done? You were busy for just over two days.''

"Aaron helped. But he wasn't happy, Hogan. You may have to help him with his Savanna-problem.''

"Oh, no. He's in that by himself." He glanced at the African violets sitting on his north windowsill and at Jemma's notes by the telephone. He saw Simone's name and stilled; he hadn't had time to talk with Simone, to cut the light flirtation link between them. "Any messages?''

"I handled a few business things while you were gone. I hope you don't mind. Jared said he needed a decision on a franchise offer, and Hogan, he really seemed to want to meet me. He offered to come here—''

Hogan made a mental note to call Jared and declare Jemma off-limits. "What's this?" he asked, noting figures on the pad.

"You're going to get mad. I thought the offer was good, and I gave him the go-ahead. The deal was on the table and hot and at a good price. You're going to get *really* mad, aren't you? Boy, if there is one thing I know how to do, it's to step on Kodiak toes—''

Her instincts about the deal were solid and she was right—he would have lost money by waiting. Hogan turned to her. "I can take it, if you can. Can you?" he challenged, needing that bit of comfort from Jemma.

She came to rest against him so softly that she frightened him. Hogan held her gently in his arms, letting her rest against him. Jemma was not a woman to openly show her needs, dismissing her independence. "I'm so sorry, Hogan. I've made so many mistakes."

"We've made mistakes together." He was just settling in to tell her of his love, when Jemma stiffened, tore herself away, and ran into the living room.

"Oh, Hogan. That's Ben's pickup. He's coming here—" She turned to him, her body outlined by Ben's headlights. "Go get dressed. Oh, Hogan, you've got to hurry—"

So much for a pushy woman promising not to shove, Hogan thought happily as Jemma pushed him into the bedroom and started sorting through the clothes closet. He reached out and tugged her squirming body against his. "Take your time. Get dressed. I'll treat Ben to some carrot juice."

"But he's never been here, Aaron said so. And now here he comes, and I'm not ready—Hogan, do you know what this looks like? I'm in my nightie and you're standing there in your shorts, and you're—"

"True. I'm wanting to be in that bed with you. But I can wait." Then to hold him until later, he filled his hands with her soft bottom and took her mouth.

The feel of her bottom clad in silk-ruffled panties lasted Hogan while he tugged on jeans, drew on a T-shirt, and walked to open the front door. For once, he didn't dress to prod Ben that he was an artist and not a rancher. Hogan didn't bother to hide his good mood from Ben, who definitely looked uncomfortable.

In the doorway, Ben held his hat in one hand and with the other, shoved a plastic-covered pie at Hogan. "Dinah wanted to know if Jemma's okay."

Hogan took the pie and smiled. He knew that it was Ben's concern for Jemma that had brought him here. "Come in."

Ben looked out to the fields, clearly uncertain. "That's a nice little milk cow there. Aaron said you've got chickens now. Dinah always wanted chickens. Wonder how milk and eggs are going to mix with tofu?"

He looked past Hogan to Jemma. She hurried toward them, dressed in an oriental-styled, long cotton dress, splashed with jade bamboo and slit up to her thighs. Her feet were bare, and she'd applied light cosmetics; large gold combs lifted her hair up and away from her face, and allowed the back to cascade in rich, dark red curls. Jemma was inserting Hogan's earrings into her lobes as she smiled at Ben. Shifting comfortably into a hostess mode, Jemma did not appear insecure or wary as she had just moments ago. She nudged Hogan aside with her shoulder, and drew Ben inside, closing the door behind him. She looped her arm through his and drew him to the couch, sitting with him. "We're glad you came, aren't we, Hogan?"

"I brought an apple pie. Dinah said it was your favorite. I'd better be going . . ." Ben did a double take at the sewing machine and the clutter of tropical plants with Jubal's horns over them. "Poor old Jubal," he said, holding his hat against his chest as if mourning a best friend. He squinted at the horns. "What's that yellow ribbon on them?"

"A sewing tape measure." Hogan couldn't resist. "She's going to decorate them with Christmas balls and mistletoe."

Jemma studied the horns. "Mmm, maybe a eucalyptus arrangement with ribbons—"

Ben stared at her and shivered in horror. "Poor old Jubal," he said again. When he recovered, he scanned the colorful material draped across the couch. "Hogan, I always thought you'd have one of those barren, nononsense homes."

"She works fast, Ben," Hogan said, amused at himself. He'd never liked clutter or too many colorful distractions, but now the clutter seemed perfect—even the tape measure hanging from Jubal's horns. Jemma had dragged out his cherished buffalo blankets, and Hogan couldn't wait to see how she used them in his home. "You should see the rest of the house."

Jemma stared at him, clearly horrified. She leaped up from sitting by Ben and grabbed the pie from Hogan. "I . . . uh . . . wait just a minute. I'll just take this into the kitchen and . . . I forgot something. Wait here until I get back."

With a dark, threatening glare at Hogan, she hurried into the bedroom with the pie. He wondered what he'd done wrong, when Ben cleared his throat and studied Hogan's hat on the horns. "I used to do that when I was feeling good. Are you feeling good, boy?"

"Pretty good. How's Carley?" When Hogan had last seen Carley this morning, she'd been glaring at him from Jemma's van.

"Pretty mad at everyone and letting them know it. There's another hole in the roof. I needed a hideout for a few hours and stole that pie. Shall we try it out?"

Hogan wondered what he'd done to upset Jemma. "Jemma told us to stay put. I think we'd better do that."

"She took the pie into the bedroom and not the kitchen," Ben noted, looking around the living room, cluttered with decorating magazines, sewing, and plants.

He eyed the plastic sack of white fluffy stuff. "Pillow makings. Dinah's been making them while Carley was gone. She sure came back in a mood, ready to take everyone apart. Mitch is sulking around like a whipped dog."

Hogan had faith in Carley seeing reason; she was set to make her mark, making the rest of them see her as an independent woman. "She'll even out. She's just getting it out of her system."

"I know, but I'd sooner do anything than live with a wrought-up female," Ben muttered. "Dinah cried the whole time. They've started to argue, mother and daughter, and that war would scare even you. Dinah told Carley that she needed to rest and that set Carley off—she's not wanting anyone to tell her what to do. . . . I like that eagle. Now that's a man's thing, even if it is wearing a beret."

Jemma hurried back from the kitchen; she had circled the house from the bedroom and Hogan wondered why. "Ben," she said. "Hogan created that eagle. It's so fierce and dark like he used to be. See the pottery by the plants—that big bowl with the pinecones in it? It's got that Kodiak bear on the bottom—Hogan made it. Isn't he talented?"

She tugged Ben up from the couch. "Come on. You've got to see his studio."

As Ben moved uneasily into the studio, stepping into it as if it were a strange new world, Hogan noted the new plants and more of his work splashed around the large, airy studio. Willow's sketchbooks were on a worktable, his mat cutter beside them, and an array of new, empty frames stacked in a basket he wove long ago. Jemma looked at him. "I thought you might mat these and write 'Willow' on the mat and—"

Ben ran his callused fingers across the sketchbooks

and when he looked at Hogan, his face was haunted. "I was dead wrong. I should have told you. I guess I didn't know how to share what was in my heart."

Old, fierce resentment instantly simmered in Hogan, and he pushed it away, turning abruptly to view the night beyond his house.

Jemma stood on tiptoe to kiss his cheek and then Hogan's. "Everything is just going to be fine."

"Why did you go into the bedroom and come out of the kitchen?" he whispered.

Jemma scowled up at him and stood on tiptoe to whisper back, "Would you want him to see my lacy underwear hanging out from your chest of drawers? Or the bed, the way we left it?"

Clearly Hogan had much to learn about living with a woman, but he wasn't backing up. "They'd better stay that way, too."

Then Ben moved to Hogan's drawing table, studying the Fire Feathers necklace design. His fingers hesitated a moment, then reverently traced the sketch. "That would be her, all right."

"It's beautiful, isn't it?" Jemma asked, her arm around Ben's shoulders. Hogan noted how easily she moved into taut situations, how her touch visibly settled Ben. For just an instant, Hogan felt that old isolation, and then Jemma's hand slipped into his and she looked up at him and the darkness slid away.

"It's you, honey. All fiery and touched by the wind," Ben murmured.

"Me?" Jemma turned to Hogan, then peered closely at the sketch. "It's so different from your other work. Is that really how you see me?"

"It's you. How I see you." He'd never felt so exposed; his heart and soul was hers, and in Fire Feathers, his emotions showed.

Her fingertip prowled over the sketch. "It's so exotic and almost pagan, yet very feminine. The feathers seem almost alive." When Jemma's tears shimmered in her eyes, Hogan picked her up and held her close. With a nod to Ben, he carried her into the living room and sat with her upon his lap. Jemma's quick soft kisses all over his face left him a little light-headed and he knew he was grinning.

"I can't go home yet," Ben said moments later as he carried in the pie plates. "I thought I'd sneak in after bedtime. Carley and Dinah have got to wear down sometime. Maxi ran out to see her sister. The boys and I had to cook and do dishes tonight."

"What about a game of chess?" Hogan asked. It seemed natural with Jemma beside him to offer Ben solace, a "hideout." "The set is in that wall closet." Jemma yawned sleepily, her head nodding, and Hogan eased her to lie down, placing her feet in his lap. He massaged her feet—a comfort to him as well—and with a sigh, Jemma began to sleep.

Ben placed the set on the coffee table. He traced the inset stone and the black-and-white onyx pieces. "Nice. I suppose you made it."

Hogan nodded and drew a light woven fabric over Jemma's legs. "Your move."

"That felt good," Ben said later, after another piece of pie and a slow, satisfying game which Hogan won. Ben looked at the sleeping Jemma, her hand curled beside her face. "Poor thing. She's all worn-out—and Aaron, too. She shopped the hell out of him and then ran him all night. He'd just get started on one thing and she'd shove another at him. He didn't have the heart to put a stop to it, but said she was all wound-up and worrying about Carley. But now, he's too tired to see Savanna, and that's going a bit. He said he's had all the hot-tempered women he can handle for a while. Savanna is balking at the corral gate. She's smart, too—Aaron would run all over her, if she let him."

The black kitten climbed up Hogan's jeans and tee-tered up the length of Jemma's body, to snuggle against her stomach. Hogan petted the kitten and looked at Ben. "He's got time on his side. We need to draw him out."

Ben cursed softly. "I knew something was wrong—couldn't pin it, though. One minute she was like any other tomboy, and the next, like a shadow."

Flashes of that night hit Hogan and right then, he was glad that Ben hadn't known what Carley had looked like—it would haunt him, too.

Ben looked at the single headlight searing Hogan's windows. "Late for visitors, isn't it? Stay put—don't disturb Jemma." He rose and looked out into the night. "It's Mitch, riding that motorcycle like he was bound out of hell."

Ben opened the door and signed for Mitch to be quiet, pointing to Jemma sleeping on the couch, her feet in Hogan's lap. Mitch nodded and followed Hogan's pointed finger to a closed wine cabinet. He lifted an expensive bottle, studied it, and, with a silent okay from Hogan, poured three glasses. Mitch served the wine, set the bottle on the table, and sprawled into a chair. "Women," he said in a hushed, frustrated tone. "Women."

"Amen," Ben added darkly.

Mitch leveled a look at Hogan. "I'd appreciate you not interfering with Carley and me."

Hogan lifted his glass, studied the fine amber swirls. Mitch was on edge, ready to fight anyone, anything, and he wasn't ruining Hogan's pleasant mood. "How so?"

"She pushed me into telling how I got these scars. She kept digging until she set me off, and I told her things I've never told anyone . . . '' Mitch's face was dark with anger. "You're to blame, Hogan. Then she kissed me goodnight as if nothing had happened."

Ben shielded a smile, and Mitch refilled the glasses of wine. "You think I'd want Carley to know those things about me—how bad it was? You're sitting there smiling, and none of this is funny, Hogan. I felt like I was spreading garbage all over her—she's too sweet and innocent, and—"

Hogan ached for Carley, tearing through the shielding layers they had wrapped around her. "Carley wants the truth from now on, Mitch. It's only fair. You know all about her nightmares—maybe she wants to know about yours."

Mitch glared at Hogan. "Fine. Now she does, now stay out of it." His temper eased, Mitch took a long slow look at Hogan's living room. "Holy—No wonder Aaron is dragging his butt. I knew he was running all over the countryside buying carrots, but she must have—"

Hogan lifted his glass in a toast; everything seemed to be just right somehow. "To Aaron and old Jubal and the almighty carrot juice—Ben, you're taking a gallon of that home."

# seventeen

"Carley has been picking at Jemma all day. Jemma has been taking it, like she deserved it. But now she's starting to snarl—" Aaron nodded to where Carley had just leaped from her saddle. Dressed in jeans and chaps and a Stetson, she'd been driving cattle to the temporary branding station. Now the rope stretched tautly between her saddle horn and the calf. Near the branding fire, Ben flopped the calf to the ground and expertly whipped a rope around its legs. Dinah inoculated it and Hogan burned the Bar K brand on its rump.

Hogan freed the calf and as it scrambled away, he downed another that Mitch had just driven into the branding station. It was ten o'clock in the morning, and they'd worked since four, driving the cattle into the pasture. Hogan ran his forearm across his sweaty face. The roundup and the exercise had momentarily relieved the tension of Carley's stalker, and Hogan was enjoying the physical strain, the familiar ritual of ranch life. "We're late with this, Ben. July heat and branding fires don't mix."

"Should have been done two weeks ago, but I had my mind on other things. First of July is okay in a pinch," Ben said, releasing the branded calf. An inspector would check the brand, if cattle were sold or transported to another county. "There. That ought to keep the cow cop happy."

"Other things? Such as?" Hogan couldn't resist teasing Ben about Dinah, just to see him get flustered. It was a new, enjoyable entertainment, watching Ben try hard to change for his lady love.

"Hogan, damn it, you're just as perverse as ever. You know that Aaron and I have been reading books about men and women's relationships—and watching soap operas to see what gets to women. All that takes time. It's like hunting—you've got to know the game and how they think. You and Mitch seem to have a handle on that, but Aaron and I are just catching up." Ben straightened and rubbed his back as Carley tromped up to Jemma, who was on foot, hugging and shooing a calf toward them. "Holy—Here it comes."

Hogan stood up and reached for the jar of iced water Dinah had just handed him. Carley had been pushing Jemma since early morning, the first time that they'd been in the same area for a week. He hated the helpless feeling as Jemma worried about Carley and mourned their friendship. Jemma's floppy Panama hat and cutoff shorts were suited to the sweltering July morning, and her temper was just as hot. From the look of Jemma, she'd passed the point of apologizing and backing away from Carley's mean mood. Hogan had been waiting for just that wide-open, fire-woman look from Jemma, and it was time. "Let them go. We can't settle it for them."

Ben's blue eyes skipped to his son's black ones. "Fine talk for someone who's been sheltering Jemma for the past week. Carley is in an evil mood, hammering at everyone. She's mad as a hornet—I think she's jealous that you haven't come around on her side. She's mean enough now to take on that stalker and scalp him.''

"I'm not choosing sides on this one. Jemma knows that. Carley is just working to get it out." Hogan had confidence in Jemma's strength, that she would survive without Carley's friendship. But would she leave him, if that relationship and tie to his family was gone?

"You're in this, no matter what you say," Ben noted. "That woman of yours has got you stirred up. Son, you're almost emotional. You've got that damned if I do, and damned if I don't look."

"I'll be glad when it's over. Both the argument between Carley and Jemma, and getting the stalker," Hogan admitted grimly. The sight of Jemma crying over the dinner he had cooked the night before—which reminded her of a Carley-time—had been unnerving. Waking up at two or three in the morning to hear the juicer humming, or to find Jemma sitting on the couch and crying over old movies had been frightening. He'd put a television set into the bedroom, so he could hold her close while she watched movies. Massaging her body had relieved her taut nerves, but had caused his body to ache.

"Well, we've got to know each other a bit during all this mess. That's one good thing," Ben said reverently. "You're a fine man, Hogan Kodiak. I'm proud to call you my son."

Hogan nodded, shielding his face by looking off to the arguing women. But his heart was full, and maybe he was a bit emotional. Just maybe he was close to forgiving his father; it would take a hard heart to hold on to the old grudges when Ben was trying as best he knew, and when he was so happy with Dinah and his family.

"Well," Hogan said finally, in the style his father used, "maybe I've got a good man for a father."

Ben's hissing breath told Hogan that he had been caught unaware by the return. When Hogan turned to look at him, Ben winked. "I'm wanting those grandkids out of you. I need some crayon drawings on my refrigerator, like every other grandpa I know."

Hogan shook his head and grinned. "When she's feeling up to speed, she's a fast mover."

Ben returned the grin. "You'll have to catch her on the run and get a ring on her finger. She's changed, too. The two of you are good together—one running at top speed, everything wide out in the open, and the other steady as a rock—that's a good team."

Hogan removed the sweaty red bandanna wrapped around his forehead and tossed it aside. Jemma feared having children, feared the restraints of a relationship, and Ben was a definite condition. Hogan studied his father. "You did the best you could, Ben. I made it."

"It was a poor sad life for a child with you carrying most of the burden, and me drinking for that spell."

A quick flash of his dark childhood slid across Hogan's mind, then dimmed. He'd found more in his homecoming than he'd expected. He saw Ben differently now, recognizing a love for a woman in another man. Hogan had reminded Ben of Willow every day, and that must have hurt terribly. If anything happened to Jemma, Hogan wasn't certain of how he would feel, or what he would do—but he knew that part of his heart would be gone. That must have been how Ben felt with Willow's death and when Dinah left him. "I'm working it out. I'm looking forward to playing a bit when this is over—with Jemma. Do you think you can work it out?"

"Stop telling me what to do!" Carley shouted. "I'm sick and tired of you. 'Take it easy with the baby calves' isn't what we're here for, Miss Prissy Jemma.''

Experienced in Carley's wrath, Mitch settled back into the shade of Ben's pickup with a jar of ice water; he looked as though he would wait out the brewing thunder-and-lightning argument and hole up a safe distance away. Aaron, Ben, and Hogan came to lean against the pickup with Mitch, each sipping his ice water. A scarf tied around her head and dressed in a simple cotton blouse and jeans, Dinah stood stark still, pale and shaking. She covered her mouth with both hands. Ben walked to her and wrapped his arm around her.

A few yards away, Carley's voice hitched up a note. ''Don't you tell me how to treat my family. They're not yours.''

''They have been my family.''

''Squatter,'' Carley shot at her.

Jemma took off her hat and slapped it against her bare thigh. ''We've been all through that. You told me to think of them as my family, and I did. You put an offer on the table, Carley, I took it. It's too late now to kick me out so easily. You want some of this? Well, I'm good and ready. Come ahead.''

''You've stuck your nose into my life for the last time. I don't need your protection. I never did. You were always there, making nice for me—''

Jemma's face was white, her ponytail a sunlit mass of vibrant, shaking curls. ''I did what I thought was best—''

''You thought! *You thought*! I can do my own thinking—'' Then Carley leaped upon her and both women went down into the dust.

''Do something,'' Dinah cried softly. ''They've been friends for so long. They've been more like sisters.''

''They're sorting things out,'' Hogan said, and prayed that they would be friends again. Every cell in him wanted to tear them apart, to make them listen to reason, but both were set in their path. They had circles under their eyes, and Jemma's nights in his bed were restless, her mind distracted during the day. He wanted all of her with him, not a shell. "They can't settle if we're in there keeping them apart."

"When this is over, I'm getting married," Aaron said longingly as the women rolled over and over, dust clouds flying up around them. "I'm building a better house on my land and setting up an office. I miss Montana too much. And I want kids, and a porch swing. Why do you think it's taking the stalker so long to make his move?"

"He hasn't had a chance to get to her. He'd be smart not to tackle her now, not with the butt-burning mood she's been in." Mitch sighed slowly and shook his head. "I thought I might buy a little section of land out here for a boy's ranch—kids from the inner city, like me. I've decided I'm going to adopt Jimmy, one way or another."

"What's that they're arguing about now?" Ben asked, frowning at the brawling, yelling women in the dirt.

"Carley is really getting it all out—she just said that when they were twelve, she wanted to see a horror movie and Jemma wouldn't let her see that much blood."

"Mitch, why are you buying land when you've already got a good share of the Bar K?" Ben asked, without looking away from his daughter and Jemma.

"That's Kodiak land. I didn't think—"

Ben cursed. "Those two are scrappy, full of it. You think we should separate them? Mitch, I don't want to listen to any manure about you 'just being adopted' or your share of Kodiak land. We'll figure out the best spot for what you want and build the damn thing," he said, leaning down to watch Carley and Jemma. "How long do you think this is going to go on? Bets?"

"Stop it, Ben. You boys get over there and put an end it it," Dinah ordered, tears in her eyes.

"Now, honey. Hogan is right. They need to burn this one out."

"You?" Carley yelled. "You need me, Jemma Delaney. You can no more fish than you can butt out of everyone's business. You've got about as much patience as a fire in a fast wind. I'm going to show that producer the real stuff—I know how to camp and I know fishing."

"Oh, no, you're not. I set this up. I'm running this show. And you're not taking that plum away from me. I've done all the prework, and I'm making a mint on that show."

Hogan shook his head and emptied his jar of ice water over his head. He looked out onto the Bar K's pastures, to the snowcapped mountains in the distance, and wished he were in his studio where life made sense. He couldn't bear another night of Jemma calling out to Carley in her sleep, of the tears in her eyes as she stood watching the Kodiak ranch house. He wasn't certain if Jemma stayed with him because she'd been exiled and her producer was due to arrive, or if she really wanted to be with him. At any rate, he wanted Jemma to concentrate on him, and it had been a long stretch between lovings. While Jemma tossed in the late hours, he'd been sketching, trying to find the images swirling within him.

He surveyed the bawling, restless herd; Kodiak tempers were stretched too thin waiting for the stalker to make his move. The oil rag had belonged to Jackson Reeves, who blurted out—under Hogan's prodding—that he didn't know who paid him well for the use of the truck. Jackson would park it in a wooded clearing and come back to find a fat envelope on the seat. The truck had been gone the day of Joe's death.

Hogan inhaled slowly and gauged the yelling match, which didn't look like it was winding down. To keep himself from interfering, he would keep busy—if he could. "Let's do it," he said, swinging up on Moon Shadow to run down another calf.

It took all Hogan's willpower not to go to that creek bank and see if the two women were all right. He realized through the branding process that he was frightened of what Jemma would do, if she were accepted back into Carley's arms and into the Kodiak ranch. He wanted Jemma with him, in his life. He wanted to protect her, but for her own good, she had to settle with Carley. Jemma was a woman who made up her own mind.

With the air of a man who had just discovered he was very fragile, Hogan sighed and set back to work.

At noon, Jemma and Carley came over the bank, walking a distance away from each other. Both were looking like thunderclouds. Jemma pulled out the tiny brush she had stuck in his back pocket and began untangling her hair. Hogan waited and when she pushed the brush back in his pocket, he smiled—everything was back to normal, but with an equal spin for Carley and Jemma. This time Carley could hold her own.

"I'm going home to take a nice long bath, eat a ton of chocolate, sleep on your fancy satin sheets, and forget about Carley's evil temper," Jemma said darkly.

Hogan stood very still. Jemma had said "home." *She was coming back to stay with him.*

"You're not going anywhere, you sissy," Carley muttered. "Unless you can't take it."

"I can take it." Jemma caught Hogan's face in her muddy hands and looked up at him as though nothing mattered but him. She tugged him close for a hard kiss.

"Thanks. I know it must have cost you not to interfere, but I think we'll make it now."

She returned his brief kiss and gave him another one, because he suspected she wasn't letting anyone do more than her. "I'm sorry that you haven't been able to work and that I've kept you so busy. You've been very patient—except that time you yelled at me for getting up on the roof to clean the skylight. And when I wanted to rearrange the furniture—and a few other things. You're a man who doesn't like changes, Hogan. I know it must have been hard on you, waking up at midnight to find me cleaning."

"Are you better now?" he asked Jemma while Carley bent her head beneath the water-cooler spigot and let it run over her.

"Much. She still loves me," Jemma whispered in his ear. "We'll be okay . . . Hey! Water girl, save some of that for me."

"Lay off, Miss Priss," Carley volleyed back without menace.

Hogan hooked Jemma back against him, holding her tight. He loved Jemma, and her happiness was his. He buried his face in her throat and caught that feminine scent that could set his body humming. He wondered if she was wearing those tiny slinky panties—or nothing at all, but he intended to find out. "Let's go swimming down the creek when this is over—naked."

"You're on."

"I intend to be on and in," he drawled softly, just to watch her blush. Jemma looked away to Carley, who had just leaped upon Mitch, bearing him to the ground. She locked her arms around him and kissed him until he groaned, his hands lowering—

"That's enough, ladies." Hogan chuckled and tipped his hat back. He stopped smiling when Jemma turned to him—He went down in the grass, happily flattened by Jemma's squirming body and heated by her wild, hungry kisses.

*Damn them.* The Kodiaks were playing in the middle of hard ranch work. They should have been frightened— they knew what *he* could do, he'd sent them warnings. The Kodiaks were living as though they were not frightened, and that stupid arrogance infuriated him. He'd make them fear him. Carley had just leaped upon that outsider, Mitch. "You shouldn't have done that. That only makes me more angry. He isn't worthy of you, dear Carley. Only I have the right to—"

The stalker frowned darkly and lowered his binoculars. An expert at driving down the country road and using the binoculars, or his night-viewing ones, he wouldn't be noticed. "You really shouldn't have done that," he repeated.

He'd seen Carley at the drugstore, blushing as she glanced at him. Recognizing the flat, small plastic pill container, he knew what the pharmacist had put in that little white sack. *Carley had set her mind to having sex with the outsider.*

A wave of pure rage burned through him, his fist hitting the steering wheel. Carley was meant for him—she should have kept herself pure for him, not opening her body for that foreign-looking Chicago tough.

*He* could have offered her so much more—with him, she would have everything . . . And now she'd have to pay—if she was defiled . . . He spotted a rabbit, feeding in the middle of the road, and because hatred ruled him, he accelerated, killing it.

Just as he would kill anyone who kept him from Carley.

\*     \*     \*

Aaron flipped the old tarp on the ground, a distance away from the house. The earth was fragrant with the gentle mist that had passed, bowing the heavy heads of the grazing grass. He lay down on the tarp and folded his arms behind his head, letting Montana, sweet and gentle, flow upon his mind. He'd missed this, the lonely hours, filling himself with Montana, drawing her strength into him.

He'd wanted Savanna on selfish terms, and he hadn't considered her softer needs. She'd shamed him into considering his life. When he'd looked back, it was nothing but the empty picture of a man in motion—flashy status jewelry, expensive clothing and jaded, uncaring women. Hogan had moved into the circle of life, no longer an observer. Aaron smiled softly—Jemma had dragged Hogan into life; she'd been good for him.

A shadow fell between Aaron and the silvery moon. "Hi, Mom. Welcome to my parlor."

Dinah settled onto the tarp, and together they watched the moon. "We used to do this when you were a baby— your dad and I. It was like we were so filled, so complete, and then Carley came along and everything was that much better. We're getting married again—when Carley is safe."

"I expected that. Dad has always loved you."

Aaron enjoyed the sight of his mother blushing. She ran her hand over his hair, as she used to do, soothing him when he was a little boy. "This is really our first time to talk in months. How are you? Really."

He was ashamed of himself for avoiding her, for resenting how she'd left Ben. "Are you going to forgive me, Mom?"

Her hand stopped moving on his hair and then began again. "What for, Aaron?"

"For coming back here, leaving you."

"You came because your heart told you to. You were a twelve-year-old boy missing his father and the rural life and animals. How could I resent that?"

The answer was so simple that Aaron closed his eyes, his chest tight with emotion. "I just dug in. Once I'd latched onto the idea that you'd left Dad when he needed you—"

Dinah pointed to a horse with two riders. "There goes Hogan with Jemma. He loves riding with her at night. They seem so complete, a single unit, her arms wrapped around him. Sometimes they just ride to a knoll and sit, outlined against the moon. They ride bareback without reins, and he guides the horse with his knees—Hogan was always good with animals, and you are too. You were so special and bright, eager for life, while he held back . . . Ben and I made bad mistakes. We hurt you children with our pride. It was our mistake, Aaron. Not yours."

"I want something more, Mom. I've changed since I came back. Everything is so full here, more meaningful. I don't think I'm going back to that rat race based on an hourly schedule and high-performance appraisals, company mergers, and stock tender deals."

"And Savanna?"

Aaron thought of Savanna, not in the fast heat he usually craved her, but in a softer, gentler way as though she were locked in his heart. "She's the best game ever, Mom. Better than chasing a big client with a fat bonus. She keeps me on my toes. A real bona fide challenge and the mother of your future grandchildren. Right now, I'm not looking too appealing to her."

Dinah winked at him. "Try the old-fashioned, romantic courting scheme, like Ben did with me. Hasn't failed yet. There isn't anything that appeals to a woman's heart like taming the playboy type into husband material. Try some of Hogan's patience. Let her come to you. You keep jumping her and not letting her have a chance to breathe, and she won't come around—give her some thinking room and romance.''

Aaron rested there under the stars, the soft touch of his mother's hand soothing him. He knew that he'd been telling Savanna what filled his heart all along, but with his body. "I'm good at learning new skills. She hasn't a chance.''

The hot July morning told of a hotter afternoon and in another week, Jemma was set to woo the television producer into a series. Life with Jemma when she had a project churning wasn't a predictable experience. Hogan had decided to sink into his own projects and try to forget that Jemma would be spending time with another man.

Hogan smoothed his newly purchased mare's spotted rump, letting her know the feel of his hands. He absorbed the strong, fluid shift of her muscles beneath the mottled hide, a concept circling him. In his mind, he saw the mare running with other horses, mottled spots blending above the stream, their reflections riding through it. Designs and colors shifted within the gleaming, sunlit spots, waiting for him to discover them. The breeze caught the mare's mane, and the coarse strands laid out another image, blending with trees. Rose turned to look at him, her eyes liquid and reflecting his image, the man whom owned her, who she must accept and who respected her.

He traced the proud arc of her neck and found it meshing with the rolling foothills, another design within a concept, intricate, appealing, challenging.

Restlessly seeking the creative needs within him, Hogan knew that his days for producing commercial designs were ending. Where once he'd wanted metal and stone, now he wanted color and movement and life.

Jared had yelled when Hogan told him the necklace was his last, that he wanted to stop all marketing plans. "Hogan, you're tossing away a fortune. Simone said the design will outsell anything we've got."

Simone hadn't liked Hogan's order not to call him, until he'd resolved the roadblocks of his life. A complicated, sophisticated woman, Simone had known instantly that Hogan was in love. He'd told her that he would make the necklace for Jemma. He smiled at Rose. "I think you'll like her. She's demanding and tough, but fair. Then there's that softer side, and she'll be there when you foal. Jemma doesn't run from trouble—she meets it."

He smoothed Rose's mottled rump again, feeling the creative images swirl around him in the clear Montana morning; they blended, colors and motion moving within a central theme.

One look at Carley's dark expression as she rode toward him told him that peace was over. Riding beside her, Mitch's face was grim. She swung down from the saddle and charged right into her mission. "Hogan, you've got to do something. I just called that producer guy and—"

She scanned his house and surrounding grounds warily. "Jemma is in the chicken house," Hogan said, still amazed that she would place her hand beneath the hens to draw out not-so-clean eggs. Of course, the bucket of soapy water she prepared prior to collecting the eggs helped.

"That guy Parkins is after her body. He as much as told me so. He's no more interested in doing a show with her than—than Mitch is. Parkins likes the long, slim, active kind."

Hogan fought the instant rise of anger, the bitter clench of his stomach. He wouldn't say anything; he wouldn't interfere. Jemma had to make her own decisions—

"Leave me out of this," Mitch grumbled. He looked apologetically at Hogan. "Carley wants to protect Jemma. The proverbial shoe is on the other foot."

Hogan realized his fist was tight in Rose's mane. While he trusted Jemma, he knew exactly how a man could use a small space like her van—

Carley's fist shot out to punch his arm. "Do something, Hogan. That guy has been playing her along. He's even slicker than she is, and that's going some. When she had to, Jemma has used flirtation to help her business deals, but this guy is out to get her. He makes my stalker look like a plotless fool. Which he is. He's going to be here next week—"

"Who?" Both men asked together.

"That TV guy, not the stalker," Carley clarified impatiently. "What are you going to do about it?"

"Jemma makes up her own mind." Hogan would remember that statement when he met Les Parkins the next week.

Driving a low red sports car and wearing mirrorlike sunglasses, Les wore his shirt open to reveal a heavy gold chain. At midmorning, he sprawled on Hogan's front porch, drinking very fine wine with the air of a beer guzzler. "So you two are living together, hmm?" he asked, eyeing Jemma's tight, leggy jeans as she settled with her cup of herbal tea.

Jemma caught Hogan's dark, hot look, quickly shielded, and knew that she had to get Les to safety. Hogan's mouth was too set, and he hadn't said anything about her plans for the television show. He'd adopted that cold, stoic cloak again, but at night, his hunger was wild, erotic, and almost desperate. She sensed that he was very close to picking Les up and shaking him—especially when Les eyed her yellow blouse, knotted at her midriff. She'd wanted to appear country, yet knowledgeable, and Hogan's citrine and carnelian earrings, bangle bracelets, and casual hairstyle added to her simple cotton blouse and faded jeans. She'd taken care with her makeup, enhancing her eyes and contour-shading her cheeks, to demonstrate to Les how good she would look in front of the camera.

Hogan had taken one look at the makeup she rarely used when she was with him and had snorted, walking out to his horses. That snort did not bode well for Les, nor the flaring of Hogan's nostrils now as he caught her perfume. He withdrew his hand from hers as she attempted to soothe him. The informal business meeting was not going well, and she had a fortune invested in the project. Carley had washed her hands of the whole thing, saying Jemma "should know better than to tempt a sick creep." Jemma had counted on Hogan, but with each of Les's leers, that support had withered. She had to warn Les that he couldn't upset Hogan—Hogan was really very delicate.

*Life with an emotional, delicate man was not easy.*

"I've been thinking we might refocus the project. Montana has so much more to offer than fly fishing. I've got some ideas in my van—I'll just go get them."

"I'll come with you," Les offered, immediately strolling off the porch and to the van.

She glanced at Hogan, who was looking like a thundercloud. "You're not going to interfere, are you? I spent a fortune on this—"

He didn't answer, but rose slowly, coldly and walked inside the house. So much for a discussion, she thought, hurrying after Les. She'd managed tight business situations before; she could again. If she could survive the brooding, stormy Kodiaks and Carley's new over-the-edge independence, she could—

"Oh, hi, Les," she managed, stepping into the van to find him nude and searching through the cabinets. Jemma shut the van's door; she knew that if Hogan were to see him—"Les, you've got the wrong idea."

When he leered and lunged at her, Jemma sidestepped him. "Don't make me hurt you, Les," she said cheerfully. "Get dressed and we'll forget this happened. We'll both profit by my ideas."

Hogan sat in his studio, moccasins up on his sketch table. If Jemma wanted to carry on her career as a wheeler-dealer, that was fine. If she wanted a television series bad enough to—Restless now, he rose to peer out at the van, which was now rocking. "I'm not going to interfere. She knows what she wants—I am not going to interfere . . . The hell I'm not."

Sitting at the sewing machine, Jemma tore the old clothing from Mrs. Coleman's box. Mending for the thrift shop would help her unstable nerves. Hogan had gone into his cave again—he had shocked himself, unprepared for his temper, and now he was brooding in his studio.

He'd jerked open the van's door with enough force to almost tear it away. He stepped into the van and immediately the whole room seemed much smaller, quivering with the violence within Hogan. "Get your pants on," he'd ordered Les. He took one scalding look at Jemma's torn sleeve and the fishing net she'd just slammed over Les's head. "Having trouble, dear?" he asked in a terrifying cold, evil, dark way.

"None at all," she'd replied brightly, fearing for

Les's body parts as Hogan towered over him. "I can handle it."

"Out." Hogan's simple command, directed at Les, sent him hopping out of the van, one leg in his pants and the other trying. Hogan had slammed the door, enclosing Jemma with him. He had leaned back against the counter and crossed his arms over his chest, studying her. "Are you going to marry me or what?"

Now, automatically checking the pockets of Mrs. Coleman's discarded garments, Jemma frowned as she found the envelope in the old raincoat. *"Are you going to marry me or what?"* wasn't exactly a romantic proposal, but Hogan wasn't looking sweet and dreamy. She'd tramped after him into the house, opened her mouth to burn him, and Hogan had wrapped his arms around her. He'd pulled her down on top of him—they'd made love on the floor, there in the bald square of sunlight on his varnished floor. Shaking in the aftermath of Hogan's hungry lovemaking and the ignition of her own wildfire passion for him, she had floated back up into reality and found his expression tender.

At the sewing machine, Jemma smoothed the sealed envelope and knew that Hogan's riffled and beautiful feathers were going to take some stroking and comforting—she'd order a book on shiatsu and Swedish massage and how to construct a Swedish steam house. She'd seduce him until he was blind. *"Are you going to marry me or what?"*

"You need a wife who wants children. I don't," she whispered.

From what she had seen of Hogan and Ben, that relationship was mending. Both men deserved more than a woman who felt suffocated by the idea of children—

The envelope crackled in her fingers, and five tickets spilled out onto the smooth wooden floor.

# eighteen

"Hogan . . ." His name was no more than a trembling whisper, yet it staked his body with ice and raised the hair on his nape. He looked up from his rough, overlapping, intricate sketches to see Jemma standing in his studio doorway, her face pale. "Hogan, look—" she whispered, her eyes wide with fear as she held out small white tickets to him. "They were in an envelope marked 'Richard.' "

He hurried to her, wrapped an arm around her and studied the—"Airline boarding passes," Jemma said, as though a giant hand were squeezing her throat. "I found them in the pocket of a coat Mrs. Coleman had ready for the thrift shop . . . I was just going to patch it up a bit. She must have wanted us to know—Oh, Hogan, I think they match the dates when Carley got those messages from the stalker."

Just as he reached for the telephone to check on Carley, Jemma gripped his hand. "She was supposed to be with Savanna. I just called Savanna, and Richard came to pick her up. They're going hiking up to Willow's cabin—oh, Hogan, that's where the winds are so haunting, where the legend is—"

Her eyes widened as Hogan cursed, striding to his office to open the file Jemma had made. He ran his finger down the lists of dates, carefully comparing them to the tickets, as Jemma leaned against him, her hand upon his chest. "You were right. They match," he said, and felt the hair on his body lift, a chill passing through him.

"What are we going to do? He's had her for four hours, and it's late afternoon."

Hogan punched in Ben's number and slammed the receiver back onto the cradle. He slapped his hand flat against the wall, clearly frustrated and worried. "Today was Mitch's day to watch her. Aaron, Dinah, and Ben are taking care of the last of the branding. Mitch wouldn't have left her—"

He picked up the telephone and rang Savanna. She answered immediately. "Mitch has gone after them— up the mountain. Carley sent him on an errand—we were going to eat pizza, and then when Mitch had gone, Richard came by. He said he only had a few hours and couldn't wait. Carley thought Mitch would understand. What's wrong?"

The plastic receiver in Hogan's hand creaked, protesting his white-knuckled grip. With Carley in danger, there was no time to ease gently into suspicions with Savanna. "Savanna, Richard may be Carley's attacker, and I think he's killed several times before. We have boarding passes that match the dates of Carley's Seattle stalker."

He outlined his suspicions briefly and the silence on the other end of the line said Savanna was circling the idea, not dismissing it. She spoke shakily, "He's been gone several times, but doctors usually do conferences and seminars. I thought nothing of it. Yes, those girls that were murdered were his patients but he's the only doctor in town."

Savanna sucked in air, the hissing sound revealing that she had reason to suspect Richard, too. "He's my brother, Hogan. Half brother. His father raped my mother during a routine examination. She didn't want anyone to know, and Ben kept that secret. That's why he was never a patient or allowed any of you to be treated—Oh, God, I've been telling Richard everything about Carley, about where she'd be—My mother told me how demented old Doc Coleman was, how he kept rambling about finding that old mine. When Richard was a boy, his father marched him up those mountains to find that old mine—*Oh, what have I done?*"

Hogan pushed aside his fear and tried to think logically—fear and panic would not save Carley's life. "Savanna—think. How would they travel—by horse or hiking or does Richard have an all-terrain vehicle?"

"An all-terrain, but that won't carry two people. What do you want me to do?"

"Stay by the phone. We may need you."

Hogan remembered how the all-terrain vehicle tracks were near the old cabin that they'd burned—He glanced at Jemma, who had just cried out to him and gripped his arm, her fingers digging in. "That ring he gave her that summer she was attacked. Hogan, it's carved jade and very expensive. He's been wanting her to wear it— he thinks she's actually his."

"Wait here—" He wanted Jemma safe; if he found Richard, he wasn't certain what he would do, and mentally unstable, the doctor could hurt her. He prayed that Carley was alive—

"I'm going." Jemma was already running out the door to his pickup.

Jemma held Hogan's free hand as they raced onto the road, where Hogan paused. To the left lay the trail to the mountains, and they would need horses and to the right was—"He's got her at his house."

"But Savanna said they were hiking into the mountains—"

"He'd want her where his precious collections are. Richard is a collector, Jemma. He places his collections together. He considers Carley to be his possession. He'll want to enjoy her visually with his other things."

"And when he finds out that she isn't a virgin?"

Those girls that were murdered were his patients. He was furious . . . and then they were dead, Savanna had said. Despite his fear, Hogan calmly managed to reassure Jemma, "Nothing will happen to Carley. We'll get to her first."

On the way to the Coleman house, Hogan concentrated on driving fast but safely—because they were Carley's only chance. He glanced at Jemma's pale, taut face, her hands clenching his single one so tightly the bones showed. Because he loved her and there was no going back from the bond they had formed, and because now—with Carley's life endangered—his life stood out boldly. He'd been in the shadows, coddling old pain and resentment. Jemma had brought him sunshine and meaning to his life; she was a part of him now, as much as his soul. He lifted the chain that held his mother's ring over his head and placed it in Jemma's hand. "I want you to wear my mother's ring. It's important to me now."

"Hogan, I can't . . ."

"If something happens—if something goes wrong, and I'm . . . We don't know what Richard will do, sweetheart, and it's important to me that you wear her ring. It's a circle, a circle of life and eternity. Life goes on, no matter what happens to interfere with it. I want to know that you're wearing my ring, that you know you're in my heart. You give me peace, Jemma. You fill me.'' Then he bent to kiss her quickly, the other half of his heart. ''Left hand, third finger, Jemma.''

''You pick the worst times—like when you threw those earrings at me.'' Shakily, Jemma freed the ring and slid it on her finger, a perfect fit. ''I'll give it back when this is finished. Ooo, I'm so mad. It's just like you to think on so many levels, when I can only concentrate on one and right now, that has to do with Carley. I feel like I'm getting ambushed. You're just so intense and pushy. You're so emotional. You're so—just you.''

''Uh-huh,'' Hogan murmured, but promised that when Carley was safe, Jemma would still be wearing his ring.

At the Coleman house, Hogan stopped to release Richard's two Rottweilers. They silently obeyed his firm command and touches as he let them know he respected them, but he was in control.

A sound caught him, stilled his senses—a cry of an owl, too early in the day—or was it a memory, a fear of Joe's owl legend? Or was it the truth, that the owl had come to take Carley's spirit away?

He forced himself to push away the fear and stood looking at the house, trying to draw cool logic into him. He absorbed every detail, then silently turned the glass knob to the parlor door. Jemma gripped his shirt as they entered the Coleman house and Hogan patted his thigh, pointing to the Rottweilers and then down the dark hallways to Richard's collections. The dogs padded off and Hogan whispered to Jemma, ''Go find Mrs. Coleman.''

''But Carley—'' He shoved her gently and with a worried backward look at him, Jemma hurried upstairs. As the Rottweilers began pawing and circling a huge chest in the collections room, Hogan motioned them to him. He quietly ushered them outside, and returned to

Jemma's whispered, "Mrs. Coleman is sleeping."

Hogan nodded and eased the chest aside. "The dimensions on the inside of the house don't match the outside. There's something behind this chest."

Carley's scream echoed upward and Hogan prayed— He found the button that released the paneled door and revealed a stairway leading to the basement. Quietly Jemma followed Hogan down the stairs to find Carley tied to a huge dragon-backed carved chair, decorated in red-silk tapestry. In the small, candlelit room, ornately decorated with precious Chinese jade and erotic paintings, she was dressed in a long gown, her eyes wide with fear. The heavy scent of incense spread over the opulent setting. Richard was dressed in black silk, sprawled upon a chaise lounge and watching her with half-closed eyes. Enlarged glossy pictures of Carley hung about the room.

Carley's eyes begged Hogan to help, and then, following her stare to the intruders, Richard leaped to his feet. "She's mine now, the sweet, innocent flower of the Kodiaks. Their precious baby."

He lifted a long curved knife over Carley. "My dogs usually let me know when I have visitors. They've been bad boys and will have to pay."

"Listen you—" Jemma stepped forward, and Hogan drew her back. Richard was too close to Carley.

Hogan moved in front of Jemma. One dark glance told her that he wasn't arguing. "Richard," he said, "only a weak man would do that to a helpless woman, attack and stalk her."

"*I am not weak!*" Richard raged, and the knife glinted, turned toward Hogan.

"You are. We've all known that you are. You're jealous of the Kodiaks, aren't you, Richard?" Hogan spoke slowly, methodically, the deep sound hypnotic in the ornate, heavily scented chamber.

Carley's eyes were wide with fear as Hogan moved closer to Richard, towering over him. Jemma wrapped her hand in Hogan's tooled Western belt and held tight. If she had to jerk him back to safety and defend him, she would. As if sensing her thoughts, Hogan looked down over his shoulder at her. "Don't," he said in a too-pained tone. "Just don't."

Then he turned back to Richard, and Jemma couldn't bear to think about that knife sinking into Hogan's beautiful body—her beautiful body, because he belonged to her. "What are you muttering about?" he asked in a low frustrated tone.

"If you get hurt, I'm never going to forgive you. I love you."

Hogan stiffened, but didn't turn. She wondered if he'd heard her. "Hogan, I said I love you," she whispered. "I've never said that to anyone before."

"I'll get back with you on that," he whispered harshly after a heartbeat of silence.

"I had to tell you. What if we don't live? You'd never know how, how—"

"Shut up, Jemma . . . sweetheart, light of my life, and keeper of my heart," and then louder to Richard, "Give me the knife, Richard. Everything will be fine. I'll see that—"

Richard jabbed at Hogan with the knife. "Stay back. You Kodiaks thought you were kings—but I've had what you'll never have. I've had the best. You swaggered around with girls swooning after you, but even then, I knew that I would have the best prize of all. I took Carley from you. Nothing could stop me, not even the almighty Kodiaks. Carley is mine. She knows it. She's waited all these years for me."

"You killed Joe Blue Sky, didn't you?" Hogan asked in a too-soft tone that raised the hair on Jemma's nape.

"Of course. I thought that was a nice reminder to you that you were very vulnerable to me. Joe was disposable—just a matter of withholding his medication for a few moments—no trouble at all."

He ran his free hand across Carley's short hair. "You really shouldn't have cut your hair, my dear."

"Has she really waited for you, Richard?" Hogan continued talking softly, distracting Richard from Carley. "Have you seen how she looks at Mitch?"

"I'll kill him, too, after I finish you. Then Carley is mine!"

The blast from a revolver echoed in the small chamber. With a disbelieving look at the slight elderly woman standing on the staircase, Richard crumpled to the floor.

While Hogan freed Carley and held her close, Mrs. Coleman used her cane to totter to her son. She bent to smooth his hair. "He didn't know I could walk. I hid that from him, because I knew that someday, I would have to—He was mad, just like his father. I knew Richard was building something down here, but he collects so many things, I thought he just needed more storage room—I mean, he *used* to collect."

Jemma helped Mrs. Coleman to stand. With tears shimmering in her faded eyes, Mrs. Coleman used her cane to walk to a carved Buddha. She stroked it lovingly. "I knew when he brought this home . . . it was Harry Medford's. Poor Harry's place was burned the night he died. Harry always loved me, you know. He was such a sweet man. He was going to help me. I wanted to live with my sister, Anna, and Richard wouldn't hear of it. Don't expect me to cry. I can't. He probably gave the girl the same medication he used on me."

"Maybe you could live with your sister now," Jemma

said gently, searching Carley's pale face and the way she hugged Hogan tight. Jemma knew how safe Hogan could make her feel, and that was important now, when she was still trembling.

Hogan turned Carley's face up to his, searching it. "He's given her something—probably to allow him to dress her and prepare for the grand event."

Carley shuddered. "He wanted to get something here first, before we took that hike. He offered me a glass of lemonade, and then I couldn't hold my eyes open. I woke up, and—"

Jemma placed her hand over her racing heart, fear still racing through her. She stood looking at them, trying to subdue the fear that her best friend and Hogan could have been wounded or killed. They were beautiful, standing like that—Carley's fair hair against Hogan's dark skin. Perfect parts of Jemma's heart were all safe and living for tomorrows. Carley would marry Mitch and have children, and Hogan would—be Hogan . . . strong, safe, enduring.

Carley looked so safe now as Hogan gathered her closer. "It's over now. For good. Jemma, take Mrs. Coleman upstairs and make some calls, okay?"

Jemma couldn't move, still locked in fear, her cold body beginning to tremble. "It's over?"

Hogan's expression was grim and frustrated, yet he spoke gently. "It is. Jemma, you've come this far. You've saved Carley's life. You've done everything right, and everyone is safe. Take Mrs. Coleman upstairs and make those calls, okay?"

Moving mechanically, doing what she must, Jemma seated Mrs. Coleman in a rocking chair near the telephone. Still icy-cold and locked in the terrifying scene, Jemma made calls to the police, and Savanna came to take Mrs. Coleman to a friend's home.

Mitch had skidded to a stop, flying to hold Carley tight against him, tears running down their cheeks. He'd be angry later, telling her how foolish she'd been, but for the moment, Mitch had his love safely in his arms. "We're getting married," he ordered shakily, "and no buts about it."

"Not now, Mitch," Hogan had said quietly. "Try her again when she's up to it."

Jemma had stayed with Hogan through the police questioning, gripping his hand like a lifeline . . . and then she fainted.

That night, they rode Moon Shadow to the top of a knoll overlooking Kodiak land, the big Bar K iron gate visible in the moonlight. Jemma sat behind Hogan on Moon Shadow's bare back, her arms around the man she loved.

She held him tighter, and Hogan placed his hand over hers, one finger smoothing Willow's wedding band. Jemma did not want to return it, not just yet, because part of her was still locked back in the terrifying scene in the Coleman basement. Hogan took her hand, kissed it, and placed it over his chest.

He was wearing the shirt she'd made, marking a special occasion. Hogan treated everything she did for him with reverence, as though he couldn't believe she would think so carefully of him. In quiet moments, when he thought he was alone or unnoticed, he often smoothed the fabric in a treasuring caress.

After the police questioning, Jemma remembered Hogan carrying her to his pickup and locking one arm around her as he drove. When they arrived at the Bar K, Hogan carried her into the house. Mitch arrived minutes later, also carrying Carley into the house. They sat in silence, Carley's terror silently vibrating through the sunlit room. Dinah, Ben, and Aaron had arrived from branding and the three had looked like a family, Aaron's arm draped casually around his mother, Ben's face aglow—

That happiness died when they saw Carley and Jemma, and Mitch and Hogan's grim expressions.

Three hours later, Ben hadn't wanted Hogan and Jemma to leave, but they'd needed the healing time together.

Now, on the moonlit knoll, on a ride like any other, they were silent. Hogan's storms seemed to settle on their midnight rides, and Jemma enjoyed them, too. It was as if Moon Shadow carried them into one life— together, without words or explanations.

The solid beat of Hogan's heart beneath her palm reassured Jemma that life would go on. "Carley is really safe now, isn't she?"

"I should have seen it. The way Richard looked at her—he's always looked at her like that, as if she were—" Hogan's jaw locked, his features hardening in the moonlit night. "But then, I love Carley, too, and I— I should have paid more attention."

Jemma rubbed her cheek against Hogan's back. "It's all over now. Tell me what you see when you look out there at the moonlit pastures and foothills and the mountains?"

"Images, blending together, colors and form separate and yet one within a concept . . . Peace. I've find peace. Here with you."

Because her heart was so filled with love, Jemma could only snuggle closer.

Later, in bed, Hogan held her close after lovemaking, as though he'd never let her go, as though his heartbeat needed hers to survive . . . She smoothed his hair and sighed, the motion bringing her breast closer into his hand. "You're a good man, Hogan Kodiak . . ."

"I'm staying here," he whispered drowsily in the aftermath of lovemaking and the terrifying, stark painful day. "Make this your home, Jemma. Here with me. Come and go as you like, but always remember that I'm here for you. I love you."

She wondered how she could ever leave him, this wonderful loving man, who would give his life for his family. She continued smoothing his hair, listening to his sleeping breath, and knew more deeply than ever how much—"I love you, too."

He was sleeping now, and she drifted along, unable to sleep. "I've always loved you, Hogan Kodiak. You've always had my heart. Just maybe I will marry you and maybe—just maybe we'll make a family."

Hogan sighed and stirred, his hand sliding down to cover her lower abdomen, opening upon it. Before Jemma slid off into sleep, she wondered how she could be so blessed to know and love Hogan, a beautiful man, inside and out.

She never felt the curve of Hogan's pleased smile and kiss against her throat.

# epilogue

*The healing time*

Hogan sat on his front porch, untangling Jemma's usual mess of leaders, lures and fishing line that lay on the rough wood table in front of him. At the beginning of September, a chill had settled onto the land, foretelling of fall, when the fur would be thick upon bears in the high country.

With the aspens turning fiery yellow, frost would be touching the small grave by Willow creek, soon to be covered by snow, driven by the haunting winds. Hogan had come home to find his peace, his soul, and he'd found love.

It was a healing time, the cycle of ranch life holding a steady thread through lives that were changing and a family mending. Carley was now impatient for marriage; Dinah and Ben had been remarried quietly, immediately.

Mrs. Coleman was financially independent and wanted nothing from the Coleman house. She'd signed all her goods to Mitch with the condition that he sell them and use the proceeds to build a boys' ranch for inner-city children. Carley had set her mind to be Mitch's partner in the venture, helping him in his unique talent for saving children.

Aaron had started to build on his land nearby, and he'd settled in for a long, determined, romantic pursuit of Savanna.

As for Jemma—she still wore Willow's ring, and Hogan wasn't insisting. Every day brought them closer, and the images moved more surely within him now. They'd come to him at first in sketches and then in watercolor, but they were still his secret, coddling them until he was certain that was what filled his artist's spirit—

*Jemma*. He treasured every day that she stayed, slept with him, and rode the moonlit pastures at night. She filled his heart and gave him peace—even when they were fighting—he'd learned to battle her outright, just to stir her up, to watch her ignite, his fire woman.

He'd found what he sought, as an artist, and as a man. He needed this balance in his life—Jemma, the land that he loved, and the discovery of the images in his life, the sketches that settled his need to create, to blend colors and shapes.

Inside the house, Jemma stood in the shadows, watching Hogan survey Kodiak land, at peace with himself. She turned Willow's ring on her finger and slashed away the tears dripping from her cheeks. Could she give him what he needed and he deserved? She loved him so, this gentle, caring man. He'd fought his past and won, he'd tried to understand Ben, and that breach was mending every day.

He turned to look at her through the glass, placing his large hand against it, and she matched it with her trembling one. He seemed to sense her moods, know her fears, and Hogan was always so safe. While they argued, they also shared quiet times, like now. He'd let her grow into him, and they'd blended together into an easy schedule. At times he cooked and cleaned, and they shared household duties. She helped him on the small ranch, and the nights were long and tender, each day better than before.

She allowed him his private cave, of course. He spent the afternoon hours sketching away in his studio, and she enjoyed sharing her business deals with him. A quiet evening, sharing the lush rug in front of his fire, brought her more peace than she'd had in her lifetime.

They were a family, she thought, a tiny perfect family. She wasn't ready yet, but she did want Hogan's children—glossy-haired little miniatures of him—to nestle within her. She'd found the end of her quest—she'd found her love.

They were already a part of each other, in their hearts, and after that all else would settle into place. The healing time had begun—a quiet acceptance of life's unending circles.

Savanna's small car pulled into the dirt driveway of Aaron's new home place. The entire Kodiak family was racing against winter. Jemma was happily giving orders; Hogan walked by to kiss her mouth closed, then place her firmly aside as he and Mitch lifted two-by-fours and carried them to another section of the stark framework with rough flooring.

Aaron had been very good to Mrs. Coleman, relocating her with her sister, taking care of her paperwork and handling her finances. On the other hand, he'd been too proper with Savanna, his body shaking, but controlled each time he kissed her good night. Their relationship and her frustration had deepened. He was very careful of her—and very proper, giving her flowers, small, unique gifts, and taking her shopping and picnicking.

Savanna took off her sunglasses and frowned. But no sex. He'd been very careful, though her body recognized the heat within his.

Aaron had changed, and Savanna enjoyed him as a man and as a friend.

She found him high on the newly shingled roof, his shirt open, his chest gleaming, and a carpenter's tool belt slung around narrow hips.

"You're drooling," Jemma whispered next to Savanna, as Aaron spied her and swung down from a rafter. He vaulted over a stack of boards and swaggered toward her, a boyish grin on his face.

"Click," Savanna whispered to Jemma, then strolled off to kiss the man she intended to marry.

"Hello, honey—mmft!" Aaron gave himself to Savanna's scorching kiss.

She pushed him back and held his shirt with her fist. "Tonight. My house. Topics—sex and marriage. Sex first. I want to get pregnant right away, and I'll want my baby wearing an Aaron Kodiak name—got it? Oh, and one more thing—just so you know . . . click."

Then she strolled away, hips gently swaying in her tight red dress. She winked at Jemma. "Click," Savanna said again with a low, sultry laugh, and bent to kiss Jimmy's cheek as she passed.

The boy flushed, made yucking noises, and tried not to look full of himself. "Women," he said to Mitch, who had just adopted him. "Weird."

Aaron stood for a long time, clearly confused, frowning, and his hand rubbing his heart as though it had just left his keeping. "Yahoo! I am getting married!" he yelled, and spread his arms wide to the blue sky of Montana.

Two days later, Ben, Aaron, and Mitch sat under the Bar K's big metal gate and faced Hogan's house. With a long, doomed sigh, Hogan swung up on Moon Shadow's bare back and rode to meet them. They glowered at him. "Do something with Jemma," Aaron ordered.

"She's going to kill us," Mitch grumbled.

"Take her off someplace until all the weddings are done," Ben added darkly. "She's got the womenfolk all worked up into a frenzy—me, walking Dinah down the aisle in full wedding garb. Hell, we're already married. Caterers, engagement parties, showers—"

"We'll stop work on my house and make your cabin ready for winter. We'll chop wood and put in a stove and running water. We'll build a warehouse to store her business deals. Take her up there—"

"I get the picture. Hasn't she always been in the middle of everything? Did you expect less from her?" Hogan asked, amused at the desperate expressions of his father and brothers. He enjoyed Jemma's fast mind, the way she charged into life, emotions wide-open, nothing hidden.

"She's yours. Do something," Ben ordered before the four turned and rode away.

Hogan shook his head and washed his hands over his face when he heard Jemma call, "Ben! Aaron! Mitch! Come back!"

Moon Shadow sidled away from the pickup that skidded to a stop. Jemma leaped out and circled it, tugging a big tarp-wrapped object to the lowered tailgate. The bright red huge bow gleamed in the sunlight. "Since you're all here, help me with this."

Hogan swung down and walked to Jemma, and with the air of a man accustomed to a woman of many interests asked, "What is it, honey?"

"Pull the ribbon—but save it for later, sweetheart."

Hogan's body hardened immediately—jolted by the image of Jemma wearing nothing, but the ribbon. She flipped back the tarp to reveal a brand-new iron sign—

The Double Bar K. For your land, Hogan.''

Ben began to laugh, the sound of his pleasure rolling over the Kodiak pastures. ''Well, let's do it, son.''

Jemma's cries stirred Hogan's hardened body as he massaged her bare legs on their bed. He ran his hands up to her bottom, found the lace covering them, and eased it away. Turning her, Hogan bent to find her breasts, nuzzling her gently, licking and suckling and enjoying the soft unsteady catch of her breath. Her hands locked in his hair as he moved lower, opening his mouth over her navel, flicking it with his tongue.

He took her hand, pressing his face to it, sucking each finger in turn, delighting in the sudden upthrust of her hips, the scent of her tightening the skin of his body. He gently sucked the incredibly sensitive portion of her thumb, just where it joined her hand. Jemma responded immediately with a ragged sigh. ''You're so sensual, Hogan. I feel as if you're devouring me. As if your lovemaking is a promise.''

''It is a promise.'' He'd share his life with her, honor her, and love her all the days of his life. He turned her to lie facing him, his hand caressing her breasts slowly, the long curve of her legs, the jutting ridge of her hip-bones. When her hand found him, drew him near, Hogan could wait no longer and surged into her, pinning her to the bed, moving slowly upon her, his hands capturing hers.

''Are you my heart?'' he asked roughly, needing the reassurance that the woman who held his body, knew she also held his heart.

''I am, and are you mine?'' she demanded, matching his need before passion took them both.

The ritual served as their vows, easing Hogan's need for a marriage certificate. When it came to Jemma, his patience was endless. He trusted her to work through their relationship to the basics—that they loved each other. But Jemma needed time, adjusting to living with him. She moved easily within the framework of their lives, unhampered now by the tethers she feared.

Later, as he lay naked in front of the fire, waiting for his love to come to him, Hogan smiled slowly as she yelled, "Hogan! Hogan!"

She tore from the kitchen, dark red hair streaming away from her. She carried his matted and covered watercolor paintings. "We'll make a mint! Limited editions, right? Only so many prints, each numbered? Art gallery showings, you with your artsy Native American look, me in—" She frowned and eased to sit beside him. "A turquoise gown, I think. Full-length, off one shoulder."

"For me?" he asked, and she blinked. Jemma could be undone when she was on a full roll. He thought of the Fire Feathers necklace and how it would look on her Christmas morning—

She slapped his hand lightly. "Bad boy. Down," she added, as he began to toy with the edge of the towel wrapped around her breasts. "What is it, Hogan? I mean it's beautiful, all the horses and wild animals, blending with mountains and scenery, and Native Americans— but it's so unusual, everything is involved, flowing into reflections and the other images."

Her gray eyes widened. "This is it, isn't it? This is what's inside you. The images you say stir you? Oh, look, that's a foal within a mare! Oh, my. It's so intricate, so intense—you've found what you wanted. They're so beautiful, Hogan."

She came to the watercolor of a tall, fair-skinned woman, a blaze of fiery hair waving up and away from her face. Amid flowers that moved about her nude body, the woman . . . "It's me. Is that how you see me? Like a fairy goddess? No, more earthy, more sensuous—"

"You are woman to me. It's called camouflage art, and yes, I'm very intense about you. I love you."

Jemma smiled softly, bent to meet his kiss, and asked a question he'd asked her, "Are you going to marry me, or what?"

Hogan inhaled the crisp dawn air, at ease with his life. Dressed only in jeans, he stood on his porch and watched the steam shoot from the horse's nostrils. It was a good time, a healing time. He wrapped contentment around him and smiled as Jemma came from the house to wrap her arms around him. Dressed in a long white robe, knotted at the waist, she snuggled against him. "Come back to bed."

Hogan smiled against her hair. "Would you like that?"

"Mmm." She snuggled closer. "You know I would. You've got that edgy look, dark and secretive and that's when you're the most volatile—Hey, what are you doing?" she asked as Hogan swept her up in his arms.

He hurried to Moon Shadow and plopped Jemma on his broad back, then swung up behind her. He wrapped one arm around her and drew her close as he guided Moon Shadow by a tug of his mane. "Okay, I'll ask," Jemma said, impatient as always. "You're not going to tell me. Where are we going?"

"To have breakfast with Dad and Mom and the family, of course."

"I'm in my robe, sweetheart," she reminded him, turning to wrap her arms around him and snuggle close. "Did you say, 'Dad'?"

"I did, and does it matter what you're wearing today?'' he asked, feeling as if he were floating in pure Montana sunlight.

''Not a bit. Not as long as I'm with you,'' she said, holding him tight like she would for a lifetime.

Hogan scanned the rolling fields, the cattle and horses, and Montana's clear blue sky. He gathered his love closer and smiled. ''Home,'' he said simply. ''I am home.''

# Discover Contemporary Romances
## at Their Sizzling Hot Best
### from Avon Books

❧❧❧

**WIFE FOR A DAY**         *by Patti Berg*
80735-1/$5.99 US/$7.99 Can

**PILLOW TALK**         *by Hailey North*
80519-7/$5.99 US/$7.99 Can

**HER MAN FRIDAY**         *by Elizabeth Bevarly*
80020-9/$5.99 US/$7.99 Can

**SECOND STAR TO THE RIGHT**   *by Mary Alice Kruesi*
79887-5/$5.99 US/$7.99 Can

**HALFWAY TO PARADISE**         *by Nessa Hart*
80156-6/$5.99 US/$7.99 Can

**BE MY BABY**         *by Susan Andersen*
79512-4/$5.99 US/$7.99 Can

**TRULY MADLY YOURS**         *by Rachel Gibson*
80121-3/$5.99 US/$7.99 Can

Buy these books at your local bookstore or use this coupon for ordering:

Mail to: Avon Books/HarperCollins Publishers, P.O. Box 588, Scranton, PA 18512     H
Please send me the book(s) I have checked above.
❏ My check or money order—no cash or CODs please—for $_____is enclosed (please
add $1.50 per order to cover postage and handling—Canadian residents add 7% GST). U.S.
and Canada residents make checks payable to HarperCollins Publishers Inc.
❏ Charge my VISA/MC Acct#_____Exp Date_____
Minimum credit card order is two books or $7.50 (please add postage and handling
charge of $1.50 per order—Canadian residents add 7% GST). For faster service, call
1-800-331-3761. Prices and numbers are subject to change without notice. Please allow six to
eight weeks for delivery.

Name_____
Address_____
City_____State/Zip_____
Telephone No._____             CRO 0999

Dear Reader,

Next month, we have some wonderful romantic treats in store for you, beginning with a fantastic Avon Treasure by a writer destined for stardom — Victoria Alexander. Her unforgettable Regency-set romance, *The Wedding Bargain*, is witty, sensuous, and completely tantalizing. A society scoundrel strikes a wager with one of the most eligible ladies of the *ton*. If he wins, he gets her hand in marriage. If he loses…you'll have to read to find out!

Lovers of contemporary romance won't want to miss *A Kiss to Dream On*, the latest from Neesa Hart. Neesa's trademark blend of heartfelt emotion and memorable sensuality are in full force here, as a toughened journalist falls under the spell of an idealistic teacher. Remember to keep your tissues handy, because I guarantee that *A Kiss to Dream On* is a laugh-and-cry romance.

Adrienne deWolfe makes her Avon debut with a smart, sassy western, *Scoundrel for Hire*. A sexy scoundrel is hired to break up the marriage of a wealthy young woman's father and his gold-digging bride-to-be, never dreaming that he'd begin to have designs of his own in this saucy heiress. Filled with delicious twists and turns, you won't want it to end!

If you love headstrong heroines and maverick men, you won't want to miss Rebecca Wade's *Unlikely Outlaw*. A young western miss is ordered to get married, or else, by her father. So she picks the worst possible prospect for a husband…only to discover that opposites are sometimes the best match.

Until next month, happy reading!

*Lucia Macro*
Lucia Macro
Senior Editor